James Henry is the pen name of James Gurbutt and Henry Sutton.

James Gurbutt is a publisher at Constable & Robinson, R.D. Wingfield's original publisher in the 1980s.

Henry Sutton is the author of seven novels under his own name. His latest, *Get Me Out Of Here*, was published by Harvill Secker in January 2010. He is the Books Editor of the *Daily Mirror*, and teaches creative writing at the University of East Anglia.

After a successful career writing for radio, R.D. Wingfield turned his attention to fiction, creating the character Jack Frost. He published six novels featuring Frost. The series has been adapted for television as the perennially popular *A Touch of Frost*, starring David Jason. R.D. Wingfield died in 2007.

'James and Henry have captured my father's style superbly. Fans and newcomers alike will not be disappointed.'

Philip Wingfield, son of the late R.D. Wingfield

First Frost

A DS Jack Frost Investigation

JAMES HENRY

CORGI BOOKS

TRANSWORLD PUBLISHERS
61–63 Uxbridge Road, London W5 5SA
A Random House Group Company
www.transworldbooks.co.uk

**FIRST FROST
A CORGI BOOK: 9780552161763**

First published in Great Britain
in 2011 by Bantam Press
an imprint of Transworld Publishers
Corgi edition published 2011

Written for the Estate of R.D. Wingfield by
James Gurbutt and Henry Sutton
Copyright © The Estate of R.D. Wingfield 2011

James Gurbutt and Henry Sutton have asserted their right under the
Copyright, Designs and Patents Act 1988 to be identified as the
authors of this work.

A CIP catalogue record for this book
is available from the British Library.

Addresses for Random House Group Ltd companies outside the UK
can be found at: www.randomhouse.co.uk
The Random House Group Ltd Reg. No. 954009

The Random House Group Limited supports The Forest Stewardship Council
(FSC®), the leading international forest certification organisation. Our books
carrying the FSC label are printed on FSC® certified paper. FSC is the only forest
certification scheme endorsed by the leading environmental organisations,
including Greenpeace. Our paper procurement policy can be found at
www.randomhouse.co.uk/environment

Typeset in 11.5/15pt Caslon 540 by Falcon Oast Graphic Art Ltd.
Printed and bound by CPI Group (UK) Ltd, Croydon, CR0 4YY

4 6 8 10 9 7 5 3

A Note from Phil Wingfield

As you can imagine, the embryo idea of a new Frost novel written by someone other than my father filled me with mixed emotions. What would friends, family and fans think? What would he have said? A great idea, a sensible move, betrayal? I knew that if we went ahead with the project it had to be right. When I read the book, I had to admit that James and Henry had done their homework and made a superb job of capturing my father's style – no mean feat. I did feel a significant twinge of guilt thinking this, which only increased as I found myself immersed in the story.

Jack Frost's route to fame is as full of twists and turns as the books themselves. He originally surfaced in the novel *Frost at Christmas* in 1972, which was rejected by the commissioning publisher. The novel was then transcribed for radio and *Three Days of Frost* was broadcast in 1977. My father's agent, Jacqui Lyons of Marjacq Scripts, continued to promote the manuscript, and her efforts paid off in the early eighties when *Frost at Christmas* was published in Canada. UK publication finally came in 1989 and Jack Frost was home again. By 1992 the then three Frost novels had been transcribed for TV and the series *A Touch of Frost* made Jack a household name.

Over the years, Rodney continued to write for radio as he much preferred this medium. But as demand for radio lessened he turned back to the printed word. He always said that he found novel-writing an ever-increasing chore, but ironically his books turned out to be increasingly marvellous reads. He wrote a further three before his death in 2007.

So, in conclusion, I think it is a wonderful and fitting tribute to my father and his work that James and Henry are breathing new life into his creation and bringing back Jack Frost in this prequel. In my humble opinion, fans and newcomers alike will not be disappointed by *First Frost*.

Phil Wingfield

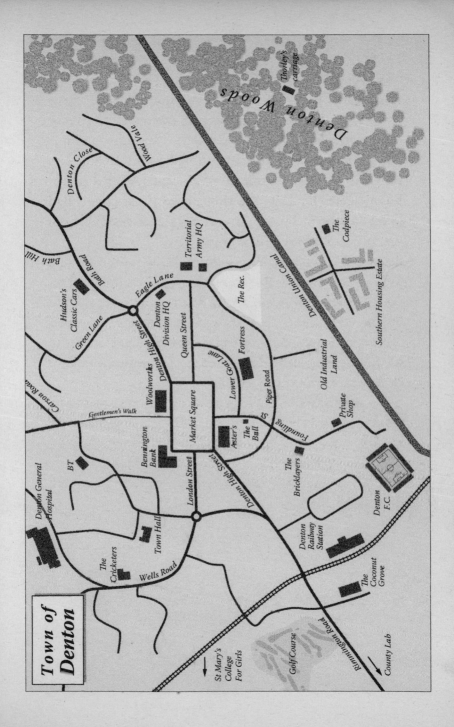

Town of Denton

Denton Woods

Thorley's carriage

The Codpiece

Wood Vale

Denton Close

Bath Hill

Bath Road

Hudson's Classic Cars

Green Lane

Eagle Lane

Territorial Army HQ

The Rec.

Denton Union Canal

Southern Housing Estate

Denton Division HQ

Woolworks

Denton High Street

Queen Street

Lower Goat Lane

Fortress

Piper Road

Old Industrial Land

Carson Road

Gentlemen's Walk

Market Square

Aster's

The Bull

Foundling St.

Private Shop

Bennington Bank

BT

Denton General Hospital

London Street

Denton High Street

The Bricklayers

Denton F.C.

The Cricketers

Town Hall

Wells Road

Denton Railway Station

The Coconut Grove

St Mary's College For Girls

Golf Course

Rimmington Road

County Lab

Prologue

He followed them up the escalator to the third floor – children's clothes and lingerie. The woman was in no hurry. He was, but he knew he had to be careful. He'd spotted a security guard on the ground floor. Couldn't see one on this floor, yet.

Saturday afternoon and the place was heaving – perfect. Perhaps he was in luck.

He thought there should have been a guard on every floor, big place like this. This was no way to run a department store, recession or not. If only things had been as slack when he was a player. Then he wouldn't be in this mess. He'd be living the high life, a big happy family in tow. El Dorado. That's how it should have been.

They were looking at school uniforms. Short, grey pleated

skirts. Navy sweaters. Crisp white shirts, bearing the logo of St Mary's College for Girls. So that was where his girl went.

He pretended to be browsing through the duffel coats, aware he was the only man on the floor. He played with a toggle, wondering what it would be like to fasten a child into such a garment, snug as a rug. To give her a kiss and a cuddle, hold her tight. He'd missed a lot. But it wasn't too late. He was still young and fit. He'd made good use of the indoor facilities.

The girl had removed her own coat and was trying on a sweater, out on the shop floor, under the bright spotlights, in front of everyone. He couldn't believe how tall she was, for her age. They grew up fast nowadays, all right.

Music was coming from somewhere. What a racket. When he was younger and into all that stuff at least they knew how to play proper instruments, and sing in tune. None of this electronic nonsense. Or boys dressing as girls. He was amazed at how so much had changed in little over a decade. Changed for the worst.

She had picked out a skirt and was holding it against her waist. Not out here, my angel, he thought. Surely her mother had to say something, get her into a changing room. This wasn't right. Who knew who could be watching? He couldn't stand it. He shuffled further behind the rack of coats, breathing heavily. His head was throbbing. It was all going wrong already.

About to blow his cover, a large, buxom, middle-aged woman, wearing the store's colours (a black skirt and a pale-green blouse, which was at least two sizes too small for her) *walked up to the mother and child. He couldn't hear what was said but this woman – the floor manager? – pointed to a far corner. The changing rooms.*

He had been thinking everything was lost but now a new opportunity suddenly presented itself. The girl sloped off towards the changing rooms, clutching an armful of tiny skirts and tops, while the mother drifted across to the lingerie. That woman hasn't changed, he thought. The tart.

He hung back for a couple of minutes; then, with his heart thumping wildly and his right hand clasping the still-damp handkerchief in his jacket pocket, he walked quickly across the floor, and slipped behind the partially drawn curtains leading to the cubicles.

Surprise was going to be his best weapon. Plus a bit of luck. It was about time things went his way: he'd already paid a heavy price.

Saturday

Detective Constable Sue Clarke sat on the edge of a soft, black leather armchair, across the living room from Mr and Mrs Hudson, who were slumped at either end of a matching settee. Mrs Wendy Hudson, a pretty, curvy fake blonde, in her late thirties, was clutching a tissue. Mr Steven Hudson, of a similar age, but with a slim, boyish build, and also with blond highlights in his hair, fashionably tufty on top and long at the sides, was drawing heavily on a Silk Cut.

It was eight o'clock at night. Pitch black and raining hard outside the neat, warm Hudson home.

DC Sue Clarke said, addressing Mrs Hudson, 'I know this is hard for you but try to remember everything as clearly as possible. You never know what might be useful.' Having just turned twenty-five, and recently promoted to CID, Clarke was anxious to play it by the book, and not make any mistakes in her questioning.

'I'll try,' said Mrs Hudson, looking up. Her voice was tired and shaky.

'Tell me about the last time you saw your daughter, Julie. This was in Aster's, the department st̶o̶r̶e̶ ̶ in centre of D̶e̶n̶t̶o̶n̶. I̶ ̶

'Yes,' said Mrs Hudson weakly. 'We were in the school-uniform bit, on the third floor – Julie needed a new skirt. She went to the changing room with an armful of stuff, and that was the last I saw of her.' The woman choked back a sob.

'You were waiting outside the changing room?' asked Clarke, her notepad in hand.

'Not exactly.' Mrs Hudson was now keeping her eyes on the floor. She was wearing surprisingly high-heeled shoes, of a not dissimilar colour to the lurid orange-patterned carpet.

Clarke pressed on. 'Where were you, then?'

'I suppose I'd wandered over to another section – there's this new lingerie bit.' The woman coughed into her tissue. 'But Julie's a big girl, she's very nearly thirteen. It's not like she needs me watching over her at all times.'

'No, of course not,' said Clarke, noticing Mr Hudson flinch. 'But how long was it before you realized she was missing?'

'I don't know. It couldn't have been more than twenty minutes. I went to find her in the changing rooms, and she wasn't there – nobody was.'

Mr Hudson was now staring at his wife, and not, Clarke thought, out of sympathy or concern. He was angry. 'Twenty minutes?' Clarke repeated, careful to not sound accusatory.

'Julie always takes her time in front of a mirror,' explained Mrs Hudson.

'There was ... , said Mr Hudson. ... ance to the changing rooms, I take it?' said Clarke.

'No, there weren't many staff about at all.'

'But the shop was busy?'

'I've seen it busier.'

'You would know,' muttered Mr Hudson, standing up, stubbing his cigarette out in an ashtray on the glass-and-chrome coffee table, then sitting straight back down again. He was a short man, shorter than his wife. 'The amount of time you spend in there, running up my account.'

'Did you see anyone suspicious?' asked DC Sue Clarke.

'What do you mean?' said Mrs Hudson, shifting uncomfortably on the settee.

Clarke's eye was momentarily distracted by the enormous television in the corner of the room. Beside it were a new VCR machine and a stack of video cassettes. From where Clarke was she couldn't read the titles. 'Men,' she prompted. 'Men behaving oddly.'

'You mean like perverts?' Mrs Hudson gasped.

'Do you think she could have been snatched?' said Mr Hudson, getting to his feet again.

'We have to keep an open mind,' said Clarke. 'But it would be very unusual.'

'I didn't see anything, anyone behaving like that,' said Mrs Hudson quickly. 'I'm sure I would ha-, noticed.'

'Most likely she'r m sure she'll come bursting through your front door any moment.'

'What if she doesn't?' said Mr Hudson.

'Well, first of all we need to contact all her friends – see if they know anything. I'll need a list.'

'She wouldn't do that,' said Mrs Hudson. 'Just disappear like that.'

'I wouldn't be so sure,' her husband disagreed. 'She can be a right stubborn little cow at times.'

'She can't have run away,' sobbed Mrs Hudson. 'Why would she do that?'

Clarke looked at her, the tears now rolling down her cheeks, and then hard at Mr Hudson. He was giving her the creeps. 'Is she generally happy?' she asked. 'Are things OK at home?'

'She's in a world of her own,' said Mr Hudson, sitting down once more. 'All she does is play records and get dressed up. Spends most of her time in her room.'

'She's a good girl,' said his wife. 'Headstrong at times, but who isn't at that age?'

They all looked up to see Detective Constable Arthur Hanlon appear in the lounge doorway, red-faced and very out of breath. Though he was still in his thirties, Clarke had always thought her chubby colleague could easily pass for being two decades older; it wasn't just his weight and thinning salt-and-pepper hair, but his old-fashioned moustache, and cheap, unfashionable clothes.

Hanlon had been searching the girl's bedroom, and was holding a framed photograph in his large, podgy hand. 'I take it this is Julie?' He waved the picture around.

'Yes,' said Mrs Hudson quietly.

Clarke strained to see a photograph of a desperately slight girl in school uniform. She had hazel eyes, prominent cheekbones and a pointy nose. There was a streak of red in her shoulder-length, mousey hair. Clarke didn't think she looked much like either of her parents.

'Can we borrow this?' Hanlon asked. 'We'll need to get some copies made.' He turned the frame over in his hands.

'Someone's taken her, haven't they?' Mrs Hudson suddenly wailed.

'I'm sure they haven't,' said Clarke, hoping to God they hadn't – such a vulnerable, impressionable-looking girl – and rising to her feet, not knowing

17

whether she should walk over and comfort the woman. Her husband wasn't going to.

'She'll show up soon enough,' Hanlon added cheerily. 'I expect it's all been a bit of a misunderstanding.'

'Don't bet on it,' Mr Hudson said sharply, standing again also.

Sunday (1)

'Whatever next?' Desmond Thorley muttered, fumbling for the Harvey's Bristol Cream. It didn't feel like he'd been asleep for long. The bottle appeared to be empty so he slumped back on his bench.

However, the high-pitched shrieking, which had so rudely and painfully woken him, seemed to be getting worse. It sounded like a child. A young child. But not at this hour, in the middle of the woods, surely.

His mind was playing games again, yet he couldn't just go back to sleep and he found himself sitting up again and peering out through a badly smudged and cracked window-pane. There was daylight, already, not that he could see much except tree trunks and branches and the sodden ground.

He gathered his mound of threadbare coats and moth-eaten blankets tighter around him. Winter was fast approaching. He looked over at the old wood-burning stove, knowing the chimney was blocked solid with tar, like his lungs, no doubt.

Scratching his head, he then noticed, lying on the dirty wooden floor, his tin of tobacco – open and all but empty. Not even one shred of Old Holborn.

Just at that moment his old railway carriage was rocked by that blood-curdling noise again, worse than anything he'd ever encountered on stage or screen; his bit-part acting career, though in the distant past, was still a vivid memory.

It was no good, he knew he wasn't going to get back to sleep. Clasping his tatty covers around him, he swung his legs off the hard bench and let his feet fall to the sticky ground. He was already wearing his boots, what was left of them. Slowly he made his way to the end of the carriage. Pushing open the rickety wooden door, he blinked in the soft light. The freezing early-morning air making his bloodshot eyes water.

The frantic, terrifying noise was coming from some way off, to the left of the end of his track, behind a wall of rhododendrons and a vast copper beech, its last few leaves still clinging on for dear life.

Feeling a mixture of outrage and apprehensive curiosity, Thorley stepped gingerly down from his carriage and on to the forest floor. This was his home, his kingdom. How dare they wake him in such a manner.

He was used to wind and rain battering Denton Woods, but it was strangely calm, which made the noise even more penetrating and unbearable. He heard a rustle coming from the bushes – he was certain of it. He walked to the end of his track, where it joined the main path, and while he was debating whether he should attempt to go straight through the middle of the rhododendron bushes, or take the less obstructed but longer route round, he heard short, heavy panting breaths behind him.

Quickly turning, and managing to lose his grip on his blankets and outer garments at the same time, he was faced with the vision of a tall, perfectly built young woman jogging towards him. She was wearing clothing so tight it left little to the imagination. Every bump and crevice was shockingly revealed. What was it with these female keep-fit types and their Lycra?

Yet it was wasted on him: women weren't his thing.

The woman was clearly startled, though rapidly seemed to feel reassured. Desmond Thorley knew he couldn't have appeared much of a threat.

She nodded a hello before passing and then increasing her pace.

He had seen her before, he was sure – with even less clothing on. Down by the north car park, that was where they came to do it, in the summer. Groups of them, sometimes. Men and women.

* * *

'Ladies and gentlemen, your attention please,' Super-intendent Stanley Mullett said loudly. He was standing between a desk and an incident board at the front of Denton Police Station's scruffy briefing room. 'Gather forward, gather forward,' he added, noticing the lack of personnel, even for a Sunday.

Mullett self-consciously fiddled with his papers while there was the noise of people slowly shuffling forward and changing seats. The new divisional commander was already regretting his decision to come to the station, straight before the golf club, despite the fact that his beige trousers were sharply creased and his Pringle sweater was neatly pressed too.

However, when the Sunday newspapers had dropped on to his doormat Mullett had realized he needed to be at that morning's briefing. And there wouldn't have been time to change into uniform and then back into his golfing attire, and there was no way he was going to miss the tee-off time. Despite his exalted position in Denton, he was still very much the new boy at the Royal Denton Golf Club.

'It has come to my attention that certain members of the fourth estate are already making enquiries about twelve-year-old Julie Hudson,' Mullet said, suspecting there was a leak from the station.

'The Southern Estate, did you say?' coughed some-one to his side.

'No, the fourth estate,' repeated Mullett. He

continued, 'The press, the press.' He paused. 'By the way, where is everyone?' There were fewer than a dozen officers in the room. A scattering of plainclothes and uniform.

'The clocks went back, not forward, last night,' snapped Mullett. 'There really is no excuse.' He slapped the *Sunday Mirror* on to the desk. Lifting his head, in an attempt at conveying superiority, he caught a couple of people bemusedly studying their watches.

Only six months into the job, Mullett was having a desperate time trying to gain control of the over-stretched and under-resourced station. The Denton Division had been the laughing stock of the county. No one, except possibly Detective Inspector Jim Allen, had a clue what they were meant to be doing. But Allen was in the middle of a walking holiday in the Peak District, and Detective Inspector Bert Williams, who should have been in charge this morning, was nowhere to be seen.

It was just as well that Mullett had made the detour between home and the club. 'See this,' he said angrily, unfolding the rag, and holding it up for the benefit of the half-empty room.

'You're holding it upside down, sir,' prompted the long, pale face of PC Pooley.

Flustered, Mullett turned the paper the right way up. 'What it says, right across the front page – and I quote – is, "COPS BEATEN BY CHILD MOLESTERS". Inside, the paper details what it claims are the mistakes police, right up and down the country, are making by not monitoring paedophiles. We're being accused of rape and murder.'

A terrible squeaking sound was coming from the middle of the room.

'These seats, sir. Sorry,' apologized Detective Constable Arthur Hanlon. 'There must be something wrong with them.'

Mullett was not going to enter into a discussion about the new office furniture. He was aware that people had already been grumbling, the ungrateful slobs.

'When I want your opinion, Detective, you'll know about it.' Mullett's stride was well and truly ruined – and it was only ten past nine in the morning. He looked about the room, hoping DI Bert Williams might have materialized, ready to take over with the finer details, as per his duty. But he was still nowhere to be seen.

Right, Mullett said firmly to himself; he was not going to be derailed by a lack of attendance and discipline. 'Now, while the nature of Julie Hudson's disappearance bears some similarities with the case of Miranda Connelly – the girl who was snatched from a department store in Bath last July – there are enough differences for me to believe at the moment that there is no connection. Notably, Miranda Connelly was a good four years younger, and the store in question had virtually no security. I don't like to say it, but it was a case of somewhat easy pickings. Aster's, as we all know, is a famously well-run ship – the pride of Denton.'

There was a titter from the floor, but Mullett didn't bother to look up. 'I doubt very much that Aster's was being targeted by a paedophile. No. In fact, I don't believe Julie Hudson was snatched by anyone,' he continued. 'And the last thing I want is for the press to start printing such nonsense.' He paused, running his fingers down his newly trimmed moustache. 'Where's DC Clarke?'

'She's off duty today, sir,' replied DC Hanlon, accompanied by more of the awful squeaking.

'Taking a well-deserved rest,' someone else chipped in. 'Frisky little thing.'

As a further bout of tittering subsided, Mullett said calmly, 'Hanlon, you were with DC Clarke when she interviewed Mr and Mrs Hudson together yesterday evening at their home. I've read Clarke's report – am I right in thinking there are good grounds to believe that Julie has in fact run away?'

'That's the impression we both arrived at, sir,' said Hanlon. 'As you will have read, Mr and Mrs Hudson appear to have a number of personal issues, to say the least. Frankly, they could barely look each other in the eye. And the girl's bedroom was suspiciously tidy, as if one of the parents had hurriedly cleaned the place up.'

Mullett wasn't sure how much he trusted DC

Clarke's intuition; she seemed rather immature and impressionable. Or Hanlon's for that matter. The great oaf was too fat to take seriously. Yet he was willing to give them credit here. A girl running away from home seemed straightforward enough, even for them. What he didn't need was pressure from the press drumming up hysteria. He knew how pernicious they could be, having been bitten once before – it had nearly ended his career.

'Thank you, Hanlon. One of the reasons why I wanted to be here this morning, having been alerted to what our friends in Fleet Street are trying to cook up, is to make sure we approach this case with an appropriate and proportionate response.'

Mullett's mind flashed to the evergreen fairways of the Royal Denton Golf Club, and the impressive men making up this morning's foursome. 'I shouldn't have to spell it out,' he said, knowing that was exactly what he'd have to do, 'but we don't want any unnecessary attention. Which would distract us from our proper investigations.'

'Does that mean, sir,' asked DS Frost, slumped in a seat at the back, puffing away, 'that you don't want us to go public on this missing Julie Hudson?'

'That's exactly what I'm ordering – for the time being. I don't want public lynchings breaking out in Denton, just because a few tabloid hacks have it in for the police. DI Williams is in charge of this case. When he gets in. For the time being ...' Mullett quickly glanced about the tatty room. It was going to take a lot more than the addition of a few modern comforts to get the place up to a standard befitting a modern division. 'For the time being,' the station commander repeated slowly, 'DS Frost will be handling the investigation.'

Mullett doubted Frost could do a worse job than DI Williams, and he was, worryingly, the highest-ranking officer present. 'I suggest, Frost,' he added, 'you and Hanlon get straight over to the Hudsons' home and get this matter ironed out.'

As he was heading for the exit Mullett suddenly stopped in his tracks, and shouted over his shoulder, 'Oh, and I'd also like to remind everyone that the canteen will be shut as of tomorrow, when we embark upon the next stage in the station's renovations. A replacement trolley service will be coming round throughout the day.'

With that Mullett was out of the briefing room and marching down the corridor, only to feel a tap on his arm.

'A quick word, Super.' It was DS Frost. 'Bert, sorry, DI Williams, had asked me to process the October crime clear-up stats for County, which, as you know, are due in tomorrow first thing. But with me taking over the Hudson case, I don't see how I'm going to make this deadline. There's an awful lot of paperwork.'

There was a strong smell of tobacco, and cheap

aftershave. The detective sergeant looked smart enough, if a little crumpled – suited, but the Paisley tie had seen better days. He was of medium height and build, with thinning, light-brown hair, intense dark eyes and an almost permanent grin on his face. Mullett could never be sure whether Frost was being mocking or friendly. 'You'll get it done, Frost,' he said. Though dismayed, Mullett was not surprised to hear that Williams had tried to pass on yet another one of his duties.

'Enjoy your golf, sir,' Mullett heard Frost shout from the other end of the corridor.

'Any sign of Inspector Williams?' Mullett asked irritably, not even looking in Station Sergeant Bill Wells's direction, as he was striding across the lobby.

'No, sir,' said Wells, from behind the front desk. He was quickly shuffling the duty roster over his Pools coupon. 'No sign, sorry, sir.'

'Keep trying.' A few paces on, Mullett added, 'Sunday morning or not, it wouldn't do any harm if you looked a little more alert. And this lobby is a bloody disgrace. But not for much longer – the decorators will be starting in here too in the next few days. I want the public to feel not just welcomed when they visit the station, but to realize we're in a properly organized division too. It's not a tatty social club, you know.'

With that Wells watched the tall, straight-backed Mullett, in his ridiculous golfing gear, delicately push his way through the lobby doors, which Wells had to concede could do with a lick of paint, and march across the yard to his gleaming Rover, neatly aligned in the super's special parking slot.

It's all right for some, Wells thought, retrieving his Pools coupon: golf, Sunday dinner, followed, no doubt, by a long snooze. He looked down at the scruffy receipt. He definitely hadn't won.

The phone rang the second Wells was reaching for his tea mug. Control was putting through calls to the front desk because they were understaffed – part of Mullett's bloody new cost-cutting regime, which was hitting the weekends worst.

'Can you speak up,' Wells said. 'What was that? You've just seen a van circling Market Square?'

'Yes,' the softly spoken male voice replied. 'At least half a dozen times.'

Wells thought he could detect a trace of an Irish accent. His heart skipped a beat. 'What colour was the van?'

'White. It was white.'

'Any idea of the make?'

'Ford Transit. No doubt about it.'

'I don't suppose you got the licence number?' Wells asked hopefully.

'Yes, I did.'

'And?'

'Hang about a moment. Yes, here it is: N16 UES.'

'Wait a minute.' Wells fumbled for his pen and the

call-register log. 'Can you repeat that, please? Hello?
Hello?'

The man had rung off, before Wells had had time to
slide open the panel behind him and alert PC Ridley,
the duty controller, to listen in. *Bugger*, he said to himself. All he could remember of the licence number was
that it had an 'N' and an 'S' in it, and maybe an eight
too.

'Look who we've got here – it's the Old Bill.' Frost
had appeared in the lobby, making for the exit.

'Hello, Jack, off somewhere nice?'

'You know me, Bill, and my love of the great out-
doors. Talking of which, I don't suppose Inspector
Allen's rung in from his hols? There's some info missing from the crime clear-up stats I'm meant to be
processing for County HQ. Maybe I'll leave the lot on
his desk for his return, and he can join up the dots.'

'Jim Allen's not going to like that. Nor is the super,
Jack, if it's late. Allen's away for another week.'

'They get paid more than us, Bill. Let's not forget.'

'I haven't, Jack.' As Frost was nearing the exit, Wells
added, 'Oh by the way, Jack, it probably isn't anything,
but a man just rang in to say he'd seen a white van
being driven round and round Market Square.'

'I don't suppose he kindly supplied the licence
number as well?'

'No . . . not all of it. But he said it was a Transit.'

'Did he now? Well, nothing to worry about then—'

Wells watched in horror as a disgusting mound of

rags and bones entered the station and collided with Frost.

'Jesus,' a winded Frost spluttered, immediately starting to brush his mac. 'It's Steptoe without his son.'

'Sorry, Mr Frost, I didn't see you,' croaked Desmond Thorley.

'Looks like times are treating you as well as ever, Des,' said Frost. 'Amazing what riches lurk in Denton Woods.'

'You'd be surprised, Mr Frost.'

'I'm sure I would. So what brings you back to the land of the living?' Frost had paused by the exit.

'I want to report an incident,' said Thorley.

'Don't tell me. On a dark and stormy night,' said Frost.

'It was morning, actually. And very cold too.'

'Is that right? Well, old Bill Wells over there is ready and waiting with pen and paper. Spin him a good one and he might even fetch you a cuppa.'

'You'll be lucky,' muttered Wells.

Sunday (2)

Detective Inspector Bert Williams made one final lunge for his radio. Having been knocked from its holder, it was hanging near the bloodied handbrake. It should have been easier to reach there, but Bert was never going to be able to grab it from where he was, half in, half out of the car. He could barely move. Besides, he had no idea whether the radio still worked.

It had taken him the best part of he didn't know how long just to shift his upper body closer by a few inches. Time had lost relevance. Life seemed to be slowing to a standstill. He knew he was shutting down for good.

He wheezed, bracing himself for another wave of

pain to spread tightly across his chest. *Flaming arse-holes, it hurt.*

Perhaps it would have been better if he'd been killed outright. Now he was left in the middle of nowhere to digest the fact that he'd fucked up. He was a better copper than that.

His mind flashed to Betty, making him wince. The compensation coming to her would be pitiful. He should have saved more carefully, planned for his retirement. At least then she would have been sitting on a tidy sum. The things he should have done – all very well to think about that now. What a bloody idiot he'd been.

And who would pick up the pieces? It was big, all right. He thought of Frost, his deputy. Was Frost up to it?

One way or another it was all there in the mountain of paperwork on his desk, back at the station, a fat file crying out for attention. Lucky, in some sense, that he never threw anything away, and rarely handed stuff back to Records.

But no one, not even Frost, would find what they needed – in time, anyway, to save him. Though just maybe, hopefully, in time to save other lives. Those bastards had to be put away. He'd never known a more ruthless gang.

Bert tried to pull his hand back and make himself more comfortable. His shoulder and his head were resting at an awkward angle against the side of the opened driver's door. The handset was definitely closer, almost within reach now. If only the door hadn't opened and he hadn't all but fallen out. If only he had the strength for another lunge. If only . . .

Arseholes, he was tired. He tried to focus, not on the blood still seeping from his chest, but on the dense hedge, the other side of the ditch. The tree-tops beyond that. Denton was far in the distance. No one would ever come down here – that's why he'd chosen it.

Sunday (3)

'Steady on, boss,' said DC Arthur Hanlon.

Frost had mounted the pavement while rounding Green Lane, as it led into Beech Crescent. He wasn't even going fast. 'Tight corner,' he exhaled heavily.

Frost disliked driving. It had taken him three attempts to pass his Advanced Police Speed and Chase Proficiency Test, quite a few years back, when he was still in uniform. He wouldn't have bothered had it not at the time been obligatory. When Frost was with Detective Inspector Bert Williams, as he normally was, Williams drove, insisted on it, whether he was pissed or not. The inspector said it helped him think. Frost himself couldn't do both – think and drive.

'Here we are, boss,' said Hanlon, once Frost was slowing on Carson Road.

Nosing the unmarked Cortina to a stop outside the Hudson house, Frost managed to scrape the hubcaps noisily along the kerb. Hurriedly he clambered out and lit a cigarette, taking two long, hard puffs, before throwing the smouldering remains on to the crazy paving.

Sensing something was wrong before he even reached the smoked-glass front door, Frost suddenly increased his pace. What was strange was the fact that there was no one anxiously peering out of a window to see who had pulled up, that the house was oddly still. The curtains were not drawn, the windows were shut. Frost stuck his finger on the bell, heard a ding dong and waited. Nothing. Impatient, he rapped on the glass, to no effect.

'Doesn't look like anyone's home, boss,' said Hanlon behind him, still catching his breath.

'I'd rather you didn't call me boss, if that's all right, Arthur. It might give me ideas above my station. You wait here, I'm going round the back.'

Left on his own, Hanlon bent down and peered through the letterbox. He caught a whiff of Alpine air freshener – he didn't remember that from yesterday evening. He heard nothing and saw only an empty hall. Standing up, he tried the door. Locked. Turning round he noticed a neighbour, a young woman, in a house across the way, staring at him from behind half-open curtains, then he noticed someone else, older, in another front window, and another. It felt like the whole street was watching him.

From the back of the house he heard the sound of breaking glass, then a thump and a muffled crash.

'Jack?' he shouted, knowing he couldn't leave the front door, having been told to wait there. He braced himself. 'Jack?' he repeated, alarmed.

Hanlon bent down once more to peer through the letterbox. Something about the stillness inside unsettled him too. On the verge of retreating to the car to call for back-up, Hanlon watched, relieved, as the distinctive form of Frost, shrouded in his mac, approached the other side of the smoked glass.

'Shit,' he heard Frost say.

The detective sergeant clearly couldn't open the front door from the inside either. It must have been double-locked, the key missing.

'Call an ambulance!' Frost shouted. 'And get Scenes of Crime and uniform down here pronto, then come round the back. The kitchen door's open.'

Frost quickly returned to the kitchen and to, he presumed, Wendy Hudson. A fully dressed blonde woman was lying unconscious, in a pool of blood, on the black-and-white chequered linoleum floor. She had been badly beaten around the head, but she was still alive, just. Frost could detect a faint pulse. He took off his mac – a recent present from his wife, Mary

– and gently laid it over the unconscious woman, before removing his jacket and laying that on her, too.

Hanlon appeared in the kitchen. Frost had had to smash one of the small windowpanes on the back door to release the catch and bolt.

'Oh dear me,' said Hanlon, rushing forward. 'The poor woman.'

'It's her, is it?'

'Yes, it's her, all right. And she was a looker, too.'

'I saw her foot from the window,' said Frost. 'Had to break in. All the doors and windows were shut tight. No sign of forced entry. The back door was bolted also, which means that whoever did this most likely let themselves out of the front door, and then double-locked it.'

'Out of habit?' said Hanlon.

'Could be,' said Frost, troubled. The woman was in a terrible state. It had been a brutal, frenzied attack, though given her untouched clothing it didn't look like she'd been sexually assaulted. 'I'd like to know where Mr Hudson is right now. And, more importantly, where the hell Julie Hudson is.' A case of a missing child, a presumed runaway, had suddenly become a lot more complicated.

'I'll alert Control, get them to put out a search for Steven Hudson right away,' said Hanlon, still short of breath. 'I noticed his car wasn't out the front.'

'That's what they pay you for, Arthur. Sharp insights like that.'

'It was there yesterday evening,' said Hanlon. 'A flashy, bright-yellow TR7.'

'A man of taste,' Frost shrugged.

'Steve Hudson's in the motor business. That place out on Bath Road – nearly new sports cars. They've got some beautiful motors.'

'Wouldn't know one if I saw one,' said Frost, crouching and feeling yet again for Wendy Hudson's pulse. Although he occasionally felt like giving Mary a quick slap, the little firebrand, he knew it took a certain sort of person to actually hit a woman, again and again until she was an unconscious mess of raw meat. Frost suddenly remembered it was his wedding anniversary on Friday, and if he didn't come up with something special for Mary he'd be in for a hiding, all right.

When Hanlon returned from calling Control for the second time, Frost said, 'Wait with her. I'm going to snoop around.'

Frost could already hear the ambulance's siren in the distance. It would be there shortly – there was little traffic about at this time on a Sunday morning, especially as the clocks had gone back. Most of Denton was still in pyjamas.

'You sure no one else is in the house, boss?' he heard Hanlon calling, as he was climbing the stairs.

The upstairs layout of the semi was all too familiar to Frost: three bedrooms, an airing cupboard and a bathroom. Frost only glanced into the first and smallest room, which was being used for laundry, with a large clothes horse, ironing board and piles of washing. The next he entered. It was the marital chamber, and what a tip. A Scandinavian duvet lay on the floor. What looked like pieces of a broken vase were strewn on top of it and across the rest of the room, along with assorted make-up, hairbrushes, hairbands, jewellery.

It looked to Frost as if someone had made a clean sweep of the dressing table, which was now bare, with the drawer gaping. The built-in wardrobe had been ransacked as well, with clothes, women's clothes mainly, and shoes and other accessories scattered nearby. In one corner lay a mound of lacy underwear, some of it appeared ripped and in shreds.

Some bust-up. Frost wondered whether somebody had been looking for something.

Down the narrow landing was the girl's room, which, in contrast to the master bedroom, was in perfect order. The walls were smothered in posters and magazine pull-outs of pop stars. There was that lanky bloke from The Boomtown Rats, and a lad in make-up with stuff tied in his hair, dressed as a pirate. *Adam Ant* it said. Behind the pictures Frost could make out pastel-pink emulsion and traces of a floral border.

He sat down on the narrow bed and pulled out a crushed pack of Rothmans from a trouser pocket. As he did so he accidentally kicked over a pile of magazines stacked at the side of the bed. He reached down and picked up the nearest. *Smash Hits*. A whole magazine devoted to pop music. He sighed. He wasn't into music, of any description, though Mary was always playing records, or listening to the charts on the radio, as if she were still a teenager. Drove him nuts.

Frost's mind had wandered. He glanced over his shoulder, back at Adam Ant, and there in a corner was a poster he hadn't spotted before, of Charles and Di. Good luck to them, he thought. They were going to need it. Any bloody marriage did.

As he felt around for his matches he heard a rustling out in the corridor, as well as the ambulance siren getting much louder. *Blast.* His matches were in his mac, which was downstairs covering Wendy Hudson. Standing, he returned the fag packet to his trouser pocket just as the bedroom door swung open. In ran a long-haired, dusty black cat, causing Frost to leap backwards into a chest of drawers. A large radio cassette recorder toppled over and fell on to the carpeted floor with a thud.

Frost eyed the cat warily. He didn't like cats. The feeling seemed mutual. The moggy jumped on to the bed and crouched menacingly by the pillow. Frost gave it a wide berth as he quickly exited the room, and bumped into Hanlon on the stairs. 'I thought I told you to wait with the injured party.'

'I heard a crash. I thought, I thought that—'

'Never mind,' said Frost, 'you better meet the ambulance out front and direct them round the back.'

As Hanlon turned clumsily on the stairs and began the brief descent, Frost said, 'When you and the lovely

Sue interviewed the Hudsons yesterday evening, did you get upstairs?'

'Yes, of course. I do know my procedures, Jack. I had a good look in the girl's room. Weirdly tidy.'

'You're right there. Did you get a butcher's at the marital chamber?' Sirens blared outside.

'Well, no, I didn't. It didn't seem appropriate. Why?'

'The kid's disappearance is troubling me more and more by the minute. Mullett's not going to be able to keep this quiet for long. We'll have to make an appeal for witnesses.'

'Yes,' said Hanlon, making his way through the kitchen and out of the back door. 'But it's the mother I'm more worried about right now.'

'She'll live,' Frost called after him, not at all convinced she would. He reached down to feel her pulse again. There was a faint but steady beat. While crouching he fished in his mac pocket for his matches, retrieving them just as the ambulance men and Hanlon hurried into the kitchen, followed by a couple of uniformed PCs.

'DC Hanlon will fill you in on the details,' Frost said, leaving them to it. He entered the hallway and poked his head round the corner of the lounge-diner. Dominating the room was a lurid orange-patterned carpet. Aside from the functional G-plan table and chairs at one end, and a fat leather sofa and matching armchair at the other, there was an enormous television, a VCR and a neat stack of video cassettes in a corner.

Frost ambled over to have a closer look. That lot, he decided, must have cost a small fortune. It was state of the art. Yet it was, by the looks of it, still all there, untouched. The cassette at the top of the pile was *Star Wars*. Hadn't everyone seen *Star Wars* at the cinema?

'There's clear evidence of a break-in,' Frost heard, coming from one of the uniforms in the kitchen. 'What's been taken? Where's Scenes of Crime?' the PC continued.

'Hold your horses, lad,' said Frost, finally lighting a fag, and poking his head back into the kitchen, while exhaling a cloud of smoke. 'It's not a burglary. Nothing's been nicked. There's jewellery and knick-knacks all over the place upstairs and a stash of top-notch electrical gear in the front room. It's a domestic, of one sort or another.' He coughed.

'Unless it's something more complicated,' Hanlon interjected.

Frost ignored him, believing the only complication was his own forced entry. At the very least it would involve another load of paperwork. But the woman was in a terrible state . . . 'You and I,' he said to Hanlon, 'had better quiz the neighbours while we're here. This is prime curtain-twitching country.'

Hanlon gave a knowing nod. 'You're right there.'

'You finished with these?' Frost said, addressing the ambulance men, who were preparing the stretcher. Before waiting for an answer he grabbed his jacket and mac, which had been half shoved across the kitchen floor. 'It ain't half nippy out.'

Shrugging his garments on and emerging into broad daylight he realized his new coat was bearing smudges of blood. At least blood was easy enough for the missus to remove. Though why Mary fussed so much over his appearance he had no idea. There were far more important things for her to worry about.

'Let's save time and split up,' said Frost once on the pavement, aware that despite its brightness the sun was not warm. Winter would soon be upon them.

'Good idea,' said Hanlon.

Detective Constable Arthur Hanlon, almost as wide as he was tall, waddled down Carson Road. Frost made his way across the road to the semi directly opposite the Hudsons'. He rapped gently on the door, waiting briefly before repeating the knock.

Nobody in, he was thinking. The sirens surely would have been enough to wake the dead. Looking about him his eyes settled on a low-slung, dark-blue Jag in the drive, the chrome trim glinting.

A dulled yet clearly cross female voice from within the house finally reached Frost, followed by the rattle of the lock.

'Yes?' A tousled brunette peeked through the crack – hazel-coloured eyes looking out suspiciously. There was a thick intruder chain holding the door.

'Denton CID.' Frost held out his warrant card.

'What do you want?' she said aggressively.

'Can I have a word, please, miss?'

'I'm not decent.'

'Don't worry about that,' said Frost, 'I'm not a church warden.'

'Hang on a minute.' The door was pushed shut.

Frost looked up at the sky, breathed out, thought there were still some perks to the job.

The door was then opened, the chain removed and the young woman, standing in the hallway in a very short, maroon-coloured silk dressing-gown, was saying, 'Yeah? What do you want then?'

Heat and heavily perfumed air leaked out of the house. 'The house opposite, the Hudsons'?' Frost gestured over his shoulder to where the ambulance had backed on to the drive. 'Know them?'

The girl peered quizzically round Frost. 'No. Haven't been here long, as it happens.'

She had a strong south-east London accent. 'Down from the smoke?' asked Frost. He couldn't keep his eyes off her legs, which went on for ever.

'Yeah,' she said, 's'pose.'

'What brings you to Denton?' Frost thought she couldn't have been more than twenty-one, twenty-two.

'I'm not sure that's any of your business,' she sneered, pushing the door to.

Frost jammed his foot in the way before it was completely closed. 'Just being friendly,' he said. 'I see you've left your manners behind, if you ever had any.'

'Piss off,' she said.

'What's your name?'

'I don't have to tell you.'

'No, you don't, not if you want me to haul you in for obstructing police business.'

'You can't do that.'

'Yes, I bloody well can.'

'All right, all right,' she laughed. 'It's Louise. Louise Daley.'

'Look, Miss Daley,' said Frost, now pushing the door open a little further. 'I've no time for prima donnas. A woman's been subjected to a very violent attack – in that house just over there, the Hudsons'. She was damn nearly killed. Sometime last night or early this morning. Did you happen to see or hear anything at all? This is no laughing matter.'

'No,' she said immediately. 'Was out last night – got back late. I sleep like a log.' She paused, looked down at bare feet. 'Now can I get back to bed?'

'Anyone else at home?' said Frost.

'No mate,' she said, smiling slyly. 'It's just me.'

'Your car, is it?' Frost glanced back at the Jag in the drive.

'Yeah, what of it?'

'Bit flash for a young thing like you?'

'I got expensive taste,' she said, smiling again.

'I bet,' Frost said, removing his foot and letting Louise Daley shut the door. 'Keep your nose clean.' He heard her reattach the intruder chain. Turning, he saw Hanlon crossing the road towards him.

'Nothing of interest yet,' shouted Hanlon. 'Bloody amazing, isn't it – these people spend all day and night peering out between their curtains, but when it comes to something important they see bugger all.'

'Always the way,' said Frost.

'And looks like the neighbours immediately next door to the Hudsons', number forty, are away,' continued Hanlon, now standing next to Frost. 'There's a pile of post in the hall.'

Frost fumbled for his cigarettes and said, 'A couple more houses each, then, and let's get back to the station.'

'OK with me,' agreed Hanlon.

'Flighty mare, that one.' Frost nodded in the direction of Louise Daley's home just behind him. 'She's got a few issues.'

'She not see anything?' said Hanlon, surprise in his voice.

'So she says,' said Frost, lighting his cigarette.

'She was gawping out of the window when we first got here,' said Hanlon.

'Was she now?'

They watched silently as Wendy Hudson was loaded gently into the ambulance and the vehicle took off at speed.

Sunday (4)

Behind his counter, Station Sergeant Bill Wells jumped as Frost barged through the doors, allowing them to swing back into DC Arthur Hanlon. That man is never going to keep up with Frost, thought Wells.

'Right, Arthur,' Frost shouted over his shoulder, 'run along and fetch us a tea, will you, while that canteen's still open for business – two sugars – and I'll see who I can reach at Aster's. We need to check out their security arrangements.'

'But Jack,' Hanlon protested, 'it's Sunday.'

'What of it?' said Frost, making for the corridor. 'I'm not suggesting we go to the store.' He paused, stared back into the lobby at a new poster alongside the fading Colorado Beetle warning. 'What the hell's that, Bill? An advertisement for the annual Denton Halloween Ball?'

'No,' said Wells, looking behind him at an angry Alsatian, foaming at the mouth, 'Crufts are putting on a Christmas special in Denton.' He laughed at his own joke.

Hanlon shuffled dejectedly across the lobby, giving Frost a wide berth, disappearing into the safety of the dilapidated building.

'What's up with him?' said Wells.

'He's hungry,' said Frost. 'Missing his elevenses.'

'Actually, Jack, glad I've caught you. There is something I wanted to—'

'Not now, Bill. Could you get me the name and home address of the Aster's manager?'

'Easy,' Wells said proudly. 'That'll be Ken Butcher. My missus plays darts with his wife, for the ladies' team at the Bricklayers Arms.'

'Debbie chucks arrows? Whatever next.' Frost sounded genuinely surprised.

'Ladies' regional final tomorrow night. They're playing a team from Rimmington, which was runner-up in the nationals last year,' Wells said with a grin, before returning his gaze to the new rabies warning poster behind him. It had already lost its fixing in the top-left corner.

'That's one place I'll be steering clear of, then,' said Frost, heading for his office.

Wells had just finished re-sticking the corner of the poster when a call came through.

The woman at the other end of the line was hysterical. 'Please calm down, love,' said Wells, trying to open the call register and grab a pen. He was sick of having to man the phones alongside an understaffed Control. 'I can't hear you,' he found himself shouting into the mouthpiece.

As she quietened a little, before explaining herself more clearly, Wells could hear a young child crying in the background.

'Attacked?' Wells finally said loudly. 'In the garden? By a fox, you think?' Wells looked up at the new poster, an uneasy feeling sweeping through him.

This morning was giving him the jitters: first there'd been an Irishman, giving him a registration number, which he immediately forgot, of a van being driven suspiciously round and round Market Square, and now here was a woman claiming her child had just been mauled by a wild animal.

Rabid was his sudden thinking, having just put up that damn poster. A stack of them had been lying in the cupboard under the counter for weeks, following a county-wide rabies warning. Except Wells had promptly forgotten all about them. Until he'd accidentally stumbled upon them that morning, while looking for a new biro. And now his mind was jumping to all sorts of worrying conclusions.

Many minutes later Wells had managed to write

down an address and was attempting to reach Frost –
to no avail. Pressing the button on the Tannoy and lifting the microphone to his mouth, he said, crossly,
'Detective Sergeant Frost to contact the front desk at
once.'

Where the hell was Frost? He'd only just been in
the lobby and now he'd disappeared.

Sunday (5)

'This is a call for uniform, surely,' said Frost, grumpily reversing the Cortina in the police yard. Even on a Sunday afternoon, and without Mullett's gleaming chariot taking pride of place, it was impossible to turn around and not scrape something. 'Why are we having to check this out?'

'Mullett's new Sunday staffing rosters,' huffed Hanlon. 'What uniform there is seems to be tied up at the Hudson place.'

'So the super thinks that because it's a Sunday coppers aren't needed,' said Frost, clunking through the gears. 'Bloody ridiculous. He should know by now that there's no rest for the wicked.'

'Doesn't help, I suppose, with Bert not being in, and Allen on holiday.'

Frost sighed loudly. 'I expect even lovely Sue Clarke will have her legs up – if not apart. While we're off to investigate an attack on a nipper, by apparently a bloody fox. Where's Johnny Morris when you need him?' Frost accelerated up Eagle Lane.

'Hold on a minute, Jack, you wanted that last right, towards Denton Woods – Forest View?'

'Oops, silly me,' said Frost. 'Can't turn round now. Not with the turning circle on this heap of tin. Let's take the scenic route.' Frost pulled straight across the Bath Road, making for the ring road, relentlessly crunching through the gears.

'Bloody clutch'll go, carry on like that,' Hanlon said under his breath.

'You complaining about my driving? Ah, look, Hudson's Classic Cars. Thought it was around here. May as well pop in. See what's on offer.'

'Jack, there isn't time,' Hanlon said, pulling nervously on his seatbelt. 'According to the Old Bill, this young child, it sounds serious. We can come straight back here.'

'A little prone to hysterics is the Old Bill. Don't worry, we'll only be a minute, Arthur.'

'You planned this, didn't you, you devious sod?' Hanlon's jowls jiggled as the Cortina bumped up the kerb.

'Right,' Frost said cheerily, climbing out and

peering over the roof, across to the forecourt. 'Sunday's the day for leisurely pondering a new motor, isn't it?'

Strung above the entrance to the forecourt was a fancy banner, swirly gold lettering on a British Racing Green background: *Hudson's Classic Cars*. In a corner of the forecourt stood a tatty Portakabin.

Bit quiet, Frost thought, surveying the gleaming, brightly coloured stock. Then he spotted a lanky young man in a large anorak, sitting on the step of the Portakabin. He was cupping a cigarette.

'Why don't you stay here, Arthur, and I'll go and have a word with the lad. Don't want to make him feel hemmed in.'

At that moment the radio crackled into life and Hanlon squeezed back into the passenger seat of the Cortina.

'If that's Control,' said Frost, 'tell them I'm taking a leak.'

Frost ambled across the forecourt, his mac flapping in the breeze. He found himself squeezing between a bright-red Datsun sports car and a green Volkswagen Golf.

'Hello there,' Frost said amiably, approaching the Portakabin.

The lad got to his feet, adjusting the front of his anorak and flicking the cigarette butt aside. Frost could see that he was wearing a suit under the parka.

'Thinking of trading in my Ford, over there.' Frost

nodded in the direction of the Cortina. 'For something a little more stylish.'

The young man peered over Frost's shoulder at the car, and sighed, nodding his head. 'Yeah? What did you have in mind?'

Frost swung round, pulling a Rothmans out of the crumpled pack. 'How about that bright-red one? Got a light?'

The young man handed over a Zippo, eyeing the Cortina again. Hanlon was slowly climbing out, and shaking crumbs off his jacket.

Noticing the lad's bemused frown, Frost added, 'Need a car that can support a bit of weight. But it's also got to have enough oumph for a quick getaway.'

Still looking surprised, the lad said, 'The Datsun? Nice motor that – a 260z. Two owners from new, only 50K on the clock. Goes like the clappers.'

'Does it indeed? Well, it might just be for me then, I'm always in a hurry. Can I give it a whizz?'

The man's face fell. 'Can't,' he said.

'Why ever not?'

'Haven't got the keys. Slight problem there. Sorry. Can I take your details and give you a bell later?'

'In a bit of a rush, I'm afraid. To be honest, I've seen something else I'm keen on. Going for a second look at it – in fact, this very afternoon.' Frost paused, surveyed the forecourt once more. 'What's your name, by the way?'

'Brendan.'

Frost thought he'd detected an Irish lilt to his voice. 'Well, Brendan . . . I'm a little confused. Sunday is surely the best day of the week here. You've got all these smart motors begging for new owners. Yet you don't have the bloody keys.'

Now looking a little forlorn, Brendan said, 'The boss has the combination to the safe. He's very particular about not giving it out. And he's not showed up yet. Truth be told, he hasn't rung in either. I can't even get into the office. Turned loads of people away already.'

'Is that right?' said Frost doubtfully. 'Steve Hudson? He's your boss, yes?'

'Yeah, that's him.' Brendan suddenly looked on guard again.

'Does he often simply not turn up?'

'He's a busy man.'

Frost was picking up odd vibes from this lad. 'When did you last see him?'

'What is this? An interrogation? You the Gestapo?'

'Just answer the question,' Frost said sharply.

The lad's brow furrowed. 'So, he left work yesterday lunchtime. He was in a hurry.'

'Why? Why the hurry?' Frost prompted.

Brendan pulled out a pack of smokes.

'Don't mind if I do,' Frost said, reaching for one of Brendan's fags. He'd just crushed a butt-end underfoot. 'Haven't had one of those for a while.' There was a thick, horizontal green band on the packet and the word *Major*. 'From across the water, right?'

'Yeah,' the lad said, not looking up. 'Originally.'

'Prefer the weather over here?' Frost asked.

The lad peered up at the sky. Heavy clouds were tumbling in from the west. 'Yeah. Every minute of it.'

'Steven Hudson, then – where was he dashing off to yesterday?'

'Who knows?'

'You can do better than that.'

'Why should I?'

Frost looked over at Hanlon, who was leaning against the Cortina. 'Don't think I need to spell it out, do I?'

'All right,' Brendan said calmly, 'I didn't hear everything but it looked like he had a blazing row with a customer, over that very car, the Datsun. Then he says he's got an appointment out of town, and that I can have the rest of the day off. So I'm out of here, too.'

'What time exactly?' Frost said.

'One thirty, two? I don't know. I didn't hang around, that's for sure. It was pissing down. And the boss isn't usually so generous.'

'Who was the customer?' asked Frost. 'Seen him before?'

'Seen *her* before, you mean. It was a she.'

'A woman?' said Frost, surprised.

'Yeah, she was pretty, too. But you'd be surprised at the number of women who come round here, looking for something fast and sporty. Mr Hudson seems to have a way with them.'

'That so?' said Frost, backing away. 'Well, I'll leave you to enjoy the rest of your Sunday. Don't work too hard. And if Mr Hudson does turn up with the combination give me a call right away. I can just see myself in the Datsun.' He dropped his card at the lad's feet.

'I know all about you lot,' Brendan said quietly.

'Sorry, didn't catch your last name ... Brendan who?' Frost called back. But the lad either didn't hear, or didn't answer. Frost flicked away the rest of his Irish smoke and made his way across the forecourt. Hanlon had already squeezed himself into the Cortina's driver's seat, and the engine was ticking over.

'Jack, Control have been on twice,' said Hanlon breathlessly. 'This Liz Fraser has called a number of times wanting to know where we are. She's frantic. She thinks that whoever, or rather whatever, attacked her baby might strike again. She's too terrified to leave the house.'

'I thought it was a fox.' Frost climbed into the passenger seat, relieved that he didn't have to drive. 'She should have called Rentokil, or that bleeding Johnny Morris for all I care. This is still not a job for CID.' He paused, fished for a fresh cigarette. 'That lad back there, Brendan, something about him I can't quite place. Not sure he's on the level.'

'Ah, Forest View,' Frost said as Hanlon swung the car into the secluded but scruffy cul-de-sac. 'Mary's always nagging on about wanting to move here. I can't see the attraction myself. Flamin' countryside with its rampaging wildlife. There's enough to deal with in the sodding town centre.'

'What's that, Jack?' Hanlon had been quietly humming along to 'The Winner Takes It All', which was blaring from the radio, annoying the hell out of Frost.

'Never mind. What number?'

'Two. Think we've just passed it.' Hanlon braked and reversed up the unmade road. 'Here we go . . . Jesus! What the . . .'

A dark-brown Mini Metro sped past, spraying gravel and clipping the Cortina's wing mirror.

'What number did you say?' Frost asked, blithely unconcerned.

'Two . . . wait a sec.' Hanlon dug out his notebook. 'No, twelve. But blimey, people shouldn't drive so fast down lanes like this.'

'Unless of course you think you're being chased by a rabid monster. C'mon, let's take a look anyway.'

Hanlon slammed the car into first, then abruptly stopped as quickly as he'd pulled away.

'Flaming hell, Arthur, you steady on now!'

'But it's criminal damage,' Hanlon said. 'At the very least dangerous driving. Besides, you're meant to stop at the scene of an accident – it's the law.'

'Forget it. He probably didn't realize he'd hit us,' said Frost. 'These things happen. Mary's always scraping our car.'

'And you're not?' said Hanlon, opening his door.

For someone so fat Arthur Hanlon could, on occasion, take Frost by surprise and move very quickly. The detective constable was out of the car and steaming up the overgrown garden path before Frost had got to his feet. 'Hang on,' Frost shouted after him, slamming the car door.

'Nobody in,' Hanlon wheezed as Frost caught up by the front door. Hanlon pressed the bell again and began rattling the door handle. 'Locked, too, not surprisingly.'

'Patience, Arthur. Give her a chance.'

Hanlon stepped back from the door and craned to his left and right, clearly working out the best way round the back.

More breaking and entering, thought Frost, just as he detected movement inside. 'Hold on, Arthur.' Frost could see that a large woman was slowly approaching the front door. 'Take your time, love,' he muttered.

'At last,' she said, opening up. 'You took your bloody time. Get better service in Sainsbury's.' She was youngish but very dishevelled, wearing baggy clothes in drab colours and no make-up. Strands of lank hair were stuck to her round, sweaty face. She had wire-framed glasses, the lenses badly smudged.

'Why didn't you trouble them, then?' said Frost, thinking if she lost some weight and tarted herself up a bit she could almost have been attractive. Perhaps she once was. 'Could have stocked up on Frosties at the same time.' Frost exhaled. The hallway, or perhaps it was the woman, smelt of stale sweat and urine. 'And toiletries.'

Hanlon gave Frost a hard look. 'I'm Detective Constable Arthur Hanlon, and this is Detective Sergeant Jack Frost, of Denton CID,' he said, pushing forwards. 'Mrs Fraser?'

'*Miss* Fraser. Liz Fraser.'

'Sorry,' said Hanlon. 'Liz Fraser. We understand your child's been' – he coughed – 'attacked.'

'By a hairy beast,' Frost added under his breath, wondering whether he should just alert Social Services and save himself wasting the next twenty minutes.

'You better come in,' Liz Fraser said. 'Becky's calmed down a lot. But she has some nasty scratches.'

'Scratches? No bite marks? No severed limbs?' Frost quipped before he and Hanlon were led through to the back of the house. There was a bright sitting room with large French doors, closed, leading on to a patio. Outside Frost could see a sand pit full of children's toys, and a revolving washing line. The yard was contained by a five-foot-high wooden fence. Beyond were the tall, dark trees of Denton Woods.

The sitting room appeared to have been hastily tidied, but it was dirty. Toys, clothes and piles of paper were in heaps in the corners, while the laminate floor was coated in grime. Sitting in the middle, chewing on a dummy, was a little fair-haired girl, two or so years old, in a dirty pink top, and red trousers. She looked happy enough, though there was an ugly bruise on her left cheek, and a bandage on her right wrist. She appeared also to have a faint bruise on her forehead. But there was no sign of anything that looked like a bite or a scratch.

'Hello, sweetheart,' Frost said, bending towards her. The toddler look startled and began to whimper. Frost pulled back. 'Nasty bruise, all right,' he said, addressing the mother. 'Shouldn't you have taken her to the doctor?'

'Try finding one on a Sunday.'

'The hospital? Could have got an ambulance out.'

'It wasn't that serious; I used to be a nurse,' Liz Fraser said. 'And I have a first-aid kit on the premises. For my job . . . I'm a childminder.'

Frost studied the place with renewed interest, taking in the quantity of kiddies' playthings, inside and out. It made sense.

'Why the great emergency?' said Hanlon. 'Why haul us all the way out here?'

'My little girl was attacked, in the garden,' the woman said nervously. 'Whatever sort of animal did this needs to be caught before another child is seriously hurt. Or worse.'

'You told the station,' said Hanlon, stepping over to the French doors, 'that you thought it was a fox.'

'Yes, that's what I first thought.' The woman followed him over to the doors. 'But I now think it might have been bigger – a big cat sort of thing.'

'A what?' exclaimed Frost. He was surprised to see Hanlon easily open the French doors – so they weren't locked, then. If the woman was genuinely afraid of something outside, she'd have at least secured the property.

Hanlon stepped into the yard, over the toys, walked round the sandpit and towards the high fence. Frost didn't think it would have been that easy for a fox to leap over, but what did he know?

'Yes,' Liz Fraser continued, 'a large cat. You know, perhaps one of those panthers.'

'A panther?' spluttered Frost.

'There were those sightings not so far from here, weren't there, near Wells last summer,' Liz Fraser insisted.

Frost was sure she was blushing. Her pale, greasy skin was turning blotchy.

'But I didn't see much, of course,' she added. 'I was in the kitchen tidying up, and Becky was having her nap in the pushchair, out the back. But as soon as I heard her scream, I ran outside.' She took a deep breath, and continued shakily, 'There it was, dark and hairy, disappearing over the fence.'

'Wasting police time is an offence, you know,' said Frost dismissively. He'd had enough. 'I suggest you get your story straight.' He made for the hallway, then paused by the lounge door. 'Who else lives here? The child's dad?'

'Chucked him out,' Liz Fraser said quietly. 'I live on my own now.'

'When did this happen?' said Frost. 'When did he go?'

'The other day,' she almost whispered.

'Where's he live now?' said Frost.

'Don't know and don't care.' Her bottom lip was quivering.

'Does he have a name?'

'Simon, Simon Trench.'

'You weren't married, then?'

'No, thank God.' Liz Fraser walked over to Becky, who'd begun crying in earnest, and picked her up, saying, 'It's all right, sweetheart.'

'You want to tell me exactly when you last saw this Simon Trench?'

'As I said, I chucked him out the other day. Haven't seen him since.'

She seemed to be avoiding looking Frost in the eye. Frost didn't see the point in pushing the woman on her relationship problems any further right now – he had an idea where it was heading. She was in all sorts of denial, and he was no shrink or social worker. What he suddenly wanted to do was to get the child into some type of proper care right away.

Hanlon was still in the backyard studying the fence and beyond. Frost thought the detective constable was being ridiculous, appearing to take the wild-animal nonsense seriously. But it gave him an idea, as he pictured in his mind the rabies warning poster Bill Wells had just stuck up in the lobby, back at the station. 'All right,' he said, 'we better get your daughter checked out by the experts.'

'But I was a nurse,' Liz Fraser said, panic – or was it fear? – creeping into her voice. 'I'm an experienced childminder.'

'So you've said,' said Frost.

'She doesn't need to see a doctor,' Liz Fraser gabbled. 'I've attended to her wounds. It's what's out there that I'm worried about. That's why I called the police.'

'It's what's out there that I'm worried about, too,' said Frost, looking away. 'We'll give you a lift to Denton General.'

'It's really not necessary,' Liz Fraser said, clutching her child tighter to her chest.

'Yes, it is,' countered Frost, as Hanlon stepped back into the lounge.

'But why?' Liz Fraser bleated.

'There's been an alert: rabies,' Frost said gravely. 'Young Becky will have to be tested and quarantined.'

'Oh,' was all Liz Fraser could say.

'I'm sure everything will be fine, but better to be safe than sorry,' said Frost. 'Come along, James Hunt here' – Frost nodded in Hanlon's direction – 'will drive us.'

Sunday (6)_____

Above the dreadful squeaking sound their shoes made as they all walked down the hospital corridor, Hanlon said in Frost's ear, 'I know what you're thinking, Jack, I got the measure of that woman too, but I'm not convinced an animal didn't do something. There were some strange marks on that fence.'

'We can't put the whole of Denton on alert for a rampaging black panther, with or without rabies, just because a mother's having a few personal problems,' said Frost loudly, not bothering who else heard. 'There'd be panic on the streets. Besides, it would play havoc with Mullett's golf. They'd have to shut the course. Come to think of it . . .'

'But even a hint of a rabies scare . . . what if that gets out to the public?' said Hanlon.

'Let's leave it in the hands of our good friend Doctor Philips here, for now.'

The consultant paediatrician, a white coat over his shirt and tie, had followed them to the end of the corridor. 'To be sure we'll need to isolate her for forty-eight hours,' Dr Philips said, smiling. 'We'll, of course, be able to accommodate the mother for that time as well.'

'As long as you keep a good eye on them both,' said Frost, 'and make sure those bruises are thoroughly looked at.'

'I think I know where we stand,' said Dr Philips. 'For the good of the child.'

'Good man,' said Frost, as he and Hanlon left Dr Philips, pushed through double swing-doors, out of the children's ward and into another corridor.

It took Frost and Hanlon less than three minutes to find the Lister Ward, where a young, fresh-faced WPC was keeping Wendy Hudson company. But it was a one-way street. Wendy Hudson, smothered in tubes and bandages, and surrounded by a phalanx of drips and monitors, had yet to regain consciousness.

According to the duty nurse, Mrs Hudson's condition, though very serious, was improving and she was able to breathe unaided. She had a fractured skull, a broken jaw and three cracked ribs.

'Been doing your nails?' said Frost to the freckled WPC; he couldn't remember her name. She had a pen in one hand and a notepad open and ready in the other.

The WPC flushed. 'No, sir, of course not.' She paused, then added, 'She hasn't moved an inch.'

'Well, don't you move, in case she does stir and decides to say something,' said Frost.

'I'm not going anywhere.'

'Good girl. If you need a tinkle, ask the nurse for one of those bedpans, and squat behind that curtain.'

The WPC flushed again, then stammered, 'Yes, sir.'

'Come on, Hanlon, let's hit the safari park,' Frost said. 'We've got a couple more calls to make before we get back to the safety of the station.'

'What about lunch, Jack?' said Hanlon anxiously. 'It's nearly three and I haven't had anything to eat since . . . well, I can't remember when. It might suit you to keep running around on empty, but it's not good for me to miss a meal.'

'We don't want that.' Frost playfully elbowed Hanlon in the stomach. 'Must take some filling.'

'I've got a healthy appetite, is all.'

'Some might say unhealthy,' mused Frost, thinking back to a couple of nights earlier and Mary having a go at him about his own diet. How he never had time for proper meals.

'Better than chain-smoking,' said Hanlon. 'I'm surprised you can still breathe.'

'That reminds me, there's another call we'll have to make. I'm out of fags. For some stupid reason they don't sell them here.'

Sunday (7)

Superintendent Stanley Mullett was sipping tea in his warm, cosy study, looking out over the sodden garden, when the phone went. He let it ring four times before picking it up. 'Yes?'

'Super, sir, it's Sergeant Wells, at the station.'

'Yes, Wells?' prompted Mullett.

'Sorry to bother you at home,' continued Wells.

'This had better be good,' said Mullett. He hated the autumn, the dampness, the dark – the fairways were in a terrible state today. And he hated being disturbed at home, when he was off duty, even more.

'It's just that, well . . .'

'Spit it out, man.'

'I still can't get hold of DI Williams. To be honest,

his wife hasn't seen him since yesterday morning. His car's missing as well.'

'I imagine that's something of a relief for her.'

'Oh no, sir. She's sick with worry. She wouldn't want me to be saying any of this, not to you – the last thing she wants is to create a fuss. Or get Bert into trouble. Apparently he's been off the booze for some time now.'

'Why are you even telling me all this?'

'I thought perhaps we should put out an alert to all units.'

'For God's sake, DI Williams is a grown man. OK, he should have reported for duty this morning, and I'll take issue with him about that when he does turn up, but it's not as if, by all accounts, he hasn't gone AWOL before. We've got enough trouble trying to locate a missing girl, and now these new developments, as it is.'

'Fair enough, sir,' said Wells. 'I just thought I'd pass it by you. And there's something else. A couple of things, actually . . .'

'This is all highly irregular, Wells.' Mullett was beginning to fume. 'Where's Frost right now? I thought I'd left him in charge.'

'Last time I saw him he was off to Forest View. A nipper's been attacked.'

'Attacked? What the hell do you mean, attacked? By whom?'

'A fox.'

'A fox? And this is a matter for CID?'

'Sunday staffing, sir. A lot of doubling-up is going on. We're all rushed off our feet.'

'Is that so, Sergeant. Well, keep up the good work.' Mullett slammed down the receiver, and quickly took another sip of his tea, but it had gone cold.

DC Arthur Hanlon followed directions up to the manager's office. He didn't quite understand what Frost was playing at, leaving the little girl at the hospital – seemed a risky ploy. Rabies. Still, he was the boss, for now at least. He felt on safer ground quizzing the Aster's store manager about the missing girl.

'Ken Butcher?' said Hanlon, walking into the manager's office and extending his hand.

'Yes, that's right,' said Butcher, a smartly dressed, bearded man in his early forties. 'Found your way up OK?'

'A lad showed me, thanks. A lot of staff about for a Sunday, considering the store's closed.'

'We're stocktaking.'

'Oh yes, your wife said so on the phone,' said Hanlon. Frost had detailed Hanlon to make arrangements for them to interview Butcher as soon as possible.

'We're getting ready for Christmas. Now, if you wouldn't mind getting to the point. We've still got a lot to do before the end of the day.'

'Yes, yes, of course,' said Hanlon.

But Butcher didn't seem too frantic – there was an open copy of a Sunday paper on his desk. 'It's just you, is it?' he said, leaning forward, and trying to cover the paper with his arm. 'Only, I was told a couple of detectives were on their way.'

'My colleague DS Frost is still downstairs, talking to some of the staff.'

'Hope he learns something useful. Not sure what help I can be. This is about a missing girl?'

'Yes, last seen on these premises, yesterday afternoon.'

'Do sit down, Detective.'

'Thanks,' said Hanlon, squeezing into a small plastic chair. He immediately regretted doing so. Aside from the discomfort, he was now having to look up at the bearded store manager. 'I'll need a list of all staff present yesterday,' he said firmly.

'Oh, really?'

'And perhaps you can outline to me your security arrangements, and which store detectives were on duty. We believe the girl, Julie Hudson – she's twelve, nearly thirteen, tall for her age, skinny, shoulder-length fair hair, with a dyed red streak – disappeared from the school-uniform floor.'

'And lingerie,' interjected Butcher.

'I'm sorry?'

'Uniforms and women's underwear are on the same floor.'

'Yes,' said Hanlon, 'of course. Interesting arrangement, by the way.'

'We thought it would help mums who were sorting out uniforms for their kids,' Butcher explained, stroking his beard. 'This way they'd be able to get the boring stuff done and dusted, and then treat themselves to a little luxury or two.'

'Underwear is viewed as a luxury?'

'We're talking fine, top-of-the-range lingerie. This is not Woolies. The initiative has already paid dividends: the lingerie takings have almost doubled in the last month.'

'I can give you some photos of Julie Hudson to circulate to all those who were working yesterday,' Hanlon said, eager to get the discussion back to Julie.

'On Saturdays we employ a lot of casuals and part-timers,' continued Butcher. 'In the current market it makes sense. Full-time staff are a huge burden for a company our size. That list you want might take a while.'

'Not too long, I hope,' said Hanlon. 'Everyone will need to see the picture. And that includes all cleaners, canteen staff, loading-bay attendants, you name it. Might jog someone's memory.'

'I'll do my best.'

'What about your security arrangements, then?' pressed Hanlon. The chair was killing him, worse than the new orange seats at the station. He half wondered whether it was a faulty item from the children's department. 'Store detectives?'

'Not in today. Obviously no point on a Sunday, with the store being closed to the public.'

Hanlon was finding Butcher increasingly obtuse. 'Yesterday is when I'm talking about. How many – names and levels of experience?'

Butcher fidgeted uneasily in his chair. 'There were two on duty, I believe. Keith Nelson, our full-time store detective (been with us for years), and Blake Richards, who's on temporary loan from Security Guard. Good solid chap, though. I'd hire him if we had the funds.'

Hanlon was incredulous. 'Two . . . and one of those not even a full-time member of staff? This is a multi-storey department store, the biggest retail concern in Denton!' *The pride of Denton* was how his mother, and practically everyone else for that matter, still referred to Aster's.

'Christmas might not be too far off,' said Butcher stridently, 'but we are in the middle of a recession. Maggie will pull us through, of that I'm in no doubt. Have a lot of respect for that woman. Give her time, that's what I say, and she'll transform this country.' Butcher was becoming increasingly animated.

Fortunately for Hanlon, who hated talking politics, Frost now walked straight into the room, saying, 'You the boss, then?'

'Yes,' said Butcher, remaining seated behind his desk. 'I'm the store manager of Aster's.'

Frost didn't offer his hand. 'We are seriously

concerned about the safety of a twelve-year-old girl, last seen in this store.'

'I don't doubt it,' said Butcher, 'but I'm still not sure what help we can give. If she's run away, it's hardly our fault, is it? Aster's has numerous exits.'

'Who said anything about running away?' said Frost, now looking at Hanlon.

'Well, I presumed . . .'

'We want to know who might have seen Julie and her mother yesterday afternoon,' said Hanlon, rising to his feet at last. He couldn't remain in that stupid chair a second longer.

'And we particularly want to know if anyone saw Julie on her own, or even with someone else,' said Frost.

'A man, say,' said Hanlon. He looked at Frost. But Frost had turned towards the window and was lighting a cigarette.

'Where would your store detectives have been positioned?' said Frost, exhaling, and not bothering to face the room.

'There would always have been one near the main front door on the ground floor, and frankly, the other one could have been anywhere – patrolling at random,' explained Butcher.

'Is it possible the man on the front door might have seen something if, say, a girl rushed out, distressed?' Hanlon asked.

'I suppose, yes, if she was making a big song and

dance about it,' said Butcher. 'But my security staff are trained to capture shoplifters, not runaways. Sorry for saying this, gentlemen, but would your attention not be better directed at the girl's friends and family?'

'Do you think,' said Frost crossly, 'your security staff would have noticed a young girl being dragged out of the store, by a man?'

'Against her will,' Hanlon added, he knew, stupidly.

'They are not imbeciles,' Butcher said, getting up. 'Now if that's all, gentlemen? I'll see the photograph is circulated tomorrow.'

'Not quite,' said Hanlon. 'We obviously need contact details for' – Hanlon flicked back through his notebook – 'Nelson and Richards.'

'And one more thing,' added Frost, by the door, 'any other way out, apart from the ground-floor doors?'

'The fire exits, I suppose. Access to them is clearly marked on every floor.' The store manager looked at his watch, a fancy gold piece with a crocodile strap. 'I'll show you, if you like,' he offered, suddenly sounding helpful. He walked round from behind his desk.

'Thanks,' said Hanlon.

'Let's go straight to where the girl was last seen,' said Frost.

'Uniforms and lingerie,' said Hanlon.

'Yes,' said Butcher, taking the lead.

'Tell me,' said Frost, as Butcher took them down the back stairs, 'why are uniforms and knickers on the same floor?'

'I'll fill you in,' said Hanlon.

Butcher was soon pushing open the door to the third floor. He flicked a panel of light switches.

'No stocktake going on here, then?' Hanlon asked.

'We're doing one department at a time,' Butcher said. 'We're working on the toy department today. Here you go, school uniforms. And there' – he indicated to his left – 'are the changing rooms.'

Frost, Hanlon noticed, was looking intently across the shop floor, in quite the opposite direction.

'At the back of that curtained-off area is the fire exit,' Butcher continued. 'See, it's all properly marked as such there.' He pointed to a small sign.

Hanlon and Butcher made straight for the changing rooms, with Frost following a few yards behind. Butcher then pulled aside the curtain to reveal, at the end of a row of cubicles, a fire door. They paused for a moment before walking further forward.

'Is the exit alarmed?' Frost asked from behind Hanlon's back.

Butcher stopped still. 'Yes,' he said, sounding unsure.

'Right, so anyone barging through these and you'd have known about it,' said Frost, moving to the front. He began rattling the doors. 'What's the system? Mains or battery?'

'Battery,' said Butcher nervously.

'How often do you check it's all operating properly?' said Hanlon.

'Oh, very regularly,' Butcher said.

With a clang the doors sprang open. 'Not regularly enough,' said Frost, engulfed by a blast of icy fresh air. 'I wonder what the fire department would have to say about this.' He quickly pulled the doors shut.

'And Julie Hudson's parents,' added Hanlon.

'The battery must have just gone,' said Butcher hurriedly. 'But it wouldn't have made any difference. Because there's always a changing-room attendant on duty – on Saturdays anyway. No one could have simply let themselves out and walked down the fire escape.'

'OK, Arthur,' said Frost, 'I've seen enough. For the time being. Best leave Mr Butcher to get on with his stocktaking. We don't want him ruining Christmas for everyone.'

The light was beginning to fail and there was drizzle in the air. Frost was niggled. Liz Fraser and her poor, bruised little girl had clouded his focus on Julie Hudson. He was missing something obvious, he was sure.

Hanlon piped up, as if reading his thoughts, 'Why didn't Wendy Hudson report her daughter missing while she was at the store?'

The fat detective constable was deftly and swiftly reversing the Cortina out of its tight parking space next to the loading bay at the back of Aster's.

'I don't know, Arthur,' Frost said. 'Flaming hell! Why didn't you ask her last night?'

'She was in a right state.'

'Obviously,' Frost said. But he could see why she might not have immediately informed the authorities. Past experience had taught him how often kids that age stormed off in a huff. Any parent would give it a bit of time before ringing the cop shop, surely, not wanting to create a fuss. Hoping for the best.

Frost wanted to try the hospital again, to see whether the mother had communicated anything yet. There was still no news of the father, despite numerous alerts having been put out, and all the relevant agencies and Controls having been informed.

'Roger that,' Hanlon said before replacing the handset, and bringing the car to a sudden stop, then indicating, as if to do a U-turn.

'More bad news?' Frost asked. He'd been miles away.

'Disturbance on the Southern Housing Estate. Control want us to check it out.'

'You *are* joking. It's nearly five, and apart from everything else I've got to get that paperwork done – the crime clear-up stats? Where's the bloody area car?'

'Kids terrorizing some oldsters,' continued Hanlon blithely.

'Nothing new there, then.' Frost sighed, relieved, and not for the first time in the day, that he wasn't a proud dad. Mary, of course, was still hoping for a miracle. Perhaps it would stop her nagging him. He looked through the Cortina's windscreen, slick with fine rain. 'But where the bloody hell are uniform?' he said, livid.

'Shift changeover, apparently, and as we're out and about, Control thought . . . it being a Sunday and everything . . .'

'Sod Control,' said Frost, sparking up. 'We're within spitting distance of Eagle Lane. I'm not trekking out to the Southern Housing Estate, even if there's a flaming riot.'

'There's a good chippy out there,' said Hanlon, licking his lips.

'I've promised the missus a takeaway, from that new tandoori. Uniform will get there in the end. Here, hand me the radio, and I'll tell Control where to stuff it.'

PC Derek Simms left his smaller and older colleague PC Baker, who was still pissed off because he hadn't had time to finish his tea, inside the panda, and made his way over to the fish and chip shop.

The rain had increased with the wind, which was blasting through the dismal, low-lying estate, and forcing Simms to squint as he dashed across the road. Outside the Codpiece was a small gang of teenagers, half a dozen or so boys, in jeans, tracksuit tops and Denton FC scarves, of various colour and slogan combinations. They appeared unfazed by the weather, or the sudden presence of the police, and were more than enjoying themselves as they heckled an old couple shuffling stiffly up the road. Chips were being lobbed at the pensioners' backs.

Attempting to make his presence felt, Simms brushed at the rain on his uniform jacket. He was tall, broad-shouldered, with a crooked nose and a crew cut. He was twenty-four years old and felt invincible.

He waited until the old couple were well out of harm's way before he barged through the gang and entered the chippy. Ignoring the queue and passing straight to the counter, Simms said, to the diminutive spotty proprietor, 'How long have your friends outside been hanging around?'

'An hour or two,' the man replied without looking up. Simms watched him slide golden battered fish into the hot display alongside an array of saveloys.

'They often here, at this time?'

'Where else have they got to go on a Sunday evening?'

Simms was going to say *Home*, then thought better of it. Scrutinizing the yobs through the shopfront more closely, he was pretty certain he recognized two of the more boisterous boys: Kevin Jones, a skinny little sod with spiky, peroxide-blond hair, and Sean Haynes, a short, fat thug with a babyface. They were always in trouble, yet too young to be prosecuted. It meant a ton of paperwork, and the heavy hand of Social Services breathing down the division's neck at every stage. And everyone knew it.

One of the smaller boys had a BMX and kept shooting off into the middle of the wet, dimly lit road, pulling wheelies.

'Give me a couple of bags of chips, will you?' Simms said, searching his pockets for loose change.

Clutching the hot bundles he stepped back outside. All quiet – the gang had suddenly disappeared. Or so he thought.

Just before he reached the panda he felt something hit him in the back. Swiftly turning, and dropping the chips in the process, he faced a barrage of missiles: balls of newspaper, sauce sachets and empty Coke cans.

PC Baker was out of the car in a flash, hand on his truncheon, but before the constables could give chase, the kids had streaked off, laughter echoing around the dark corners of the rotten estate.

Back in the car, with the remains of the chips, Simms said, 'I think I know who two of them are. Time for a couple of house calls?'

'What's the point?' said Baker, relaxing into his seat.

'We could take them down a dark alley and rub their faces in a bag of cold chips – something like that,' said Simms.

'And then get the boot for our troubles? Everyone saw you in the chip shop.'

'Can't wait to get out of this uniform,' Simms was desperate to become a detective.

'You'll be lucky, with this new chap Mullett in charge. I hear he does everything by the book. What's more, I hear there's been a freeze on promotions – cost-cutting, apparently.'

Sunday (8)

Bert Williams felt very cold. Night had fallen once again, thick and wet and freezing. He was drifting in and out of consciousness.

The tall hedge the other side of the ditch had become an impenetrable brick wall. A prison wall. He was now a prisoner. The metallic smell, the clanking noise. The cramped spaces. The bars and uniforms and pasty, blank faces. The tables had finally turned.

All the scum he'd once put away were on the outside, in the warm sunshine, with their wives and families, their dolly birds and little bastards, drinking and laughing. Living it up on the Costa del Sol. The world was upside down.

Bert tried to clench his fingers, tried to pull himself

back to the present. But all he kept thinking was that the wrong people were always one step ahead. That he'd been playing a game of catch-up all his life.

Yet Betty, bless her, had stood by him, hadn't she, through thick and thin. His mind wandered back to when they first met. He was on leave after Dunkirk, a welcome-home dance. There she was across the hall, blonde hair shimmering . . .

His body was numb. The pain had all but gone, leaving just this terrible chill.

He'd tried his best to keep Betty happy, to keep Denton safe. There was just too much evil in the world.

There . . . Williams thought he could make out a light in the distance, moving his way, but he couldn't keep his eyes open long enough to focus. Was it a flashlight, car headlamps?

No, there was no one. No one was coming to his aid. He was going to die here, and very soon. He should have been more flaming organized. But he only had himself to blame.

Why he'd become so hooked on smashing this gang, all by himself, he really didn't know. Because he'd been handed a lead on a plate . . . maybe? Because all along he hadn't known quite who to trust . . .

Also, he supposed, he hadn't been sure whether he was on to something at last, whether he was about to crack the case of a lifetime, one that would see him retire with his reputation restored. Or whether he was barking up the wrong tree. He'd grown scared, scared of the truth.

And then the truth got scared of him. Three people he hadn't been expecting at the usual rendezvous. That was a shock.

He couldn't stay awake. *Sorry, Jack – you'll have to find your own way now.*

Sorry, Denton.

Sorry, Betty.

Jack Frost sat in the Cortina, eating a chicken vindaloo straight out of the aluminium tray, plastic fork practically melting from the heat. The curry, from the new Denton Tandoori, was so hot it was nuclear. But very tasty. He hadn't been able to wait to get home before tucking in. He checked his watch – just gone ten.

Once more he peered through the windscreen at 8 Denton Close, a nice, detached modern house, with a steep pitched roof and a large chimney, and crazy-cladding running up the side of the building. A soft orange glow was coming from the curtained front room. There were shadows behind the curtains: people moving about. A weak light in one of the upstairs bedrooms went on again.

Suddenly lights were going on and off all over the house as though the building itself were flashing out Morse code. But there was nothing in the way of either loud, antisocial noise, or indecent behaviour, from what he could see and hear.

Having been bollocked by Control earlier, Frost felt he couldn't ignore a request to check out a disturbance in Denton Close, seeing as he was heading home that way. Not that he'd rushed here, stopping to pick up the curry first.

He took another mouthful of his and Mary's dinner. The station on this Sunday evening was so under-staffed that they'd had to send a detective on what should have been an area-car dispatch. Still, he was enjoying his dinner with no one nagging him.

What's more, there didn't appear to be much of a disturbance.

That Mullett had decided to channel resources towards lavish office furnishings and a new paint job, rather than paying for more staff and overtime, was not something he was going to worry about now, either.

The radio crackled into life. Frost gave a start, swallowing rapidly.

'Jack? Anything to report?' It was Station Sergeant Bill Wells.

'Bill? You still at the helm? It's gone ten,' Frost managed to reply, his mouth burning. He should have got a drink as well, a take-out can of lager.

'Bloody well am,' said Wells. 'Just about to leave, though. Johnson's finally turned up. But first, those two things you asked about,' continued Wells. 'Blake Richards, the temporary Aster's security guard, is an ex-copper, ex-Met. Some problem in the past there. And second, the girl's father, Steve Hudson? His uncle is Michael Hudson, the manager at Bennington's Bank.'

'Thought so,' said Frost.

'Word is, he's the money behind his nephew's car business, not to mention quite a few other ventures around town.'

'Bill, you are the fount of all knowledge,' Frost added, pleased with the information.

'Well, the fount has now run dry, until tomorrow anyway. What's with the disturbance?'

'Quiet as a mouse here.' Frost licked his fiery lips. 'No doubt whoever rang it in had another agenda. Still, I'll hang around for a few more minutes.'

'That's good of you, Jack.'

'Do what I can in these straitened times. What's keeping those area cars so occupied, anyway?'

'Charlie Alpha's tied up in Market Square, and Tango Bravo has a puncture.'

'A puncture? I'll try telling that to Mary,' chuckled Frost, peering more keenly through the rain-splattered windscreen. 'I'll tell her to give you a tinkle when she doesn't believe me.'

'Oh, and Jack, I should warn you, Mullett was on the phone earlier this evening, wondering where you'd left the crime clear-up stats. He needs them first thing.'

But something had caught Frost's attention. 'Got to go.' Replacing the handset with one hand and reaching for another chunk of naan bread with the other, Frost made out a shape, a figure crouching behind the pampas grass on the front lawn of number eight. Had it, had he, or had she been there all along?

Frost watched as the front door was suddenly flung open by a man in what looked like nothing more than a silk dressing-gown. He was tall and athletic, no older than thirty, his receding hairline lending him a noble air. Even from this distance he looked to Frost like a right stuck-up toff.

Lurid red light now seeped out, gently bathing the neat lawn and the shrubbery in its glow. A young couple, fully dressed, emerged from the hallway, and stood for a moment with the man in the dressing-gown by the open front door. Much to Frost's surprise, both then kissed the toff goodnight, and hurried down the path towards a small sports car, an MG, which was parked with two wheels on the pavement, on a sweep of the close, just a couple of cars away from Frost's Cortina.

Frost attempted to slide down in his seat, but it was not easy with the curry perched on his lap.

He heard the sports car drive off slowly. Carefully pulling himself up, he returned his gaze to the house. It took him a moment to regain his focus, partly because the front door was now closed and one of the upstairs lights was out. Yet he could still see silhouettes downstairs, behind the curtains. Seemed like people were dancing, slowly.

Moving his gaze to the front garden, he realized he had now lost sight of the crouching figure, if indeed someone had actually been there. Perhaps he'd been imagining things. This curry was certainly powerful stuff. He was sweating profusely.

Then something made him look in the rear-view mirror, just in time to catch a glimpse of a person passing around the side of the Cortina. Frost quickly leant over and flung open the passenger door.

There was a shriek of pain – or was it surprise? Female, anyway. Frost watched as a slightly built woman, with long straggly hair and clad in dark clothes, began sprinting away to the middle of the close and towards the narrow public alleyway that ran between the two central houses.

Before he had time to even contemplate giving chase, Frost was acutely aware of a damp, burning sensation in his lap. 'Flaming arseholes!' The vindaloo was everywhere, the dish upturned.

Frost leapt from the car and into the middle of the road as if possessed, brushing away the lumps of meat and sauce. By the time he looked up the woman was long gone and the close still and deathly quiet.

Monday (1)_____

Denton Union Canal at 7.25 a.m., Monday morning, was deserted. Vanessa Litchfield found herself increasing her pace along the rutted and rubbish-strewn towpath. There was black, stagnant water to her left and the notorious Southern Housing Estate to her right. It was barely light, the sky blanketed by heavy, hunkering clouds.

She usually ran through Denton Woods but twice now she'd come across the mad old tramp who lived in the railway carriage. He gave her the creeps, so she thought of trying the canal again. During the summer the stench from the canal had got so bad that she was unable to breathe. Now in the autumn the empty towpath was not as smelly but the looming menace of the Southern Housing Estate was still there.

In charge of PE at St Mary's School for Girls, Vanessa was a fitness fanatic. Each morning she embarked upon a six-mile jog before a hearty bowl of Alpen. Then she spent her day supervising the girls in the gym and on the playing fields.

This morning she would not have any appetite for the Alpen. At the loneliest stretch of the canal, between the two road bridges, she saw something floating in the foul, still, dark water.

She stopped, suddenly out of breath and gasping with horror. But there was no mistaking it. A man was floating face down towards the far side of the Denton Union Canal. She could clearly see the back of his head, his arms and his legs, encased in drab, sodden clothes.

Vanessa Litchfield couldn't understand why no one had spotted it, had spotted him – it was hard to think of it as a him, as a human being – earlier.

Looking up and down the towpath, and across to the far side, she realized, in growing panic, why of course. People seldom came this way. A violent housing estate one side of the canal, and scrubby, vacant land, interspersed with derelict warehouses on the other.

Checking over her shoulder once more briefly, she sprinted off in the direction she had been going, hoping there'd be a call box soon.

She paused to catch her breath a short while later, then lifted the receiver in a heavily vandalized phone box covered with graffiti – PAKIS GO HOME, KERRY IS A FAT SLAG, among other remarks scrawled everywhere. She couldn't help wondering whether taking the job at St Mary's had been a terrible mistake, and whether she should have accepted a more junior post at Cheltenham Ladies' College instead.

Monday (2)

Superintendent Mullett smoothed his moustache with his two forefingers, then drummed nervously on his newly installed mahogany desk. There'd been some tough times already at Denton. Now rabies? *Surely to goodness not.* The continent, yes, that was crawling with all sorts of diseases. God help the country if they ever built a tunnel. There hadn't been a death from rabies in the UK since the turn of the century.

Nevertheless he'd had a courtesy call from the very head of Denton General to say a young child was being tested for rabies. She'd been brought in yesterday by a DS Frost. She was in isolation and the tests were continuing.

'Morning, sir,' said Frost.

At last, there he was in front of him, but what on earth was he wearing? A pair of faded, flared jeans and a strawberry-red jumper a couple of sizes too small. 'DS Frost, I would remind you to knock before entering.' Mullett quickly glanced at his watch: nine twenty.

'I did, sir, but there was no reply.' The DS helped himself to a visitor's chair, and pulled a cigarette stub from behind his ear and poked it in his mouth.

'Well, that doesn't mean you can just stroll on in,' said Mullett, finding himself shoving a heavy, cut-glass ashtray in the detective sergeant's direction. He certainly didn't want ash on the new Wilton. 'Quite a catalogue to discuss already, Detective. First of all, though, where are the crime clear-up statistics? They were meant to be on my desk first thing. I don't see them. Do you see them?'

Frost made a big show of scanning the enormous, sparse desk.

Mullett was not amused.

'No, you're right,' said Frost. 'I don't see them either.'

'Well, why not?' bellowed Mullett, as Frost casually slumped back into the fine-leather chair. 'And this had better be good.'

'To be honest, sir,' pleaded Frost, 'I need clarification over a number of cases, from DI Allen. I thought he'd sorted this all out before he went on his hols. Not like DI Allen to be anything other than ruthlessly efficient. But it seems there are quite a few holes only he can fill: I guess it'll just have to wait until he's back.' The detective took a couple of long drags on his cigarette before continuing, 'He's on a walking holiday, isn't he? The Lakes? Offa's Dyke? The Pennine Way?'

'Let's leave DI Allen out of it for the moment,' sighed Mullett.

'Fair enough,' shrugged Frost.

'A progress report is what I want.'

'Yes, sir. Well, DC Hanlon and I interviewed the Aster's manager, Mr Butcher, and—'

Mullett cut him short with a raised hand. 'Aster's? I'm not interested in department stores! The little girl who's being tested for rabies. What exactly is going on?'

'Going on?' Frost looked bemused.

Mullett realized he'd always found it hard to take the detective sergeant seriously. 'Yes, going on?' he snapped. 'I had a call from the head of the hospital who told me a little girl was being tested for rabies. This could have national implications.'

'Just a precautionary measure, sir.'

'Just a precautionary measure, you say?' shouted Mullett.

'There's no actual rabies as far as I'm aware,' said Frost. 'You can't have been fully informed.'

'Not by you I haven't.'

'Never thought that hospital was very well run. I

just arranged for the little girl to be kept out of harm's way for a couple of days. At the time it seemed like a good idea. Would never have happened so quickly if we'd turned to Social Services.'

'I'm not sure I'm with you, Frost.' Mullett leant forward.

'The little girl, Becky Fraser, has, I believe, been seriously neglected by her mother, a Liz Fraser, and quite probably subjected to considerable physical violence by her father, a man, yet to be located, called Simon Trench. Over a considerable period of time, I wouldn't doubt.'

'Considerable physical violence?' repeated Mullett.

'A Dr Philips is doing me a favour and looking into the extent of her injuries,' Frost said gamely. 'Thought best to see exactly where we were before any serious questioning got underway and we had to issue an arrest warrant. We wouldn't want to make a mistake with a minor: you know how touchy Social Services can be, especially where parents are concerned.'

'But what's all this rabies nonsense about, then? Why was I rung up by the head of the hospital himself?'

'Bit of a smokescreen, to be honest, sir. How I managed to get some cooperation from the child's mother. She said her daughter had been attacked by a wild animal, and I told her we were in the middle of a new rabies alert – you see, Bill Wells had just put up a new poster in the lobby – and that the child would have to be tested.'

'This all seems highly irregular to me,' huffed Mullett. 'The head of the hospital doesn't even know what's going on. What if the press get wind of it? Young child being tested for rabies in Denton General, they'd love that, all right.'

'Well, as I said, Bill Wells has just whacked up a warning poster in the lobby.'

'I *have* seen it.'

'If anyone tries to say they weren't warned—' continued Frost.

'Frost,' interrupted Mullett, 'I seriously hope you know what you're doing. The last thing I want to do is read some scare story in the *Denton Echo*.'

'Of course not. Wouldn't want to panic the good citizens of Denton, would we?'

Mullett stroked his neatly trimmed moustache again. 'Where are we with the missing girl?'

'Nowhere, I'm afraid,' said Frost promptly. 'The mother hasn't come to her senses yet, poor thing. And there's still no trace of her husband, Steve Hudson. The usual alerts are in place. All ports are on the case.'

'Steve Hudson, hey? Possible, I suppose, that he'd been interfering with his daughter, she runs off and the mother finally confronts him.' Mullett rubbed at his moustache once more. 'Unlikely we'd get him convicted for that, though – you never do. Our best bet is assault, but that's only if his wife wishes to press charges. Or maybe she'd been having an affair.'

Mullett paused again and briefly looked up at the

ceiling. 'I wouldn't waste a lot of time on this one, Frost. The girl will turn up sooner or later. As will the father. He's well connected around here, I believe. In fact, you'd do well to remember just that.'

'The woman was nearly killed, sir,' protested Frost. 'You should have seen her, battered and bruised beyond recognition. Lying in a pool of blood—'

'I gather there's an issue with contaminated evidence. It's been reported to me that neither you nor DC Hanlon was properly attired. And I'm not just talking about a failure to don Andy Pandy suits. For heaven's sake.'

'I don't know who could have informed you of such a blatant lapse of procedure, Mr Mullett,' Frost said, rising from his chair, as if to go. 'But the situation was critical – a woman was dying on the kitchen floor. Our priority was to save her life.'

'Which is why you smashed your way through the back door,' sighed Mullett.

'There was no other way, sir.'

'No, there never is.' Mullett suddenly felt weary. 'Before you go, Frost, could you please explain why you're not properly dressed today?' Mullett thought he looked like a New York hoodlum. 'I wasn't aware of any undercover operations this morning.'

'Still in the planning, sir.'

'What do you mean, "still in the planning"?'

'Thought I'd check out Steve Hudson's second-hand sports-car place. I was going to pose as a customer.'

'And you couldn't do that in a suit?'

'This garb seemed more in keeping. Didn't want them to have any idea I was a copper.'

'Don't think they would have,' Mullett said drily. 'Well, try not to bother anyone too respectable.'

As Frost was disappearing from the room, Mullett suddenly called after him, 'By the way, you haven't heard anything from your chum Williams, have you? I gather he still hasn't reported in for duty.'

But Frost either hadn't heard Mullett, or chose not to stop and answer.

Bright and early Monday morning and the gloom had already poured in. *What a mountain to climb to get this place in order.* Mullett stifled a yawn, knowing it would be pointless issuing Williams with a written warning. He was retiring in just a matter of weeks, and frankly his presence usually only confused operations. It was probably better that he was out of the way. Not that that was the point.

Mullett stood up, cracked his knuckles. 'I wonder whether he realizes his pension could be at stake,' he said aloud to himself.

Frost ambled out to reception. Must get over to Bert's, he thought, but he needed something to eat first.

'All right, Bill, when does this trolley service kick into action? I'm starving.' He glanced at the desk, but there was no one in sight. 'Hello, hello?' he shouted. 'Jesus!'

Ghost-like PC Pooley had popped up from behind the counter, his stare as vacant as ever.

'What's this, the Hammer House of Horrors?'

Pooley said nothing, but grinned crookedly.

'Where's Bill?' Frost asked, patting his tight jeans pockets for his fags, to no avail. He must have left them in his office.

'Sick,' said Pooley.

'I wasn't asking about you,' Frost replied. 'Where's the Old Bill?'

'Very funny, Mr Frost. Like I said, he's off sick.'

'Nothing catching, I hope.' Frost's attention was drawn to two men barging through the main door and depositing large metal tins underneath the notice board.

'Mr Mullett's paint,' Pooley explained. 'Gallons of the stuff.'

'Oh yes, the new decor. What's he gone for? Battleship grey?'

'Magnolia, I believe.'

'Magnolia? Bleeding hell.'

'Apparently it wasn't him that chose it,' Pooley said mournfully. 'It was his secretary, Miss Smith. She picked the new chairs as well. Thinks she's some kind of interior designer.'

'I've heard enough already,' said Frost, turning and making his way back into the interior of the building, and to his and Hanlon's office to fetch his coat.

Hanlon was at his desk, reading the *Mirror*. More stories about paedophiles.

Frost glanced towards the door to Bert Williams's office, which was not really much more than a cubicle in the corner of CID. He was half wondering whether he should have a quick rustle around the inspector's desk, see if Bert had left any indication as to where he might be. But knowing the mess in there Frost wasn't sure there was any point. Besides, there was a quicker and easier option he hadn't yet explored.

'I'm off,' Frost declared, grabbing his mac. 'Before I get refurbished.'

'Hey, wait a minute, Jack,' Hanlon said, shutting the newspaper and looking up. 'You can't just—'

'I'm going round to Bert's, won't be long. I'll come back for you after the briefing. I've just had my own private audience with his lordship so I don't feel I need another earful already. Then we'll pop into the bank, see what Steve Hudson's uncle knows. Seems to be the only close relative around. And it strikes me money might be part of it.'

Despite Mullett's conviction about the Hudson case being nothing more than a simple domestic, Frost wasn't going to drop this one.

'What's with the mufti, Jack?' Hanlon shouted after him. 'You auditioning for *Saturday Night Fever*, part two?'

Betty Williams was on her fourth mug of Gold Blend, and her fifth B&H. She was staring out of the kitchen window, at the washing line. A couple of Bert's shirts and some of her slips were flapping in the breeze. She was pleased she'd been able to get the washing outside. The weather this time of year was so unpredictable. She expected it would rain later. It usually did, if it hadn't started out wet already.

She had hoped to get round to a little gardening later. Get out while she could. The front garden was a mess and everything needed pruning before the winter really set in.

Taking a large sip of coffee, she told herself off for being so negative. *Always think the worst, that's you, Betty. Pull yourself together.* It wasn't as if Bert hadn't gone off on a binge before. Once he'd disappeared for four days, eventually returning with some tall tale about being stuck undercover in east London. He'd stunk of booze. The station had been calling incessantly, trying to track him down, saying they knew nothing about his whereabouts.

Much like now, except the calls from Control hadn't been so frequent, because, she supposed, they'd all grown used to Bert's little disappearances, and were taking his misdemeanours less seriously. He only had a few weeks left in the job. They'd make allowances, let him bow out quietly.

Betty wasn't going to make allowances, however. Something else was niggling away at the back of her mind, and she was worried stiff. For her, for them, for him.

As she was taking another sip of coffee, the doorbell

rang, making her jump and spill Nescaf on the clean, Formica-topped kitchen table. Her limbs suddenly felt very heavy as she walked to the front door. She could see a man on the other side of the glass, of medium build and height, casually dressed. Window cleaner?

She cautiously opened the door. 'Jack,' she gasped, immediately relieved, and then almost as quickly not relieved. 'What are you doing here?' She looked at him hard, at his clothes, and added, 'And on your day off.'

'Hello, Betty. Can I come in?'

'Of course, of course. Come through to the kitchen. I was just having a coffee. Can I get you one?'

'That'd be lovely. Two sugars.'

Betty filled the kettle, while studying Frost. She couldn't make out his expression, he was looking so intently through the window into the back garden. As if he was withholding something. 'How have you been?' she asked nervously.

She couldn't remember the last time she'd seen Jack, or Mary. There had been a period when the Frosts had often dropped by for a drink and a takeaway.

'Busy, as ever, with this new super,' he said, lighting a cigarette.

'Oh, yes, him,' she said.

'No rest for the wicked, as they say.' He coughed. 'I'm not on my day off, either. To be honest, I had a slight accident with . . . actually you don't want to know. Bert about?'

'No,' she said, also reaching for a cigarette. 'Sorry, Jack. He's not here.'

'When did you last see him? Because the super's on the warpath, and, well, I thought I'd do what I can. Get to him before Mullett does.'

'Still trying to make his mark, is he?'

'You could say that.' Frost coughed again as he exhaled.

'You should give up,' Betty said. 'Young man like you. Everything to live for.' Betty had a soft spot for Jack. He was one of those lads who always caught the eye of women of a certain age. It wasn't just a mothering thing.

'That's what Mary keeps saying. She's at me about it night and day. But in this job, you've got to have some vices. Wouldn't surprise me if she wanted me to start jogging next – it's all the rage.'

She watched as Frost puffed out his chest, and winked at her. 'I haven't seen him since Saturday,' she found herself saying. 'He went out just before lunch, said he wouldn't be long, and that was the last I saw of him. He took the car, too.'

'That's a bloody long time,' said Frost, scratching his chin. 'But he's gone on benders before, hasn't he?'

'Not normally for this long. A night maybe. A day. Sometimes two. I expect he'll come through that door any minute, stinking to high heaven, looking like he's been sleeping rough, which he probably has. What am

I to do, Jack? He can't go on like this. How can I get him to dry out?'

'I don't know, Betty. I really don't. I'm sorry.'

'The thing is, he hasn't been drinking that much recently. Part of me hoped he'd got it back under control. I didn't want to make a big deal about it. You see, he's been very preoccupied about something. I wondered whether it was his retirement. I don't know. Work-related was my guess.' It pained her to reveal anything intimate about Bert. Though Jack was almost family; if anyone could help it would be him.

'I'll check around,' said Frost. 'Try some of his old haunts. Put the word out.'

'There is something else,' she said, sure it was nothing, but feeling that odd niggle at the back of her head again. 'He keeps popping out to the phone box, down the road. I've watched him. But we have a perfectly good phone here. At first I thought he was nipping off for a drink, so I followed him one day last week. Thankfully he didn't see me. You don't think he's . . .'

'He's what, Betty?'

'You know, having an affair?'

Frost laughed. 'At his age? Can he still get it up?'

Betty found herself laughing too, first time in days. 'You'd be surprised.'

Monday (3)

A pretty, young secretary showed Frost and Hanlon into a smartly furnished, wood-panelled office, not at all dissimilar to Mullett's lair at the Eagle Lane cop shop.

'The manager will be with you shortly,' she said, with some anxiety. 'But he only got back from holiday this morning and he says he wasn't expecting you. I keep his appointments diary, you see.'

'Thank you, love,' said Frost. He didn't want to get this pert young thing into trouble. 'Arthur, you did telephone ahead to say we'd be coming in?'

Hanlon looked blank.

'Never mind. I'm sure the manager of such an esteemed bank wouldn't have wanted to keep the fuzz waiting out in the cold. We'll make ourselves at home.' Frost took in the plush surroundings and pulled out a Rothmans. 'Good to see our hard-earned cash has been so wisely invested.'

'I'll leave you to it.' The girl smiled uncertainly and left, leaving the door ajar.

'Think this Michael Hudson will know anything useful, Jack? By all accounts he's an awkward sod.'

'He's a bank manager,' said Frost. He wandered over to the enormous desk in the centre of the room and took a closer look at the various curios that covered the green leather-topped surface.

Presently in hurried a short, plump, grey-haired and blue-chinned man, wearing a pinstripe suit.

Frost replaced a fancy-framed photograph on the desk, accidentally dropping some ash as he did so. He then tried his best at what he thought was an ingratiating smile, and stuck out his hand towards the approaching bank manager.

Michael Hudson took Frost's hand in a surprisingly limp fashion, as if he was afraid of catching something. 'Sorry to keep you. I've just got back from a short break. What can I do for you, gentlemen?'

Frost said, exhaling smoke, 'Hope you don't mind us dropping in. I'm Detective Sergeant Frost and this is Detective Constable Hanlon.'

'Yes, yes, I've been told who you are – though your dress, Sergeant, did throw me. Are you, as they say, "undercover"?'

'We're detectives,' Hanlon said weakly.

'How can I help? Is it about this spate of armed robberies hitting the county?' Michael Hudson suggested, suddenly animated.

'Not unless you know something I don't, Mr Hudson,' Frost said. 'We've come about your nephew, Steven.'

'Steven? Haven't seen or spoken to him in . . .' He paused, rubbed his prominent chin, and continued, 'Quite a while. Truth is, we fell out. I thought that was common knowledge in Denton. Though I suppose there's no reason why you should know.'

'No,' said Hanlon.

'So when were you last in contact with him?' Frost asked, wandering over to the window.

'A year or so ago. Why on earth do you ask? Is there a problem?'

'You could say that,' said Frost, moving closer. 'His daughter, Julie, has disappeared, his wife, Wendy, has been beaten to within an inch of her life, and now there's no sign of your nephew – or of his silly yellow car.'

'Oh God, dear me,' said Michael Hudson, slumping into his seat. 'You mean he's taken Julie?'

'No,' said Hanlon, who had pulled out his notebook. 'We don't think so. Julie went missing on Saturday afternoon. I interviewed your nephew and his wife about her disappearance that evening, and then yesterday morning Wendy Hudson was found in a pool of blood on her kitchen floor, and Steven had also vanished.'

'How is Wendy now?' said Michael Hudson quietly, obviously shaken.

'Last time I looked she was still unconscious,' said Frost. 'Her face has been completely smashed in. But she'll live.'

'God help her – the poor woman.'

'Which is why,' said Frost, 'it's imperative we find her husband as soon as possible. When exactly was the last time you had any contact with Steven?'

'As I said,' replied Mr Hudson, still quietly, 'a year or so ago. There might have been one or two business communiqués since, but nothing personal.'

'Your wife, what about her?' said Hanlon. 'Has she had any contact?'

'Not as far as I know. I'd be very surprised if she had: they've never exactly seen eye to eye.'

'I'm sure I don't need to remind you of the serious-ness of the situation,' Frost chipped in.

'No, no,' protested Michael Hudson, 'of course not.'

'What sparked this falling-out between you and your nephew?' Frost moved back to the window, peer-ing through the Venetian blinds and out on to Market Square. He was just in time to see a buxom young woman in a very tight Bennington's Bank uniform wiggle across the street and into the main entrance two storeys below.

'I'm not sure I can remember exactly,' said the bank manager.

'You haven't seen or spoken to your nephew for a year and you can't remember *why*?' Frost scoffed.

'Not to do with money, then?' added Hanlon.

'Well,' Michael Hudson started, 'there is a business arrangement between Bennington's Bank and Hudson's Classic Cars.'

'There's a surprise,' said Frost, still with his back to them.

'There's no need to adopt that threatening tone, Sergeant.' Hudson leant forward in his chair. 'Everything's above board here – I can absolutely assure you of that.' He removed a crisp white handkerchief from the breast pocket of his suit jacket and dabbed at his forehead. 'The bank's dealings with my nephew's car business are under strictly normal commercial terms.'

'Normal terms, hey?' Frost said, finally turning to face the room. 'The same as you treat every customer, I'm sure.' He fired up another cigarette. 'What I'm still not getting, then, is why you two have fallen out – and yet you still do business together.'

'This is a large bank. I don't handle every account,' Michael Hudson said. 'As to our falling-out . . . I'm not sure I can quite remember the details, though it would have had nothing to do with business. To be quite honest, Steven is one of those people who are always rather full of themselves. Likes to be a big fish.'

'You mean he's a bit flash?' said Hanlon.

'I suppose you could say that. But family is family.

I was very close to his father, my late brother.'

'Any idea where Steven might be now?' said Frost.

'No idea, I'm afraid. I'd help if I could.'

The bank manager was still looking very pale. Yet Frost felt little sympathy for him – he just didn't seem quite concerned enough. Truth was, Frost had always distrusted bank managers. 'Any idea at all where Julie could be?' he snapped.

'No. I barely know her.'

'Well, if you hear anything, anything at all,' said Hanlon, 'we'll expect you to get in touch with us right away.'

'Yes, of course,' said Hudson, dabbing his forehead again. 'This has all come as something of a shock – we were in France. Only got back late last night. This is the first I've heard about it. I'm sorry I can't help more.'

'Not *that* sorry,' said Frost, unable to help himself.

'I beg your pardon? Superintendent Mullett happens to be a friend of mine. I'd watch what you're inferring.' Hudson eyed his large, multi-buttoned desk phone.

Frost extinguished his cigarette with his fingertips, putting the butt in his mac pocket. 'Then you'll know all about his aims to clear up crime in Denton, from domestic abuse to fraud and corruption.'

'Look,' said Michael Hudson, adopting a more conciliatory tone, 'I've always been rather wary of Steven.'

'But you were more than willing to lend him some cash?' quizzed Hanlon.

'That was a business decision. We are a progressive bank – we like to help local businesses. Anything we can do to help the economy move out of recession.'

'All right,' stated Frost, 'no need to take up any more of your precious time.' He moved closer to the desk for one last nosey. 'But if your nephew does pop by for a large withdrawal, let him know we've got all the ports covered.'

Frost, with Hanlon struggling to keep up behind, exited the grand office, passing the secretary at her desk in the executive lobby.

On the ground floor Frost saw a clutch of smart young female tellers sitting behind half an inch of bullet-proof glass. He chanced a smile in their general direction, wondering for a second whether he should have gone into high finance rather than rotten police work.

'I thought we were on to something,' he said, on the pavement. They were walking towards the car, parked in the far corner of Market Square. He stopped to light a cigarette, cupping the flame. 'I'm not so sure now.'

'You think money's behind all this?' said Hanlon.

'Doesn't look like it. Come on.' Frost increased his pace. 'Let's get over to the hospital, see how Wendy's doing.'

'And the little Fraser girl,' Hanlon added, making for the driver's door.

As they were leaving Market Square, Control bleated into life. A jogger had discovered a man floating in the canal, and the corpse was now at the county pathology laboratory. DC Sue Clarke was already there. However, as the most senior detective on duty, Frost was to join her immediately.

The sudden, mid-morning sunshine glistened on the wet, winding country road to the county lab. Frost sank further down in the passenger seat and expelled smoke, blinking at the glare. His mind was juggling the disappearances of Bert Williams and Julie Hudson, conjuring up very different emotions. And then there was the girl's father, Steven Hudson.

'I'm coming round to your new look,' said Hanlon, breaking the silence. Neither had said a word since leaving Market Square. 'Adds a certain swagger to your stride. Ever thought about becoming a villain?'

'Is there that much difference between us and them?'

'Not a lot sometimes, I suppose.'

'Well, don't get used to it. My suit'll be back from the cleaner's first thing tomorrow. If that blasted curry hasn't burnt a hole in it.'

'Hot, was it?'

'Oh yes,' said Frost distractedly.

'Bet the missus was none too pleased – when you turned up with her portion in your crotch.' Hanlon smiled.

'She's none too pleased with whatever I do.'

The radio crackled into life just as the unobtrusive, single-storey county lab building came into view. Frost grabbed the handset and answered.

It was PC Pooley, sounding grave. 'Mr Frost, is Arthur Hanlon with you?'

'Yes, the great hulk's here.'

'Got some bad news for him,' said Pooley. 'His mum's been taken ill. She's in Denton General.'

Hanlon's face fell as Frost relayed the message. They pulled in alongside DC Clarke's Escort.

'Tell you what,' said Frost, 'best you get straight off and see your mum, so take the car. The lovely Sue can have the pleasure of driving me back.'

'You sure, Jack?'

' 'Course,' said Frost, clambering out of the car. 'Go on, hop it.'

Inside the drab lab complex Frost was engulfed by cold, antiseptic air. He made his way silently across the grey carpet tiles of the lobby, not bothering to flash his credentials at the uniformed security woman at the front desk, and ventured quickly down a harshly lit corridor.

A left turn, a right turn, another left and he was faced with a set of forbidding steel swing-doors; a couple of portholes at head height revealed little. He pushed straight into the laboratory, where he was greeted by another temperature drop.

Polar-blue fluorescent lighting glared down on Dr Drysdale, the neatly gowned, and as ever neatly groomed, middle-aged pathologist, who was flanked by his assistant, a gawky, dark-haired youth of eighteen or so.

Standing a few feet away was DC Clarke, looking smart and sexy in a tight-fitting navy trouser suit, a white blouse showing at the collar, her ample breasts held snugly by the jacket. Her shoulder-length, light-auburn hair appeared full of bounce, while her cheeks showed a hint of colour.

Drysdale looked up from the corpse, beckoning Frost over. 'Better late than never,' he said crisply.

Frost felt that he and not the stiff was under the chilly spotlight: Drysdale and Sue Clarke were regarding him warily.

'Like the get-up,' said Clarke, grinning.

Frost fingered the neck of his jumper self-consciously.

'Drowned,' Drysdale sniffed.

'Really, Doc, in a canal? You do surprise me.' Frost surveyed the corpse – a male, late sixties, large bald patch, short, untidy grey beard. The poor bugger had clearly suffered a battering as well.

'With the amount of filthy water he had in his lungs,' the pathologist continued. 'Stomach contents: tea, white bread, chicken and chips. No alcohol.'

'Chips? What sort of chips?' Frost asked keenly, poking the corpse on the arm with his forefinger.

'A chip is a chip, Mr Frost.'

'A chip is *not* a chip, Doc. Oven, crinkle-cut, home-made, those little French fries you get in that McDonald's? Fat, greasy chip-shop chips? You'd be surprised.'

'Obviously your field of expertise. Here, take a look.' Drysdale pointed to a bucket by the table.

Frost quickly turned away, as did Sue Clarke. 'Not likely,' Frost snapped, 'I've got enough food for thought. When would he have last eaten?'

'I can't be exact, but would estimate around two yesterday afternoon,' said Drysdale.

'That's good enough for me.' Frost paused, automatically feeling in his pockets for his cigarettes. 'I was always warned not to go swimming on a full stomach. Sue, do we have anything else to go on?'

Clarke was brushing something off her jacket sleeve. Then, looking straight at Frost with her large hazel eyes, she said studiously, 'It seems the victim was beaten up, probably robbed, before he ended up in the canal.'

'State the bleeding obvious,' Frost grumbled, returning her stare.

Undeterred, she added, 'There was no wallet. Nothing else to identify him with.'

'Right – that makes it murder, manslaughter, aggravated robbery, or a stupid accident. Whichever, we've got an unidentified corpse on our hands. Someone's going to be upset. Time of death?'

'Doctor Maltby, who pronounced the victim dead at the scene this morning, thought late yesterday afternoon, around four or five,' Clarke said.

'For once that old soak isn't far out,' chipped in Drysdale. 'The body has definitely been in the water overnight. See the bloating, and skin coloration.' Drysdale delicately prodded the corpse's neck, before running his gloved fingers over the stiff's face. 'By the way, he wore heavy glasses.' Drysdale indicated a couple of tiny indentations on either side of the nose.

'What's that got to do with anything?' Frost snapped impatiently.

'Give me a chance,' Drysdale said crossly. 'He may have had seriously impaired vision. There's too much bruising around the sockets of the eyes – here and here – for me to be any more certain right now. I'll need to do further tests.'

'You've all the time in the world,' Frost said. 'He's not going anywhere. But initial thoughts, beyond the fact he drowned?'

The pathologist paused, straightened up and rubbed his gloved hands together. 'Bruises along the torso, the ribs, and more concentrated contusions around the head and neck,' he said calmly. 'Though the skin is not broken, apart from a split lip. A number of teeth are freshly missing, not that he had many. The skull is not visibly fractured, but I haven't yet checked for signs of concussion – where's my saw?'

Frost flinched as the assistant moved over to a side

tray, containing a gruesome selection of implements. 'Just tell us what you reckon now, could you?' Frost said anxiously.

'I would say he'd been beaten, kicked and punched, and, by the look of these contusions, by more than one person. A gang?'

Frost noticed Clarke frown, her young face betraying shock and horror.

'Though not severely enough to kill him,' Drysdale finally added. 'He was alive when he hit the water. Whether he was conscious or unconscious is another matter, and one, in my opinion, that'll determine the culpability of the people who attacked him.'

'You stick to your job, Doc, and I'll stick to mine,' said Frost, deciding he'd seen enough. 'Now, I'd like to take a quick look at the deceased's clothing, if you've not sent it to Forensics yet, and then we'll leave you to get the chainsaw out.'

Some minutes later, by the small car park, Frost said, 'Any chance of a lift, love? DC Hanlon's had to take off – his mum's been rushed to hospital. Wouldn't want to have to spend the night out here, on my own.'

'Of course,' said Clarke, unlocking the unmarked Escort.

Frost thought her tone indicated otherwise. 'Jolly good,' he said nevertheless, climbing into the passenger seat and reaching into his pockets for his cigarettes.

'Though, I'm in a bit of a rush to get back to Eagle

Lane,' Clarke said, slipping gracefully behind the wheel and unbuttoning her jacket.

Frost couldn't help glancing at her fabulous chest. It was some sight.

'All that paperwork on that dead man to be done,' she said. 'I don't like to let it get on top of me.'

'No, of course not,' Frost replied cautiously – he hadn't worked with Clarke much before. 'I'm the same myself. Love to have a clean and tidy desk. Fag?'

'No thanks, not while I'm driving.'

'Didn't realize you used to be a traffic cop,' Frost exhaled, as Clarke accelerated out on to the main road and aggressively screeched through the gears until the speedo touched 70 mph.

'Very funny. Just haven't got all day,' she said. 'What's with the red jumper and the flares?' She looked over at him, for a little too long, he thought. 'Hot undercover job?'

'Could say that.' He decided not to distract her further from her driving and to try to keep his gob shut. Fortunately the road ahead was clear – if only his mind was too.

He had grave concerns for missing Julie Hudson and the health of her mother, Wendy, and was feeling increasing frustration that Steven Hudson had yet to be apprehended. And then there was little bruised Becky Fraser now stuck in isolation, with Becky's father, this Simon Trench fellow, also not located, let alone interviewed.

And on top of all that, Frost was now faced with having to identify a battered corpse. Someone could be missing a husband, a father. Frost wondered whether it was an isolated incident or whether the gang would strike again. Whoever he was, the canal corpse, he wasn't well off, judging from his clothing, and the worn soles of his cheap shoes.

Sue Clarke, Frost decided, could at least deal with that case. She seemed especially efficient and keen, eager to get stuck in.

Reaching for his cigarettes, then realizing he was already smoking one, Frost hoped Hanlon wasn't going to be sidetracked for too long by his sick mother. Frost badly needed his assistance. DC Clarke was fine, more than fine in fact, but he thought Hanlon dependable.

Frost's mind drifted back to Bert Williams as they hammered down the autumn lanes. The inspector had failed to report for duty plenty of times before. Not so often for two days on the trot. Though it was Betty who had really spooked Frost – that business about Bert popping out to the phone box, at all hours.

Strange. Frost was as certain as he could be that Williams was not having an affair. Other women were not his passion. It was alcohol, and, Frost supposed, still some sort of commitment to the force – once a copper, always a copper. Who knew what the old fool was up to. Nothing to do with work, Frost hoped, not some wild goose chase. There were plenty of ruthless bastards out there.

Frost had told Betty that he'd look for Bert, and he would. There were the boozers of course, the old haunts, and then that mountain of paperwork on Bert's desk. Perhaps that would reveal something. Yet that was exactly what Frost now saw he'd been avoiding. Because that would mean work, CID work, and some daft hunch or other, driving Bert on, regardless of the risks. Frost knew how stubborn the inspector could be, how hung up he was about sliding disgracefully into retirement.

Fields flashed by as Frost kept glancing in Clarke's direction, weak sunlight catching her auburn hair and smooth, glowing cheeks.

'This bothering you?' he finally said, holding up his cigarette.

'No problem,' she replied, turning to face him. 'I've always found smoking rather sexy, like in the old black-and-white movies. Stupid really, but there you are.'

Suddenly feeling self-conscious, Frost reached forward and turned on the radio, whacking up the volume. Bloody Abba again. But by the outskirts of Denton he found himself distractedly tapping out the beat on the glove compartment – catchy tune.

Frost abruptly stopped, stubbed out his cigarette and stared gloomily out of the window at the rows of pre-war semis. He and Mary lived in one just like that.

As they approached Market Square Frost said, 'Pull over, love, there's something I need from Aster's.'

'Don't tell me, a new suit?'

'From Aster's, on my salary? You've got to be kidding.'

'That's an expensive new mac you're wearing over your civvies though, isn't it? Apart from the odd stain. Where does that come from?'

'It was a present,' said Frost, jumping out of the car, slamming the door shut behind him, and giving Clarke little alternative but to follow.

'I can't just park there,' he heard her say, as he pushed against the main revolving door into the store. 'I'll get a ticket.'

'Let's hurry up, then,' he shouted over his shoulder. 'We want the third floor.'

'Whatever for?' Clarke was close behind him now, Frost's progress being impeded by hordes of OAPs hunched around the bargain bins on the ground floor.

'Come on,' he shouted above the din of excited old codgers, 'we'll take the back stairs.'

The third floor was much less crowded, the school-uniform area all but empty and just a few housewives browsing in the lingerie section. Frost, with Clarke dutifully following a few paces behind, meandered through the colourful aisles. 'What sort of underwear tickles your fancy, Sue?' he asked loudly. 'French knickers?'

'G-strings, preferably black,' Clarke said crossly, struggling to keep up. 'What the hell do *you* think?'

'Only asking,' he said. 'Come over here, there's something I want to try.' He sprinted ahead.

'Don't tell me,' said Clarke, 'you're one of those men who likes to wear women's underwear.'

'The fire door,' he muttered, continuing towards the changing rooms in the far corner.

At the entrance to the changing area was a desk and an unruly pile of numbered plastic discs. But there was nobody around, and even if there had been on Saturday, Frost doubted an attendant would have been able to see what went on further down the corridor. A returns rack blocked much of the view towards the cubicles and, of course, that fire exit.

He slowly made his way down the corridor before pausing to look back. Yes, it was certainly obscured. Nobody could see a thing: the security in this place, it was a joke.

Where the hell had Clarke got to? Frost pushed on towards the green double-door fire exit, and began rattling the release bar.

'Excuse me, sir, can I help you?' came an authoritative female voice some distance behind him.

He turned to encounter a buxom, middle-aged woman bearing down on him. Christ, he thought, it's Mrs Slocombe straight from *Are You Being Served?* The buttons on her blouse looked as if they might ping off at any second.

'No, we're all right – just looking,' Frost said, again glancing around for Clarke.

'Looking at what, sir? These are the changing rooms for the lingerie and school-uniform departments. Menswear is on the second floor.'

'In that case I appear to have made a mistake,' he said, trying to avoid the woman's suspicious stare. 'This way, is it?' he said, turning back round and giving the metal bar of the fire exit a hefty shove.

A shrill, deafening ring blasted out. 'It works,' he said, surprised, walking out on to the fire escape. That bloody store manager Butcher must have had the batteries changed. There was a worrying creak, more a crack, as he peered over the edge.

'You can't go out there!' the woman was shouting behind him, trying to make herself heard above the piercing din of the alarm. 'Come back at once, or I'll have to get security.'

Ignoring her, Frost edged further out, clutching the rusty metal railing. He felt a wave of vertigo. Below him was a skip full of mannequin parts – lurid pink arms and legs and torsos, and the odd bald head. Beyond it was the loading bay, an articulated lorry parked up. The gates to the back of the building from the street – which must have been Piper Road – were wide open. There was no evidence of a security post, no one checking who was coming in and out.

The manager might have panicked and got the fire-exit alarm working again, but overall the store's security set-up was poor.

The piercing ringing, Frost realized, had now

stopped. He turned round to be confronted by the Mrs Slocombe figure. She had been joined by a burly middle-aged man in a suit, clearly a security guard. Both stood in the doorway, not venturing out on to the fire escape.

'Sure this platform is safe?' Frost gave it a good shaking before slowly stepping back inside. 'I wonder what the fire service would have to say about it.' He scrutinized the security guard more closely. He had a round, lined face, short, light-brown hair and a neatly trimmed beard. He was a good three or four inches taller than Frost, and had a heavier build. The way he was carrying himself, all aggressive confidence, led Frost to think immediately that this was an ex-copper.

'I'm guessing,' said Frost, for once a name coming to him, 'that you're Blake Richards. Hoped that bell might get your attention.' Frost pulled out his warrant card, and the security guard stepped backwards, giving Frost some space.

'Bloody hell, is this how plainclothes dress in the sticks? Yeah, I'm Richards.'

The gist of earlier conversations Frost had had with Bill Wells and Arthur Hanlon came flooding back. 'This what happens when a colourful career in the Met comes to an end?' retorted Frost. 'Spend your days mooching about the shops with a load of pensioners?'

'Beats chasing petty vandals around the Southern Housing Estate,' said Richards. 'You know what they say about Denton Division – graveyard of ambition, staffed by a load of drunks and incompetents no one else will have.'

Frost slammed Richards against a cubicle door, taking the larger man by surprise. Ignoring the startled squeal from inside, Frost firmly held him there. 'Any more lip from you and I'll run you down the nick. Insulting a police officer . . .'

'Touchy, aren't we,' said Richards. 'Perhaps I should claim police brutality.'

Frost released his grip on Richards and, straightening his mac, said, 'Really? Wouldn't put it past you.'

The buxom floor manager butted in. 'Do you think we could carry on this, uh, conversation in Mr Butcher's office?' she said brightly.

'No need, I won't be long,' Frost said. 'Just a few quick questions and I'll leave you both to get on with your busy day—' He was interrupted by a faint but determined knocking.

The two men stepped aside and a thin, purple-haired woman, clutching an armful of flesh-coloured underwear, emerged from the cubicle, looked around in panic, and scuttled off.

'All right, Richards' – Frost cleared his throat – 'cast your mind back to Saturday afternoon, if that's not too much to ask. Did you see this girl?'

Frost produced a copy of the photo of Julie Hudson, with the red streak in her mousey hair, and held it up. 'You must know the story,' he added. 'One minute she was shopping on this floor with her mum, the next she's disappeared.'

'Yes – of course. Mr Butcher informed me of your visit yesterday, and that photo's been pinned up in the canteen. But I didn't see her on Saturday.'

'How can you be so sure?' said Frost.

'I can't be,' said Richards, 'but the store was busy as usual, and unless she was trying to nick something and had been apprehended by myself or another member of staff, I wouldn't have had any cause to notice her. I don't remember everyone who comes in here shopping.'

'Let me have a look,' the floor manager said, peering keenly over.

'You not been shown this yet?' said Frost, catching a whiff of very pungent perfume. 'Your boss was left with clear instructions to distribute this picture among all staff: a girl has gone missing.'

'As I said, it's been pinned up in the canteen,' interjected Richards.

'I haven't seen or heard anything about it,' the woman insisted, looking closer.

Frost caught Richards giving her a withering look.

'You know,' she continued, 'I think I do remember her. Trying on a school uniform, a skirt – she couldn't find her size. She was awfully skinny. She was also being a little fussy. Though girls that age usually are. The skirts are never short or tight enough.'

'I need to get back to the ground floor,' Richards

said. 'Busy day, Monday – the cafeteria offers half-price meals for pensioners.'

'Off you trot then,' said Frost. 'But don't expect this to be the last you hear from me, Richards.'

Frost returned his focus to the floor manager. 'Anything else you can tell me?'

'Well, it was in the afternoon, three thirty, four-ish. The mother, I presume it was her – a rather pretty, well-dressed woman – was having a right go at the girl for being spoilt. You hear that a lot in here, I can tell you. Though I thought it was a bit rich, given that the mother clearly didn't stint when it came to looking after herself. Anyway.' She carefully ran her right hand over her bouffant hairdo, flashing Frost a clearly flirtatious smile.

'Take your time,' said Frost.

'There was mention of something that happened on holiday – boy trouble, I thought for some reason – at which point the girl sloped off to the changing rooms, and the mother went over to our new lingerie department. We do have the best lingerie department in Denton, you know.'

'So I've heard. Then what?'

'That's odd.' She fingered a heavy gold bracelet on her left arm. 'I don't remember.'

'You were doing so well,' said Frost. 'It's the next bit that I need to know about.'

'I'm trying.'

'Who was manning the changing rooms?'

'Ah, well, we had a bit of a staffing problem on Saturday. I'm afraid to say we didn't have a member of staff, or a casual, specifically assigned to that duty.'

'For the whole day?'

'That's right. Myself and the sales assistants took it in turns to keep an eye out.'

'To keep an eye out?' Frost almost shouted. 'This place is not what it used to be.'

'Mr Butcher has introduced some interesting new measures,' the woman said, looking embarrassed.

'What about your top-notch security detail? Where was Mr Richards, or the other one – the store has two guards, doesn't it – all that day?'

'That's a good point. I'm sure I shouldn't be telling you this, but normally Mr Richards particularly is only too keen to patrol this floor. If you ask me he likes to watch the women choosing their smalls.' She paused, giving Frost a knowing look. 'Now, I remember noticing him in the morning, when we were less busy, but I didn't see him all afternoon. That was definitely unusual.'

'Well, thank you, Mrs . . . ?'

'Roberts. It's Mrs Joyce Roberts.'

'You've been most helpful – though we might need to take a statement from you later.'

'Of course,' she said. 'Anything I can do to help. A missing girl . . . how dreadful.'

'Yes,' said Frost. 'We're getting worried. Now where's my colleague got to?'

Frost left the floor manager by the changing rooms and walked back into the main part of the store, where DC Clarke came rushing up to him.

'Been having a look around,' she beamed.

'For God's sake,' said Frost. 'This is not the time for frilly-knicker shopping.'

'Just what do you take me for?' Clarke said crossly. 'I was checking the other exits and the layout of the floor. You know, there's hardly any staff about. Be hard to have it all covered if it was a bit busier.'

'Perfect spot to snatch a girl,' said Frost quietly, as if to himself. 'But still, would you snatch a girl in broad daylight in a department store?'

'You think she was taken?'

'I don't know what to think,' said Frost. 'Come on, back to the nick for us. We'll need to get out the drawing board, see exactly what we've got so far.'

They pushed their way back through hordes of doddering pensioners, and emerged into the fresh Denton day, Market Square thronging with lunchtime shoppers. Here Frost had a better idea. 'Seeing as the canteen's out of action – fancy a pickled onion and a quick pint?'

Monday (4)

'Well, well, well,' said PC Baker. 'Look who he's trying it on with now.'

'What?' PC Simms lifted his head from the ragged copy of *Auto Trader* that had been kicking around the filthy floor of the panda car for weeks.

'Frost and Sue Clarke.' Baker took another bite of his sandwich.

'What the hell are you talking about?' Simms flung the paper on to the back seat. 'Where?'

'You should keep your eyes open, that's what we're paid to do. You've missed them.'

'Where?' Simms repeated, craning his neck over the dashboard.

'Stumbling out of the Bull and into the Bricklayers.

Arm in arm. Well, almost,' Baker said, his mouth full.

'You're kidding? Jack bloody Frost and Sue?'

'Reckon so.'

Simms strained his tired eyes on the street ahead. He could see the two pubs and a few pedestrians, but neither Frost nor Sue. Was Baker pulling his leg?

They'd been parked up in the panda on the corner of Foundling Street and Lower Goat Lane for the last ten minutes or so. Dispatch had told them to keep a look-out for two men who'd been spotted loitering at the rear staff entrance to the Fortress Building Society. A member of the building society staff thought them suspicious and, given the Rimmington hit, had dutifully reported what she'd seen. But the PCs had seen nothing untoward, so had decided to remain where they were and eat their sandwiches.

And now Derek Simms realized he'd missed the only thing of note. 'That little slut,' he said quietly.

'What was that?' said Baker.

'Nothing.' Simms thumped the dash. He couldn't just sit there, while his bird was with another bloke, even if it was a CID officer. Sue Clarke and her frigging ambition – it was driving him crazy.

Making matters worse was the fact that the more Simms wanted to be with Sue Clarke, the less keen she seemed. Despite their nights of passion she was still reluctant to acknowledge that they were going out with each other.

'Frost and Sue,' said Baker, laughing. 'Who'd have thought it?'

'Right,' huffed Simms, 'about time the Bricklayers was checked for underage drinking.' He made to get out of the car.

'Leave it, Derek,' said Baker. 'No need to upset the licensee. We don't want a fuss.'

'All right then, who's to say the men we're on the look-out for aren't having a pint in the Bricklayers?'

'They'd have every right. Don't be ridiculous: we don't even know what *they* look like. We were meant to keep an eye out – that's all. We haven't seen anything remotely suspicious.'

'Oh yes we have,' snapped Simms. 'Frost with my woman. I'm checking out the pub.'

'Wait a minute. Look, just beyond that telephone box, getting into a dark-blue motor.'

'What, Frost and Sue?' Simms stared morosely ahead.

'Not Frost, you berk. A couple of blokes – big, bald geezer in a sheepskin carrying a bag, and a wiry little fellow in a leather jacket. A Jag – over there. The smaller man's climbing into the back, the other into the front passenger seat, so someone else is driving.'

'Got you,' said Simms at last. He watched the car pull quickly into the road, and promptly stop by the junction to Market Square, indicating right. 'Do we follow? Or pull them over?'

'No, I've got the number,' said Baker, replacing his

notepad in the pocket of his shirt. 'We had no orders to intervene, unless there's obvious illegal activity, and we can't follow in this.' He drummed on the steering wheel of the panda. 'Down to plainclothes – Frost and your bird.'

'Bugger off,' said Simms. 'I'm still going in that boozer. I need a piss.'

As he was climbing out of the vehicle, the radio crackled into life. 'Charlie Alpha, there's a disturbance in Denton Park. A large dog is running amok, terrorizing a group of mothers and toddlers. You are urgently requested to attend the scene. Over.'

'Saved from making a tit of yourself,' said Baker, with a smirk. He turned the ignition key.

'The only dog I'm worried about is in that pub,' sulked Simms, slumping back into his seat.

Monday (5)

The CID office was in chaos. Mounds of paper everywhere. Crisp packets, styrofoam cups growing mould, soiled napkins, half-eaten sandwiches, newspapers, cigarette ash. The drawers of the filing cabinets were open, over-stuffed files bursting out. The blinds were stuck halfway down and skewed at forty-five degrees, revealing grimy windows and the rapidly approaching night.

Frost's mood was darkening with it. He had been trying to pull together the threads of the Julie Hudson case, but was making little progress. He still couldn't decide whether Julie had simply run out of Aster's on her own, or been dragged out, quite possibly down the fire escape. He wanted another word with Blake

Richards, the security guard; Frost had taken an instant dislike to him.

And just as perplexing was the fact that Julie's mother, Wendy Hudson, had been so savagely beaten, sometime later on the Saturday or early Sunday morning, most probably by her husband, and Julie's father, Steve Hudson. What was the motive? The ferocity of the attack had Frost believe it more complicated than a run-of-the-mill domestic.

Frost shoved a pile of paper across his desk so he could pick up the phone, which was trilling annoyingly – probably his wife about to nag him for something or other. But no, it was an excited DC Clarke, telling him that the dog pound had just called her about a Labrador picked up by Charlie Alpha earlier that afternoon in the park.

The dog was in fact a guide dog, though behaving in a severely distressed manner. Checks were being run to find the owner. But Clarke was already wondering whether this had anything to do with the dead man found in the canal – could he have been partially sighted? Blind? Drysdale, the pathologist, had mentioned he'd worn glasses.

Clarke informed Frost the animal was being tested for rabies.

'Rabies?' Frost said, before remembering about Liz Fraser and Simon Trench's little girl, Becky, currently having those tests at the hospital – the smokescreen. Rumours of a rabies outbreak, it seemed, were spreading far and wide already. 'Shit,' he muttered, wondering about the wisdom of his ruse, knowing Mullett would go ballistic if this went any further.

Once the call had ended, Frost quickly lit a cigarette, blowing smoke all over the paperwork in front of him. Try as he might, he couldn't concentrate. He looked at his watch; close to five. Frost dialled Police Sergeant Webster's extension in Records, just as Grace with the tea trolley poked her head around the door.

'Evening, Mr Frost,' she said, 'last orders.'

'Double Scotch,' Frost said, with the phone still clasped to his ear; it didn't seem like Webster was in.

'Can't do that,' said Grace, a little round woman in her late fifties. She was wearing a floral housecoat and a hair net. 'PG Tips and a Kit Kat any good?'

'Do I look like a bloody chimpanzee?' said Frost.

'Sorry?' said PS Webster on the phone. 'That you, Jack?'

'All right, Grace, tea it is, please,' Frost said, this time holding the phone away from his mouth. Replacing it, he said to Webster, 'Has DC Hanlon been on to you about a bloke called Simon Trench – father of a battered little girl called Becky Fraser? And her mother, Liz?'

'Yes,' said Webster. 'We're working on it. Got an address: in Forest View, Denton.'

'I know that. *We* gave it to *you*.'

'But do you know about all the call-outs to that address?'

'Apart from ours yesterday, no,' said Frost, as Grace placed a mug of tea and a Kit Kat on the edge of his desk, before pulling her trolley out of the room. Frost waved her goodbye.

'These go back months,' said Webster. 'An area car was twice dispatched to the house in the middle of the night because this Liz Fraser thought she'd seen someone snooping about outside. Nothing came of it.'

'But this Simon Trench,' said Frost, taking a careful sip of his tea, which was scalding, 'no form?'

'Haven't unearthed anything so far.'

'Workplace? Vehicle? What else you got?'

'Not a lot,' said Webster apologetically. 'We've been prioritizing Steven Hudson. 'Though I have found out that Simon Trench owns a Mini Metro.'

'Chocolate brown?' said Frost distractedly, remembering the car that had clipped the Cortina's wing mirror in Forest View.

'Just says brown,' said Webster.

'Thought so.' Frost took a bite of the Kit Kat. 'Get an alert put out, can you?' he said, mouth full. 'For whatever good that'll do. They still haven't stopped Steve Hudson, and his motor's bright yellow.'

'Plenty of heat on Steve Hudson, though,' said Webster. 'Allegations of ABH, threatening behaviour, fraud – you name it.'

'So why wasn't he on my radar?' said Frost.

'Most of it was from years ago, and nothing stuck.

Appears to have been keeping his nose clean for a while.'

'I wonder why?' said Frost. 'Leopards don't change their spots.'

'They just get more crafty. Well, I'm off down the pub, then,' said Webster.

'Before you go,' said Frost, slumping back in his chair, 'see what you've got on a Blake Richards, formerly of the Met.'

'Funny you should ask about him,' said Webster. 'Bert Williams wanted everything I could get on him only the other week. In fact, Williams should still have the file somewhere – it was sent down from London. Thick as a telephone directory, it was.'

Monday (6)

Superintendent Mullett was giving his office a final once-over: the ornaments on the desk were in precise alignment, the in-tray empty, the telephone, having been dusted by his own handkerchief, was shining brightly. If nothing else, order and cleanliness always provided him with a certain comfort.

With something approaching a satisfied smile on his lips, he tapped the edge of the desk for luck, then headed out of the inner sanctum, turning off the light, only to walk straight into PC Simms, who'd obviously been loitering by Miss Smith's desk.

'What the hell, Simms! You gave me quite a shock,' said Mullett.

'Sorry, sir. It's just that I was hoping to have a word with Miss Smith.'

'But as you can see, she's not here.' Mullett looked at his watch – he was going to be late for dinner yet again. 'She left over an hour ago.'

'Yes, I can see that now. What I mean is . . .' The constable was flustered. 'I thought maybe she'd popped to the canteen, so that was why I was waiting.'

'You know the canteen is out of order at the moment.'

'Oh, yes, of course it is. I'd forgotten.'

'It seems to me you've forgotten quite a lot, like the time Miss Smith finishes work for the day.'

'I suppose so, sir. Sorry.'

'Sorry? What did you want with my secretary anyway?' Mullett didn't have time for this, but then he certainly didn't have time for any untoward behaviour in his station. A tight ship, that's what he ran, not a knocking shop.

'It's a personal matter, sir,' said Simms.

Mullett was not in the least surprised. 'Personal?' he shouted. 'This is not a bordello, lad. Pull yourself together.' Mullett then set off down the corridor, thinking that Simms needed a cold shower. If not a good caning. As head boy at Charterfield, Mullett had loved thrashing the juniors.

Monday (7)

Jack Frost and Sue Clarke were hurrying to Wendy Hudson's ward, down yet another squeaky corridor. Frost's head was throbbing, the lateness of the hour and the bright fluorescent lighting not helping matters. He felt a twinge in his lower abdomen, probably down to the three pints he'd had at lunch.

Hospitals were even worse at night, Frost found himself thinking. The long, empty corridors, bereft of patients, nurses, visitors. The stink of loneliness, fear and death. 'Did you see *The Shining*?' he asked, the atmosphere really getting to him.

'No way,' said Clarke. 'I hate horror films. Though I wouldn't mind seeing *An American Werewolf in London* – apparently that's really funny, not just scary.'

'Just trot down to Denton Woods,' said Frost. 'On a full moon. You'd be surprised what you'd see.'

Lister Ward was in darkness apart from a light at its far end. They continued down the corridor past the occasional groan, moan or snore, until they reached the nurses' station.

A redhead was sitting by an Anglepoise lamp.

'Hello, love,' Frost said politely. 'We've come to see Wendy Hudson – I'm DS Frost and this is DC Clarke, Denton CID. We got a call a short while ago, saying Mrs Hudson had regained consciousness.'

To Frost's extreme annoyance he'd also discovered that the WPC in attendance had been relieved of her duties much earlier in the day because Mullett thought it a waste of resources keeping a constable by an unconscious woman's bedside. So when Wendy Hudson did wake up there'd been nobody on hand to record anything she might have said.

'Yes, that's right.' A faint, Irish brogue drifted up from under the light, while the nurse continued to write carefully in a ledger.

Now he was here, Frost was even more livid. Mullett wasn't just a stingy bastard but an incompetent one as well. 'Can you remind me which bed is hers?' he asked. 'It's a little dark out there.'

'But you can't talk to her now,' the nurse said, raising her angelic face.

'Why ever not?' Frost said, still trying to be polite.

'Lights-out is at ten. As you may have noticed,

everyone is asleep. Or trying to get to sleep.' She smiled up at him, as if it were the most obvious thing in the world.

'Listen to me, sweetheart' – Clarke was tugging at Frost's sleeve, but he ignored her – 'it's been a very long day, we're in the middle of a particularly serious police investigation, so go and wake her up again. She's a big girl, I'm sure she stays up after ten when she's at home.'

'She's still heavily sedated.'

'Then why the flaming hell,' he said, almost spitting as he leant over her desk and turned the beam of the lamp directly in her face, 'did you call us to say she's awake?'

'Come on, Jack,' Clarke murmured behind him.

'Firstly, I didn't call anyone,' said the nurse, tapping his hand off her lamp with a biro, 'I only came on at ten, and secondly, as I understand it, she *was* awake – briefly.'

Frost stepped back from the desk. 'Thank you so much for your help,' he barked. 'The next time she happens to wake up, perhaps you would do me the favour of letting me speak to her, so that I might have some chance of finding not just the person who damn nearly killed her, but her missing twelve-year-old daughter, who could be in serious danger.'

The nurse looked down at the notes she'd been writing, saying nothing.

'If it's not too much trouble, of course,' Frost added,

144

barely able to contain himself. 'Nurse . . . ?' He couldn't read her badge.

Finally she began to speak. 'It's sister, actually . . . please keep your voice down.'

Frost had already turned his back on her and was marching towards the exit. He could hear Clarke scampering after him. He needed a cigarette, and a drink. 'Why does the whole of Denton seem to be filling up with Irish? And none of them any bloody help.'

'Sorry?' Clarke asked, confused.

'Never mind.'

Once out of Lister Ward, and on another, more brightly lit corridor, Frost had an idea. 'Where's the kiddies' ward?'

'*They*'re certainly going to be fast asleep,' said Clarke.

'It's not the kids I want to have a word with. Come on.' They had reached an atrium of sorts, with signs pointing in all directions. Frost realized he had no idea where the Fraser child was now being kept, in isolation.

Still he led Clarke towards the clearly marked paediatrics section of the hospital. After a couple of flights of stairs and more dismal corridors they came to the internal paediatrics lobby.

Commanding the main desk was a fearsome-looking matron in a sharp blue uniform, complete with white hat. Frost knew in an instant that, warrant card or not, he wasn't going to get past this one.

'I've had enough people snooping around this ward today,' said the matron, before Frost had even opened his mouth, 'with all manner of excuses and lies.'

'Sorry to hear it,' said Frost.

'One chap even tried to bribe me, he did,' said the matron. She looked at Frost keenly. 'I know what you two are up to – on the hunt for a story. Well, you're barking up the wrong tree with me. You're not going to get another inch down that corridor.'

'Wait a minute, love,' Frost protested, alarm growing. 'Just because I wear a raincoat doesn't make me a scavenging newshound.'

Finally having established his and Clarke's identity, the matron was surprisingly forthcoming about Becky Fraser's predicament. 'The poor mite's obviously being kept in a room all of her own, and we've set up a bed for her mother to be by her side; didn't seem any point in keeping her out.'

'No, of course not,' agreed Frost, though suddenly worrying about Liz Fraser, and whether he'd got it all wrong and that it was her and not the child's father who had been abusing Becky. Frost had too much on his mind – he was losing sight of what was really what, losing his edge, his conviction.

'I think they've been together all day, playing happily,' said the matron.

'I see,' said Frost.

The matron looked around her, before whispering, 'The tests are continuing, but we won't know anything until tomorrow afternoon at the earliest.' She winked.

Frost could sense that Clarke was on the verge of giggling. He had no idea how much the matron really knew, or whether she realized the child's isolation had actually been orchestrated by a Denton CID detective both for her immediate protection and to gain some precious time.

'And the consultant?' Frost suddenly couldn't remember the doctor's name. 'Can I have a word with him? Is he about?'

'No, Doctor Philips has long been gone for the day,' the matron said, adding quietly, 'though I do believe he tried to contact you at the station this afternoon.'

'Is that right? Well, the message never got through.' Frost tried to remember whether it had or not.

'He'll be here in the morning,' said the matron more sternly.

'Good, I'll contact him then.'

'Do you want to see whether the mother's still awake? You could perhaps have a word with her.'

'No,' said Frost. 'No need to bother her. It's Doctor Philips I should talk to first.'

Frost also knew he had to get on to Social Services sharpish.

Standing outside the hospital, in the cold night air, under the car-park lights, Frost held out a match for Clarke. She cupped his hand and leant forward, cigarette between her teeth, but shivering as she did so.

'Feels like winter is well and truly on its way,' she said. 'It's bloody freezing.'

'I like the winter,' said Frost, 'clears my sinuses.' He paused, looking towards the bushes. 'But what I don't like are sneaky old hacks.'

'I'm sorry, not with you.'

The rustling Frost thought he'd heard became more pronounced.

'Jack!' rang out from the shadows, as a tall, slim man stepped into the light and walked towards them. Frost realized he'd been expecting as much.

'Hello, Sandy,' said Frost dismissively. 'What brings you to Denton General this time of night – I hope you're not as ill as you look?'

'Fit as a fiddle, actually,' the tall man said.

'Sue, allow me to introduce you,' said Frost. 'DC Clarke, this is Sandy Lane, *Denton Echo*'s one and only hack.'

'Hello, DC Clarke,' Lane said, taking his time over shaking Clarke's hand.

'So, why are you skulking about out here?' Frost asked, wheezing slightly as the chill air got right inside his lungs.

'My mum, taken bad a couple of days ago. They think she's had a stroke.'

'Sorry to hear that,' said Frost, trying hard to sound like he meant it.

'She's doing all right, though. Made of stern stuff, us Lanes.' The reporter paused. 'Funny bumping into you, Jack. She's in a ward with another old dear, a Mrs Hanlon. Been chatting to one of your colleagues this afternoon, as it happens – DC Arthur Hanlon.'

With a sinking feeling Frost had a good idea what was coming next. Though thorough and diligent, Hanlon wasn't always as sharp and on his guard as he could be.

'Rabies in Denton. Now, Jack, that's a big scoop,' said Lane smugly. 'Of national interest.'

Frost said nothing. Reached for another smoke. Working out his line.

'Care to comment?'

Frost knew the presses for tomorrow's paper would have run by now, and that anything he said would be largely irrelevant. 'What have you set in motion, Lane? Be awful for you if it turned out to be nothing more serious than an errant squirrel cosying up to a nipper.'

'Come on, there's a little girl in there undergoing tests for rabies, and that's a fact.'

'Can't argue with that,' said Frost.

'See, see, I knew it was true!' cried Lane. 'That bloody lying matron.'

Had Frost simply confirmed Lane's suspicions? 'Hold on a minute. A test is one thing – confirmation's another. Besides, how do you know there aren't other reasons why she's here as well?'

'But Jack, you don't get it, do you? Whether there really is rabies in the county is neither here nor there. The possibility that it *might* be here is enough of a story. Doctors, tests, isolation wards. It's a bloody big story too – with pictures, interviews. We've got more than enough.'

'Interviews?' Frost laughed. There was only so much that Lane could have cobbled together. Though standing in the shocking cold, pushing eleven at night, Frost was almost beyond caring. 'You and that rag of yours, Lane' – Frost tapped Clarke on the arm, gesticulated towards the Escort – 'you'll be begging us for the real story one day. For *any* real story. So, in the meantime, just remember the public, those people who'll be too terrified to leave their houses, to go to school, to the doctor's, to do their shopping. All because you couldn't be bothered to check the facts. They'd be better off reading the bloody *Beano*.'

Once in the Escort, the engine being warmed by Clarke's keen foot, Frost asked, 'How about a nightcap? We should just make last orders. I'm frozen from the inside out and the Cricketers is just around the corner from here – believe there's a bit of a darts match going on.' It was also just possible, Frost hoped, that Bert Williams could be there; it was one of his regular haunts. Or if he wasn't, someone might have seen him very recently.

'Can't,' said Clarke. 'I'm already late.'

'Aye-aye – who's the lucky chap?'

'As if I'd tell you.'

'Amount of gossip flying around that nick, could be one of many,' said Frost, laughing.

'Not everyone mixes work with pleasure.' Clarke accelerated out of the hospital car park.

'No, but you're a copper. Coppers don't have much time for anything other than the job.'

'Yes they do, if they're quick about it,' said Clarke, turning to smile at him.

'That's my problem, then. I always take too bloody long.'

'There'll be a lot of women who think that's an advantage,' she said, turning on to the Rimmington Road. 'I'll drop you off, if you like.' The Cricketers appeared up ahead.

'That would be grand, thanks.'

'Do you ever go home?' she asked.

'Something always seems to crop up first,' Frost said.

Tuesday (1)

'What the blazes is this?' Mullett slammed the newspaper on Frost's desk, sending paperwork and cigarette ash everywhere.

Frost looked up, doubting whether he'd ever seen the super so angry. Mullett's face was puce above the starched collar of his white shirt. His magnified eyes seemed to be popping out of their sockets behind his horn-rimmed glasses. Frost glanced across at Hanlon, who immediately rose from his chair and made a dash for the door.

'Desperate,' Hanlon muttered, clutching his vast stomach and backing away down the corridor.

Frost unfolded the *Denton Echo* and read the headline: RABIES IN DENTON! BABY CONFINED IN

GENERAL. The story was accompanied by a huge photo of a rabid dog – the image looked familiar. 'Wonder where the snap came from?' Frost said, mostly to himself, lighting a cigarette.

'Balls to the photo!' Mullett shrieked as he paced the cramped CID office. 'Have you any idea what this means? We'll have every vulture up from Fleet Street now, all right.'

'I thought they were here already,' said Frost. 'On the hunt for paedophile-aiding-and-abetting coppers.'

'That's more than enough of your lip, Frost. I've already had the Chief Constable on the phone. Give me one of those.'

Frost slid the Rothmans over. 'I don't know anything about it, sir. Presumably the hospital isn't airtight. One of the nurses, maybe?' The superintendent was making him feel even more defensive than normal.

'What do you mean, you know nothing about it?' Mullett barked. 'That hack Sandy Lane told the Chief Constable first thing this morning – the Chief Constable no less – that he'd spoken to one DS Frost outside the hospital late last night, and you'd all but confirmed it was true. For heaven's sake, Frost!'

'It was unfortunate that Lane was skulking about there. His mother's ill, apparently.'

'I don't give a *damn* about his mother,' said Mullett.
'No, sir.'

'No, sir?' Mullett shouted. 'This whole rabies

nonsense has got completely out of hand already, for which you, Frost, are entirely to blame.'

'It was the health and safety of a little girl, Becky Fraser, that was my most pressing concern,' said Frost. 'Thankfully she's being well cared for right now. To be honest, an opportunity arose and I went for it. At least it's given us some time.'

'No, Frost, that's exactly what we don't have – time. Not now. What the hell were you doing at the hospital late last night anyway? Presumably little Becky Fraser was safely tucked up in bed.'

'I was checking on Wendy Hudson, sir. The woman who was nearly battered to death?' Frost said angrily. 'We had a call yesterday evening – after you'd gone home, I presume – saying that she'd woken up. All on her own.' He looked his superior in the eye. 'With no bloody WPC at her bedside, ready to record anything she might say, because someone wasn't prepared to sanction any further overtime. So when I eventually get there—'

'Oh yes, the case of the missing girl.' Mullett frowned, stubbing out his cigarette and looking at his watch. 'Have we found the chap yet? The husband? This thing should have been wrapped up by now.'

'No, sir.'

'How hard can it be?'

'I'm more concerned about the girl, Julie Hudson. Her mother was nearly clobbered to death – her disappearance has to be related.' Frost paused. 'We'll pick her father up soon enough. But it's Julie Hudson's safety I fear for. She's not even thirteen.'

'She's still on the run, is she?'

'She's still missing, if that's what you mean,' said Frost, despairing.

'Well,' said Mullett, 'you'll have to make do with the resources at hand. Unless you're as stupid as you look, you must realize we're suddenly facing a very grave personnel crisis at the station, and when the whole of Denton is about to explode with anxiety over rabies scare stories. DI Allen, as you know, is on annual leave for the rest of this week, and there is still no sign of DI Williams – I don't suppose you have any idea where he is? You're his partner in crime, aren't you?'

'No, sir, sorry. I've no idea where DI Williams is. Some sort of domestic crisis, I imagine.'

'It had better be good. By God.' Mullett scratched at his moustache, before resuming, 'I need time to think and plan a course of action, before this morning's briefing. Just don't go opening that great mouth of yours again, not to anyone, or you can kiss your job goodbye. Call yourself a detective? At least you're wearing some approximation to a suit today.'

With that Mullett made an about-turn, only to bang straight into Grace's tea trolley, which had silently appeared in the doorway.

'What on earth . . . ?' said Mullett, kicking the trolley away.

'Cup of tea, sir?' Grace asked.

'Tea? Tea? I haven't got time for tea.' Mullett rubbed his knee and made off down the corridor.

'What's got into him?' said Grace.

'He's been bitten by something horrible,' said Frost, lighting another cigarette, straight off the butt of his last one.

'Needs a nice cup of sweet tea to calm him down, I should say.'

'He needs something, darling,' said Frost, thinking hard. 'I'll certainly take a cuppa.'

'Biscuit?'

'Why not.'

Sipping his tea, Frost thought that Liz Fraser really had quite a lot to answer for. News that she'd made previous dubious calls to the police, and that the father of her child, Simon Trench, had no obvious form (though at least they knew he had a chocolate-brown Mini Metro) was beginning to worry him more and more. With Mullett on the warpath and Denton gripped by fear – at least according to the *Echo* – the stakes had been raised considerably.

It would almost have been funny had it not been for the child. Which reminded Frost, he still hadn't yet spoken to the paediatric consultant, let alone dug around in Social Services' records. Now that Hanlon was back on duty, his mother thankfully not as seriously ill as first thought, Frost knew exactly who could do the legwork there.

Just as he was contemplating putting in an

appearance at the briefing – he didn't see the point in giving Mullett any further ammunition – the phone went. It was Drysdale, the pathologist.

'Good morning, Doc, someone back from the dead?' said Frost.

'Detective Frost, I'll get straight to the point. The man pulled from the canal? Having done some further tests and consulted a top Harley Street eye surgeon, who happens to be a very good friend of mine—'

'Go on, get to the flaming point then,' snapped Frost.

'He was blind.'

'Are you positive?'

'Yes, there's no doubt at all.'

'Thank you, Doc. I just happen to know where his dog is.'

The briefing-room door squeaked open and Sue Clarke glanced round in time to see Jack Frost sneak in, a biscuit between his teeth. He raised his eyebrows at her, before sitting down next to PC Derek Simms.

She returned her attention to the front, where Superintendent Mullett had moved on from rabies and his contingency plan, and was discussing Julie Hudson, and why the devil her father hadn't yet been apprehended, and this distracting, domestic mess all sorted out.

Clarke was amazed that the super seemed more concerned at this stage with finding Steve Hudson than Julie. But she supposed he had his reasons. She continued to take notes.

'Clarke, Hanlon, Frost?' Mullett was suddenly saying.

'Yes, sir?' she replied nervously, looking up and realizing she was the only one of the trio to reply.

'Anyone checked out the girl's school yet?'

'No, not yet, sir,' she said. Why hadn't she thought of that yesterday? Too busy boozing at lunchtime with that rascal Frost, only to be spotted by Derek Simms, who, drawing the wrong conclusion, had given her a right earful late last night. Simms was the jealous type, that was for sure.

'We've made arrangements to meet the head-mistress within the next hour,' said Frost, much to her surprise. 'DC Clarke and myself. Thought it would be good to have Clarke there, you know how prickly these women teachers can be around men.'

Mullett looked confused. Clarke turned to Frost, who gave her a wink.

'Err . . . yes . . . that's right, sir,' she said, turning back and addressing the divisional commander. She'd forgotten what school the girl went to. Oh, where were her notes? It was all very well scribbling everything down, but if you couldn't find the right page, or even read your own handwriting . . .

'Just make sure the staff don't go blathering to the *Echo*,' Mullett instructed. 'I still want this kept quiet – operational reasons dictate as much.'

Clarke didn't know what he was talking about.

'God forbid,' Mullett continued, 'that the press get hold of this one, as well as the rabies nonsense, then we're all done for.'

'Yes, sir,' she said. 'We'll be very discreet.'

'As always,' sighed Mullett. 'Now, this body dragged out of the canal. Where are we with that?' He looked enquiringly around the room.

Clarke hadn't done anything about this, since mooting the idea to Frost yesterday that the man may have been blind. She felt badly out of sorts today, her disastrous late-night date playing havoc with her concentration.

She'd have to shape up if she was to grab one of the new promotions Mullett had dangled in front of the division at the start of his tenure. With two DIs down, now was a chance for her to shine, surely.

'We'll be able to confirm his identity at least very shortly – if not the exact cause of death,' piped up Frost again. 'The pathologist has just confirmed that the poor man was blind, which was only what DC Clarke had already deduced. And, fortunately, PC Simms here' – Frost patted the PC on the back – 'has a way with dogs, ensnaring, I believe, what was the man's guide dog in Denton Park yesterday afternoon. The mutt had been disturbing some mothers and kiddies.'

Clarke stared back at Frost. She was delighted that her speculation about the man being blind had been proved correct, and also that Frost had given her the credit in front of Mullett. But – feeling her cheeks burning – was that reference to Simms having a way with dogs anything to do with her? No, surely not.

'You look dreadful, Wells.'

Station Sergeant Bill Wells sat up straight. Mullett had appeared from nowhere.

'Touch of the flu yesterday,' he said. 'Haven't completely shaken it but thought I'd struggle in, knowing how short-staffed we are at the moment.'

'Very good of you, Sergeant.'

Wells watched Mullett brush his moustache with his forefingers, a puzzled look creeping across his face. 'What are they doing there?' the super asked sternly, pointing to a stack of paint tins in the corner of the lobby.

'Your paint, sir?' Wells answered feebly.

'I know *what* it is, you fool – why is it *there*?'

'Nowhere else to put it?' Wells had no idea. 'It turned up yesterday, when I was at home, ill.'

'Where's your initiative, man? It's in the way – can't you see that? Someone could trip over it, and then we'd have the union come down on us like a ton of bricks.' Mullett stood in the middle of the lobby, hands on hips, pouting. 'Still no sign of DI Williams, I suppose?'

'No sir. Not a peep.' Wells watched Mullett glare at the paint, as if it signalled everything that was wrong with his life. Though of course it was the super's half-brained idea to tart up Eagle Lane in the first place.

Mullett marched off, leaving Wells wondering just what he had really wanted. To check on the tidiness of the lobby? The sort of welcome the division now offered the good citizens of Denton? Simply to moan? It was all getting more ridiculous by the day.

Bleeding hell, Wells had a headache – his throat was raw, too. Having had a more than deserved lie-in yesterday (*that'll teach them for giving me two double shifts in a row*) he'd gone and got hammered last night at the Cricketers. Bumping into bloody Jack Frost while he was at it. At least Mullett thought he looked ill.

The phone rang, again.

'Nice safe place, Denton,' said a quiet Irish voice.

'I beg your pardon? This is Denton Police, front desk.' Was Control still putting outside calls straight through to him when they were jammed solid?

'I said it was a nice safe place, Denton.'

What on earth? Wells's head was throbbing like a bastard. 'Excuse me, what did you just say?' But who-ever it was had hung up.

Struggling to keep the contents of his stomach down, Wells tried to get his head around the signifi-cance of what he'd just heard. It was the second peculiar call he'd taken from an Irishman in the last couple of days, the first being the one on Sunday about a van being driven slowly around Market Square.

He was thinking back to something Frost had said

in the pub last night – something crass about the pope and then how he'd better keep his voice down because Denton was suddenly crawling with Irish.

Wells found himself thinking about the hunger striker who'd died back in May and that IRA bloke who'd escaped from prison in the summer, and the resulting number of security alerts Scotland Yard had issued. He scratched a sideburn thoughtfully.

The station sergeant reached for the call log, his pen and blotter, but was disturbed again by Mullett, who reappeared in the lobby with Pooley. The super was gesticulating wildly at the paint, while Pooley looked on vacantly. Finally Pooley seemed to get the message and gingerly picked up a couple of tins.

'Sir, Superintendent Mullett, sir,' Wells said, as loudly as he could manage.

The super spun round. 'Yes?' he snapped.

'While you're here, thought I should mention this call I just received.'

Mullett glared at him across the lobby. 'You know the procedure, if it's important . . .' The super looked away.

'I know, sir, but Control seem a little stretched again, and DS Frost is not at his desk, and as I said, while you're standing right there, thought I'd—'

'I don't have time to listen to your burblings, Wells,' Mullett cried out, with a look of disgust as he watched the laden Pooley struggle down the corridor.

'Sir, I really—'

Wells couldn't finish what he was going to say, because Mullett suddenly marched up to the desk and sniffed loudly. 'DI Williams is not hiding behind that counter, is he? I smell whisky.'

Tuesday (2) _____

Speeding along Denton High Street, Frost noticed a couple of punks, pink hair silhouetted against the black-and-white facade of the new Andy's Records. He frowned. 'I don't mind the fact they've raided their mum's make-up box, but I don't understand the gobbing.' He glanced over at Clarke.

'They're letting us know how pissed off they are,' she said. 'Showing their disrespect for the world they live in.'

'Well, that's not going to make it any better, is it?'

'They're just kids.' She smiled. 'You must have been rebellious when you were younger.'

'Who's to say I've changed?'

'That's true,' she said. 'Thanks, by the way, for earlier.'

'For what?'

'You know, for crediting me with spotting that the body in the canal was a blind man, in the briefing. And for saying we'd already organized this meeting at Julie Hudson's school.'

'I was saving my bacon too,' said Frost. 'I should have thought about the damn school yesterday.'

'It was good of you, anyway.'

Frost coughed, suddenly relieved that she wasn't going to castigate him for his joke about Simms and dogs; she was a good sport, all right. Could take it. 'Steady on, love,' he said, as she sped on. This was going to be another hair-raising ride.

For once Frost felt some results were coming in. The blind man had quickly been identified as Graham Ransome, a resident of the old folks' flats on the Southern Housing Estate's Arberry Close.

A frogman had pulled a guide dog's harness from the canal on Monday afternoon, which was linked to both Ransome and the black Labrador Simms and Baker had found in the park the same afternoon. Initial studies of the harness, torn and frayed, indicated that there had been some kind of scuffle, probably leading to the distressed animal breaking free, running off and later causing havoc in the park.

Frost's focus now was on how exactly Ransome had ended up dead in the canal, given Drysdale's account of him having been badly beaten.

Something crossed Frost's mind. 'Why didn't Scenes of Crime seal off the canal bank?'

'It didn't appear to be necessary, I guess,' Clarke said. 'Looked like an accident,' she added lamely.

Frost supposed she was covering her back. 'Not even the odd footprint?'

'Too many fire service and frogmen, trampling all over the place, trying to fish the body out.' Clarke slowed, a little too late, and narrowly missed a wobbling cyclist. 'I don't know, Jack. I supposed I messed up. I mean, I was the first officer at the scene.'

'Don't worry, love. We've all been there. The thing is, best never to admit it. I can keep a secret.'

'I'm glad I can be of some help this morning.'

'Seemed the obvious thing to do, bring you along,' coughed Frost. 'A school full of ripe young girls – wouldn't be appropriate for a healthy young man like myself to go wandering around on my own.' He lit another Rothmans, inhaling deeply. 'Anyway, Hanlon says he's got a stomach bug. Thinks he'll have to go home.'

'I heard about his mum. That got something to do with it?'

'His mother – how do you mean?'

'Has he caught something?'

Frost laughed. 'He's caught something, all right – it's called keeping a low profile having put your foot in it.' Though not completely surprised, Frost still couldn't believe that the great oaf had blabbed to a bunch of old biddies in the hospital about rabies. 'They think his mum's had a very minor stroke. She'll live.'

Clarke overtook a sugar-beet lorry.

'By the way, I liked your thinking about the poor bugger being blind,' said Frost thoughtfully. He was glad he was with Clarke, now, rather than Hanlon. 'That was smart.'

'Thanks.'

'Before you know it, you'll be a DI. We're certainly short of them at the moment.' His mind leapt uncomfortably to the fact that Bert was still missing.

'I'm in it for the policing, not the promotion,' Clarke said. 'I want to serve and protect the public.'

'I bet you do.' Frost didn't believe her for one minute, but there, looming in front of them, was St Mary's School for Girls. The school, once a Georgian stately home, was set back from the main road. Topiaries separated the long drive from the opulent grounds filled with ancient oak and yew trees. It was imposing and impressive, and reduced both Frost and Clarke to silence.

The car rounded the corner and came to an abrupt stop on the gravel drive.

Frost, sweaty from his alcohol intake the night before, found his eyes drawn to a gaggle of girls in shockingly short skirts standing by a low wall to the left of the main building. A teacher, a lithe brunette in a tracksuit, seemed to be admonishing one of the girls.

The altercation held the attention of the others.

'That's Mrs Litchfield,' said Clarke. 'She's the woman who discovered the dead man in the canal. I forgot she was a teacher at St Mary's.' She paused. 'I'm surprised she hasn't taken a few days off work . . . after such an experience.'

'Can't say stumbling upon a stiff would put me off turning up for work here,' Frost mused. 'Oh, the privileged few . . .' He glanced at the notes he'd hastily compiled after the rushed call to the school – following the briefing. 'The headmistress is a Mrs Rebecca Sidley. This could be fun.'

Walking away from the Escort, Frost was aware that he and Clarke had caught the attention of the schoolgirls. One or two of the teenagers glanced flirtatiously at Frost. He straightened his back to increase his height as he climbed the steps leading to the main entrance.

Once inside Frost and Clarke were immediately met by a frail, grey man of about sixty – some kind of porter, Frost guessed – who'd been sitting on a bench in the dim lobby.

'Yes?' the man asked, raising one lopsided eyebrow.

'We have an appointment with Mrs Sidley,' Clarke said.

The man looked stonily at them for a moment, before stepping aside to let them into a vast hall. It was quiet and musty-smelling. A chill draught blew through.

'You can't do that in here, sir,' the porter said coldly, gesturing at Frost's cigarette.

Frost took a deep drag before looking around for somewhere to stub it out. His eyes alighted upon an aspidistra in a tall china stand, which he moved towards.

The man quickly leapt forward with a small glass ashtray he'd plucked from his pocket. 'I shall advise Mrs Sidley you're here,' he said and abruptly disappeared.

'Crikey, it's like something out of the Victorian age,' Frost said, looking up at a mangy stag's head on the wall. 'Hard to guess who's the oldest, Mr Cheerful with the ashtray, or the moose.'

After five minutes or so of Frost and Clarke pacing the huge hall and eyeing tatty, out-of-date issues of *Country Life*, piled high on an oak side table, the old man returned and beckoned them down a long corridor, to a study at the back of the building.

The room was lined with bookshelves and a handful of stuffed raptors were mounted on plinths. Frost, for all his experience in police work, found something particularly unsettling about taxidermy, with both the process and those who collected the beasts. Outside, through a couple of floor-to-ceiling windows, he could see a formal garden, with playing fields beyond. Gaggles of girls stood about on the grass, drifts of cigarette smoke here and there.

'Sherry?' The voice behind him was refined.

'Don't mind if I do,' said Frost, turning. A tall, thin woman, with greying black hair wound into a tight bun, and with a face dominated by an aquiline nose, had appeared from a side door. 'I am Detective Sergeant Frost,' he offered, momentarily disarmed by her regal appearance. Holding out his hand, he added, 'And this is Detective Constable Clarke.'

'Rebecca Sidley. How do you do,' she said.

'Lovely view.' Frost pointed his thumb back towards the girls outside the window, trying to recover his composure.

'Isn't it,' she smiled calmly. 'I do like to watch the girls at play.' She opened a drinks cabinet, discreetly situated amid the bookshelves, and poured two large schooners from a cut-glass decanter. One went to Frost and the other was set down on her desk. Clarke she appeared to ignore.

Mrs Sidley picked up a heavy desk lighter and lit a long, thin cigarette. 'So, how can I be of assistance?' she asked, sucking at her cigarette. 'I believe you are worried about one of our pupils?'

'Yes,' DC Clarke said, rankled. 'We are very concerned for Julie Hudson's safety, following her disappearance at the weekend.'

Mrs Sidley inhaled deeply, properly turning her attention to Clarke for the first time. A faint smile fluttered across her face. She gracefully tipped the ash from her cigarette and moved towards the window. Queen of all she surveyed, Frost thought.

'Jenkins,' she called, without raising her voice.

Seemingly from nowhere the stooge appeared. 'Yes, ma'am?'

'Fetch me Mrs Cooper.'

'I believe Mrs Cooper is on break duty,' the man replied.

'The girls will manage just fine without her.' Mrs Sidley smoothed back a stray strand of grey hair that had escaped the tight bun. 'Don't you think so, Mr Frost? Besides, it's nearly eleven thirty, bell-time.'

Frost's gaze had drifted back out of the window, to a couple of girls, nearby, doing handstands in short skirts. He half wondered whether the acrobatics were for his benefit.

'Mr Frost?' Mrs Sidley repeated, amused.

'Yes, impressive facilities, Mrs Sidley,' he said, turning to face the room.

'Do sit down, please.'

Frost and Clarke sank into a chesterfield. It was particularly hard and uncomfortable.

'Mrs Cooper – she's Julie Hudson's form teacher – will be with us shortly.' Mrs Sidley slowly eased herself into the deep red-leather chair behind her desk.

Back trouble, Frost suspected. Had she been turning cartwheels in her spare time? When she was younger?

'Mrs Cooper will be a lot more help than I. We have over four hundred girls here. Now, I do believe you have a new superintendent,' Mrs Sidley queried. 'A Mr Flounder?'

'Mullett,' said Frost sharply – he didn't have time for small-talk. As he felt his pockets for his cigarettes, there was a knock on the door.

'Ah, Mrs Cooper, do come in,' Mrs Sidley called.

Frost watched as a short, plump blonde in her early thirties, wearing a ridiculously tight, flared purple-corduroy trouser suit, stepped hesitantly into the room.

'Mr Frost and his colleague here,' said Mrs Sidley, addressing Mrs Cooper, 'are asking after Julie Hudson.'

'Oh,' Mrs Cooper said. 'Well, Julie was absent yesterday and today.'

'I could have told you that,' said Frost.

'It's usual if a child is sick for the parents to call in,' Mrs Cooper persisted. 'We've not heard anything and, yes, we were starting to become concerned.'

'You're not the only one,' said Frost. 'So you tried to contact the parents?'

'Yes, we've rung a couple of times. But there's been no answer.'

'No surprise there,' Frost said.

'How is Julie in general? Attentive? Happy?' DC Clarke asked.

'She's certainly a bright girl and normally seems happy enough. Though I have to say she's possibly been a little distracted of late,' answered Mrs Cooper, glancing at the headmistress. 'I have been worried about her weight, too – she's very thin.'

'May I ask about the reasons for your concern for Julie?' Mrs Sidley interrupted, looking straight at Frost.

But it was Clarke who answered, blurting out, 'She disappeared sometime on Saturday afternoon, we think from Aster's department store.'

Frost frowned at his colleague. He hadn't intended to reveal all the specifics, not straight away.

'Shopping – that's all these girls are interested in nowadays,' sighed Mrs Sidley.

'Disappeared? Oh dear. The parents must be distraught,' Mrs Cooper said.

'You could say that,' Frost said sternly, deciding that perhaps shock tactics were the best option. 'Problem is, Mrs Hudson is in Denton General – beaten to within an inch of her life. And Mr Hudson has gone missing.'

Mrs Sidley gave a sharp intake of breath. 'Goodness. You don't think he's had anything to do with it, do you?'

'I've always found Mr Hudson to be rather charming,' said Mrs Cooper, flushing slightly.

'We aren't ruling anything in or out at this stage,' said Frost. 'What's important is that you tell us anything about Julie, and her family, anything at all that you think odd or unusual, or that might be useful.'

Mrs Cooper looked thoughtful.

'You said Julie's been a little distracted and reserved of late?' prompted Clarke.

'Well, there is maybe something you should know,' the teacher began, looking at her boss, clearly asking for approval. Mrs Sidley nodded. 'It has been said, among the girls that is, that Julie's father is not her natural father. But you know what girls are like. They can be very cruel.'

'Is there any bullying at this school?' asked Clarke.

'I should think not,' said Mrs Sidley sharply.

'When did you first hear this?' said Frost, ignoring Mrs Sidley and directing his question to Mrs Cooper.

'Recently. Let me think, last week? Perhaps the end of the week before.'

'Who from exactly?' Clarke asked.

'Oh, more than one girl. It's just something I've overheard.' Mrs Cooper was looking increasingly flustered.

'The timing could be very important – please try to be more specific.' Frost was vexed: a whole new scenario was materializing.

'I'm afraid we've all had a rather shocking couple of days, as I'm sure you are aware,' Mrs Sidley said, taking control. 'It's not every day that one of our teachers discovers a dead man in Denton Union Canal.'

'If you are referring to Mrs Litchfield – is it? – she seemed fit enough to come to work today,' countered Frost.

'We saw her talking to some girls out front,' added Clarke politely, 'as we arrived.'

'That's as maybe. But we were all rather shocked and upset nevertheless.'

'However you look at it,' said Frost, 'better a dead old man, than a young girl ... kidnapped, raped, murdered, you name it.' He paused. 'What about Julie's mother? What can either of you tell me about Mrs Wendy Hudson? There must be a lot of contact with the parents at a posh place like this.'

'She always seems very keen to do the best for her daughter,' said Mrs Cooper, being careful, Frost thought, not to look at Mrs Sidley. 'But, how can I put this? She seemed maybe a little too anxious to fit in. It's a class thing, I suppose. A lot of our girls come from very privileged, county backgrounds. I'm not quite sure that the Hudsons were from quite the same social strata – they do, I believe, live in Denton itself. And Mr Hudson is a second-hand car dealer, isn't he?'

'And Julie?' asked Clarke. 'Were you aware of any special friendships? Boyfriends even?'

'Boyfriends?' Mrs Sidley snorted dismissively. 'Boys are not even allowed on the grounds. We have none of that sort of nonsense here.'

'All right then,' persisted Frost, unabashed, 'what about girlfriends? I think you know what I mean.'

'I most certainly do not!' The headmistress rose to her feet. 'Jenkins,' she shouted. Then more quietly but equally firmly, 'Detective, I think this appointment has come to an end.'

The old stooge appeared in the doorway.

'Jenkins, see these people out, please,' Mrs Sidley said sharply.

'I'm sure we can find our own way,' said Frost. 'Sue, how's your geography?'

'Got an A,' Clarke answered smugly.

Leaving the study, and the great hall, and making their way to the car, Frost and Clarke appeared to have hit the end of break-time. Girls were rushing everywhere. Frost didn't know where to look, bumping smack into a slight young Asian girl, nearly knocking her to the ground. 'Sorry,' he said. 'Didn't see you there.'

'Are you our new Head of Games?' she asked.

Tuesday (3)

DC Hanlon replaced the receiver and scanned his notes. This, he thought, should at least get him off the hook with Jack Frost – and Mullett, for that matter. Progress of sorts, but he could kick himself. Telling his mum that there was someone in the same hospital being tested for rabies, what was he thinking of?

He'd supposed that his mum, lying wired up on a hospital bed, wasn't taking much in. But of course she was – only to blab to the old biddy in the neighbouring bed. Next thing Hanlon knew, he was being chatted up by slimy Sandy Lane.

Hanlon greedily tucked into a second sausage roll; at least it was providing some comfort. Handy this business of Grace with a trolley, he thought, no need to trek all the way to the canteen.

'If you've got a dodgy belly you should go easy on those sausage rolls,' said Frost, entering the office. 'What with you and the ailing Old Bill on the front desk, the place is fast becoming an infirmary.'

'Jack, hello, I've got some good news . . . what do you mean, "go easy"?'

'Just been chatting to a man from Rentokil in the car park. Since they gutted the canteen, they've found the place is crawling with rats,' Frost said chirpily.

'Rats?'

'Yes, hundreds of the buggers.'

'Ah, but they'd have been there all along,' Hanlon said hopefully. 'Haven't had a problem yet, and I've eaten enough meals there over the years.'

'That was before we had rabies.'

'Right,' said Hanlon. 'Look, about the *Echo* story . . . I can explain, Jack.' Hanlon watched Frost move round to his mess of a desk and begin foraging in a drawer.

'Too late, the damage's done.' Frost retrieved an old Bic lighter, which he began shaking vigorously. 'Anyway, cheer me up. What's this good news, apart from the fact your mum's got perfect recall?'

'Forensics isolated an intriguing set of prints in the Hudsons' kitchen.'

'How do you mean?' Frost, still in his mac, which was suddenly looking very much the worse for wear, pushed a pile of paperwork aside and perched on the edge of his desk.

'They made a match.'

'A match? Arthur, I could forgive you anything.' Frost beamed, much to Hanlon's relief. 'Someone with form?'

'Could say that,' said Hanlon. 'They belong to one Lee Wright – with a string of convictions, most seriously armed robbery. He was released on parole three months ago. Just spoke to his probation officer in Bristol.'

'Let me guess: a no-show last week?'

'Spot on. And what's more, he's a Denton boy. Birth certificate says Denton General, 1948.'

'So he's come home to wreak havoc,' said Frost.

'Looks like it, but why? And where is he now exactly?'

'You were doing so well, Arthur. Thought you were going to tell me all that.' Frost shrugged, dug his hands into his pockets. 'I wonder if he's settling an old score?' He scratched his head. 'Or he's come to collect what's his?' He paused. 'Any contact address for him in Denton? Any living family?'

'That's where it begins to run a little dry,' said Hanlon apologetically. 'His last-known address was with his parents, off New Lexington Road.' Hanlon didn't even have to look Frost's way, before continuing, 'Yes, Jack, I've checked it with Records. The Wrights gave up the lease over ten years ago and moved out of town – around the time, I guess, when their son was banged up good and proper. Probably couldn't stand the embarrassment.'

'Children today,' muttered Frost, 'ungrateful sods. Never could see why Mary's so bloody keen.'

'Come on, Jack,' said Hanlon, 'that's not what you used to say.'

'Still,' said Frost, 'might be worth going round there to see if the current owners know anything about the Wrights.'

'Nearly a decade on, and in that part of town?' said Hanlon. 'Hey, where are you going now?'

'To see if I can trace Grace and the flipping trolley. Fancy one of those sausage rolls myself. Something tells me we're in for a busy afternoon.'

The second Frost left the office the detective sergeant's phone went. Hanlon reluctantly picked it up. 'Yes?'

'Can I speak to Detective Sergeant Frost urgently, please?' It was a man's voice, clear, authoritative.

'I'm afraid you've just missed him,' said Hanlon. 'Who's speaking?'

'It's Doctor Philips, from Denton General. Paediatrics.'

'Right,' said Hanlon. 'Can I help?'

'No, probably not,' said the doctor firmly. 'It's a very sensitive matter. I need Mr Frost. I've been trying to speak to him since yesterday evening.'

'If it's regarding little Becky Fraser and the rabies

tests, I'm working on that case with DS Frost,' Hanlon said eagerly.

'Whom am I talking to?'

'Detective Constable Arthur Hanlon. I brought her to the hospital with DS Frost on Sunday.'

'Are you the large chap?'

Hanlon looked at the half-eaten sausage roll in front of him. 'Yes, I suppose you could say that.'

'I suppose you'll do, then,' said Doctor Philips. 'OK, well, Becky Fraser has two cracked ribs, burn marks on her back, and one on the sole of her right foot, a fractured wrist and, of course, there's the bruising to her head.'

'I see,' said Hanlon, suddenly feeling rather sick. Frost had been spot on, while for a moment or two he himself had actually considered the fact that the girl might have been attacked by an animal, rabid or not. 'She couldn't possibly have been bitten by an animal, then?'

'Not as far as I can see.'

'So what happened to her?'

'That's not really for me to speculate on,' the doctor said. 'My job's to fix her injuries – which have been attended to. We've done all we can for the moment. She's ready to be released.'

'Some parents, unbelievable,' muttered Hanlon.

'Look, I was happy to do what I could when she came in, irregular as it might have been. But now that the public have been alerted to a situation involving a rabies scare – even if it was spurious to begin with – we are being besieged. And it's not just the press. Many people are clamouring for a rabies test, saying they've been bitten by this and that. We fear the situation could get completely out of hand.'

'Right,' said Hanlon.

'We really do have to release her,' reiterated Dr Philips. 'For the good of the community. We have to show that there's no real outbreak of rabies in Denton.'

'Could you please hang on to her until at least the end of the day,' pleaded Hanlon, then adding, 'For her own safety?'

He needed Police Sergeant Webster's latest leads on the possible whereabouts of Liz Fraser's ex-partner Simon Trench; Hanlon was almost certain that Frost hadn't got anywhere with this yet. No doubt Frost would be expecting him to pick up the pieces, but would have somehow forgotten to inform him of any such details. Hanlon sighed heavily, knowing he would find himself trailing in Frost's wake.

Then there were the relevant people at Social Services to contact – always a nightmare. Plus Liz Fraser would have to be formally interviewed.

All this, which was suddenly so much more urgent, on top of trying to track down Lee Wright, which had to be the priority now they had proof that he had been in the Hudsons' kitchen.

'I'll see what I can do,' said Dr Philips. 'But no promises.'

Hanlon rose from his desk but, not sure what to do first, promptly sat back down again and picked up the remains of the sausage roll.

'But just what were you doing slinking around boozers all afternoon with Jack Frost, anyway?' said PC Derek Simms.

The drizzle had dampened Simms's fair hair, making his large oval face all the more boyish, and innocent, Sue Clarke thought, knowing of course that he wasn't exactly innocent – childish, maybe.

She was leading the way along the narrow, over-grown path, being careful not to get her shoes too muddy, yet they were in a hurry. 'Derek, I can't believe you're still going on about this. Not after that row last night. And it wasn't all afternoon, anyway. Look, I really appreciate you coming down here with me in your lunch hour. But you didn't have to.'

'I don't understand,' said Simms, 'how you could even have a half with him. He's notorious, can't keep his hands off any bit of skirt. I've seen him. The way he leers at women, all those crude jokes.'

'Don't be ridiculous. He's not like that. He's married, anyway.'

'That hasn't stopped him in the past, or so I've heard. He's never ever at home, that's for sure,' Simms continued. 'I bet he tried to kiss you, didn't he?'

'For God's sake, Derek, it was work, OK? CID

stuff.' She knew that would wind him up. 'Jack's all right – just committed to the job, that's all.'

'Jack, is it now? Jesus Christ!' exclaimed Simms. 'I've had enough of this. You can make your own way back.' He turned to go, but hesitated.

'Look, forget about Frost for a minute, can you. He's a colleague, simple as that.'

'Like me,' said Simms, moodily. 'I'm just another colleague too, am I?'

'Let's not go down that road right now. Besides, it's not as if I'm the only one.'

'What the hell does that mean?'

'You know exactly what that means,' she said, then adding quietly, 'Mullett's secretary – *Miss* Smith.'

She trudged on, pleased to notice that Simms was following again. Out of guilt? Despite his stupid, childish jealousy, she was glad he was with her and in uniform. There was no one else about, and the semi-derelict warehouses, overgrown shrubs, stagnant black water and memory of the floating corpse were giving her the creeps, big time.

'What are we looking for, anyway?' asked Simms eventually.

'I don't know,' said Clarke, fully aware that she was bending procedure. She shouldn't have been here without informing someone in CID, and she certainly shouldn't have hoodwinked Simms into accompanying her.

They had reached the spot where Graham Ransome's body had been pulled on to the bank by frogmen. It was a muddy mess. Large puddles had formed in the path and the surrounding undergrowth had been well trampled over by Scenes of Crime. There was rubbish everywhere. Clarke flinched as the wet finally soaked through into her shoes. The bottoms of her trousers were speckled with mud.

'Hey, what about this?' said Simms.

Clarke looked up. He was by the very edge of the canal, his foot parting a clump of grass. Gingerly she stepped over to him. 'What? I can't see a thing.' Though it was only the middle of the day the light already seemed to be fading.

'There, that,' said Simms, prodding the grass with the toe of his right foot and revealing a piece of maroon-coloured material.

Clarke crouched down, reaching out.

'Don't touch it,' snapped Simms. 'Didn't they teach you anything?'

'I wasn't going to,' said Clarke. How dare he undermine me, she thought. 'I was just going to move the grass more out of the way.' She fished a biro from her jacket pocket and used that to part the grass further. 'Looks like a piece of a scarf.'

'Clever girl. Any idea what sort of scarf?'

'A woolly one?'

'Don't you know anything? Denton Town FC, away colours.'

'Of course I knew that,' she lied. 'What I meant was the material: it's wool, knitted.'

'Hasn't been there long.'

'What makes you think that?' Clarke stood up.

'That's obvious, isn't it?' said Simms. 'Looks like it's in good nick to me.'

Clarke crouched down again, noticing that the piece of scarf had a ragged edge. 'Well, yeah, does seem newish.'

'Has to be, anyway,' said Simms.

'Why?'

'Those away colours only came in two weeks ago, when the *Echo* started drumming up support for Denton's first FA Cup game. Seemed a bit optimistic to me, but the *Echo* paid for it.'

Clarke smiled at her on-off boyfriend. Maybe he was detective material after all. But could she ever really trust him to be faithful? Not that she wanted to make any big commitment – to anyone – at the moment.

She retrieved a plastic evidence bag from her jacket pocket and with her pen carefully gathered up the piece of material.

'Rats? Are you sure, Miss Smith?'

'Quite sure, Superintendent, that's what the man said. Oh look, there he is, by his little van. He's been back and forth all morning.'

Mullett peered through the blinds adjacent to his

secretary's desk. There was a direct view of the car park, perfect for keeping an eye on the station's comings and goings.

'*Hundreds*, he said,' she added, as she pulled out a Tupperware box containing her lunch.

'Hundreds – it would be,' Mullett sighed. 'Well at least he's dealing with it . . . Wait a moment, whose car is that?' He watched as a spanking-new silver Jaguar calmly pulled into the slot next to the Rentokil van. He didn't know why he'd bothered to ask Miss Smith whose car it might be. He knew exactly.

'Miss Smith, where's Bert Williams's file? I need to check a few details about his pension.'

Miss Smith, now biting into a stick of celery, didn't have time to answer before the phone rang. 'Superintendent Mullett's office,' she said, still crunching.

Mullett winced.

Holding the phone away from her ear, she said, 'It's Sergeant Wells, on Reception . . .'

'I know full well where he is,' said Mullett crossly.

'He says the assistant chief constable is here, and he's already on his way up to see you.'

'Fantastic.' Mullett grimaced. That was another person he wished would retire. Unlikely though, as the assistant chief constable was not much older than himself. Perhaps someone would snatch *him* from a department store. 'Well, dig out Bert Williams's file for me anyway, please.'

Without knocking, Nigel Winslow, the thin, bald, pointy-nosed and bespectacled assistant chief constable, strolled into Mullett's suite of offices. 'Stanley, sorry to drop in on you unannounced like this.'

'Not at all, Nigel. Pleasure to see you. Tea?' Mullett held the door open to his inner sanctum. He followed the assistant chief constable in.

'No, thanks,' Winslow said in his strong nasal voice. 'I say, do you have a rodent problem?'

'No, no, no. A preventative inspection, I believe,' Mullett said quickly. 'Part of the renovation programme.'

Winslow raised his eyebrows. 'Oh – that's odd. The Rentokil chap implied you had an infestation, in the canteen, of all places.'

'Really? News to me. What a nuisance.'

'Fortunately, I've had my lunch,' said Winslow. 'Very good restaurant out on the Wells Road. Anyway, there's something rather sensitive I wanted to talk to you about. Thought it best in person.'

'Please, take a seat, Nigel.' Mullett gestured to one of the fine, leather visitor's chairs, and watched the assistant chief constable eye the chair as if it were somehow contaminated, before finally settling on it.

'It's not regarding the crime clear-up statistics, I'm sure you'll be happy to know, or this damn rabies palaver,' Winslow huffed, 'but that raid on the building society in Rimmington a couple of weeks ago, the so-called *Star Wars* heist.'

'Oh yes?' said Mullett, fully aware of the material details: a gang of four, all armed, and all wearing Darth Vader masks. It had already been linked to another building society heist two months previously in the town of Wallop, where the raiders had disguised themselves in headgear that looked like it belonged on a medieval battlefield – the Wars of the Roses Robbery. How the press had loved that.

'Not easy to say this, Stanley, so I'll get straight to it. Through a number of local informers, and an undercover operation, it seems that someone in the force, and I'm afraid to say, Superintendent, from your division, must have been in on it.'

'What the hell do you mean, "in on it", Nigel?'

'That someone from your division has been helping this gang with their planning. You see, Stanley, in both raids the gang knew about the recently installed CCTV – aerosol paint on the camera lens – and the new security arrangements, which effectively were OK'd by us in the first place. What's more, they seem to have had prior knowledge of our response times. Frankly, they've been brazen.'

'I don't know how the hell you've come to that slanderous conclusion!' Mullett exploded. 'Any fool would know about the CCTV as soon as they stepped into the building society. As for the security arrangements – damned if I know – but I can assure you that there are no traitors working here!'

'Could you just remind me, Stanley, who *is* working

here, apart from the decorators, and the Rentokil people? Weren't you saying just yesterday at County that you're chronically understaffed, and were in fact missing two senior detectives?'

'Ah, well, that's right. DI Allen and DI Williams are on annual and sick leave respectively.'

'Annual leave? At a time like this? A rabies scare. A missing girl. And who knows what else you're having to deal with. Cancel it right away.'

'What do you take me for? Orders to that effect have already been issued.' Mullett reached over to his in-tray and riffled through some papers. He had no idea if he could get hold of DI Allen, on his blasted walking holiday, or not – but now he was going to have to bloody well try.

'Leaving you with just DS Frost in charge of CID, is that right?' enquired Winslow, pushing his wire-framed glasses further up his sharp, shiny nose.

Right then Mullett would have liked to shove them up his arse. 'Yes,' he coughed.

'Always thought rather highly of Frost.'

'Is that right, Nigel.' Mullett felt a migraine coming on.

'Bit of a maverick, that's for sure,' said Winslow. 'Though he and old Inspector Williams pulled in some results. Williams off sick, you say? When exactly does he retire?'

'He's laid low with the flu – apparently.' Mullett couldn't help coughing again. 'In fact I was just about

190

to sign off his retirement date and pension paperwork. It's one thing hiring someone, but the paperwork involved in retiring them is even more rigorous. Easier to sack them.' Mullett tried to laugh.

'What about uniform?'

'Sorry, I'm not with you.'

'Any strange behaviour? People behaving out of character? Anyone you don't trust implicitly?'

'For God's sake, Nigel,' Mullett said, exasperated, 'I run a very tight ship. Impenetrable. How many times do I have to tell you? There are no weak links here.'

'I hope you're right. The thing is,' said Winslow, 'that's not what my people are hearing, and with this armed gang on something of a roll, we need to put a stop to them before someone's killed. I surely don't need to remind you that in both robberies a couple of female tellers were brutally pistol-whipped. It's only a matter of time before we're dealing with murder as well.'

Mullett had the distinct impression he wasn't being told everything. He reached for a Senior Service, before offering the pack to the assistant chief constable, who refused.

'What I suggest, Stanley,' Winslow continued, 'is that you go through every member of staff's credentials and their working practices with a fine-tooth comb. Check, and check again. Personnel records, the works. You'll need to do it yourself, of course, can't let on what we're up to.'

How much time did Winslow think he had? His headache was getting worse by the minute. Mullett felt his forehead creasing under the strain.

Miss Smith pranced into the room, with news that the tea trolley was on its way, and did anyone want anything.

'No,' said Winslow sharply.

Mullett tiredly echoed him, his mind wandering briefly to Simms in his office suite last night, and that guff about waiting for Miss Smith. 'I'll do as you say,' said Mullett to his esteemed visitor, once his secretary was out of earshot. 'But don't get your expectations up.'

'Good man,' said the assistant chief constable, rising from his chair and adjusting his heavily embossed cap. 'Tell me' – he paused by the door – 'what's the latest with this rabies business? You should know for sure today, shouldn't you? People are starting to get rattled. I've had enquiries from both Fowler and Heseltine's offices.'

'Yes, that's right,' said Mullett, realizing both that he hadn't heard a thing about it from Frost, or anyone else in CID, for hours, and that Winslow, like himself initially, was addressing the scare with much more seriousness than it obviously warranted. If Winslow found out it was a ploy by Frost to circumvent the system he would undoubtedly bring Mullett's judgement into question. Mullett couldn't believe he'd let it slide. 'Fingers crossed.' He smiled lamely.

'I hope you have your contingency plans as well defined as your renovation job,' the assistant chief constable said smugly.

With his head splitting, Mullett watched Nigel Winslow amble out of his office. What more could possibly go wrong now? He pressed the button on his intercom. 'Miss Smith, could you come back in here right away,' he spat. 'I'd like a word.'

Tuesday (4)_____

Frost was waiting for Clarke as she finally walked out of the Ladies, tucked away at the back of the station. 'It's not that bad in there, is it?' he said. She looked as if she'd been crying.

Colour instantly rose to her cheeks. 'New make-up. I think I'm allergic to it. What are you doing loitering around the women's toilets, anyway?'

'Waiting for you. Can't find a woman, chances are she'll be in the bog. Come on, we're off to the hospital again. Wendy Hudson's perked up and there's a consultant I need to see.'

'You need more than a consultant, Jack Frost.'

'Less of that, love.' He led the way, lighting up as they went. 'I hear the assistant chief constable's been in,' he said. 'Something's going on.'

'Mullett for the high-jump?' Clarke said.

'If only. Can't see what that sod's done wrong, apart from breathe.' Frost took a deep drag. 'I'd watch your back, that's all.' He exhaled though gritted teeth. 'Don't go chatting up the wrong blokes, if you know what I mean.'

'No,' huffed Sue Clarke. 'Don't know what the hell you mean.' She'd flushed again.

Frost noticed she had mud all over her shoes and the bottoms of her trousers. 'Been rolling in the hay again?' he said. Clarke ignored him so he continued, 'Sometimes it's your closest friends who turn out to be your worst enemies.' They were now walking across the lobby where Station Sergeant Bill Wells was on the telephone.

They pushed through the double doors to the car park just as a panda car sped through the gates, siren blaring. 'Still, don't think they'd be able to catch you, not with your driving,' said Frost, as Clarke unlocked the Escort.

'Actually, Jack,' she said, getting comfortable behind the wheel, 'I've got something to tell you. A bit of luck.'

'You're getting married?'

'Don't be ridiculous.'

'Oh, well, that's a relief. I'm still in with a chance, then.'

'I thought you were married?' She swiftly reversed

the car out of the tight parking slot, rammed the gear stick into first and accelerated forward.

Frost found himself, once again, clutching the sides of his seat. 'On paper.' He began humming, before suddenly stopping, remembering that it was his wedding anniversary on Friday. What a stretch already.

He looked over at Clarke, taking in her young fresh face. Fortunately she appeared to be concentrating on the road ahead. 'So what did you have to tell me, then?' he said.

'I went back to the canal – where the blind man, Graham Ransome, was found.'

'When?'

'Earlier today.'

'DC Clarke, you should have informed either Arthur or myself first. Attractive young woman like you – the canal is not the safest place to be on your own, in plainclothes. Look what happened to poor old Graham.'

'Who said I was on my own?'

Frost laughed. 'Don't tell me, while you were *in flagrante delicto* – as they say in Spain, or is it Italy? – you came upon a piece of evidence, which should have been spotted the day before.'

'Forget the *in flagrante* stuff, but yes, I did find something. It's already with Forensics.'

'Don't spare me the sordid details, then,' said Frost. 'Reveal all.'

* * *

Bill Wells had tried calling after DS Frost, but Frost seemed preoccupied with DC Clarke as they'd sauntered through the lobby on their way out of the building.

Control had dispatched an area car to the scene now, anyway. A fatality, RTA probably, down a farm track some eight miles from Denton, wasn't really a matter for CID.

Though the fact that the body was found in a Cortina was making Wells feel decidedly uneasy.

'Hello, Mrs Hudson,' said Frost gently. 'Been in the wars, have we?'

Propped up in bed, the woman's face was mostly obscured by bandages, bruising and tubes, though she did manage to nod a grim affirmative.

'I'm DS Jack Frost, from Denton CID, and this is my colleague DC Sue Clarke, who you've met before.'

Clarke smiled at the woman.

'We'd obviously like to ask you a few questions,' continued Frost, 'if you are feeling up to it.' Or not, he might well have added.

The woman nodded. She still hadn't opened her mouth, and Frost was suddenly beginning to think she couldn't, with a broken jaw among her injuries – the duty nurse hadn't volunteered any such information, nor, he realized, had the consultant. It was a wonder anything got done in this hospital at all.

Frost looked at his watch; Julie Hudson had

been missing for almost exactly seventy-two hours.

'I hope they're looking after you OK,' said Clarke. 'Got everything you need?'

Really, thought Frost, there was a time and a place for such inanities and this wasn't it. He'd brought Clarke along because he knew the questioning would get personal and Wendy Hudson might be more willing to open up to a woman – plus Clarke had interviewed her originally.

As it was, Wendy Hudson wasn't opening up to anyone.

'Mrs Hudson,' said Frost, moving closer to the woman's bed, 'Mr Hudson, that is, your husband, Steve, is now missing, as well as your daughter. You're in here, beaten black and blue. So what's been going on?'

Wendy Hudson stared straight ahead and slowly shook her head from side to side. She appeared to try to lift her right hand, but could barely raise her fingers from the blanket.

'Perhaps she's not able to talk,' said Clarke, who was now on the other side of the bed with all the various drips and attachments, and reaching for the woman's left hand, which she lightly took hold of.

'You won't get any useful information from feeling her pulse,' muttered Frost, turning away. 'She is alive.' The tatty Venetian blinds were askew, those that were still in place, that is, revealing a view of the rain-swept car park, three floors below. A van with a very large aerial protruding from the roof sat in a far corner. Squinting, Frost could make out the letters *BBC* on the side.

'Was it Steve,' Clarke was saying, 'who did this to you?'

Frost looked back and noticed the woman twitch. Was that a yes or a no? 'Seems like you've got the magic touch, Sue,' he said. 'Ask her again.'

Clarke repeated the question and the response was much the same. 'What the hell does that mean?' said Frost.

'I think it means: maybe,' said Clarke, smiling kindly at the woman.

'We're not going to get much of a statement, are we?' sighed Frost. He lit a cigarette, only to spot a large no-smoking sign as he exhaled, advertising prosecution for offenders. He took another deep drag and carefully stubbed the cigarette out on the sole of his shoe, putting it back in the packet.

'Is your husband with Julie?' he asked, bending back towards the desperately sick woman. 'Has he got her somewhere? Has he done something to her?' Frost coughed.

Wendy Hudson suddenly began shaking her head. Again and again. Frost found just watching the poor woman exhausting enough.

'I think that's definitely a no,' said Clarke.

'Can she write?' Frost asked. 'Hand her your notepad and pen, love.'

Clarke promptly did as she was told, shifting round the bed and trying to rearrange Wendy Hudson's fingers so she could clasp the pen on her own.

She held on to the pen, all right, Frost could see, but didn't appear to have the dexterity or the energy to write anything legible. 'We're not getting very far,' he said, as much to himself as to anyone.

Clarke said again, 'Has Steve got Julie? Has he done something to her?'

There was a distinct shaking of the head.

'But he beat you up. Is that right?' pressed Clarke.

The response this time was different. Both a nod and a shake. Meaning, Frost suddenly decided, that Steve Hudson had attacked her, but Wendy Hudson felt somehow to blame. He could see pretty much exactly where this was heading, thinking again of his earlier suspicion, voiced to Hanlon, about Lee Wright coming back to Denton to claim what was his.

Taking a deep breath, Frost said, 'He beat you up because he suddenly found out, after – what is it? – thirteen years that Julie was not his kid. That right? Julie's real father being one Lee Wright – nice fellow – who just so happens to have been released from prison a few weeks ago and who paid you a visit, I'm guessing, just the other day. Popped round for a cup of tea, did he?'

Frost glanced over at Clarke, who looked startled. He continued, hearing Wendy Hudson begin to sob surprisingly loudly, 'Sorry to be blunt, Mrs Hudson, but we urgently need to get to the bottom of this. Julie needs to be safely accounted for, and as far as I'm concerned, it doesn't matter whose father Steve Hudson is, or isn't. Anyone responsible for beating up a woman with such brutality needs to be behind bars.'

Wendy Hudson was shaking her head one moment and nodding the next, giving Frost the impression that she disagreed.

'You can't blame yourself for everything,' said Clarke.

Frost was pleased that the DC seemed to have picked up the same idea. Wendy Hudson was sobbing harder.

'It'll be all right,' said Clarke, holding her hand again, 'once you're better and feeling stronger.'

'And Julie?' Frost coughed again. His mind was a little less clear, less made up on this point. 'Is she with Lee Wright, her natural father?'

That nodding and shaking again, which Frost took to mean she didn't know. He looked at Clarke again.

'No?' Clarke prompted.

Wendy Hudson seemed to nod more affirmatively this time.

Yes, thought Frost. 'Lee Wright's got her, hasn't he,' he said triumphantly. He still had no idea whether Wendy Hudson had known this all along. Perhaps she had made up the story about her daughter disappearing from Aster's for Steve Hudson's benefit. Or maybe she didn't know for sure, but just hoped Lee Wright had her, and was keeping her safe.

Either way, Frost couldn't imagine that an armed robber, recently released from a very long stretch inside, would make much of a father. 'I need the phone,' he said.

'Yes,' said Hanlon crossly, picking up the phone and half expecting it to be the hospital again, saying that Becky Fraser had in fact been discharged.

'Hanlon!' barked Mullett, clearly in a rage. 'Where's Frost?'

'Sorry, sir, no idea.'

'No idea?' Mullett shouted. 'He's in charge of bloody CID at the moment, I need him *now*. There's been an accident.'

'An accident? What—' started Hanlon.

'Yes – a fatality. I want Frost,' repeated Mullett, 'urgently.'

Hanlon pushed aside the Fraser paperwork.

'It's one of ours,' the super continued, a little more quietly this time. 'Dead behind the wheel.'

Thinking there was no time like the present, Frost made for the payphone behind the tatty newsagent's and gift shop in the lobby of the hospital's main entrance.

While he dialled the station, Clarke wandered over to look at the magazines.

He was put straight through to Hanlon. 'He's got the girl,' Frost said immediately, 'as I suspected. Came back for what he thought was rightfully his. What was that last address you have for Lee Wright in Denton? He's somewhere close, I can feel it in my bones.'

'Jack,' said Hanlon. 'Wait a minute, wait a minute. Where the hell are you? Everyone's looking for you. Mullett's frantic.'

'I'm at the hospital; Wendy Hudson's been nodding out some answers.'

'Well, brace yourself. I have some bad news.'

'A body's been found? Not the girl? Oh shit. Armed robber or not, he was her bloody father.'

'No, Jack.'

Frost could barely hear Hanlon. The line was terrible. 'Speak up, Arthur,' he said.

'It's Bert,' said Hanlon.

Frost felt something give in his chest and his head immediately began to spin. 'What do you mean, it's Bert?'

'He's dead, Jack.'

Frost momentarily held the phone away from his head, looked out through the lobby doors, at the heavy grey sky on the near horizon. With his left hand he reached for his cigarettes. 'Where, how?' he asked calmly.

'It was an accident, Jack. Rimmington way, a lane in the middle of nowhere.'

'What the hell was Bert doing out there?'

'That's all I know, Jack. Look, I'm really sorry. I know what he meant to you, especially.'

Frost thought of Betty, their two grown-up children. 'Does Betty know?'

'No,' said Hanlon. 'A farmer called it in an hour or so ago. Charlie Alpha is at the scene. Mullett's on his way.'

'What about Scenes of Crime? Maltby?'

'It was an accident, Jack.'

'No, it bloody wasn't!' shouted Frost. 'What's the exact location, I'm on my way.'

'Jack, hold on a minute. Dr Philips, the paediatric consultant, rang some time ago. About Becky Fraser. You should at least have a word with him before leaving the hospital – he wants to release her. Says the rabies business is getting out of hand.'

'Rabies?' Frost was for an instant confused, the thought of Williams dead had wiped everything else from his mind.

'And that she has some burn marks on her body, on top of quite a catalogue of other injuries,' said Hanlon hurriedly. 'It's abuse, all right. But we haven't got any further with tracking down the father, Simon Trench . . .' Hanlon paused, took a breath. 'And that's if it was him, and not the mother. We need to bring Liz Fraser in for formal questioning and let Social Services—'

'Arthur, haven't I already asked you to deal with this?' said Frost, cutting him off. 'Look, just give me the location. Where is Bert?'

Frost hung up and ran across to Clarke, who was flicking through a magazine by the newsstand. 'I need the car – the keys – won't be long,' he said breathlessly, holding out his hand. Clarke passed them over, not bothering to question his motives.

'Small task for you, while you're here,' he called over his shoulder, barging through a group of pregnant young women. 'Tell that Dr Philips up in Paediatrics not to discharge the rabies child on any account, and don't let the mother out of your sight. Hanlon will fill you in.'

Reaching the exit, Frost was accosted by a man who shoved a microphone in his face. Frost sent the microphone flying, and sprinted across the car park towards the Escort.

Tuesday (5)

Mullett climbed out of his Rover, checked his cap was straight and marched towards the cluster of officers. There were two panda cars and an ambulance on the scene. A tractor sat further up the wet lane. It was quickly getting dark, raining off and on. The superintendent shivered.

'All right, Simms,' he said, approaching, 'anything been touched? Moved?'

'No, sir,' said PC Simms eagerly, holding a reel of police tape. 'Well, not exactly. When we arrived and spotted the body, I did check for a pulse, though it was pretty obvious that he'd been dead for some time. I recognized him straight away, sir,' he added.

'Anything immediately suspicious?' Mullett asked,

scrutinizing the young PC. Could Simms be bent, leaking information? Seemed ludicrous. 'Anything to suggest it wasn't an accident?' Mullett knew he had to go through the motions, at least show the right level of concern and gravitas, given they were dealing with a dead detective. It was by far and away his worst day as superintendent of the damned Denton Division.

'No, not that I can see,' said Simms.

Mullett walked over to the car, which was half in a ditch to the side of the lane; the front end was badly dented. Mullett moved round the vehicle, catching his first sight of Williams's body slumped awkwardly against the opened driver's door, his right arm and leg hanging out of the car. *Christ*, Mullett thought, it must have been quite a prang. Williams's chest seemed to have taken the brunt of the impact, probably against the steering wheel.

'What a lonely place to die,' said Mullett to no one in particular, wondering whether the door had opened on impact, or whether Williams, having initially survived the accident, opened the door, but was then unable to climb all the way out.

Looking up he saw a fire engine making its way down the lane. Some distance behind the fire engine, but catching up fast, was an Escort, one of the station's, with a flashing light slapped on the top.

'The ambulance men want to know whether they can remove the body, sir,' said Simms, 'what with it getting dark.'

Mullett looked at the corpse again, and at the car, how it was positioned, or rather how it had ended up. He walked round once more and peered at the opened driver's door, noticing that the radio handset was dangling out of its holder. The impact could easily have dislodged it, though Mullett wondered again whether Williams might have survived the accident, might have tried to reach for help. But what the hell was he doing down this dirty little lane? 'Tell them they'll have to wait,' he said to Simms.

'Yes, sir.'

'Where does this lane go?' Mullett's geography of Denton and its surroundings was not all that it should have been.

'Back road to Rimmington, sir, not used much now.'

'Right.' Mullett paused. 'Get on to Control. We'll need arc lights, a tent. I want Scenes of Crime here and Doctor Maltby.'

'Yes, sir,' said Simms again, this time sounding confused.

'Accident or not, we owe it to Williams's family to get to the bottom of what happened here,' Mullett stated. If such an investigation showed, as Mullett expected it to, that Williams was drunk behind the wheel, and veered fatally off the track, then so be it. The division was heading in a new direction. There was going to be transparency all the way up to the top.

Hearing a screech of breaks, Mullett looked over to

see the Escort skid to a stop behind the fire engine. 'Jesus Christ,' he muttered to himself as DS Frost hurriedly clambered out, wrapping his mac around him.

Without acknowledging his superior Frost headed straight for Williams's Cortina.

Mullett kept his distance as Frost walked slowly around the car, peered through the windows and the opened door, and then crouched down by Bert Williams's body. From where he was Mullett couldn't see exactly what Frost was doing, but shortly puffs of cigarette smoke, caught in a spotlight now being angled from the fire engine, began drifting up into the freezing, damp early evening air.

Frost's actions seemed to affect the other officers present, along with the ambulance and fire crews. Suddenly there was quiet and stillness and Mullett found himself solemnly removing his cap.

'Bastards!' Frost shouted, breaking the peace and emerging from his crouched position by the far side of the car, fag in the corner of his mouth, the glint of tears on his cheeks. 'I'll get the bastards who did this.'

'Hang on a minute, Jack,' Mullett said, walking towards his detective sergeant. 'I understand you're upset. We're all upset. This is a tragic accident. Bert was . . .' Mullett couldn't think what to say next. 'He was unique, in his way. One of our own. One of the family.' Mullett coughed.

Frost wiped his face on the sleeve of his mac. 'I

don't care what you thought of him,' said Frost, 'but this was no accident. Where are Scenes of Crime, Doc Maltby? Why aren't uniform on their hands and knees, combing the area? Call themselves coppers? And what's that ambulance doing there, bang behind the Cortina, destroying any tracks? And your Rover, sir, right in the sodding way too.' Frost fumbled for another cigarette.

'Jack, there's no need for hysteria. All the proper measures are being taken. That's why I'm here, to see to it all.'

'Where are Scenes of Crime?' Frost repeated.

'Jack, calm down.' Mullett was aware of uniform observing the altercation and the raised voices. 'I promise you, this accident – this incident – will be investigated properly. I'll personally be in charge, until DI Allen's back.' Despite what he had implied to Winslow earlier in the day, Mullett now realized he really had no option but to try to haul Allen back from his holiday. All leave would have to be cancelled.

'You'll get to play your part,' Mullett said, 'don't worry. And for your information, Scenes of Crime and Maltby are on their way.'

'Right,' said Frost.

'Believe me,' Mullett continued, 'we'll get to the bottom of this.'

'One thing, Super,' said Frost, 'I want to tell Betty.'

Mullett was only too keen to acquiesce. 'Of course, Frost.'

'Oh and another thing,' Frost walked back over to the damaged Cortina, which, slick with rainwater, was glinting surreally under the spotlights. 'I want a news blackout.'

'A news blackout?'

Frost turned to face Mullett, his eyes filled with anguish. 'Yes, a blackout. I don't want whoever did this to know we're on to them yet.' Frost placed both hands on the damaged wing, head bowed, as if physical contact would reveal the cause of the tragedy.

Mullett paused for thought – he would have to be careful how he played this. 'On to them? Yes, quite.' He looked at his watch. 'But Jack, let's not get carried away with this. Wait and see what the autopsy throws up. What Forensics find. Besides, you know what the press are like: they'll say what they want anyway. Too many people know about this already.' He looked across at the fire crew, the ambulance men. 'Try keeping that lot quiet.'

'No mention or public statements from us about suspicious circumstances, then,' Frost carried on. 'This could be crucial.'

'Fine chance gagging that lot from the *Echo*,' said Mullett. 'Just how the hell do you propose we do that?'

'By giving them the real story about the Hudson girl.' Frost turned and began trudging down the dark track towards the Escort.

'And what's that, Jack?' Mullett called after him.

'Twelve-year-old kidnapped by convicted armed

robber, out on parole. That'll get them excited. Doesn't make the probation service look very competent, either.'

'What? What are you talking about, Frost? Come back here. Come back here at once. That's an order!'

Hanlon knocked again on the tatty front door. On the hunt for Lee Wright, he was chasing up the only address they had, which was over a decade out of date.

He was about to give up when the door opened to reveal a thin, bespectacled middle-aged man wearing a stained white shirt and a scruffy pair of old suit trousers. He was barefoot. 'Yes,' he said politely, scratching his wild hair, 'can I help you?'

'Denton CID, sorry to disturb you, sir.'

Looking bemused, but not remotely concerned, the man yawned and scratched his head again. 'Yes?'

'Would you mind if I asked you a few questions?'

'Fire away,' the man said. He had a clear, well-educated accent. Again something Hanlon hadn't been expecting, not in this part of town, not with the man looking so unkempt.

'How long have you lived here, sir?'

'Now there's a very good question,' the man said. 'You see, I first moved in, gosh, must be around ten years ago, but I've been away since, on secondment, in the United States twice, and once to Japan, and once to the Soviet Union. All for periods of no less than six months, but no more than three years. So you see, I haven't actually lived here for anything like ten years.'

'I see,' said Hanlon. He'd needed to get out of the station, to clear his mind, to let his emotions about Bert Williams steady, and thought he might as well check out the only address he had for Lee Wright, second-guessing Frost's orders. Now he was stuck talking to some bloody boffin, who obviously had plenty of time on his hands. 'But you are the tenant?'

'I do believe I'm now the owner. I'm rather embarrassed to admit that I've taken advantage of Denton Council's Right-to-Buy scheme.'

'Can I ask the nature of your business?' Hanlon continued, unsure why he hadn't just got to the point. Curiosity? Delaying tactics, so he didn't have to rush back to the station, which would be in a state of shock?

'Business is not quite the right word. Theoretician would be more accurate. I'm an academic, for the Open University.'

'Right,' said Hanlon. So he was a proper boffin.

'Do you want to come in?' the man said.

'No need, unless you're harbouring a man called Lee Wright.'

'It's only me here, I'm afraid, and the cats. Lee Wright, you said? Funny you should mention that name.'

'Oh yes?'

'A couple of people were here only yesterday evening, looking for a Mr Wright. A rather rough-looking chap, big, shaven head, lots of gold rings on his fingers – I'm sure you know the type. And a short, wiry, Irish fellow. There was someone else with them too . . . I think.'

'You think?' said Hanlon.

'Well, there was a car parked close by, and its engine was running. You wouldn't leave a car parked with the engine running, would you? So I assumed there was someone else, a driver—'

'What sort of car was it?'

'That I couldn't tell you – cars aren't my thing, I'm afraid,' the man said.

'I'm sure not,' Hanlon said sarcastically; the fellow was getting on his nerves. 'Colour, perhaps?'

'Black, I think, or was it dark blue? Yes, could have been dark blue. It was quite a big, smart-looking car.'

'That's something, I suppose,' Hanlon said. 'What exactly did you tell these gentlemen?'

'I have an aversion to intimidation, of any sort. I said I'd never heard of a Mr Wright. I could tell it was only going to lead to trouble.' He smiled, weakly.

Hanlon glanced behind the man to see that the dimly lit hallway was lined on either side with stacks of books and papers. Higher up, garish paintings and posters hung on the walls.

'They quickly went on their way,' the boffin continued. He laughed. 'Perhaps I scared them off.'

'So you've never heard of Lee Wright?'

'Oh yes, I lied to them,' the man said, scratching his head again. 'Of course I've heard of Lee Wright. He used to live here with his mother, until he was locked up for armed robbery. I moved in pretty much straight after the Wrights left. Or rather Lee's mother left. She wasn't called Wright any more then, but Joan Dixon – been married a few times. One of the neighbours told me about her. I have a very good memory for names.' He smiled. 'I don't think she had the stomach for the scandal, which was why, I presume, this place became available.'

Hanlon was suddenly excited. 'I don't suppose you have a forwarding address, for the mother, for this Joan Dixon?'

'Oddly enough, I do, or did. I never throw anything away. I had a quick look last night, after those thugs paid me a call. Didn't find it, but that doesn't mean I won't. It's in the kitchen somewhere. There's just quite a lot of paperwork to wade through . . .'

Hanlon looked at his watch. At least he had a new name. He handed the man a card. 'If you find it, please ring this number immediately. A girl's life could be in danger.'

Tuesday (6)_____

'What's that doing there?' said DC Sue Clarke, walk-ing into the lobby. 'Oh, oh no. Not Bert?'

Wells looked around from behind a small vase of flowers, and a faded photograph of Bert Williams propped up against it. He'd swiped the flowers from Miss Smith's desk – she was always receiving flowers – and removed the photo from the awards notice board. It was Wells's small tribute; a bit hasty, he knew, but stuck on the front desk he felt desperately out of the action. He nodded sombrely at the detective constable as she came forward.

'When?' she said.

'I'm not sure, exactly,' said Wells. 'They found his body this afternoon. There'd been a car accident, out towards Rimmington. A farmer rang it in. Charlie Alpha was dispatched. Weird thing was, I immediately had a feeling it was Bert.'

'Anyone else involved?'

'No, he seems to have gone into a ditch.'

Clarke looked at him questioningly. 'A ditch?'

'Apparently. Look, all I know for certain is that the inspector is dead. Longest-serving member of this division,' Wells said. 'According to your friend Simms, Mullett's gone into overdrive. Wants to know exactly how it happened – for the family's sake. Word is, though, if it proves to be either a mechanical failure, or if Bert was responsible in some way, then the Force won't have to cough up the life assurance.'

'Typical. So that's what you get for all those years of service,' said Clarke. 'Makes you think about just who's watching your back.'

'Or stabbing you in it.'

'What if it wasn't an accident? If he was, you know, cut down in the line of duty?'

'Blimey,' said Wells, wiping his brow. 'But don't see how that's possible. Cost the division a packet if it was, though.' He found himself smiling grimly.

'What was he doing out there, I wonder.' She shook her head, retrieved a muddy handkerchief from her bag and blew her nose hard. 'I can't believe it. The poor bugger, and he was about to retire, too. He's got a wife, hasn't he, and a couple of grown-up kids. Grandchildren?'

Wells watched as Clarke gently touched the photograph. With Bert gone, the place would never be the same. He'd not been in it for himself, but for the good of the division, the good of the people of Denton. And he'd never forgot to have a laugh. They didn't make them like Williams any more.

'Are you going to answer that?' said Clarke.

Wells hadn't realized the phone was ringing. 'Good evening, Denton Police,' he said hoarsely.

'Nobody's safe,' said the voice on the other end.

'Sorry, can you speak up. Can't hear you very well,' Wells shouted.

'While the British occupy our land.' It was a man, sounded Irish.

'What?' said Wells. 'This is Denton Police.'

'You're running out of time.' There was a click.

'Who was that?' said Clarke. She was still by the front desk. 'A crank? It's about that time in the evening.'

Wells sighed heavily. 'I hope so – God, what a day.' He'd log the call. Go through the motions. Try yet again to get someone to pay attention. It was well beyond a joke: three calls now, all coming from men with Irish accents. But not, he thought, from the same man. He'd tried to talk to Mullett about it twice, of course, but the super had waved him away. He'd have to badger Frost, but Frost was going to be in no mood to deal with dodgy calls, whoever they were from.

'Sue,' he said, just catching her before she disappeared into the building proper, 'you, CID, haven't heard anything about any IRA activity in the county, or in Denton?'

'No,' she said, surprised. 'Should we have?' Wells watched Clarke step back into the lobby, interested. 'That call? I wouldn't be too worried. The whole country is twitchy. Besides, why on earth would the IRA want to target Denton?'

'Because it's got a large Territorial Army base?' announced Hanlon, taking both Wells and Clarke by surprise. He'd appeared from nowhere and was waddling across the lobby, soaking wet. 'Because it's been designated a new town and has been earmarked for twenty million quid of government money?' he continued, shaking the rain from his hat. 'Because we're about to get an Intercity train link to London. Whole load of reasons.' He stopped abruptly by the counter and gazed at the flowers, the picture.

'We're in the middle of a recession,' Clarke said scornfully. 'Denton's not going anywhere.'

'Except down a league or two,' said Wells.

'What was that?' Clarke said.

'Bloody Denton Town FC – got ideas above their station because they've got a new striker,' said Wells, aware the conversation was drifting, that they were avoiding the subject on all their minds, the dead inspector.

'Oh yes,' said Clarke, 'and they were given a new away strip for their efforts. Even I know about that.'

'They'll never get anywhere in the Cup.' Wells

stood back from the counter as Hanlon closed in on Williams's instant, makeshift memorial. The portly detective bowed his head.

'At least there's no rabies in Denton,' Clarke said.

'That's a relief,' Wells sighed.

Hanlon turned back to face the room and Clarke, and said, 'But we've got a problem with child cruelty, though, haven't we?'

'Afraid so,' said Clarke.

'Just back from the General?' said Hanlon.

'Yeah,' she replied. 'Jack and I were there to see Wendy Hudson. Before he dashed off, Jack said I should find Dr Philips.'

'That was good of you. They're still hanging on to Becky Fraser?'

'Yes, but it took some effort,' said Clarke. 'Dr Philips is swamped with people thinking their children have rabies. Nevertheless, they'll keep her in until tomorrow.'

'I don't know how you did it, but well done, Sue,' said Hanlon, 'that'll really help.' He looked over to Wells, and said, 'You can pull that poster down now, if you want, Bill. Alert over.'

'Am I right in thinking you never thought this little girl could possibly have caught rabies?' Wells said to Hanlon.

'Could be,' said Hanlon.

'Bloody hell! And I thought I was for the high-jump, for not having stuck up that alert from County earlier.

But the mother who rang in said her daughter was attacked by a fox – what was it, then?'

'Turns out she was attacked,' said Clarke, 'but by a human. Dr Philips found numerous bruises, and burns on the soles of her feet, on her back – poor little thing – that could only have been inflicted by another person, on purpose. She had a couple of cracked ribs as well.'

'What did Miss Fraser have to say for herself?' asked Hanlon. 'We need a formal statement from her, get some charges put on the table.'

'I agree. But I didn't want to push her there,' said Clarke. 'Once Social Services are on hand, let's bring her in. I reckon, though, her partner, this Simon Trench, was the violent one. She seems scared stiff of him, and more than happy to stay at the hospital with her daughter for another night. That's not to say, though, that she didn't know it was happening. I wonder if the story about the fox was another cry for help.'

'Jesus,' said Wells. 'And I thought Forest View was a nice place to live.'

'Grown women get bullied and abused, too – wherever they live,' said Clarke.

'What do you reckon,' asked Hanlon, 'neglect? Aiding and abetting?'

'First off, we need to let the public know that there's no rabies,' countered Clarke. 'That's the least we can do for Dr Philips. As I said, he took some persuading.'

Wells looked at Clarke. She seemed to get what she wanted readily enough.

'Be good to pick up Simon Trench, then, before they're out of the hospital,' said Hanlon. 'More work. And have we got to worry about the IRA as well?'

Wells watched Clarke follow Hanlon into the warren, and wondered whether he'd have to spend the rest of his career stuck on the flaming front desk. But looking at Bert's picture he knew there were worse things. He tapped the photo, muttering, 'Rest in peace, mate.'

Frost stopped the car just before the phone box. The freezing rain was now lashing down. He switched on the interior light and pulled Bert Williams's bloodied notepad from his pocket. He couldn't believe no one else had removed it first.

Williams's writing was illegible at the best of times. But as Frost flicked through the pages some of the names were clear, and some of the numbers. He had no idea whether the notes referred to one case, one investigation, or many – but somewhere was the information he needed. He also knew that, if he could call in a favour at British Telecom, it should be possible to check the numbers in the notepad against the numbers dialled to and from the public phone Bert kept disappearing to. He needed to see what correlated.

He slowly climbed out of the car and headed towards the small terraced house, clasping his mac around him and dipping his head against the rain. He could see a light was on in the front room, though the curtains were tightly closed. Betty would be frantic but still hopeful. He was going to shatter everything.

Frost knocked gently on the glass of the front door.

She was on the other side almost instantly, fumbling with the locks. 'Jack.' Betty pulled open the door, her voice shrill with anticipation.

Frost looked at her and he didn't have to say anything more. He stepped inside and took hold of Betty, who was already shaking, and pulled her into him, wrapping his arms around her fragile body. She seemed so small, so slight, so old. Her life suddenly devastated.

Eventually, Frost said, 'He was cut down, Betty, doing the job he loved – you have to believe me. They'll try to make out it was an accident, but it wasn't.' He sniffed, sucked in air. 'He was the best flaming copper that Denton's ever seen. He was a good man, Betty.'

Frost knew he was rambling. 'Those calls he'd been making from the phone box' – he paused, breathed in the cold, sodden night air that had followed him into the hallway – 'the fact he'd not been himself recently – he was on to something, I know it. Something big. Don't listen to whatever anyone else from the station might tell you. Give me a little bit of time. I'll find the bastards who did this, I promise you that, Betty. I promise you that.'

Tuesday (7)_____

'Mother of God,' muttered Desmond Thorley, turning over on his hard, damp, narrow bench. The foxes, or were they badgers, were at it again. Would he ever get a good night's sleep?

Struggling to get comfortable, he suddenly flung the threadbare covers to the floor, angrily swung his thin frame round and got up. He didn't think he could have been asleep for more than an hour or two.

He stumbled across the carriage, to the grimy window. Rubbing the condensation away he peered out. Couldn't see a thing. But he was damned if he was going to venture outside in this freezing cold. What he needed was an air-rifle, he decided, so he could shoot the buggers. Wouldn't want to kill them, just give them a nasty sting.

Just as he was about to crawl back to his hard bed, he saw a figure, over by the rhododendrons. He gasped. Then he saw another one. They were both dressed in bulky dark clothing. They appeared to be carrying something heavy. A bag?

Slowly, quiet as a mouse, he crept back across his carriage, climbed on to his bench, pulled the covers on top of him, and shut his eyes tight.

Jack Frost rubbed his eyes then looked at his watch. The time, eleven forty, slowly came into focus. Hanlon had only just left, and at last Frost was alone, in Bert's office. He was sitting at his late friend's desk, lit only by a knackered Anglepoise.

Behind the Rolodex he spotted the top of a picture frame. He reached over, spilling the full ashtray as he did so, and picked up the photograph, which he didn't think he'd ever noticed before. It was a black-and-white shot of Bert and Betty, on their silver wedding anniversary. Not a very good picture – Frost had taken it himself, with Mary's Instamatic. When was it: '71, '72? Christ, how Bert had aged over the last ten years. They all had.

Frost stifled another yawn, carefully placing the picture in front of the Rolodex and doubting whether he and Mary would make their silver. Nothing and everything had changed.

He scooped the spilt ash and cigarette butts into his cupped hands and tipped the mess back into the ashtray. Leaning closer and blowing the rest of the ash away, he made out that the dark-blue card underneath was not blotting paper but the tatty cover of a fat Scotland Yard personnel-department file.

'Ah, Jack, I thought it might be you in here.'

Frost gave a start and looked up to see Mullett looming in the doorway. 'Mr Mullett – you spooked me. Bit late for you, isn't it, sir?'

'Day like today, routines go out of the window,' Mullett sighed.

A little too obviously, Frost thought.

'And I've a mountain of paperwork. It's not only you lot who are continually snowed under.' He stepped closer, peering over. 'What have you got there?' Mullett gestured towards the blue file Frost realized he was clutching.

'Nothing, nothing.' Frost looked at the file as if he'd never seen it before in his life, then casually dumped it on top of a stack of papers behind him. 'We're getting somewhere with the canal stiff; some crucial evidence has been found,' he said, trying to distract the super. 'And there's been another breakthrough with the Hudson case. Just got a call from our friends in Dover.'

'Yet more developments? Thank God for some good news.'

The super pulled up a chair, then retrieved a packet

of Senior Service from his jacket pocket. He offered it to Frost first.

'Steve Hudson has been arrested at the Dover Hoverport, alone.' Frost lit up. 'The sod was on his way to Calais. An alert Customs official spotted the motor. Should be here by the morning.'

'Well, that is good news,' Mullett said unconvincingly.

Frost continued, 'God knows where he was really headed – Spain? That's where they all end up, isn't it? By all accounts, Steve Hudson used to keep some pretty unsavoury company. Not sure I trust his uncle much, either. You know, Michael Hudson, manager of Bennington's Bank. Bailed his nephew out once too often, I reckon.'

'I know it's been a long, tiring day, Jack,' said Mullett. 'But it's always best to temper your hunches in this business, and keep things professional, especially when referring to local dignitaries.'

'Local dignitary, Michael Hudson?' Frost tried to laugh, but his heart wasn't in it.

'Gathering solid evidence is what we deal with – *all* we deal with.' The superintendent leant forward, flicking ash into the overflowing bowl. 'And that goes for Bert as well,' Mullett continued. 'Jack, you simply must try to keep your emotions out of it. I've said we'll get to the bottom of this, and we will. The truth will prevail, believe you me.'

Frost shook his head. He was exhausted.

'So let's not go barking up the wrong tree, making all sorts of insinuations. The division needs to pull together, especially at a time like this. This is not a place for people who think they know better – for people to betray our trust in them. God forbid.'

'Yes, sir.' What was Mullett banging on about? Frost was too tired to argue.

'Good. So we're agreed: no wasting valuable time looking for something that isn't there.' Mullett ran his forefingers through his moustache. 'And Frost, when you make significant breaks on cases, can you please immediately inform me.'

'It's a bit late for me, sir,' Frost yawned. 'What case exactly are you referring to?'

'The Lee Wright connection to the Hudson case. I knew about the prints, of course, but not that he's Julie's father.'

'Ah, yes, sir. Well, there wasn't time. I went straight from Wendy Hudson's bedside at the hospital to that lane where Bert was found. You were one of the first to know.'

'That's as may be.'

Would it ever be possible to please the man?

'Are we, then, any closer to locating this Lee Wright?' said Mullett, stubbing out his cigarette.

'I'll let you know the minute we get any closer,' said Frost.

'Damn those parole boards,' said Mullett, quickly adding, 'He could be armed. We'll need to make sure we're fully prepared and go in with tactical support.'

'Yes, of course.'

'And the girl – you think she'll be unharmed?' Mullett asked.

'He's her father. I bloody well hope so.'

'Let's not forget, Frost, that Wright has been more than ruthless in the past. He shoved a gun into an innocent person's face.'

'These people usually operate by different rules when it comes to their own,' Frost said.

'All the same, let's keep an open mind and be fully prepared until we know she's safe. And it wouldn't do any harm to go easy on Steve Hudson, until we can be certain of what his intent was. According to DC Clarke, his wife was very confused. Plus it must have come as something of a shock to suddenly find out you're not the father of a child you'd always taken to be your own.'

Frost supposed Clarke had written her damn report already. 'No excuse to pulverize a defenceless woman,' he pointed out.

'Maybe not, but we get it wrong, and we could all be made to suffer.' Mullett rose to leave. 'Night then, Jack.' He reached over and put a hand on Frost's shoulder. 'Get some rest.'

Frost got up to shut the door after his boss, retrieved the thick blue Met file and sat back at the desk.

It detailed Blake Richards's chequered career in the Met. The chippy new Aster's security guard, the man who Frost had had a run-in with only yesterday, was no saint. Frost had wondered if his neatly trimmed ginger beard was an attempt to mask all sorts of flaws and discrepancies.

The file contained a commendation for his under-cover work relating to the famous £5-million Ealing heist, then a reprimand for intimidating a female wit-ness over a bank job in Chelsea. A much more serious allegation of rape hadn't stuck. Another commend-ation for undercover work during a gangland killing spree in the East End. Then there were unfounded allegations of collusion with the Flying Squad's notorious Inspector Dickie Brent, who'd been dis-missed and eventually charged with murder and bribery.

As he was fighting to stay awake, another all too familiar name suddenly caught Frost's attention: George Foster. Beefy, thuggish, notoriously violent, Foster had been a bouncer at Denton's seedy strip joint the Coconut Grove, before ramping up his organized-crime operations and heading for the big smoke. Frost hadn't seen or heard of him for many years.

Foster's name was mentioned here in connection with an investigation into a series of bank jobs in south London and the Croydon area. Richards was leading the investigation, but the case was eventually dropped due to tainted evidence.

On the same page Williams had written another

name in the margin. Whether it was the light, the hour, or Frost's eyesight, he couldn't make it out. He'd have to get Forensics on to it, but quietly. He didn't want any more bloody lectures from Mullett about not following hunches.

Plus Bert had had his reasons for keeping this quiet. Frost would have to tread carefully.

Wednesday (1) _____

'Jack?' Hanlon pushed the door further open and walked into Bert Williams's office. Frost's head was resting on a blue file amid the mountains of paperwork which littered the late inspector's desk. The detective sergeant was fast asleep, and snoring loudly.

It was 8.30 a.m. Hanlon, still in his hat and coat and clutching a warm bacon sarnie, sat down in the scruffy spare chair opposite the desk, took his sandwich out of the greasy paper bag and tucked in. Swallowing, he said again, more loudly, 'Jack.' Adding, 'Rise and shine.'

Frost stirred.

'Jack,' Hanlon said once more. 'Wake up, you sod, we've got one hell of a day.'

Slowly Frost lifted his head, clocked Hanlon, sat back in Williams's old office chair, and fumbled for his cigarettes. Lighting up, he said, exhaling, 'Where's my breakfast?'

'I didn't know you were going to be here already, did I?' apologized Hanlon. 'Not like you to be so punctual. Here, you can have half of this if you want.' Hanlon went to rip off a corner of his sandwich.

'Don't worry, I'll wait until Grace pops by with her trolley. It's liquids I need, not solids.'

'Not sure you're going to have time to hang around. A couple of people we've got to find first.'

'Yes, all right, I do realize that, Arthur,' grumbled Frost. 'At least Steve Hudson's been arrested – stopped at Dover Hoverport, of all places, he was – one less to worry about.'

'Finally, considering he must have stuck out like a sore thumb in that motor of his: yellow TR7, like a huge wedge of cheese tanking down the A2. Trench's brown Mini Metro won't be anything like so obvious to track. How are we going to find that?'

'I don't know. We need another chat with Liz Fraser – she's still foxing me.' Frost laughed at his own joke. 'Clarke had a bit of a go yesterday in the hospital, apparently, but it sounds like she was too soft on her.' He paused. 'And this Simon Trench fellow, he must have mates in Denton. I bet Liz Fraser has some idea where he might be holed up, who he's with. You alerted Social Services yet?'

'Just getting on to it, Jack.'

'A right pain in the arse, that lot,' said Frost. 'I suppose we'll have to involve Social Services if we ever find Julie Hudson, too. Her mother's in no fit state to look after her at the moment. And Lee Wright – father or no father, he'll be going straight back inside.'

'Had some luck there, yesterday,' said Hanlon. 'Lee Wright's old address? Well, amazingly, the man who lives there has been there, on and off, ever since the Wrights moved out. Or rather the Dixons. Wright used to live there with his mother, who goes or went by the name of Joan Dixon. Just seeing what we've got on her, and the owner of the house is going through his paperwork. Says he had a forwarding address somewhere.'

'Good boy,' said Frost, pushing the chair back and standing.

'Interestingly, though,' said Hanlon, 'a couple of heavies paid Wright's old address a visit on Monday evening, asking for him. A large bruiser with the usual gold fashion accessories, and a wiry little Irish fellow. Oh, and there might have been someone else, stayed in the car.'

'What sort of car?'

Hanlon looked at him, wondering why he'd asked that. 'Large, dark, was all he said. Cars aren't his thing.'

Just then Bert Williams's phone went. Hanlon and Frost both jumped.

'Jesus!' exclaimed Frost. 'Someone know something we don't?' He picked up the phone. 'Yes?' he said hesitantly.

'Jack.' It was Bill Wells. 'Thought you might be in there. Heard you stopped the night.'

'Very comfortable it was too.'

'That's what Bert used to say.' Wells cleared his throat, before adding, 'There's someone down in the cells who's complaining that he's *not* very comfortable. In fact, he's making a right racket.'

'Steve Hudson, by any chance?'

'That's the one. Plus his solicitor has just arrived.'

'Have them assembled in Interview Room One, will you please, Bill,' instructed Frost. He put down the phone. 'Arthur, I have visitors downstairs: the wife-beater and his stooge.'

As Frost left Bert Williams's office, he added, 'I know you've got a lot on your plate – but don't forget to call those old dragons at Social Services.'

As DC Sue Clarke walked into the lobby, a tramp came stumbling out. He looked vaguely familiar.

'Friend of yours?' she said once inside, teeth gritted through the lingering stink.

'That man,' said Station Sergeant Bill Wells, peering through two huge, sad bouquets of flowers, 'is a right pest.'

'That why you were hiding?'

'Desmond Thorley,' said Wells, 'once performed at

the Royal Variety Performance in front of the Queen, or so he'll have you believe. Keeps coming in here banging on about strange goings-on in the woods, where he lives in a beaten-up old railway carriage. If you ask me, the only strange goings-on are in his head. Drinks like a fish.'

Clarke moved closer to the front desk where the smell of the tramp was replaced by the heady scent of lilies and roses. The desk was overflowing with flowers and cards and hastily scrawled messages. A bottle of Denton Pale Ale had even been placed by Bert Williams's photograph, a black ribbon tied around the neck.

'Has Mullett seen all this?' Clarke was taken aback by the very public and almost immediate outpouring of grief.

'Word got round. People have been adding stuff as they've come in this morning,' said Wells, rubbing his hands. 'Mullett went straight to County – big press conference trying to clear up the rabies business.'

Clarke looked at her watch. 'I'm running late, and I need to find DS Frost before the briefing. A couple of developments.'

'He should be heading for Interview Room One. Steve Hudson and his lawyer are waiting.'

'Shit!' Clarke rushed to the internal door. 'I'm all over the place this morning – I'm really not prepared.'

'Make it up as you go along,' shouted Wells after her. Then to himself, 'Everyone else does.'

* * *

'Tell me again, Mr Hudson,' Frost was saying, 'exactly how you came to the conclusion that Julie is not your natural daughter?'

'Simple. Her bloody mother told me as much.' Steve Hudson was unshaven, his highlighted hair a mess, dark rings around his eyes. He looked shrunken and a little bit scared, behind the interview desk.

'Just like that?' Frost had heard it all before: a wife-beater believing his actions had been fully justified.

'No, not just like that,' Hudson replied. 'The cow had been acting very odd. You know, late-night phone calls and stuff. Don't know what she was getting up to in the day at home, either. A man had been round last week, that's for sure. A neighbour told me.'

'Is that right,' said Frost. 'And who would that be?'

'Just a neighbour, that's all.'

'I don't see that this is relevant,' said Steve Hudson's solicitor, the slippery Henry Dobbs, who was sitting some feet away from his client, and looking increasingly agitated. Perspiration speckled the chubby man's flushed face. Frost thought he urgently needed to loosen his red spotty bow tie.

'So you confronted her?' Frost offered, making himself more comfortable – Mullett's new chairs hadn't yet made it into the cramped, airless interview rooms.

'I thought she was having an affair . . .' For the first time Steve Hudson met Frost's gaze. 'Not something any man should have to put up with.'

'Steven,' interjected Henry Dobbs, scribbling something on a yellow legal pad, 'you know you don't have to say anything at all at this stage. This is merely a formality. Detective Frost is fully aware of your rights. Aren't you, Mr Frost?'

Frost lit a cigarette, keeping his packet to himself. He then looked over to see if the tape recorder was still running; it was.

'I've got nothing to hide,' said Hudson.

'And that's why you were running off to France?' asked Frost. He was bored with this already, his mind this morning never far from Bert Williams, from Betty, her breaking down in his arms. Frost needed to get hold of his contact at British Telecom, get those telephone numbers in Bert's bloodied pocket notebook checked and cross-checked.

'Needed a break,' grumbled Hudson. 'That was all. Who wouldn't have if they'd been in my situation?'

'All right,' Frost said, 'where exactly were you in the house when you first confronted your wife?'

'We were in the bedroom, I think.'

'And this was on Saturday night, just a few hours after Julie had gone missing?' Saturday, Frost thought. Bloody Saturday.

'I was off my head with worry, of course, but Wendy was acting like everything was almost normal. Like Julie had only popped out to see a friend. She even tidied Julie's room for her, saying she wanted it spotless for when she returned,' Hudson said, his anger subsiding.

'Detective,' piped up Henry Dobbs, 'I'd like a few moments with my client in private.'

'Dobbs, why don't you save your breath for once,' said Frost, 'you know we'll get there in the end. Besides, your client keeps inferring that he's got nothing to hide.'

Frost shifted his gaze to Steve Hudson. 'Detectives Hanlon and Clarke had already been round to take statements by this stage, right? Are you then implying that Wendy was putting on some crocodile tears for our benefit?' Thoughts of wasting police time crossed Frost's mind.

Thoughts also came to him of the poor woman battered nearly to death, lying in a pool of her own blood on the kitchen floor.

'I was the one who called the police initially,' said Steve Hudson. 'You'll have that on your records. If you keep such things.'

Frost watched Dobbs frown. Never trust a man with a beard was one of Frost's favourite adages. Never *ever* trust a man who wears a bow tie was another.

'Wendy changed her tune when your lot turned up, that's for sure,' Hudson continued.

Frost noticed that Hudson's hands, out on the table, were shaking. Nerves? Signs of alcohol dependency? With his dyed, messed-up hair, black turtleneck sweater and swanky leather jacket, Frost couldn't understand how anyone would buy a used motor off him. He looked more like a footballer out on the razz. Or a failed crooner.

'If we can get back to the moment you confronted her.' Frost looked Steve Hudson in the eye. 'This was in the bedroom, right?'

'To begin with,' Hudson said.

'You made a right mess in there,' said Frost, making a point of ignoring that twat Dobbs's glare, 'before what, chasing your wife down the stairs and into the kitchen, where you proceeded to knock the bleeding life out of her?'

'Mr Frost,' interjected Dobbs, 'as you know full well, my client is under no obligation to answer such outlandish accusations.'

'Outlandish?' shouted Frost, turning to face Dobbs.

'My wife told me that I was not the father of our child,' added Hudson quietly.

'After you did what, exactly? Torture her? Beat her round the head, again and again?'

'Detective,' said Dobbs firmly, 'I really object in the strongest possible terms. My client is, at this point in time, innocent. This line of questioning is beyond the pale, and you know it.'

'If I lost my temper,' said Hudson, more strident again, 'then I'm sorry. But I was badly provoked. She . . . she came at me with a knife, for God's sake.'

'A knife?' Frost said with disbelief.

The solicitor turned to his client.

'It was self-defence,' continued Hudson.

'That's an interesting line to take,' said Frost. 'Not

sure Scenes of Crime would agree with you. What happened to this knife?'

Hudson remained quiet for some time before uttering, 'Must have got lost in the scuffle. I don't know – could have been kicked under a unit.'

'Scuffle, hey?' said Frost calmly. 'Thing is, from where I'm sitting, I could have sworn I was looking at attempted murder.'

'Now, now,' said Dobbs, 'I'm not aware of anyone pressing charges, yet.'

'Give us a chance. We thought we'd let a certain lady have her say in the matter first, but seeing as she's lying in a hospital bed, her head smothered in bandages and her jaw wired up, talking's not very easy for her—' Frost was interrupted by a hurried knocking at the door. He looked over his shoulder to see DC Clarke's lovely fresh face peering into the room.

'Sarge, can I have a word?'

'Excuse me, gentlemen.' Frost rose from his chair and grabbed his almost empty packet of Rothmans. 'Make yourselves at home.'

'Yes, love?' Frost said, firmly shutting the interview-room door behind him.

'I've just come from the hospital. Thought I'd look in on Mrs Hudson first thing this morning, seeing as I was passing.'

'I like the initiative,' said Frost. Clarke was certainly pulling out all the stops: revisiting the canal, popping in at the hospital before breakfast. 'But I take it you avoided the kiddies' ward.'

'I'm not Wonder Woman,' said Clarke.

'Well, hopefully, Hanlon's on Becky Fraser's case. So how's Wendy Hudson, then? Enjoying her Cornflakes?'

'She was a hell of a lot more alert, and able to talk a little too. At least she made herself completely clear this time.'

'Good, good,' said Frost, suddenly hoping he hadn't overstepped the mark with Steve Hudson for no valid reason.

'Gosh, you look tired, Jack. Did you get to bed last night?'

'Don't worry about me.' Frost glanced up and down the empty corridor, embarrassed. 'So what did Mrs Hudson have to say for herself? The spiv in there' – he gestured at the interview-room door – 'is now saying she came at him with a knife.' Frost rolled his eyes. Mullett had been right – the whole case had never been more than a very bloody domestic.

Clarke sighed, shrugged her shoulders. 'She doesn't want this to get out of hand.'

'Get out of hand?' Frost spluttered. 'Too late for that, I'd say.' He could never understand the human capacity for forgiveness.

'The point is—'

'Don't tell me – she doesn't want to press charges.'

'You've got it in one.'

'Afraid of the exposure?' he sighed. 'Bollocks. Bang goes our key witness. And what about her blasted daughter? Isn't she concerned for her safety, her whereabouts? Happy for her to run off with a convicted armed robber?'

'I'm not sure mother and daughter get on too well,' said Clarke.

'Jesus Christ!' Frost swiftly turned away from Clarke and opened the door to the interview room.

'Mr Hudson,' he said, entering the room once again, 'I'm afraid to say your wife remains in a critical condition, unable to communicate. You'll be held here for the time being on suspicion of attempted murder.'

'Mr Frost,' sighed Henry Dobbs, standing. 'I don't need to remind—'

'Dobbs, I wouldn't even raise the question of bail. Mr Hudson has already made one attempt to flee the country.'

'I most strongly object, yet again,' cried Dobbs, 'to your preposterous allegation that my client in any way—'

Frost turned for the door, muttering to himself, 'Where's the duty constable? I need this loser banging back up . . . and the key chucking away.'

Wednesday (2) _____

Hanlon put down the phone. 'Yes!' he said aloud, punching the air.

It was a result – of sorts. The boffin had found a forwarding address for Lee Wright's mother, Joan Dixon. She hadn't gone that far either, just across town, Denton Woods way. Chances were the woman would have moved on again ages ago, but still it needed to be checked immediately.

Except the morning briefing was in five minutes and Hanlon realized he should at least run it by Frost, before checking the address out. Wright was a convicted armed robber, could be dangerous.

Mullett would certainly insist on the involvement of the Tacticals. The whole thing could very quickly become a major operation, and when no one of interest was found at the address Hanlon would be left to look a fool. He really couldn't risk that after his rabies slip.

As Hanlon was contemplating skipping the briefing and heading straight to the address on his own – bugger the consequences – Frost and Clarke appeared in the CID office.

'Briefing's cancelled,' Frost beamed. 'Mullett's still at County, leaving yours truly in charge, and I've got nothing useful to say.'

'Nothing new there, then,' said Hanlon.

'Better we press on, Arthur,' said Frost. 'What have you got?'

'An address for Lee Wright's mother, Joan Dixon.'

'Already? You do work fast. Well, let's go,' said Frost, grabbing his mac.

'Shouldn't we inform Mullett?'

'No point wasting time,' said Frost.

Hanlon reached for his coat also, spotting that Clarke looked perplexed.

Frost, who also seemed to have noticed, said, 'Sue, man the ship, will you?'

Hanlon added, 'Social Services should be getting back to me about Liz and Becky Fraser.'

'What is it with you men and Social Services?' Clarke asked. 'It's like you're terrified of them.'

'We are,' said Frost, making for the exit.

'Hairy-scary, that's for sure. Oh, by the way, what do Forensics say about the football scarf?'

'Nothing yet,' said Clarke. 'Still waiting.'

'Hurry them up, for what good it will do.' Frost backed into the corridor, Hanlon following. 'A gang of young thugs, that's what we're after.'

'I'd come to that conclusion as well,' said Clarke, patiently. 'Just thought we'd need a bit more to go on. Plenty of gangs about on the Southern Housing Estate.'

'Be like finding a needle in a haystack,' said Hanlon.

'The guide dog's the key to that one,' called Frost, from the hallway. 'Has to be. If only we could get the dog to identify the spotty culprits in a line-up.'

Left alone in the CID office, DC Sue Clarke sat glumly at her desk and retrieved her notebook. Being stuck waiting to hear back from Social Services, with regards to bruised Becky Fraser, and from Forensics, over the piece of scarf and Graham Ransome's death, was not going to be very exciting. She knew she could be a little more useful.

She got up and walked over to the tall metal cabinet containing the recent case files, knowing she'd have to start trawling through every reported incident of violence, intimidation and aggravated robbery on and around the Southern Housing Estate. She'd then have to check known football hooligans, see if anything correlated.

Then perhaps go back to the pathologist, Dr Drysdale, to see if he had any clearer idea of how exactly Graham Ransome received his injuries – whether there was anything incriminating there.

Probably she should have already done this, but there weren't enough hours in the day. Besides, it was the chase she enjoyed, being out and about – with Jack Frost too, she realized. Not the drudgery. Perhaps she wasn't cut out to be a detective after all.

'Sue,' came the voice of PC Simms close behind her.

Startled, she spun round. 'What the hell are you doing creeping up on me?'

'I was just passing your office . . . the door was open.'

'Well, I'm busy,' she said dismissively.

'On what?' said Simms, leaning over and picking up a file.

Clarke grabbed the file from him and placed it back on the desk. 'A million things,' she said.

'That bit of scarf we found by the canal lead any-where?' Simms said.

'Don't you start.'

'Just asking.'

'A gang of yobs on the Southern Housing Estate – that's what we believe we're after,' Clarke said.

'Try the Codpiece – that chippy. Kids are always hanging around there,' Simms suggested and walked over to the open filing cabinet.

'You looking for something in particular?' asked Clarke.

Simms was running his fingers over the tops of the files. 'No,' he said, quickly adding, 'lot of paperwork in your job.'

The phone began trilling. 'If you don't mind, I need to get this.' Clarke waited for Simms to leave the room before she lifted the receiver. 'CID.'

'Sue?' It was Bill Wells, out of breath. 'There's been a bomb scare – Market Square.'

'Turn that off,' said Frost as the car radio crackled into life.

'Is that a good idea, Jack?' said Hanlon.

'I don't need any more distractions while I'm driving,' said Frost, negotiating the notorious Bath Road roundabout. 'Besides, we don't want Mullett stalling us by sending for the cavalry. Frankly, the less he knows the better.'

'Fair enough.'

Frost lit a cigarette while waiting to pull across the roundabout. 'Cast your mind back a moment, will you, Arthur. A couple of weeks. Shortly after the Rimmington heist.'

'The *Star Wars* robbery, you mean?' said Hanlon.

'If you must call it that.'

'Vicious job. But what of it?'

'Something's troubling me.'

'That's unusual, then. Hey, steady on, Jack.'

Frost had taken a corner too wide and had to swerve back on to the left side of the road. 'Not our

248

investigation, I know, but we'd just been talking about it when Miss Smith came into the office, looking for Bert – though Bert had just pissed off somewhere.'

'How could I possibly remember something like that? Everyone was always looking for Bert.'

'Said she wanted a private word with him. You know how flirty she can be.'

'Yes,' smiled Hanlon. 'Bert had a way with her, that's for sure.'

'He liked her knockers,' mulled Frost.

'Hard not to,' said Hanlon, raising an eyebrow.

'She was carrying an Aster's shopping bag,' Frost said, more seriously, 'and there was an Aster's shopping bag on Bert's desk. Miss Smith said, "Snap," or something like that, and that she and Bert obviously shopped in the right places.'

'Even if I did remember, for the life of me I don't know where this is going, Jack.'

'Neither do I, quite.' Frost suddenly pulled up right outside the old telephone exchange, recently given a new name and fancy logo: British Telecom. Right waste of taxpayers' money. 'Mind the wardens, Arthur, I won't be a minute.'

'Hey, what the hell are you doing?'

Frost ignored Hanlon, climbed out of the motor and dashed into the lobby. The once-grand neo-classical building was awash with cheap blue-and-grey carpet, fixtures and fittings. Frost went straight up to the reception desk, and asked for Mike Ferris, the chief engineer. 'He's expecting me,' said Frost, knowing of course that he wasn't.

While waiting, Frost flicked to the page on which he'd copied the four telephone numbers from Bert Williams's bloodstained notebook, along with the number of the call box. He ripped out the paper just as the friendly, heavily lined face of Mike Ferris appeared in front of him.

'Hello, Jack.' Ferris had a trace of Geordie in his accent. Of medium height and build, and in late middle age, Ferris was wearing blue work trousers with a white short-sleeved shirt and a tie. 'You should have warned me you were coming. I could easily have been out, this time of the morning.'

'Something just came up,' said Frost, looking over his shoulder. 'I need a bit of help.' He paused. 'On the quiet, if you know what I mean.'

'For you, Jack, I'm always happy to help. If I can. But is it wise you standing around here? Not worried about being seen?'

'I'm in a rush, Mike. Take a look at this, can you.' Frost handed Ferris the piece of paper he'd ripped from his notebook. 'Any names and addresses you can match to these numbers, also the dates and times of any calls between them – this one's a call box, by the way – will make me a very happy man.'

'I'll see what I can do.' Ferris carefully folded and slipped the note into his back pocket.

'I owe you,' said Frost, turning to leave.

'Don't worry about it,' Frost could hear Ferris saying. 'You've more than helped me out in the past.'

Frost smiled to himself as he left the building. Letting Ferris's batty wife off a shoplifting charge had more than paid for itself already. And if Ferris could come up with some meaningful names and addresses, not to mention dates and times of calls, Frost knew the net would be closing in on whoever killed Bert. It wasn't just a vague hope, he was convinced there was a connection.

'Not parked illegally, are we?' Frost said to Hanlon cheerfully. Hanlon was out of the Cortina, talking to a tiny female traffic warden in a uniform far too big for her, her cap comically askew.

'I was just explaining,' said Hanlon, brandishing his warrant card, 'that we're on official police business. Isn't that right, Detective?'

'Official or not,' the traffic warden said – she must have been pushing sixty – 'you still can't park here. There's no emergency that I'm aware of and you're on a double-yellow line. You're obstructing the highway, and as such are in breach of bye-law—'

'Don't tell me what I'm in breach of,' Hanlon interrupted.

'Come on, Arthur,' said Frost, climbing into the driver's seat. 'We've all got jobs to do. And that poor old dear is about to get drenched.'

'Serves her right,' mumbled Hanlon, looking up at

the suddenly leaden sky, before easing his great bulk inside the car.

Station Sergeant Bill Wells found he was biting his nails, staring at the large black phone on the front desk. With everybody at County seemingly involved in the ridiculous rabies press conference, including of course Mullett, Wells was waiting for the Anti-Terrorist Branch to confirm whether the code word used in the bomb scare was correct.

It seemed to be taking them ages.

At least Wells had just taken the precaution of calling over the Tannoy for all officers present to assemble in the briefing room. Not that he knew who would then direct the operation – if it came to that.

He couldn't raise Frost or Hanlon on any car radio. Which, as far as his panicked mind could work out, meant that the only people of rank left in the building were Clarke and himself.

The sound of hurrying feet and banging doors filled the station, as Wells felt his heart beat faster and faster.

Superintendent Mullett followed Assistant Chief Constable Winslow out of the County Headquarters press room, believing he'd managed to swing the blame on to the papers for creating all the hysteria about the rabies scare.

'Well done, Stanley,' said Winslow. 'I think Denton Division comes out of this almost blemish-free.'

'Thank you, Nigel.'

'Superintendent Mullett,' a voice hollered down the corridor. 'A quick word, if I may.'

Mullett watched with great irritation as the *Denton Echo*'s chief reporter, Sandy Lane, pushed past two WPCs and planted himself so close to Mullett that he could smell bacon on his breath.

'A quick word about that blind man who was murdered by the canal,' Lane pressed.

'Murdered?' snapped Mullett. 'I think you're leaping to conclusions, as ever.'

'I'll put it another way, then.' Lane grinned. 'Surely the police are linking his death to the recent spate of youth violence and vandalism on the Southern Housing Estate? By all accounts, the man had been subjected to a vicious beating.'

'I don't know where you get your information from, Mr Lane,' said Mullett, fully aware of Winslow's scrutinizing eye, 'but we will let you know in due course. The investigation is in full swing.'

Still undeterred, Lane continued, 'I mean, can you assure the *Echo* that the elderly population of Denton is safe? Only last month a pensioner was kicked to the ground and robbed, on the very same street where Graham Ransome lived.'

'At this stage there is absolutely no evidence to link the two incidents,' Mullett replied firmly. He could see the headline now: DENTON OAPS TOO TERRIFIED TO LEAVE THEIR HOMES. Though yobbish behaviour on the Southern Housing Estate was an increasing problem, the mugging of the pensioner was unresolved: after several line-ups it was clear the woman was both senile and a drunk and had no idea what her assailants looked like.

'When do the police expect a breakthrough?' Lane just wouldn't let it go. But fortunately for Mullett, a colleague of Lane's had materialized, slapping him on the back, and diverting the hack's attention.

'When are you going to start reporting the truth?' hissed Mullett, before rushing after Winslow.

'What a tiresome fellow,' Winslow said, once Mullett had fallen into step. 'And he was the bugger who created all that rabies trouble. I'd have a word with his editor, Stanley. Get him shifted over to the sports pages. The way Denton are playing at the moment, that'll give him plenty to contend with.'

They'd reached the double doors to the assistant chief constable's suite of offices. Mullett was about to make his excuses when Winslow tapped him on the arm and said quietly but firmly, 'Spare me a moment. Coffee?'

Mullett glanced at his watch. He wanted to be back in Denton by ten thirty at the very latest. 'Of course, sir,' he said, through gritted teeth. He was nervous enough about leaving Frost in charge of the briefing, let alone the station.

'It's important, Superintendent, and I won't keep you long.' Winslow ushered Mullett through.

Mullett sat down, placing his cap on the chair next to him. The room was large enough to host a conference.

Winslow buzzed his secretary for coffee, before fixing Mullett with a penetrating stare. 'Inspector Bert Williams,' he eventually sighed, before removing his wire-framed glasses and vigorously cleaning them with a special lens cloth. 'Very sorry to hear he's passed away.'

'Yes, it's awful news,' replied Mullett. 'Days away from his retirement, too. What a tragedy.' He didn't know where this was leading, but didn't like Winslow's tone.

'And I thought he was at home, with the flu,' Winslow tutted, replacing his glasses. 'Instead he was gallivanting down country lanes, Rimmington way.' He paused. 'Look, I'll come straight to it, Stanley. Was Williams on the level?'

Mullett couldn't help but look away from those beady eyes, magnified through crystal-clear lenses. 'On the level? Do you mean, did he have a drinking problem?'

'That wasn't what I was getting at,' Winslow said. 'Though it might not be entirely unconnected. Remember our conversation just yesterday – about a leak, in your division, connected to those brutal Rimmington and Wallop heists?'

Mullett hardly needed reminding. However, he had certainly not made any connections to Williams, the longest-serving member of the division. A drunk maybe, but he was not disloyal.

'As I'm sure you are aware,' continued Winslow, 'I was a great admirer of Bert's, but by all accounts his drinking and absenteeism had been getting rather out of hand. Clearly he could no longer be relied upon.'

'I don't know how you could know that,' said Mullett, defensively. 'Really—' They were interrupted by Winslow's frumpy secretary reversing into the room with a tray of coffee and biscuits.

Winslow waited for her to pour the coffee, proffer Jaffa Cakes and disappear, before he piped up again, 'Allegiances go out of the window with alcoholics. Besides, the latest intelligence suggests that this gang, aside from having a police insider on their payroll, have links with some seriously dangerous individuals over from Northern Ireland. You can probably imagine what I'm getting at – terrorists turned professional criminals – and I'm afraid I'm not at liberty to divulge any more at this juncture. But needless to say, it's imperative that we make headway urgently.'

'Obviously I'll do what I can,' said Mullett, more than a little exasperated. He didn't like being kept in the dark where County, or he presumed National and the Anti-Terrorist Branch at that, were concerned. 'Given what you've told me.' He coughed. The coffee was too strong for his stomach. He wondered whether he might be getting an ulcer.

'What was Williams working on when he died?' Winslow asked.

Mullett had no idea. The old biddy who'd been mugged? A possible arson attempt? An aggravated burglary? Nothing major. 'A number of routine investigations,' he said. 'With his retirement imminent, he was winding down, of course.'

'Has the post-mortem thrown anything up?'

'Too early.' Mullett took another sip of the coffee, feeling it go straight to his bowels. 'We should hear the preliminary findings this afternoon.'

'Well, keep a very close eye on it.'

'Sorry, Nigel, it's been a long morning already – what exactly are you implying?' Mullett was becoming more uncomfortable by the second.

'Come, come. Do I really need to spell it out?'

Mullett grimaced as another shockwave rippled through his bowels.

'All right, I will. Could Williams have been tipping this gang off . . . and then something went fatally wrong?' The assistant chief constable didn't appear very interested in a reply, barely pausing before he continued, 'Why not get that fellow Jack Frost on to it? If anyone has any idea about the skeletons in Williams's cupboard, it'd have to be Frost. He was his partner, wasn't he?'

'Nigel, with all due respect, I'd have thought that Frost's relationship with Williams is precisely the reason not to—'

'Oh, rubbish. If there's any question over Williams's demise, Jack Frost will want to clear his name,' said Winslow. 'Can't believe Frost is bent. And he's certainly not stupid.'

'But Nigel, there is no question mark over Williams's death, at the moment.' Mullett couldn't believe Winslow was taking this line; unless, of course, Winslow was party to some information that he wasn't. Or, unless – he shuddered – it was a test to smoke out the real mole, and someone was actually pointing the finger at him. 'I have to say, sir, that I just don't think Frost is experienced enough.'

'Precisely, precisely,' Winslow said, rubbing his hands. 'Something like this needs an untrained eye.'

Maybe, but not uncouth, Mullett could have added. Instead he said, lamely, 'We do have the very capable DI Allen.' Not that Mullett had yet been able to track him down to cancel his leave.

'Put Frost on to it, right away. There's a good fellow.'

'To be honest, sir' – Mullett was not going to let this go without a fight – 'I had thought it might be advisable if Frost had a few days off. You know, compassionate leave? He was very close to DI Williams. I don't want him making any irrational moves. He's working on a couple of sensitive cases as it is.' Mullett paused for effect. 'Don't forget the whole rabies thing started with him. I wouldn't like to put him under any more pressure.'

'Nonsense. Pressure brings out the best in a chap.'

Mullett's bowels twitched urgently for attention. 'If you insist,' he said crossly. He got to his feet, and began shuffling backwards out of the room.

Winslow's attention was diverted by his desk phone, which had started to ring and flash.

Mullett barely made it to the corridor before he heard Winslow shouting after him, 'Superintendent, you have a bomb in Market Square! Mobilize your troops – sounds like the real thing.'

Hanlon left his finger on the doorbell for a good few seconds. A pessimist by nature, he didn't hold much store that whoever answered would even have heard of the Dixon woman. He'd struck it lucky with the last address and the boffin. Twice in a row wasn't going to happen.

The fact that Frost had turned off the radio and so they were out of contact with Control was also making Hanlon more anxious and downcast by the minute. He knew that Frost had his own issues with Mullett and procedure, but he didn't see why he had to expose himself to such a serious misdemeanour as well.

And who knew what Frost had been up to when he popped into the telephone exchange? Another skirting of the rules, was Hanlon's guess. Though if, as he suspected, it had something to do with Bert Williams, then Hanlon was more than happy to forgive Frost anything. Jack might have been putting a brave face on it, but Hanlon knew what the inspector had meant to him.

'Nobody in,' Hanlon said to himself, not in the least surprised. Relieved in a way. He'd decided he wanted to get back to the station. Make his presence felt.

'Give them a chance,' said Frost, who had now climbed out of the car and was puffing away on the pavement behind him. 'Probably can't hear the bell with that racket going on.' Frost raised his eyes to an upstairs window.

Hanlon stepped away from the porch. He'd somehow missed that, pop music coming from one of the bedrooms. Frost moved forwards and gave the doorbell another go. Hanlon could now hear a voice from inside. Saw a figure through the frosted-glass door coming towards them.

A plump and kind-faced grey-haired woman, in her late fifties, opened the door. She looked suddenly resigned. 'He's not here,' she muttered.

'Lee's not our concern, right now,' said Frost presumptuously.

Bloody hell, Hanlon thought. *Jackpot*. Adrenalin was surging through his body. 'Denton CID,' he said, shoving his warrant card in the woman's face. 'Are you Joan Dixon?'

'Yes.'

'It's the girl,' said Frost gravely. 'Julie, Julie Hudson. It's her safety we're most concerned about.'

'Well, I suppose you'd better come in,' Joan Dixon said.

* * *

As the dank countryside flashed by, Mullett, gripping the steering wheel with one hand, tried yet again to reach Control on the handset with the other. The airwaves were either jammed, or Control was blocked. What the hell was going on at the Eagle Lane station? He couldn't bear to think.

'Come in!' he barked. He was at least thirty minutes away from Denton, having only just left County headquarters. *Blasted rabies*, Mullett said to himself. *Blasted Frost*. If it hadn't been for some half-baked scheme cooked up by the detective sergeant to avoid Social Services and get a little girl supposedly out of harm's way, Mullett wouldn't have been at County this morning, and could have been directing operations on the ground.

They had a proper life-threatening crisis, and not only was Mullett not on hand, but it didn't seem like anyone else was either.

His brief telephone conversation with Sergeant Wells before he left County had filled him with dread. The Anti-Terrorist Branch had confirmed that the code word, though not the most recent on their books, was a recognized one. Wells had then told Mullett that while he'd already notified the bomb squad, he was unable to raise either Frost or Hanlon, who weren't just out of the building, but out of radio contact.

It was against procedure, and now lives were at risk,

while Station Sergeant Bill Wells – yes, the station sergeant – was temporarily in charge. The man couldn't even organize the lobby.

Boiling with rage, Mullett glanced at a map of Denton spread across the front passenger seat. He was working out the best way to seal off Market Square, hoping Sergeant Wells was doing the same and directing uniform accordingly.

'Hello, hello!' he shouted into the handset, trying to keep his eye on the road, as the country lane was becoming increasingly winding. He could hear nothing but loud static. 'Come in!' he yelled, just as a small dark-brown car suddenly appeared on the rise of the hill, in the middle of the road.

Mullett threw the handset to one side and swerved the car violently to the left. There followed the muted thud of impact and the super's Rover skidded on to the verge.

'Come on down, Julie,' Joan Dixon shouted for the fifth time. 'The police just want to know that you're all right.'

'Should we go and get her?' said Hanlon. They were still crowded in the narrow hallway, with Joan Dixon effectively guarding the stairs. The pop music had only got louder.

'No, that'll scare her,' she said, looking at Hanlon, then Frost. 'She's a very sensitive girl.'

'Deaf too, is she?' said Frost.

Hanlon looked at his colleague, as if to say, *Keep your mouth shut.*

'Come on, Julie,' shouted Joan Dixon one more time, 'there's a good girl.' Turning to Hanlon and Frost again, she added, 'She's been through a lot, these last few days.'

'Suppose you don't want to go and get her, do you?' Frost suggested.

'Ah, no need,' Joan Dixon said, as a tall, very thin girl appeared on the landing and tentatively made her way downstairs.

Julie Hudson's painfully angular face was heavily made up. Tatty pieces of cloth had been tied into her mousey hair, but the streak of red it had in the photo was still clearly visible.

'Where's Lee?' the girl asked, suspiciously eyeing Hanlon and Frost. 'He's been ages.' She was wearing a ripped vest top, held together with safety pins, a tiny white PVC mini-skirt, stripy red-and-black tights and a pair of huge black Dr Martens boots.

As she reached the bottom stair Hanlon could see that her make-up was concealing a livid outburst of acne. He could also see the look of stark relief on Jack Frost's face.

'Who are you?' she said, squaring up to Frost.

'Hello, Julie. I'm Detective Sergeant Frost and this is DC Hanlon, Denton CID. We've been very worried about you.'

'Why? I haven't done anything wrong.'

'We know that, love,' said Frost.

'Tea, coffee?' Joan Dixon said, moving towards the end of the hallway, and presumably the kitchen.

'We're fine,' said Frost.

Speak for yourself, thought Hanlon. 'Tea would be grand, thanks.' Hanlon tried to smile at the girl, who was now leaning shyly against the wall. She immediately looked away. *That's gratitude for you.*

'Now, what we need to know,' said Frost, 'is how you ended up here in this house, who exactly brought you here.'

The girl looked towards the end of the hallway, as if for help, but Joan Dixon had disappeared to make tea.

'He brought me here,' she answered quietly.

'Who's he?' said Hanlon.

'My dad, I suppose.'

They moved towards the kitchen. 'Was it against your will? Did he hurt you in any way?' prompted Frost.

'No,' she said, huffing. 'Why would he do that? He's my dad, right. I wanted to come. I hate my mum.'

'He wouldn't hurt her – last thing he'd do,' said Joan Dixon, as she filled the kettle.

'Where is your son, Lee?' Frost asked her.

'He went out to get a few things, should have been back by now.'

'Seeing as he's on parole, as far as I understand it,' said Frost, 'he shouldn't be anywhere near here anyway. He should be in Bristol.'

'But he was desperate,' said Joan Dixon. 'I know it's all been a bit of a shock for Julie, but Lee's been doing everything he can for her. Spoiling her rotten, he is: new record player, portable TV, clothes, jewellery, you name it. I don't think she was very happy at home with her mum, and that man, as it was.'

'I'd still like to know how the hell Lee Wright got her out of Aster's, in broad daylight?' Frost persisted.

'You'd have to ask him that,' Joan Dixon said, suddenly less sure of herself. 'But he didn't hurt her, in any way.'

Hanlon and Frost both looked at Julie who, saying nothing, merely looked away.

'No, I'm sure not,' muttered Frost, eyeing the bare kitchen counter. Joan Dixon clearly kept a tidy, clean house.

'He'd waited a long time to see her,' she continued.

'Well, that wasn't anyone's fault apart from his own,' said Hanlon. The woman was beginning to annoy him – didn't she realize the trouble her son had caused? 'A conviction for armed robbery is not something you can easily forget.'

'Julie won't be taken away, will she?' Joan Dixon asked, her voice now beginning to quaver.

'She's still a minor,' said Frost, who Hanlon could tell was also running out of patience. 'It's not up to us. But if it was, I'd drive her straight round to her mum's. That's if her mum wasn't in hospital.'

Joan Dixon gasped. 'What do you mean?'

'What's happened to Mum?' said Julie, her face, despite the make-up, going very white. 'Is she all right?'

'Seems like someone wasn't too happy about Lee and Wendy's big secret getting out,' said Frost.

'Not Lee,' said the woman. 'He wouldn't do such a thing.'

'Anyone capable of shoving a loaded shotgun in someone's face could do anything,' said Hanlon. Julie, he noticed, was standing completely still. He regretted what he'd just said, having no idea what Julie already knew about her real father.

'That was a long time ago,' Joan Dixon said, a note of resignation in her voice.

'No, it wasn't Lee who put Wendy Hudson in hospital,' said Frost. 'But that doesn't mean he's off the hook. Kidnapping is a serious enough charge. Not the sort of behaviour you'd expect from someone who is still on parole. Looks like he'll be going straight back to the slammer.'

Julie gasped now.

'But Julie needs him,' Joan Dixon said urgently.

'Julie needs her mum,' said Frost. 'Her own home. Don't you, Julie?'

Julie said nothing, now looking at the floor.

'What on earth has happened to Wendy?' said Joan Dixon.

'What's happened to Mum?' repeated Julie. 'What's happened to her?'

'She was badly beaten – by her husband,' said Frost. 'Who, thankfully, we've now got in custody.'

'I hate that man!' Julie suddenly shrieked. She rushed out of the kitchen, and clumped up the stairs.

'Wendy'll recover,' Frost continued, addressing Joan Dixon, 'but Lee should have thought a little harder before turning up out of the blue. He went round there last week, didn't he?'

'I don't know,' Joan Dixon said. 'I suppose it's possible.'

'Couldn't he have come to a more civil arrangement with the mother of his child?' Hanlon said.

'Look,' she said, 'none of this was my idea. When he turned up here with Julie, on Saturday afternoon, I was shocked. But what could I do? I tried to make her feel at home.'

'Well, it's all over now,' said Hanlon. 'You and the girl will be accompanying us back to the station, I'm afraid. Many more questions need to be answered.' Hanlon was keen to exert some authority, given that it was his painstaking work that had located the missing girl.

'Now where's this bloody son of yours again?' said Frost, lighting a cigarette.

'I don't know, honest,' she said. 'He went out first thing this morning. Said he was just going to the shops.'

'To pick up another teenager?'

Hanlon looked at Frost sternly – yet another

inappropriate remark – and said, embarrassed, 'The whistle gone on your kettle, love?'

Joan Dixon reached round and turned off the gas. The kitchen was fast filling with steam.

'Has he got other friends in town?' Frost asked. 'He can't have been back long.'

'Look, he's done his time. He's straight now,' she insisted. 'He doesn't want any more trouble.'

'That's not what my colleague asked,' said Hanlon.

'He's in enough trouble as it is,' warned Frost, who was looking out of the window. A row of conifers closely shielded the back garden.

'He did bump into someone in Denton, not that he was too happy about it,' Joan Dixon volunteered. 'Someone he'd met in prison. Not sure why I'm telling you this – to keep him on the straight and narrow, I suppose. But Lee's changed. He's got a good heart. He needs to rebuild his life, his relationship with his daughter. He's potty about her.'

'Who was this person, this fellow ex-con he bumped into?' said Frost.

'I don't remember the name, even if Lee told me,' she answered. 'He was Irish, though, Northern Irish, that I do remember. Because Lee said the man used to be in the IRA, he used to brag about it. That's what really worried me. Lee was scared too, I could tell.'

Frost sighed, scratched his chin. The woman looked genuinely worried – not without cause, these guys were in a different league. 'Which prison was this?'

'The last one Lee was in: Dartmoor.'

Pop music – or was it punk? – could be heard from upstairs once again. 'Why don't you get Julie to gather her things,' said Hanlon, 'and let's get down to the station.' He knew Lee Wright wasn't going to walk in the front door with a Cortina screaming CID parked right outside. He'd see if he could get the house put under surveillance, while hoping Lee Wright had the sense to turn himself in.

He doubted it, somehow.

Wednesday (3) _____

'The north side cleared and blocked off, Sue?' asked a red-faced Bill Wells, relishing the drama of his new outdoor role.

'Yes,' replied DC Sue Clarke anxiously, out of breath, beside him. 'Everyone is well behind the tape. Not many people about, though, thank God.'

Wells, who was positioned on the corner of Queen Street and Market Square, peered into the gloomy distance. Couldn't see a living soul. The threat of another heavy downpour must have helped. Also Wednesday was never very busy, what with the half-day closing. 'Where's Constable Miller?'

'Securing Foundling Street,' Clarke replied.

'And Simms?'

'He's checking the west side, London Street.'

'So who's over by Gentlemen's Walk?'

'Not sure, Bill. PC Baker? I saw a uniform down by Aster's.'

'But that's the other corner. Bugger,' Wells muttered, thinking Baker was two streets away, checking the multi-storey. London Street had to be less of a priority than the pedestrianized Gentlemen's Walk, where shoppers on foot would be even more vulnerable.

However, with such a paucity of uniform, not to mention of higher ranks, Wells thought they were covering a lot of ground, given how light on officers Denton Division was at the best of times. Despite the circumstances, he was feeling almost proud.

The radio in Clarke's Escort car crackled into life through the open door. Wells swiftly stepped over, leant in and lifted the handset. 'Wells,' he said.

'Wells? At last. I'm still ten minutes away,' squawked Mullett, across a very bad connection. 'Should have been there by now but some twit crashed into me, sending me off the road. Is the area completely sealed off yet?'

'Yes, sir,' Wells shouted, looking quickly over his shoulder, as if to reassure himself. 'You've had an accident, sir?'

'Yes – but let's not bother about that now.' Mullett's voice wasn't just being muffled by the static; Wells thought there was a distinctly shaky faintness to it. 'Suspect vehicle?' the super asked.

'A white van is parked bang outside Bennington's, sir,' Wells answered. 'The bank has been evacuated. Bomb squad is not here yet. They're having to come from Windsor.'

'*Windsor*?'

'They've been rehearsing for a royal pageant,' shouted Wells into the mouthpiece.

'Royal pageant? With the country on a state of alert and the IRA on the rampage?' shouted Mullett. 'Whatever next!'

Wells looked at his watch. The bomb was set to detonate in fourteen minutes. 'Joke, isn't it?'

'No, it's most definitely not,' said Mullett. 'Sweep the area once more, then get well back. Nothing else you can do.'

Wells replaced the handset. 'Sue, you stay here and chase up the fire brigade, they should bloody well be here by now. I'll run round the square once more.'

He dashed towards the square, clutching his hat and the megaphone, quietly surprised he had it in him to move so fast.

'You can't drive down there,' said Hanlon.

'Oh yes I can,' said Frost, swinging the Cortina into the recently pedestrianized Gentlemen's Walk. He'd show his passengers what advanced police driving was all about. 'Plenty of space – no old codgers in the way, either.'

'Mind your language,' said Joan Dixon in the back.

'Mind that bin, Jack,' said Hanlon.

'Who put that there?' It was narrower than Frost had thought.

'Didn't think this was much of a short cut to Eagle Lane, anyway,' said Hanlon.

'Yes, it is,' said Frost, pulling the car to a halt, just before the junction with Market Square. 'Via Woolies. I'm out of pick 'n' mix.'

'Not really the time, Jack,' mumbled Hanlon crossly.

'I want to come,' Julie shrilled from the back. 'If I'm going to be stuck in a police station all day, I'll need some sweets.'

'Fair enough,' said Frost, climbing out, his plan to entice Julie away from her grandmother working like a treat. 'Come on, then. I'll pick, you can mix.' He stood on the slippery, wet cobbles, gathering his mac tightly around him, waiting for Julie to extract herself from the cramped rear of the car. There was a freshness to the damp, cold air. It was going to pelt down again any moment. 'Grandma, want anything?' he said, lowering his gaze.

'A pardon for my son?' Joan Dixon said.

'Depends how he can help us,' Frost called over his shoulder as he and Julie headed round the corner towards the Woolies entrance on Market Square.

'Hurry up,' he heard Hanlon shout from the car.

'So what's your dad, your real dad, like?' Frost asked the girl.

'He's all right, I suppose,' she said. 'He's not that old, but it's like he doesn't know anything about anything. And he wears these horrible clothes.'

Frost caught her heavily made-up eyes looking him up and down.

'I suppose they're not that horrible,' she added quickly. 'Just not very, you know, modern.'

'He's been away a long time, hasn't he? Like he's stuck in a time-warp?' Frost had never remotely cared about what he wore, as long as it didn't reek of curry. It was Mary who took issue with his attire.

'Now, Dad,' Julie continued, more than happy to dawdle along, 'well, whatever he is now, my mum's husband, the bastard ... anyway, he like wears what he thinks are these cool leather jackets and jeans and stuff. But he looks like a right tosser.'

He does now, all right, thought Frost, in a station cell.

'Loads of my friends fancy him, though.' She paused, peered hesitantly left and right, a gawky, less than innocent look on her face. 'He's a right sleazeball. Been shagging the woman who lives opposite us, too. Poor Mum.' Her bottom lip quivered and she looked up at Frost. 'I want to see my mum. She's OK really ... she's not that badly hurt, is she?'

'She'll be all right, I expect, given some time,' said Frost, pushing on one of Woolies' double doors. 'We'll make sure you see her later. Why don't you get her something in Woolies to cheer her up? I'll lend you ten bob.'

But the door wouldn't give. Locked? Frost put his face to the glass. No one inside, yet the lights were on. He could see a couple of shopping baskets, half full, in the middle of one aisle. He checked his watch. Very strange. Then a badly parked van, just yards away, caught his eye.

'Who's looking after my cat, then?' Julie said. Frost turned from the van and looked at her blankly, confused.

'If Mum is in hospital and you've got Steve,' continued Julie, 'who's feeding Toyah?'

DC Sue Clarke stepped away from the Escort and walked the few yards to the end of Queen Street. Squinting, she looked across the square. It was hard to make out much in the damp gloom, except the white van illegally parked outside Bennington's, half on the pavement, and which was blocking the view to the entrances to the shops on that side of the square, including Boots and Woolies – long cleared, she presumed.

Wells was nowhere to be seen. Neither, damn him, was PC Derek Simms.

Light playing on the van made her think for a second that she was seeing movement, shadows beyond, but as the first fat drops of rain began to fall she turned back towards the Escort, which she'd purposefully parked at an angle right across Queen Street.

She reached the vehicle just as Mullett's Rover pulled out of Opie Street and came roaring towards her, headlights flashing. She looked around for Wells again, but he must have been taking the long route back, checking the barriers and police tape and that uniform were all in place.

She was impressed with how quickly everything had come together – thanks to Wells's organizational skills, and her own, for that matter. But she didn't like being put on the spot. The boss made her nervous.

Mullett brought the car screeching to a stop, then leapt out, hat in one hand, a map in the other. 'All clear, is it? Everyone back?'

'I think so, sir.' Clarke gazed at Mullett's new executive saloon. There was a large dent in the off-side wing.

'What are you looking at?' Mullett said.

'Your car, sir,' said Clarke. 'An accident?'

'DC Clarke' – Mullett looked at his watch – 'a bomb is about to go off. Let's concentrate on saving lives.'

At that moment PC Baker came jogging into the street from the square. 'There appears to be a car parked in Gentlemen's Walk,' he said, gasping for breath.

'Gentlemen's Walk? But that's a pedestrian street,' said Mullett. 'What the devil is a car doing there? Disabled car, is it?' He looked at his watch again. 'Who's manning the Walk? Blocked off right back by the Wells Road, I hope. Certainly don't want a bunch of pensioners ambling into this.'

'I'm not sure,' said Clarke. She couldn't think clearly. 'PC Miller?'

'Well you, Constable,' Mullett said, glaring at PC Baker, 'go all the way round, and come back down from the far end.' As Baker sprinted off, Mullett said, 'I don't suppose the bomb squad's here yet?'

'No, haven't seen them,' said Clarke, her confidence quickly ebbing away. What could she do to rescue the situation, to impress Mullett?

'Where's the fire brigade?' Mullett scanned the distance.

'They're still on their way, too,' said Clarke, 'One of the unit's been dealing with a car on fire on the Southern Housing Estate.'

'Jesus Christ, where are we, Belfast? Another torching?'

'Don't know yet,' said Clarke.

'Either way they've got more than one truck, haven't they? This is farcical. I'll be having words with the fire chief about this.' Mullett marched up the road, towards Market Square, shouting, 'It's not every day you get a bomb in the centre of Denton.'

Clarke followed close behind, though the sound of a car reversing at speed made her look over her shoulder just in time to catch the rear of a dark-blue saloon disappearing down Lower Goat Lane, the narrow street running along the back of the Fortress Building Society. She thought that part of town had been roped off.

* * *

'The cat?' I'm sure he's fine,' Frost said, thinking about the van.

'She better be. Toyah's a girl. Don't you know anything?'

'Yes, yes, but I don't know what that old banger's doing there,' Frost said to Julie, walking just a bit further on and thumping the side of the white Transit van, parked half on the pavement, half on the road, right in front of Bennington's Bank. They'd been about to head back to Gentlemen's Walk and the Cortina, but Frost couldn't let this go, being such a stickler for legal parking himself.

Walking round to the front of the van, he immediately noticed that the tax disc was three months out of date. The condition the van was in made him doubt it would pass an MOT.

'Dad used to sell vans,' said Julie. 'My *old* dad . . . before he got into sports cars. He loved them, the nutter. I think that that was where, you know, he and my mum . . .'

Frost wasn't listening. He was trying the passenger door. Locked. He zipped round the bonnet and out on to the road to try the driver's door. Locked also. Looking inside, he was struck by how empty and clean the cab was, given the age and state of the vehicle. No sign of any papers, sweet wrappers, fag packets, crumpled drink cans, the usual rubbish. He came back round on to the pavement, where Julie was idly looking at her wet boots.

'Sorry about the sweets,' he said. 'There'll be something at the station – we've got this brand-new trolley service. Hang on a sec.' He walked to the rear of the van, tried the handle, pulling hard. It made an odd sound. No, the noise was coming from somewhere else. Was it shouting?

Frost gave the rear door one last tug and, to his surprise, it opened with a creak. What the hell, he thought, and clambered inside. Hunch or not, something was just not right about this van.

The load area was empty except for, towards the front, a large cardboard box. Stooping, Frost made his way forwards.

Wells had joined Mullett and Clarke on the corner of Foundling Lane and Market Square; they had just walked round from the end of Queen Street. Now Mullett watched as Wells put the megaphone to his lips, for a third time, trying to get the attention of that imbecile Detective Sergeant Frost, who'd suddenly appeared by the suspect vehicle. What's more, he wasn't alone.

'FROST!' echoed deeply around the square, despite the now hammering rain. 'Clear the area. Clear the area. Immediately.'

'What the hell is that man playing at?' said Mullett, peering into the dim distance as Wells's amplified voice finally died away. 'It's no time to be a hero. And who's that girl? He's putting her life in terrible danger.'

'Gosh, I believe that's Julie Hudson,' said Clarke excitedly. 'They must have found her.'

'And found their way into the middle of a supposedly secured area,' said Mullett, looking at his watch, the seconds ticking away. 'Another appalling breach of procedure!'

'Frost's timing has always been awful,' said Wells.

Mullett gave him a damning look. 'I don't care about Frost, but that poor girl's life is not going to be sacrificed because of incompetence in my division, whoever's responsible.' Mullett paused, sized up the square once more, checked his watch. It was always a little fast. 'No use standing there, bellowing into that stupid thing,' he said, setting off at a trot, but soon increasing his pace to something resembling a sprint.

Yet before Mullett had even got halfway across the square he was overtaken by DC Clarke, going like the clappers. We really haven't been making full use of her, he couldn't help thinking.

Clarke reached the van first, stopping briefly by the girl, and then climbing into the back.

Mullett reached the van with Bill Wells closing in fast behind.

The girl, standing on the pavement in an extra-ordinarily tiny skirt, but with great big boots, and with a most bizarre hairdo, gave Mullett a startled look, then said dismissively, 'They're in the van.' As if Mullett didn't know.

Wells, behind him, gasping for breath, said, 'I'll get her away. I'll get her away.'

'Don't you come anywhere near me,' the girl warned him.

'Don't think it's necessary, Wells,' said Mullett, who was by the back of the van, peering in.

'Look at this, Sue,' Frost was saying, as he retrieved a pink, bald mannequin's head from the box.

Clarke was holding a life-size plastic arm. 'Do you think they go together?'

'Hello, Super,' said Frost, at last seeing Mullett, 'found some illegally parked body parts.'

'Nothing in here's going to blow up,' said Clarke, clearly trying to adopt a serious tone and edging out of the van.

'A hoax,' said Mullett. He was almost disappointed. 'A bloody hoax.' Apart from everything else his car had been pranged rushing here – *I could have been killed*. He stood back, replaced his cap squarely, and surveyed the all but empty Market Square. Suddenly the green army bomb-disposal van appeared on Queen Street, its antiquated siren clanking away.

'Super, sir,' Wells beckoned excitedly, leaving the girl, his radio glued to his ear. Mullett couldn't make out what the station sergeant was now saying into the device, with the bomb-disposal van making a hell of a racket and its driver hooting frantically for Clarke's Escort to be moved out of the way.

'Yes, Wells?' Mullett said dejectedly.

'Control's on the line: we're getting reports that the Fortress has just been hit.'

'The building society?' said Mullett. 'I didn't hear an explosion. Whose fault is this – did we have the wrong location?'

'Not blown up, sir,' said Wells. 'Robbed, by an armed gang. They've been cleaned out.'

Wednesday (4)

'Exceptional times call for exceptional measures,' said Mullett. He surveyed the packed briefing room. Every department, from the drug squad to Records, had been summoned. He'd sent Miss Smith round the building, twice. It was early afternoon, but some progress had already been made.

'You'll be pleased to know that the Anti-Terrorist Branch are sending down a chap called DCI Patterson, because of the nature of the hoax, and County are sending over Assistant Chief Constable Winslow. Both will be seconded here for as long as it's necessary.'

Mullett was livid. The last thing he wanted was beady-eyed Winslow breathing down his neck, and this fellow Patterson – whoever the hell he was – sniffing around. It wasn't as if anyone had been killed. There hadn't even been a bomb to defuse.

This raid on the Fortress Building Society happening right behind their backs – obviously using the bomb scare as a diversion – was another matter.

Mullett pointed to the incident board, and a large-scale map of Market Square and the surrounding streets. Various photographs had also been pinned up around the map: the rear of the Fortress, the Fortress's car park, three shots of Lower Goat Lane – where DC Clarke might have spotted the getaway car reversing at speed – views of the white van, the artist's impressions of the gang that had hit Rimmington and Wallop.

Standing out was the picture of a black leather mask, with two tiny holes for the eyes, a beaky extension for the nose, and a zip where the mouth should be. The raiders had all been wearing similar masks.

Mullett began, 'This is what we know, so far.' He paused almost immediately. With so many assembled bodies, the squeaking of the new chairs was driving him to distraction. He'd have to ask Miss Smith to contact the supplier, discreetly of course. He didn't want to be seen to have procured sub-standard furniture.

Where was he? He turned to the board and back to the floor. 'The gang used a most effective diversion tactic, the bomb scare. And we haven't ruled out the possibility that the torching of a car on the Southern Housing Estate was also connected.'

'Rule it out, sir,' came a voice from the far-left corner. It was Frost.

'Sorry, Frost?'

'The torching, sir. I think we've already cleared that up,' said Frost. 'The car's been identified. It's a Datsun sports, stolen from Hudson's Classic Cars sometime last night.'

'What makes you think it's not connected, Frost?' said Mullett.

'Because a little sod by the name of Sean Haynes, with a very long history of joy-riding, despite the fact he's still in short trousers, has already confessed to nicking it. Uniform picked him up an hour ago.'

'I see,' said Mullett. 'Thanks for telling me. Where's this lad now?'

'He had to be let go,' said Frost. 'Social Services couldn't lend us another chaperone. They've got their work cut out with Liz and Becky Fraser, and they're also deciding what to do with Julie Hudson.'

'Right,' said Mullett. He scratched his head. 'But that still doesn't explain why this car was set alight this morning, at exactly the same time as the hoax and the raid.'

'Bit of local jealousy,' interjected Frost. 'Seems some other thugs thought Haynes was getting too big for his boots.'

'So they decided it was the fifth of November early,' said Mullett.

'In one, Super.'

'Well, let's leave the car out of the equation, for the moment,' said Mullett. 'This still leaves the fact that there's an armed gang out there somewhere, with both the will and the intelligence to mount a serious bomb hoax, while swiftly and brutally raiding a building society . . . of over a million pounds.' Mullett paused for effect. 'Most worrying, aside from another couple of female tellers being on the wrong side of a pistol-whipping, is the fact that they did use a recognized code word – whether it's out of date or not.'

'The thing is,' interjected chubby, ruddy-faced Police Sergeant Nick Webster from Records, 'this gang is not just going to have us after them, but the IRA as well. The Provos don't take too kindly to impersonators.'

'If they were impersonators,' said Mullett. 'DCI Patterson will be looking at the possibility that the raid was conducted as part of a fund-raising effort for the terrorists.'

'I didn't think the IRA were short of cash, not with the backing they get from the Yanks,' said Webster, who, with his tightly curled mop of blond hair, looked more like a farmer than a police officer.

'Also, would an IRA outfit have targeted three building societies in one county – presuming all these raids are linked?' asked Hanlon, sitting near the front. 'Surely they would have spread themselves wider, what with their resources. There must be a strong local connection.'

'Good point, Hanlon,' said Mullett.

'Don't think, if they were IRA,' said PC Pooley, who'd been standing to the side of the room, 'that they'd use S&M masks, even if it was for the good of the cause. You know, being Catholics?'

'Who knows,' said Frost. 'Right load of hypocrites.'

S&M? Sadomasochism? Mullett had been wondering about the masks. Now it was obvious what they were really for. Perhaps he'd been underestimating the motley bunch in front of him. 'Thank you, Pooley,' he said. 'This might well give us something to go on.' Mullett's mood was brightening considerably – he wasn't going to dwell on how PC Pooley had come to the S&M conclusion.

'But sir, even dismissing an elaborate IRA connection,' protested Frost, 'this is the third armed raid in the county in as many months. Seems to me we should have more information on the form of this gang by now. What's County really know?'

'Actually, I was just getting to that, thank you. I do understand your frustration, Frost, believe me,' said Mullett. 'As I said, Assistant Chief Constable Winslow will be with us shortly, principally to coordinate the three directly affected divisions: us, Rimmington and Wallop. It's no time for one-upmanship or petty rivalries. We're all in this together. The public only deserves as much.' Mullett was of course determined for Denton to make the major breakthroughs and come out on top.

'Bit too late, if you ask me,' Mullett heard Frost mutter, and for once he was inclined to agree.

Just what was County holding back? This business about a mole, since the raid this morning, had been sitting more and more uneasily on Mullett's shoulders. County must have had some reason for implying there was a leak – no smoke without fire. Yet Mullett was determined to prove them wrong, by God he would.

Which reminded him – he hadn't yet informed Frost that Winslow wanted him to head up the Bert Williams investigation. In his heart, Mullett still thought it would be better if Frost had a few days of compassionate leave, but there was no way that would be possible now. Even if DI Allen were to suddenly materialize, all leave had been officially cancelled as of noon today. And as it was Frost was bang in the middle of everything, worryingly indispensable.

'There are three key lines of inquiry I want the Denton Division to pursue,' Mullett said sternly. He enjoyed a good fight, and it didn't do anyone any harm being the underdog. 'I want every employee of the Fortress interviewed and scrutinized, whether they were a witness or not. I want the history of that van traced double-quick, and I want every face, scout and tout in Denton given a drilling.' There was a collective groan from the floor.

'And I want to know exactly where those masks came from,' he added.

* * *

Frost sat back at his own desk for the first time in ages, or so it felt.

'Don't know what's got into Mullett,' said Hanlon, 'but he seems to be in a surprisingly good mood, for someone who's currently without a single inspector on duty and with his arse on the line, what with these big-wigs about to descend on us.'

'Funny you should mention that,' said Frost. 'He just collared me in the corridor, slapped me on the back.' Frost wasn't going to reveal the full extent of Mullett's private exchange after the briefing – he couldn't quite believe it himself. 'I'd have preferred a good bollocking. At least you know where you are then.'

'And, by the sounds of it, I thought you'd made a right cock-up, climbing into that van, leaving Julie on the pavement. Half the division, Mullett included, looking on in horror. This is the stuff of legend, Jack.' Hanlon laughed. 'Plus there's that not insignificant matter of you insisting we keep the radio switched off. Which is why we ended up in the shit in the first place.' Hanlon chuckled again, stuffing the last chunk of a sticky-looking Danish into his mouth.

'No, it's not,' said Frost. 'If those in charge had done their job properly we wouldn't have been able to pootle down Gentlemen's Walk.'

'Come on, Wells, and Clarke for that matter, by all accounts did pretty well . . . considering,' said Hanlon, pastry crumbs blowing over the desk.

Frost was just thinking he hadn't had any lunch, having missed the last trolley round, but now he wasn't sure he was still hungry. 'Don't get me wrong. It's Mullett I blame. He thinks he's so damned organized, but his problem is he's not very good at delegating. He doesn't trust people. Thinks we're all idiots. Then he panics when the shit hits the fan.'

'Did you hear about his car?' said Hanlon, his mouth still full.

'Who hasn't? The story Mullett's putting around is that a car came straight at him, in the middle of the road.'

'And he did all he could to avoid it,' finished Hanlon.

'I wouldn't be surprised if it was the other way round.'

'Wouldn't surprise me, either. Right mess the car's in.'

'Maybe someone will make a complaint.'

'It'll be hushed up quick enough.'

'I expect so.' Frost moved over to the other side of the desk and began rummaging through the nearest mountain of folders and paperwork. What had he done with Blake Richards's blue Met file?

'Anyway, I still don't know why Mullett's so cheery,' resumed Hanlon.

'Maybe he likes proving himself. He hasn't got much option at the moment. About time he looked a little closer to home for friends.' Frost lit another

Rothmans. 'Which reminds me. I've been thinking we should let Steve Hudson go home for now.'

'You're joking. Why?'

'Well, Julie's now safely in the care of Social Services – whether she likes it or not – and her mum's still tucked up in hospital.'

'I wouldn't say "safely" in the care of Social Services,' said Hanlon. 'You should have seen them.'

'Ah, thanks for dealing with them, Arthur, but you don't need to go into details.'

'We've hardly finished with Social Services yet.'

'Oh?' said Frost.

'There is the small matter of Liz and Becky Fraser.'

'Right,' said Frost.

'The problem is,' said Hanlon, 'Social Services won't intervene while Becky's still in hospital. Some new directive has just come on stream.'

'So where does that leave us?'

'Well, seeing as we're jammed up here, I had no alternative other than to let them go home. Social Services said they'll pick it up right away, and I'll get round there as soon as I can.'

'Seems a bit risky to me,' said Frost.

'Not as risky as releasing Steve Hudson, if you ask me. Why don't we just charge him?'

'With what, exactly?' said Frost. 'Plus I don't think he'll make a run for it, not again. Far too much heat on him now. Besides, I reckon he's more use to us out and about.'

'How so?'

'That car, nicked from his forecourt, the Datsun, which was torched on the Southern Housing Estate? I've got a hunch.'

'I thought that had been resolved. You told the super as much in the Fortress briefing.'

'Yes, I know,' said Frost. 'But it doesn't quite stop there. Another car's playing on my mind – and Steve Hudson's grubby little paws don't seem to be very far away from that one, either.' He paused, scratched his chin. 'The thing about this job,' Frost continued, gathering some papers, and making for the corridor, 'that's been foxing me from the beginning, my very first days in CID, is that the minute you think you've got somewhere, you're really somewhere else entirely.'

'I don't know how your mind works, Jack.'

'Neither do I.'

'Hey, where are you going?' shouted Hanlon.

'The morgue,' Frost shouted over his shoulder, hurrying down the corridor.

'What about Lee Wright?'

Damn, Frost thought, turning not left at the end of the corridor, towards the lobby and the exit, but right, in the direction of Forensics. He'd forgotten about Wright.

As she was walking briskly down the main corridor on the ground floor of the station, making her way to the exit, Clarke suddenly felt an arm on her shoulder, someone pulling her back. She turned to face Derek Simms.

'Don't keep creeping up on me, Derek, for God's sake,' she yelled.

'Keep your knickers on,' said Simms. 'I just wondered whether you wanted any help from me tracking down that gang on the Southern Housing Estate. PC Baker and I were out there earlier, helping pick up the tyke who torched that car. You don't want to go sniffing around there on your own, I can tell you.'

Clarke doubted very much that Simms's offer of help was genuine. She didn't like the way he was looking at her. 'You keeping tabs on me, Derek?'

'No – what the hell are you talking about?'

'I can't seem to breathe without you sticking your oar in. Look, if I need back-up, I'll ask for it. There are procedures.' She peered anxiously about the corridor – she didn't want to be spotted talking to Simms like this, the way rumours spread around the station. But luckily no one else was in sight.

'You were more than happy for me to come down with you to the canal yesterday,' said Simms.

'I've thanked you for that.'

'So what's changed now, all of a sudden?'

'Nothing,' said Clarke. Even if she had been planning to drop by the Southern Housing Estate, anxious that Graham Ransome wasn't forgotten in the light of the raid on the Fortress, she wouldn't have wanted Simms along. She wasn't entirely sure what had changed between them now, but something had.

'I saw you, you know,' said Simms menacingly.

'Saw me what?'

'Leap into that van, after Frost. You could have got yourself killed. I mean, what did you think you were doing rushing across Market Square?' His voice was getting louder and angrier.

'There was a girl there too, you know. It was her safety I was worried about.'

'Not what it looked like from where I was.'

'Derek, leave it, all right? This is not the time, or place. There are a few more important things going on.'

'It was disgusting,' said Simms. He had grabbed hold of her shoulder again. 'You're disgusting. A disgusting little tart.'

Without thinking Clarke raised her right hand, knocked Simms's arm away, swung wildly and slapped him hard on the cheek.

Wednesday (5)

'Second time this week,' said Drysdale, in his usual dismissive tone.

'Lucky for you,' said Frost, stepping into the freezing lab and shivering. 'Crikey, can't you get some heating in here, given what we must be paying you?'

'If you want the place to stink to high heaven. You know, Frost, you should cut down on the cigarettes. Terrible for your circulation.'

'Don't you start.'

'Two bodies, Detective; two suspicious deaths,' said Drysdale. 'Plus this raid on the Fortress that everybody's talking about. You've certainly got your work cut out.'

'Hang on a minute' – Frost felt in his pockets for his

fags – 'you're going too fast. I say, where's your assistant?' Frost had never trusted that boy. Shifty eyes, and who'd want to work in a morgue at his age?

'He's at college Wednesday afternoons.'

'Studying what? Hairdressing?'

'Can we stick to business?' said Drysdale. 'I haven't got all day.'

'Doesn't look like anyone's leaving here in a hurry.'

Drysdale walked over to the vertical bank of steel-fronted fridges, began pulling up a handle, then appeared to have second thoughts. 'Mr Ransome – no need to bother him again. Though I expect his nearest and dearest will be getting a little impatient.' Drysdale gave Frost a piercing look. 'They'll want closure, you know, those responsible properly dealt with.'

'His mutt is being very well looked after, thank you.'

'Now, Mr Frost,' Drysdale said, opening another drawer, 'this has come as something of a surprise.' He pulled the drawer out, grunting a little as he did so. The sheet had already fallen away from much of Bert Williams's considerable upper body. Drysdale stood back respectfully. 'Personally, I always liked the inspector. A troubled man in many ways, though not without charm.'

'Get on with it,' said Frost. He was the impatient one now, unable to look at Bert Williams's bruised and bloodied torso.

'Severe trauma to his upper chest, consistent with a

296

body slamming into a steering wheel – with considerable force. It's possible to work out the speed of impact, et cetera.'

Frost sighed, looked up at the harsh lights. This was not what he wanted to hear.

'Three broken ribs, one puncturing his left lung, or what was left of it – heavy smoker, wasn't he? – another narrowly missing piercing his heart. Snapped in half almost. Very nearly didn't spot the contusions around his kidneys, and bladder, or the pounding his liver must have taken.'

This was more like it. Frost closely scrutinized the pathologist, a blackness descending. 'You're saying he was beaten? Tortured even?'

'What I'm saying is,' said Drysdale, 'and I'm going to be very particular about this, Mr Williams received multiple injuries, some more serious than others, some seemingly consistent with a car accident, some not.'

'Someone made it look like an accident, didn't they?' said Frost, not sure why the Force bothered employing Drysdale's services. He turned to leave.

'You'll need to see what Scenes of Crime, and Forensics, have to say about that. Corroboration will be essential.'

'Day, exact time of death?' Frost shouted over his shoulder, knowing it didn't really matter. It was when Bert was attacked that would help Frost the most, and he had a clear enough idea.

'I'd put it at sometime on Sunday evening, Sunday night.'

Frost was by the doors, but facing into the room. 'But he didn't die immediately, did he?'

'No, he hung on for quite a while,' said Drysdale. 'Possibly even twenty-four hours, given the amount of blood in his lungs, and the clotting on the wounds.'

'So he was fatally attacked sometime Saturday afternoon,' said Frost.

'I'd be very careful about using that word "attacked",' said Drysdale.

'Come on, Doc, was he left to die, or did they think they'd already killed him?'

'Looking at the injuries,' said Drysdale, 'and at this stage strictly between you and me – I always did have time for the inspector – I'd say they intended to kill him, eventually. Not easy to get that sort of thing just right.'

'A botched job? Amateurs?' thought Frost aloud.

'Perhaps they were disturbed. But this is all supposition. I won't be held to this. I need to do more tests and your lot need to come up with some other evidence.'

'Thank you, Doc, thank you very much,' said Frost, hurriedly backing out of the freezing room. He'd misjudged Drysdale. He vowed to give the pathologist his ear in future.

For now, though, he wanted to have a word with someone who he didn't think he'd misjudged: Blake

Richards. The Aster's security guard knew more than enough about bank jobs, intimidation, bribery, extortion, rape and murder. What's more, Richards had a link to former local bad boy George Foster – it was all there in the blue Met file.

Frost, slowly making his way across the car park, knew it was a big leap, but could Foster be back, orchestrating these heists in Wallop, Rimmington and now at the Fortress in Denton?

Bert Williams had been working on something like that, Frost could see now. And then the inspector suddenly had known too much.

While Richards's involvement and motives were still to be discovered, Foster's would be clear as day. Professional thugs like Foster didn't change for the better – they only got greedier and greedier. Until they made a mistake.

It was never a good idea to return to your old stamping ground, thinking there'd be easy pickings. Because word would get around. Somebody would see you.

Frost, now in his car, his mind flying off in all directions, thumped the steering wheel. Who else was involved? Lee Wright's mum telling him about Lee being spooked because he'd run into an ex-con in Denton, a former IRA hard man, suddenly seemed very significant. Bomb alerts, recognized code words. Terrorists turned professional criminals.

Frost lit a cigarette, turned the key in the ignition and pulled out of the car park, with the light fading, winter fast descending. He was beginning to realize just what he was up against. But heading back to Denton, aiming for Aster's and Blake Richards, Frost just couldn't understand why Bert had been acting on his own.

'Bloody Frost,' said Hanlon, gripping the sides of the passenger seat. 'Went to the morgue ages ago, hasn't been seen since.'

'You don't think Drysdale's cut him up by accident?' Clarke laughed.

'If only,' Hanlon said, watching the badly lit Wells Road speed by. Clarke's driving was giving him the jitters. But at least she was accompanying him to Liz Fraser's, even after the day she must have had, and on a case that wasn't strictly hers. Though he'd agreed to then swing by the Southern Housing Estate with her.

'Keep your eyes on the road, please, Sue,' he couldn't help saying. Worryingly, she kept looking at him, smiling happily enough, the Escort roaring ahead.

'God, I'm pleased to be out of the station,' she said. 'With everyone running around like blue-arsed flies on this Fortress investigation, it's driving me nuts. They're all in too much of a panic to make any headway.'

'That car you saw reversing on Lower Goat Lane,' said Hanlon. 'I reckon that's the best lead we've still got.'

'Maybe, but without a registration number, it's not going to get us anywhere fast. I reckon we'll get further with the masks. Can't be too many places that sell them.'

'You never know,' said Hanlon. 'There, on the left. That's the turning to Forest View.'

'Nice around here,' said Clarke, rapidly slowing the car and screeching on to the bumpy, unmade lane. 'I'd like to live near the woods. Have a big, comfy house one day.'

'It's a bit mixed, I reckon,' said Hanlon. 'You get a lot of space for your money, so I've heard, and the views of course, but much of this is still council. Here' – he pointed to number twelve – 'that's Liz Fraser's house. One day it will all be tarted up, I expect.'

Clarke had to stop a couple of houses away. Cars were parked badly all over the place, some partly in front gardens, others way out into the lane.

'Forest View's got a lot more up-and-coming to do,' said Hanlon, climbing out. 'See what I mean?'

It was suddenly very dark, as they made straight for Liz Fraser's modern but scruffy terrace. It must have been underlit at the best of times, but now a couple of the streetlamps were out.

'Wow, it's chilly,' said Clarke, wind whistling through the nearby trees. 'Feels like it could snow.'

'There'll be a frost tonight, I reckon,' said Hanlon. 'Hang about.' He walked just beyond Liz Fraser's house to a car that had been half reversed on to the garden of the neighbouring home.

It was a dark-coloured Mini Metro, brown. The driver's front wing was badly dented and there were long scuff marks along the whole of that side. Hanlon could have sworn the car wasn't damaged when it sped past them on Sunday.

'Social Services meeting us here?' asked Clarke, shivering.

'That's what they said. But I'm not banking on it – one of the reasons why we needed to get here this evening.' Hanlon made for Liz Fraser's front door. 'Looks like she's got another visitor, though.'

'You can piss off,' Frost said, rushing towards the station entrance.

'Hang on a minute, Mr Frost,' said Sandy Lane, loitering in front of a panda car in the dim station yard. 'I understand that the *Star Wars* mob have struck again. In the heart of Denton, while you were fumbling around in the back of a van.'

Frost slowed, glared at the tall, sleazy reporter. 'If you hadn't spent all your time and energy whipping up scare stories about rabies, you might have been on hand to record a real incident. Recognized code words are not taken lightly. Instead you screwed up, and you're still no better informed.'

'Well, tell me, then, what happened to DI Williams?' Frost heard Lane shout behind him. 'All sorts of rumours flying around. Come on, Jack, give me a couple of minutes.'

Frost only increased his pace, slamming through the double doors into the station lobby. It stank to high heaven of flowers, and in the middle of all the tributes was Bert Williams's tired face, in black and white, grinning hopelessly.

Frost found himself nodding at the portrait, saying, 'I'm getting there, my friend. I'll nail them.' Williams would have hated the fuss, though. The flowers, the messages. He was a man who rarely betrayed his emotions.

'What was that?' said Bill Wells, pushing aside a bouquet of already wilting lilies. 'Know something I don't?'

'Bill,' said Frost, walking straight towards the cramped, no doubt frantic bowels of the building. 'There are some vicious bastards out there, believe me.' Trouble was, with Aster's on half-day closing, Frost hadn't got any closer to them. He'd had a pint and gathered his thoughts in the Bricklayers instead.

'I hear you did a good job this morning with the bomb scare,' Frost said, 'until I buggered it up. You see, that's the problem with this game: there's always some idiot throwing a spanner into the works. I'd stick to your flower arranging, if I were you.'

Instead of turning right, towards his office, Frost made for the stairs. Taking two at a time, he barely noticed constables Baker and Miller coming the other way, and then a WPC whose name he'd forgotten, if he'd ever known it.

'Steady on, Jack,' she said, as he knocked against her arm, nearly making her drop a couple of files.

'Sorry, love.' Frost was miles away already.

The door to Mullett's outer office was open and he walked straight in, glancing at Miss Smith, who was on the phone, playing with her hair with her other hand.

'You can't go in there!' she shrieked, as he opened the door to the inner sanctum.

'Oh yes I can,' he said, suddenly facing Mullett, who was perched behind his desk, a look of angry bemusement quickly spreading across his neatly bespectacled and moustached features.

As Mullett started to rise from his chair, Frost noticed that the superintendent was not alone. Spilling over the edges of a chair opposite him was a man Frost immediately recognized.

'Trying to buy your nephew out of here, are you?' Frost said to Michael Hudson, the manager of Bennington's Bank, as he realized he hadn't yet authorized Steve Hudson's release. Perhaps he wouldn't bother now. Frost had always hated any hint of nepotism, let alone moneyed patronage and privilege.

'DS Frost,' Mullett said firmly, 'could you wait outside?' Mullett paused, turned his attention to Michael Hudson, 'I'm so sorry, Michael. This is most irregular.'

'The only thing that's irregular,' said Frost, slowly backing out, 'is Bennington's investment policies. I'd still like to know the precise terms of your loan to Hudson's Classic Cars.'

'Frost, if you must know, Mr Hudson and I are discussing local security arrangements following the raid on the Fortress,' said Mullett sternly. He had come round from his desk, and was almost pushing Frost out of his office. 'This has got absolutely nothing to do with his nephew.'

'Hasn't it?' said Frost.

'I'm seeing all the local bank managers,' spat Mullett.

As the door slammed shut in Frost's face, he heard Miss Smith, sitting at her desk in the outer office, rapidly replace the receiver. 'Don't worry about me,' Frost said, patting the pockets of his mac – where the hell were his fags? 'I can keep a secret. Who's the lucky chap now?'

Miss Smith blushed scarlet. 'If you must know, I was talking to my dad. He wanted to know the latest about the bomb scare. Whether it was safe to take his dog for a walk.'

'Nowhere's safe round here any more,' said Frost, stepping into the corridor.

Wednesday (7)

'Where does he think he's going?' said Hanlon.

They'd finally been let into the house by a flushed Liz Fraser, and were just walking into the lounge when Hanlon spotted a man in the backyard, trying to climb over the fence.

Liz Fraser looked at Hanlon and Clarke, weariness and something more sinister etched on her plump face. 'For a walk?' she said.

'For a walk – at this time of night?' Hanlon quickly moved over to the opened French doors, stepped into the yard. 'Oi!'

The man, half over the fence, turned to face Hanlon. The light from the lounge was just strong enough to pick out his features: he had a hollow face, dark squinty eyes, and very short light-brown hair. He was wearing a pair of jeans and what once must have been a smart suit jacket over a thick jumper.

'I'd come back here, if you know what's good for you,' shouted Hanlon.

'Why? Who the hell are you?' the man stayed perched where he was.

'Police. DC Hanlon, Denton CID.'

'It's her you want to arrest, not me,' he said, nervously. 'She's the nutter. I haven't done anything.'

Hanlon could see Clarke standing by Liz Fraser's side in the lounge. He wondered where the child was.

'Why don't you climb back down – Simon, isn't it? Simon Trench? – and we can have a chat?' said Hanlon, walking closer to the fence. Gusts of wind were ripping through the trees.

'No one's going to believe me, are they?' Trench wailed.

'Not if you run off.'

'Simon!' Liz Fraser shouted from the lounge. She and Clarke were now by the open French doors. 'It's over, all over. Don't make it worse for yourself.'

'Where's your little girl?' Clarke asked Liz Fraser, concern clear in her voice. 'Where's Becky?'

'She's killed her!' Simon Trench yelled. 'She's fucking killed her.'

'No,' said Liz Fraser, standing very still and staring out into the yard. 'She's asleep. We just put her to bed. Like we always do.'

Hanlon didn't like the look on Liz Fraser's face one bit; he was finding her way more disturbing than dark-eyed Simon Trench.

'Go and look for yourself,' Liz Fraser said to Clarke. 'She's upstairs.'

'You're coming with me,' said Clarke, taking Liz Fraser by the arm.

Hanlon watched them walk out of the lounge, then turned to Simon Trench. He could easily have grabbed Trench's leg, but he didn't sense he was about to drop down the other side and run off into the woods. 'Do you want to tell me what's really been going on here?'

'She scares me,' Simon Trench said. 'She's evil. You don't understand what she makes me do.' He was beginning to shake, uncontrollably.

'Arthur!' Hanlon heard Clarke shout from inside the house. 'We need back-up. The girl's dead.'

Hanlon lurched for Simon Trench's ankle, and took hold of it.

'I told you,' Simon Trench said.

'Frost!' shouted Mullett, rapping on the doorframe. 'Wake up.'

Yawning, Frost slowly removed his feet from Bert Williams's desk.

Give a yard and he takes a mile, thought Mullett.

'Hello, Super,' Frost said cheerily. 'Good of you to drop by.'

'You silly man,' said Mullett. 'If you'd heard your

blasted phone I wouldn't have had to come all the way down here.'

Miss Smith had gone home for the day, despite a blanket offer of overtime to all staff, leaving Mullett to fend for himself. He'd hoped that in this time of crisis even the admin staff would be prepared to go that extra mile. Miss Smith was more than testing his good-will, the sly little vixen.

'Phone?' said Frost, looking about the desk, piled high with clutter. 'Can't seem to find it.'

'Frost, you might be in charge of the investigation into Bert Williams's death – because, frankly, there's no one else around to do it – but believe me, that doesn't mean you can do whatever you want. Barging into my office like that.' Mullett found he was scratching his head, something he'd been doing a lot recently. Reminded him of when, in the army, there'd been an appalling outbreak of lice. 'And as for that farcical show you put on in Market Square. That won't be forgotten about in a hurry.'

'At least I saved the bomb squad from getting their hands dirty,' sniffed Frost.

'Security cordons aside, what I still don't understand is why you weren't alerted to the situation by Control.' Mullett tapped his toe impatiently.

'Beats me. Problem with the airwaves?'

'When everything dies down, there'll be a proper inquiry.'

'That'll make interesting reading.'

'In the meantime, I'll be watching you like a hawk.'
Mullett turned to go.

'Is that all, then, sir?'

'No. There is one more thing.' Mullett stepped
back into Williams's office, where Frost already looked
worryingly at home. 'I don't want you badgering
Michael Hudson again. He told me about your visit
earlier this week, when you effectively accused him of
aiding his nephew's flight from the country. I'll have
you know Michael Hudson's a particularly fine,
upstanding member of the community.'

'And the Golf Club,' muttered Frost.

'I've just warned you, Frost.'

'The thing is, bankers get on my nerves. Don't trust
them an inch.'

Mullett didn't want to hear any more but, against his
better judgement, he stayed rooted to the spot. Truth
be told, Mullett wasn't overly keen on Michael Hudson
either. The trouble was, the bank manager was indeed
on the membership committee at the Golf Club. 'Do
you trust anyone, Frost?'

'Less and less.' Frost reached for a cigarette.

'Well, don't go peddling rumour and misinform-
ation, otherwise all hell will break loose,' said Mullett.
'Especially where people like Michael Hudson are
concerned. Gut feelings and instinct have no place in
a court of law.'

Mullett, the proud holder of a law degree, left Frost
to his quagmire and headed back to the sanctuary of

his pristine office, knowing that Nigel Winslow, the assistant chief constable, and this fellow Patterson from the Anti-Terrorist Branch were due to arrive imminently. For what bloody good that would do.

Wednesday (8)

'Yes?' said Frost distractedly into the phone.

His mind was elsewhere; Forensics had just deciphered Bert Williams's scrawl from the Met file. They'd come up with a name: Joe Kelly. Didn't mean anything to Frost. Yet.

'A man's just called in,' said Bill Wells. 'There's been a serious incident, Jack, out in Denton Close.'

'Denton Close?' said Frost, still not quite paying attention.

'Sounds like murder. Aggravated burglary, gone badly wrong.'

'Sorry, Bill, not with you.' What Frost really needed were those names and, hopefully, addresses from Mike Ferris, his friendly contact at British Telecom – but they'd now have to wait until tomorrow. Blake Richards's home address suddenly would have been helpful, too. Given that Aster's had been shut since lunchtime Webster in Records was having to work on that. Frost would have to put Webster on to Joe Kelly also. Records, like everywhere else in the station, was chronically understaffed.

'A young woman's dead, Jack,' said Wells. 'Probably raped. In her own home. Her husband's just rung it in. Charlie Alpha's on its way and you need to get there too, as soon as possible.'

'Where's Hanlon?'

'Haven't you heard?' said Wells. 'Hanlon and Clarke are in Forest View. That little Becky Fraser, the rabies girl, she's also been found dead, at home.'

'Dead? No, please God,' said Frost, standing and grabbing his mac with his free hand. He felt dizzy. 'Becky Fraser, are you sure?'

'Yes, I'm sorry, Jack. Hanlon and Clarke are with the parents, a Liz Fraser and a Simon Trench. Apparently they're cooperating.'

'Cooperating? I'd like to hear that.'

'You need to get to Denton Close, Jack.'

'Right, OK. I'm on my way. Where exactly?'

'Number eight.'

'Why does that ring a bell?'

'Series of noise complaints.'

'I was thinking of a curry.' Frost replaced the receiver, adjusted his crotch and rushed out of the room.

* * *

'You know,' said Clarke, driving slowly for once, 'I guess there are some cases that you'll never understand.'

'Human behaviour,' said Hanlon. 'They don't teach us enough about that at Hendon.'

The meat wagon containing Simon Trench and Liz Fraser overtook them on the Wells Road.

'It's going to take quite a few shrinks to sort this one out,' said Clarke, watching the vehicle disappear into the distance.

'Liz Fraser's been crying out for help for some time. I suppose we didn't realize that she was the one who needed protecting, from herself.' Hanlon sighed. 'But I guess they're both responsible.'

'What's the betting he gets the longer sentence?' Clarke slowed right down for a roundabout. A Cortina thundered across in front of them.

'Yeah, I suppose you're right. She'll probably just get a stint in a secure mental institution.'

'Not sure I'd fancy Broadmoor much,' said Clarke, then adding quietly, 'what's going to haunt me, though, is the fact that if we'd got there just a bit earlier that little girl would still be alive. I can't bear to think of her being suffocated – if that is how she died. And then the way they'd tucked her up in her bed, as if for the night.'

'Social Services should have been there,' sighed Hanlon. 'Their blasted new directive – there's always one. Christ, they should have been there months, years ago.'

'We should have made a stronger case,' said Clarke.

'What would have been the point? They wouldn't have listened. They only hear what they want to hear.'

'I feel sick. Not sure I'm up for the Southern Housing Estate tonight.'

'We can't protect everyone, Sue,' said Hanlon.

Wednesday (9)

Lost behind sad, stinking bouquets of flowers, Station Sergeant Bill Wells finally had a moment to contemplate his new Pools coupon. Sighing loudly, he scanned the Saturday fixtures. Low down in the leagues he noticed that Denton were playing Rimmington at home: the local derby.

Wells was rudely torn from his football considerations by the sharp ping of the desk bell. Pushing aside his Littlewoods booklet, he glanced up to see the pointy-nosed and bespectacled head of Assistant Chief Constable Winslow. He scrambled to attention. 'Evening, sir.'

'I know DI Williams will be sorely missed, but this is a little over the top, isn't it, Sergeant?' said Winslow, gesticulating at the flowers.

'The staff wanted to express their feelings,' Wells found himself saying, knowing he was responsible for the memorial. 'Williams had been with us for a long time.'

'Too long,' muttered Winslow.

'What was that, sir?'

'Tell Superintendent Mullett I've arrived, will you?'

'I do believe Sir Peter Farnsworth, the chairman of the Fortress, has just popped by to see him,' said Wells, knowing full well that Sir Peter was in with Mullett and the super had left clear instructions not to be disturbed.

'Even more reason, then, to tell him I'm here.'

Wells tried Miss Smith's extension, half remembering having seen her leave for the day. Not surprisingly, there was no reply. Winslow was looking impatient. 'Not answering,' said the sergeant. 'Look, why don't you go straight through, sir?' At least it wasn't Wells who'd be disturbing the super.

Winslow promptly marched off, leaving Wells to return to the Pools. Yet before he had a chance to find his place, another man slipped into the building. He was in his mid thirties, solidly built, with a five o'clock shadow, shoulder-length dark hair, a scruffy black leather jacket, jeans and dirty white plimsolls.

'Hello,' the man said, approaching the front desk. The distinct Irish accent didn't make Wells any more relaxed. 'I'm here to see the divisional commander, Superintendent Mullett.'

'And you are?' Wells said.

'Patterson, ATB.'

Wells frowned.

'DCI Patterson, Anti-Terrorist Branch,' the man quickly added.

'Oh, right, of course, yes,' Wells mumbled. 'Wasn't expecting . . .'

'What?' the man enquired.

'Nothing, nothing.' Wells was too embarrassed to ask for the man's ID. 'It's just that the super's a little tied up at the moment.'

'I bet he is. Tell him I'm here, will you?' Patterson said, raising his eyebrows hopefully, or perhaps it was disdainfully. 'I've just driven down from London.'

'How was the traffic?' said Wells, picking up the phone once more, though not sure whether he dared dial Mullett's personal extension.

'A joke. Much like Denton, from what I've already seen of it.'

'Line's busy,' Wells lied. 'Why don't you wait over there.' He pointed to the bench running under the notice board.

The Anti-Terrorist Branch officer swaggered over to the bench, his leather jacket swinging open to reveal that he was packing a Smith & Wesson Special.

* * *

Frost pulled up in Denton Close, almost exactly where he'd been positioned on Sunday night, and switched off the engine. Looking at the very same house, number eight, as the drizzle now smeared the windscreen, he tried to recall what he'd seen.

Once more soft orange light was seeping around the curtains of the front room, but there was no movement inside this time. He remembered the tall, thin man on the doorstep, kissing people goodbye. Then there was the woman he'd nearly knocked over when he opened the car door, and her running away – who the hell was she? He'd clean forgotten about her. And then the sensation of hot curry in his lap – he hadn't forgotten that.

What struck him now was how still and dark and quiet it was. The only sign something terrible had happened were the two PCs stationed outside the front door.

Frost shook his head as he got out of the car; his limbs were feeling heavy and cumbersome. Fatigue wasn't the only battle he was fighting.

'Evening, boys,' he called out, squinting in the rain as he hurried towards the porch. He slowed by the entrance. 'What we got?'

One of the sentries, PC Simms, appeared desperate not to make eye contact, and continued to look into the wet night, ignoring Frost's question.

'Dead woman,' PC Baker said, sniffing, his nose reddened with cold.

'So I'd heard,' said Frost, ignoring Simms's attitude – just a boy, that one. 'And the husband . . . he's inside, is he?'

'Yes,' confirmed Baker.

'His name?' asked Frost.

'Maurice Litchfield.'

'Litchfield? Heard that name somewhere this week . . . Well, let's take a look inside, shall we? Lead the way, will you, Baker.'

Baker pushed open the front door. It had something to do with the blind man, Graham Ransome, Frost suddenly remembered.

'Husband is in the lounge, on the phone, or was.' Baker indicated a room off the hall to the right.

As Frost vigorously wiped his feet on the doormat, he cupped his hand to his ear. He could make out a broken, low voice emanating from the lounge.

'The body is upstairs. Front bedroom,' said Baker.

Gingerly stepping on to the luxuriant, deep-pile, cream-coloured hall carpet, Frost made for the lounge and peered round the corner. A man in a dark suit sat on the sofa, his head in his hands, talking softly into the phone. A tumbler of Scotch was balanced precariously on the Dralon arm of the sofa. Beside him was the source of the mellow lighting, an orange lava lamp.

He certainly appeared to be the bloke in the silk dressing-gown Frost had seen on Sunday evening: thinning hair, aristocratic profile, lanky build . . .

Frost stepped back abruptly, straight into Baker, who gave an audible start.

'Blimey,' Frost mockingly protested. 'No need to keep that close.'

'Sorry, Sarge,' Baker said, whispering, 'I was just trying to see if Mr Litchfield was all right.'

'All right?' Frost hissed. 'Of course he's not bloody all right.' Frost made for the stairs, knowing he'd have to face the worst sooner rather than later. Baker followed, but giving Frost a bit of space.

'Where is she, then?' Frost stood in the doorway of the ransacked master bedroom. Drawers had been pulled out, clothes were strewn everywhere. A jewellery box lay on the floor, along with heaps of make-up and accessories. 'Where?' Frost repeated.

'In the bed, under the duvet.' Baker pointed at the crumpled, purple-coloured bedding.

Frost stepped towards the bed, careful not to disturb the debris on the floor. Gently he pulled back the covers. 'Wow . . . what a shame.' Despite the grey pallor of death, this was a striking female corpse. Frost couldn't help thinking of a classical marble statue.

'Sorry, sir?' Baker said, hesitantly. 'What was that?'

'I said . . . forget it. What's her name, first name?'

Staring at the body, Baker appeared suddenly lost for words.

'Come on, lad, I haven't got all night.'

'Vanessa.'

An image came immediately to Frost's mind of a

very attractive young woman addressing a bunch of teenage girls outside St Mary's school. Vanessa. Vanessa Litchfield. That was it: the woman who had discovered Graham Ransome's body floating in the canal, and who worked at St Mary's School for Girls.

'Any idea when this supposed attack took place?' Frost asked, frowning. 'The thing is' – he was speaking as much to himself as to Baker – 'if she was raped, it's unlikely whoever did it would bother to undress her fully first, and then take her up to bed to do it. But it takes all sorts.'

'No clear idea when this happened,' said Baker. 'The husband was out all day, working in London.' The PC flicked back through his notepad, adding, 'He reckons she was raped *because* she was in bed, naked.'

'No confirmation there, then, I take it,' said Frost. 'I'm no expert when it comes to rigor mortis, but she's been there a while.' Frost prodded the woman's shoulder. 'Stiff as a board.'

'You certainly are no expert. Stand aside, Detective.'

'Ah, the good doctor himself.' Frost turned and grinned at Doctor Maltby, who was striding into the room, shaking the rain from his Homburg. 'Been a busy week, Doc, and we keep missing each other.' Frost had a grudging respect for the old soak.

As usual Maltby's tie was askew, his wiry grey hair still defied gravity, while his bushy grey eyebrows continued to erupt from his forehead.

Bert Williams had always been highly complimentary

about the doc – they were from the same school, in many ways, Frost thought.

'Never known a week like it, Mr Frost,' Maltby said, pulling on a pair of latex gloves.

Frost stepped back from the king-size bed to allow Maltby better access, catching a blast of Johnnie Walker Black Label as he did so – the doc's preferred tipple. 'No, can't say I'd ever want another week like it either.'

While Maltby fussed around the corpse, Frost lit a cigarette and checked out the lurid seascape that hung above the bed: a naked Venus was rising from an opened oyster shell.

'Well, she's dead, good and proper,' said Maltby.

'Thank you, Doctor,' said Frost. 'I thought she might be. You fondling her like that would surely have woken her were she asleep.'

'Been dead a while, too,' said Maltby, ignoring him. 'Rigor is at its peak. Between eighteen and twenty-four hours is my preliminary conclusion.'

Frost noticed a flashing blue glow seeping around the curtains.

Maltby was opening the corpse's mouth, sticking his fingers inside, then running his hands lightly over the woman's arms and legs. 'What do you make of that?' He lifted the right leg up slightly by the ankle.

'It's a foot,' Frost said. 'Size six, I'd guess. Wait, is that a verruca I can see?'

'There's reddening around the ankle, Mr Frost.

'Caused by chafing. And here, on the other one, too.'

'From what, do you reckon?' Frost stepped closer.

'You better wait for Drysdale's report, he's—'

'Paid more than you?' Frost finished, though feeling vaguely disloyal for mocking Drysdale's position; the pathologist had done Frost a huge favour earlier in the day.

'Quite. Her toes are disfigured, too, and there are the beginnings of bunions – probably down to her footwear.' Maltby stood back, peeled off his gloves. 'Bit of a mystery this one. She hadn't swallowed her tongue. No real sign of trauma. No bruising around the neck, though there is another slight chafing mark. Almost as if she'd been wearing a collar or necklace that was rather tight.'

'Unlike you not to have an opinion at least,' quipped Frost. 'Are you working to rule?'

'As I said, been a long week, already.' Maltby adjusted his glasses. 'Though I'll offer you this: if she was raped, she certainly didn't put up a fight. The chafing and faint marks around her neck are not consistent with any serious attempt at restraint.' Maltby made for the bedroom door. 'You'd be surprised by what people get up to in their own homes.'

'I'm not sure anything would surprise me any more,' said Frost, as Maltby left the room and made for the stairs.

'Very sorry about Bert, by the way,' Maltby called over his shoulder.

'We all are,' Frost replied, turning to face Baker, who was now bending down inside the built-in wardrobe on the far wall of the bedroom. 'Not knicker sniffing, are you?'

'What do you make of this, Sarge?' Baker said, straightening and holding up a black-leather face mask with a zip where the mouth should be. He walked over and handed it to Frost.

Frost took it, perplexed. Then suddenly he thought of S&M, and the gang that had hit the Fortress. A coincidence too far, surely.

Baker had now also discovered a black rubber basque, handcuffs, an array of large pink phalluses and a pair of thigh-high white PVC boots, so pointed that Frost found it crippling even to look at them. The thought of Vanessa Litchfield trussed up in this gear was more than enough to fuse his tired brain.

'Kinky, eh?' Baker leered, waving a huge, black strap-on penis at Frost.

'Put that back, you've no idea where it's been,' Frost said sharply. 'Forensics will have some probing questions for you after they brush that thing down.'

Baker dropped it instantly.

'Wonder if she wore it,' said Frost.

'What, that?' Baker pointed to the strap-on at his feet.

'No. The mask, you idiot. You'd be surprised what headgear people pop on to nip out to the bank.' Frost wondered if it was bought locally or by mail order. He thought one thing might lead to another and shoved the black-leather mask into his mac pocket. He moved over to the bed. The enamel on the iron frame at the head had been worn right away at various points. Through various playful restraints rubbing against it?

'Where do you get this sort of sex gear round here?' said Frost.

'There is a place at the far end of Foundling Street, blacked-out windows, a Private Shop, I think,' said Baker, deliberately not looking at Frost.

'Why don't I know about that? Don't answer. So, what's the husband's story?'

'He works in the City, a stockbroker. Up and out by five thirty every morning, back shortly after seven. Says he discovered his wife dead when he got in tonight, and dialled 999 straight away.'

Frost paced back and forth at the foot of the bed. There was a faint creak from the iron frame. 'That doesn't seem to stack up,' he eventually said. 'Of course we'll get confirmation later, but given the state of rigor I seriously doubt she died during the day today. Not even first thing this morning – which, I suppose, might at least have explained why she was naked and in bed.'

Frost went back over to the painting, Venus rising from her oyster shell. 'Why does Maurice Litchfield think she's been raped? Because she's naked, and wasn't when he left her this morning? Because he's had an exploratory sniff?'

'To be honest, he hasn't said much at all,' said Baker. 'We were waiting for you.'

'How thoughtful.' Frost lit another cigarette, exhaling heavily. 'There's something very fishy about this, I'm afraid, and I don't mean that strap-on.'

Baker winced.

'We'll have a quick word with Maurice,' continued Frost, 'see if anything more comes to light immediately, otherwise let's wait until Drysdale and Forensics have their say before we get down to any serious questioning. I want uniform posted out here all night.'

Baker now groaned audibly.

'I do believe I hear the patter of Scenes of Crime's feet on the stairs,' said Frost, turning towards the landing. 'They'll have plenty to amuse themselves with.'

_____Wednesday (10)

Sue Clarke, at home and in bed at last, couldn't keep the image of the dead little girl out of her head. Seeing Graham Ransome being pulled on to the canal bank by the police frogmen was one thing, but a dead two-year-old was quite another.

It was the way Becky Fraser's eyes were shut, and how there was almost a smile on her little face. She'd been neatly tucked up in bed – no sign of the struggle that must have ended her life.

Making it all so much worse, of course, were the parents: Liz Fraser and Simon Trench. They'd been arguing about who'd incited what, who'd pushed who into that one last, fatal time. There'd been a long catalogue of abuse, a slow, steady downward spiral.

The history of this troubled and lethal partnership would be pored over by the courts for months. But what had quickly become clear, what Liz Fraser and Simon Trench both admitted to, was that they had tucked up the small child's limp body, in bed, for ever. Then kissed her goodnight and goodbye.

Clarke threw off her duvet, found her dressing-gown, and went into the kitchen to make a cup of tea. Her mind was whirring away, coming to the conclusion that while Liz Fraser had long wanted to be caught and stopped, Simon Trench had begun to hate himself so much he didn't care what happened to him at all.

That, at least, was Clarke's bit of amateur psychology, for free.

Wrapping her dressing-gown tightly around her, she half thought about ringing Derek Simms, to say she was sorry for losing her temper in the corridor that afternoon, and would he like to come over and warm her up.

But as she sipped her hot drink, she realized she was never going to apologize to him, let alone ask him over again. He was a right prat, putting it about all over the place, too. Besides, he only ever really fancied himself.

Back in the bedroom, her thoughts turned to Jack Frost. Now there was a man who never took himself too seriously, yet he was full of integrity. She couldn't help wondering whether he was in bed right now . . . with his wife. What the hell was she like?

Clarke hoped his wife made him happy. Or one day, she might just have a go herself.

'A sex shop, on Foundling Street?' Hanlon exclaimed. 'How did I miss that?'

'Too busy looking for that bakery,' said Frost, stretching back in Bert Williams's old chair, hands behind his head, feet on the desk, a hole in both soles of his shoes.

It was late, very late, and Jack Frost, Arthur Hanlon and ruddy-faced Police Sergeant Nick Webster from Records were crammed into Bert Williams's office, the room as smoky as a nightclub.

'Blacked-out windows,' said Webster quietly, perched on the edge of the large desk. 'You wouldn't know it was there unless you were looking for it.'

'But you knew, all right,' said Frost, nodding at Webster. 'Dirty sod.'

The wind whistled outside, making the cramped, dimly lit, smoked-filled office feel almost cosy.

'The thing is, Arthur,' Webster continued with a grin, ignoring Frost, 'these places are always there if you look for them.'

'Never been detailed to Vice,' said Hanlon.

'Is that regret I hear in your voice?' said Frost.

'Grow up,' muttered Hanlon crossly.

'Pointy boots, shackles, masks and big rubber cocks aren't everyone's cup of tea, I suppose,' mused Frost. 'But give Arthur a sausage roll, and he'd do things to young Miss Smith that'd make your ears bleed.'

'Don't mean to interrupt, but did I hear the word "tea"?' asked Grace, hovering by the door. 'You men want a last one? The boss has said I can go on all night, and there'll be no problem claiming overtime.'

'I bet he has,' said Frost.

'All right, cheeky,' she said, 'but it's gone midnight, and I'm dead on my feet. Overtime or not, I'm not planning on sticking around for ever.'

'Love one, thanks,' said Frost, 'and let's see if Bert left something behind we could top it up with.' He began riffling through the desk drawers and almost instantly retrieved a three-quarters-full bottle of Scotch. 'Think we could all do with some of this.'

'By all accounts,' said Hanlon, still vexed, 'Miss Smith has enough men bothering her.'

'Wasn't aware she was complaining,' said Frost.

'Mullett's had words with her about it, apparently,' revealed Webster. 'Doesn't like that sort of thing going on right under his nose.' He paused, sniffed. 'I hear she even had a thing with Pooley, of all weirdos.'

Frost leant across the desk to top Webster's tea up with Scotch.

'And then there's Simms,' continued Webster. 'Though everyone knows he's also been poking . . .' His voice trailed off, and he took a gulp of tea.

'The way you're going on,' said Grace, 'anyone would have thought you had a soft spot for our Miss Smith.'

As laughter erupted Grace quickly pulled the trolley out of the room and disappeared down the corridor. Webster's chair, one of Mullett's new orange ones, which he'd dragged in from the corridor, then gave an alarming squeak.

Calming down, Frost said, 'Don't get married too young, that's the key, I reckon.'

'Doesn't stop some people, Jack,' Hanlon smiled.

'Well, perhaps some people shouldn't get married at all,' Frost said, flicking ash on to the floor. 'Who's for another top-up?'

'Yes, please,' said Hanlon. 'I'm gasping. Nasty business at Liz Fraser's. Sue Clarke's taken it rather badly. She was very upset.'

'Not often you see a dead child, even in this business,' said Frost. 'I should have done more,' he added, before taking a large swig of his fortified tea. 'Got that Doctor Philips at Denton General to keep her in longer. I don't know, there must have been something I could have done. Trouble was, I took my eyes off it.'

'Don't be too hard on yourself, Jack, we all should have done more. There was a lot going on, and neither Liz Fraser nor Simon Trench were on Social Services' radar,' said Hanlon. 'Social Services have a lot to answer for, too.'

'They'll pass the buck – as ever,' sighed Frost. 'Thing is, I always knew Liz Fraser wasn't entirely blameless, for the kid to be in that state when we first found her. But to kill a child . . .'

'She'd made those emergency calls in the past, hadn't she?' said Webster. 'Complaining about prowlers and suspected burglars. What was that all about?'

'Cries for help,' suggested Hanlon. 'Help from herself.'

'We're not shrinks,' said Webster. 'How were you meant to work that one out? We couldn't even track Trench's car.'

'I suppose this station's a touch overstretched,' said Hanlon, ironically. 'Anyway, Mullett doesn't seem overly concerned with the case.'

'He never was,' said Frost. 'Don't think he likes children much.'

'He just wants everything that's not to do with the Fortress investigation filed and put to one side,' said Hanlon.

'Anything to please those effing bankers,' grumbled Frost.

'Mullett doesn't know whether he's coming or going at the moment, if you ask me,' said Webster. 'You can't just leave investigations midway.'

'Mullett and his blasted paperwork.' Frost took another long sip of tea.

'He should be running a bank, not a cop shop,' laughed Webster.

'At least we don't have DI Allen sticking his oar in,' said Hanlon. 'Let's be thankful for that.'

'I thought all leave had been cancelled,' said Webster.

'It has,' confirmed Hanlon. 'But for some reason Allen has evaded the call-up.'

'That's a surprise,' said Frost.

'Maybe not,' disagreed Hanlon. 'Heard a rumour that he's having marital difficulties: Mrs Allen's got a bit bored. And that he's going through some sort of a breakdown.'

'You're joking! Bloody hell . . . can't believe you kept that to yourself, Arthur.' Frost laughed, drained his mug, looked up at the ceiling and rolled his eyes.

'Everyone's at it,' piped up Webster.

'Not everyone,' said Frost. 'I doubt Mullett even knows where his own prick is.'

'Did I hear my name?' The superintendent appeared in the doorway.

Frost attempted to hide the bottle of Scotch behind a stack of papers. 'Just talking about the old super,' Frost beamed. 'And how good it is to have a vigorous new boss.'

'Some sort of celebration going on?' Mullett said, eyeing the Scotch and wincing at the fog of smoke. 'When I sanctioned overtime, this wasn't what I envisaged.'

'Actually, sir, we were toasting DI Williams. Care for one?' Webster said, solemnly, and winking at Frost.

'Ah, yes, well,' said Mullett, 'under the circumstances I think I will. Been a hell of a week.'

Frost scanned the room for a glass, and finding

none, finished his own and proffered the tea-stained mug to Mullett, who nodded with thinly veiled distaste. Frost poured a generous measure.

'To Bert,' Frost said, raising the bottle to his lips.

'To Bert,' they all replied.

Mullett briefly hesitated before downing the contents in one.

'What a day, sir,' said Hanlon.

'You could say that,' Mullett huffed, clearly looking for a top-up. Frost dutifully obliged. 'Finally got shot of Assistant Chief Constable Winslow and DCI Patterson for the night. Though they'll be back first thing.'

'Treading on your toes, were they?' smirked Frost. 'I know just how that can feel.'

Mullett looked at Frost sternly, before glancing around the room. 'Well, gentlemen, I'll say goodnight. Let's hope for some major breakthroughs tomorrow. I want this Fortress raid cracked. Over a million was taken, firearms were used and people beaten up. We must get this resolved. The reputation of the whole division depends on it.'

'Sure you don't want another, sir?' Frost said, sensing the superintendent wasn't quite ready to depart after all.

'Go on then, just a splash,' Mullett smiled. 'We'll organize a traditional guard of honour at Bert's funeral, of course . . . Any news there, Jack? I've seen the pathologist's preliminary report – rather open to interpretation.'

'Not yet, sir,' Frost said, making a last round with the bottle. He was keeping his suspicions firmly to himself for the moment – Bert had obviously had his reasons for keeping things quiet. 'Bottoms up.'

Mullett took a gulp and placed the mug on the cluttered desk. 'Well, goodnight, gentlemen,' he said again. 'Careful driving home. They reckon there's going to be a frost tonight, first of the year. There're a lot of lunatics about as it is; someone nearly took me out for good this morning. Made a right mess of the whole of one side of my car. They didn't stop, either. Had I not been on the way to Market Square I'd have turned round and given chase.'

'Bet you haven't done that in a while,' said Frost.

'It wasn't a brown Mini Metro by any chance?' enquired Hanlon.

'Could quite possibly have been . . . it all happened so fast. Why?' said Mullett, suddenly looking a little sheepish.

'I think I know the owner.'

'Well, let's not bother him at the moment. There are more important things to be getting on with.'

Mullett was gone as swiftly as he had arrived.

'The way he reacted there,' said Frost, 'anyone would think that Mullett had been at fault.'

'Should be easy enough to find out,' said Hanlon. 'The driver's in the cells: Simon Trench.'

'Of course,' said Frost, 'the chocolate Mini Metro.'

'The chocolate Mini Metro,' Webster echoed.

'Though the way Trench drives,' said Hanlon, 'I wouldn't be surprised if he was to blame. The ratty little man's got a deathwish.'

'Bloody shame he didn't kill himself before he killed his daughter,' Frost sighed.

'I think we need another drink,' Webster said, getting to his feet. 'Allen keeps a bottle—'

'Does he now,' said Frost. 'Well, as the most senior-ranking officer here, I authorize you to gather the evidence at once.'

Wednesday (11)

Night Station Sergeant Johnny Johnson, standing behind the front desk in the draughty lobby, could hear singing coming from somewhere. He looked at his watch and yawned. It was nearly 2.00 a.m.

Was it drunken louts passing Eagle Lane? But at this hour? The pubs, of course, had shut long ago. Unless there'd been another lock-in at the Bricklayers.

It was getting louder. He turned down the portable transistor radio, which he kept under the desk for company through the long night shifts.

Suddenly the interior door clattered open and three dishevelled figures lurched as one across the lobby: Arthur Hanlon, Jack Frost and Nick Webster, the big guys propping up Frost in the middle.

'It's the Old Bill,' said Frost.

'Hello, Bill,' called out Hanlon.

'Aye-aye,' said Webster.

'It's Johnson,' said Johnson firmly.

'Johnson?' queried Frost, trying to focus in the general direction of the counter. 'Johnny Johnson, night sergeant? Well I never.'

'Where have you been hiding yourself?' slurred Hanlon.

'Strange rumours flying around this place,' stuttered Webster. 'Concerning a right randy Mrs Allen, for one.'

There was a roar of laughter.

'Out!' shouted Johnson. 'Out, the lot of you, before I have you arrested and slam you in the cells for being drunk and disorderly.'

Johnson watched in disgust as the three officers pushed open the station doors and disappeared into the freezing dark.

Barely had the doors stilled when the phone went. 'Denton Police,' Johnson said promptly.

'I know that, you fool,' said the voice on the other end. 'Tell Jack Frost,' the man quickly continued, 'there's a present for him lying in the gutter outside the Coconut Grove.' The line went dead.

Johnson rushed to the entrance, but the pissed trio were nowhere to be seen.

Thursday (1)

The Cortina had reached seventy, far too fast for this dirt track of a lane at night. Frost felt perspiration break out on his forehead as he peered desperately ahead. The rain was pelting the windscreen, and the wipers seemed useless, thudding to and fro, making a peculiar knocking sound with every stroke. The car accelerated further into the darkness.

'For Christ's sake slow down!' Frost yelled at the driver.

'But we must go faster – they're gaining on us.'

Frost looked over his shoulder, and, sure enough, the Transit was practically upon them. The van's cab light was on and Frost could make out four masked faces. The Cortina gave a further surge. Christ, he had to get Bert to hospital. The noise from the wipers was getting louder. Frost turned to his driver, and recognized the man they'd pulled out of the canal.

'But Mr Ransome, you're blind! You can't drive!'

'You can do it, Jack, I know you can,' Bert Williams suddenly wheezed from the back seat, coughing up blood.

'I hope you're feeding my dog, Detective,' Graham Ransome said with a smile, displaying his lack of teeth.

Frost woke abruptly, drenched in sweat, the rapping on the windscreen jolting him back to life. He struggled to open the Cortina window, which had frozen, and revealed the station's milkman standing in the early-dawn light.

'You all right in there, Mr Frost?'

'Yes, Neville . . .' Frost stretched his stiff limbs. 'Could you let me have a pint on account?'

'No problem,' the milkman said. 'A bit of a cold one to be camping out?' The milkman indicated the frost on the window. 'Your scarf caught my eye, it's trapped in the door. Then I took a closer look and saw the interior light on.'

'Catching up on my reading – must have dozed off,' Frost said. He got out of the car, took the pint and made his way stiffly into the station.

Thursday (2)

'You never know what goes on in people's homes,' Frost said to DC Sue Clarke as she pulled out of the lab car park and steered the Escort back towards town, accelerating hard.

It had been a difficult appointment first thing on a frosty morning, with Drysdale now presiding over four bodies, four suspicious deaths. The blind man Graham Ransome, who'd died after a struggle on the towpath. Bert Williams, who'd had his chest caved in by one or more assailants, at least as far as Frost was concerned. Becky Fraser, doped with sleeping pills and then suffocated by her own parents, seemingly acting in collusion. And a naked Vanessa Litchfield, asphyxiated in her bed at home, with no evidence of serious resistance. There had been only a small amount of alcohol in her bloodstream, but there were other fluids inside her, all right.

Christ, thought Frost, not for the first time. Two fatal beatings and two asphyxiations. Yet the circumstances of all four deaths could not have been more different, and so far they only had the culprits connected to one death. And on top of it all, Mullett breathing down his neck – bomb scares and robberies. The night in the Cortina and the Scotch hadn't been wise. But they had Lee Wright – brought in last night. That, at least, was something.

'It beats me just what some people get up to,' Frost added, thinking now of Vanessa Litchfield and glancing across at Clarke, waiting for a response. None came. 'An affair or two I can understand,' he persisted. 'In fact, I read somewhere that very attractive women are more likely to be promiscuous. But this—'

'Where would you have read that?' Clarke snapped.

'As I've said before, you'd be surprised what I read in my spare time.' Frost raised an eyebrow. He couldn't work out how Clarke was taking the news that Vanessa Litchfield appeared to have been something of a nymphomaniac.

According to Drysdale, there were clear indications that Vanessa Litchfield had consented to have sex with several men. The chafing marks around her ankles and neck had come from light restraints. Together with Frost's initial observations of what was still being referred to as the crime scene – the wear on the bedstead and all the equipment from the cupboard – everything was pointing to a sex game gone horribly wrong in a house used to host swingers' parties, orgies and S&M sessions.

Drysdale had suggested that Vanessa Litchfield had died while trying to achieve a heightened orgasm through oxygen starvation. It was a known practice, apparently.

'What you read is neither here nor there,' said Clarke. 'How are we going to break it to the husband that his wife had five different men's semen—'

'Do me a favour, one of them is bound to be Maurice's,' Frost interrupted, amazed at her naivety. 'I told you about the clobber we found at the house: handcuffs, masks, dildos, whips, the works. Maurice Litchfield would have been one of Vanessa's most grateful beneficiaries, not to mention, I don't doubt, a keen observer of all the sordid goings-on.'

'Being kinky is one thing, letting any old randy sod shove his prick inside you is quite another,' she said crossly.

'If you say so.' Frost paused briefly before adding, 'Frankly, we don't know much about her or her husband at the moment. All we do know for certain is that Vanessa Litchfield was asphyxiated, and within the last few days had at least five different sexual partners. Her husband, Maurice Litchfield, meanwhile, is maintaining that she was raped and murdered.'

There was an odd tension between himself and Clarke this morning. And he didn't think it was to do with the graphic nature of the Litchfield case. It was something else. His mind flicked back to Market Square yesterday morning, Sue Clarke suddenly clambering into the van, the look of concern on her lovely face.

Lighting a cigarette as the crisp countryside sped by, Frost remembered that Mike Ferris at British Telecom still hadn't provided him with any names and addresses for those telephone numbers from Bert's notebook.

Frost wondered whether he should get Clarke to drop him off in town on their way back to the station, but first there was another quick stop he thought they might as well make.

'We pass right by St Mary's School in a moment, don't we?' he said, flipping down the visor to cut out the low autumnal sun's blinding glare. The weather had cleared towards dawn, while the temperature had plummeted yet further, producing, as forecast, a treacherous, sparkling frost. 'Let's see if that old bat Sidley can shed any light on Vanessa Litchfield's' – he coughed – 'character.'

The headmistress was in the middle of taking a class – classics, according to the decrepit stooge Jenkins.

Clarke decided to wait in the musty hall, to mull

over the investigations on her plate, while Frost paced about on the gravel forecourt in front of the grand building, chain-smoking. Frost really seemed too pre-occupied with the demise of Bert Williams, she thought, to provide any great inspiration. That was until this morning, anyway: the Litchfield case had clearly sparked his interest.

Though he stank to high heaven of whisky, and looked an absolute shambles. He hadn't shaved and she could have sworn he was in the same clothes he'd worn yesterday, and the day before that, come to think of it. She couldn't help wondering where he'd spent the night. On the sofa? In the car?

She sighed, trying to get her mind back on track. What was bothering her was her lack of progress with the Graham Ransome investigation. Apart from that bit of a football scarf, still with Forensics, she had little else to go on. But, even though it was her case, there was no way she could have trawled around the Southern Housing Estate with DC Hanlon, or anyone else for that matter, last night. After the Forest View tragedy she'd been exhausted, physically and mentally. And she certainly wasn't going to ask another favour of Derek Simms.

Jenkins suddenly reappeared to inform her that Mrs Sidley was free to see them. Clarke went outside to grab Frost, who was now over by the car, on the radio. He waved her away, so she left him to it.

In her study, Mrs Sidley was as regal as she'd been

on their previous visit, though this time she remained imperiously seated behind her desk.

The headmistress had heard that Julie Hudson was alive and well, but had not yet heard of the death of Vanessa Litchfield. Clarke relayed the basic facts, though was careful not to mention anything about the PE teacher's sexual proclivities.

Mrs Sidley took her time to digest the news, before saying, 'That is truly terrible. I'm deeply shocked. Vanessa was such an energetic, enthusiastic young woman. And a great asset to the school.'

Frost banged his way into the room, giving both women a start. Barely acknowledging him, Mrs Sidley none the less stood up slowly and made a move for the drinks cabinet.

It wasn't yet eleven in the morning, Clarke noted.

'She was extremely dedicated,' Mrs Sidley continued, 'always the first to volunteer for extra-curricular activities.'

'Yes, I'm sure she was,' Frost chipped in.

'And a good morning to you, Detective,' she said brusquely. 'Sherry?'

'Don't mind if I do,' Frost replied.

Clarke shook her head despairingly.

'As it happens, it's her extra-curricular activities that we're interested in,' said Frost. 'Did she belong to any clubs?'

'Clubs? Do you mean a tennis or a chess club?' Mrs Sidley raised her eyebrows, clearly perplexed at Frost's question. 'I'm sure Mr Litchfield would be able to enlighten you as to Vanessa's social activities. As far as the school goes—'

'Chess wasn't quite what I had in mind,' said Frost. 'Mr Litchfield is obviously extremely upset. We haven't been able to interview him properly yet.'

Clarke still couldn't understand Frost's habit of questioning someone while his attention appeared to be focused elsewhere – he seemed far more interested in the bookshelves.

'You've met Mr Litchfield, then?' he said, peering at the spine of some old tome.

'Once or twice, socially, yes,' volunteered Mrs Sidley, returning to the seat behind her desk.

'Ah, so you do know something of the Litchfields' social life?'

'I'm sorry, Detective, I'm not quite sure what you're driving at.'

Frost reached up on tiptoes to remove a volume. 'Nine out of ten murders are committed by someone the victim knows. *That is*,' he added with emphasis, 'if indeed we're talking about murder. We're just trying to ascertain who the deceased knew. And what better place to start than the workplace. Unusual choice of literature you have here: *Justine* by the Marquis de Sade?'

'That is very valuable, please do be careful,' Mrs Sidley urged. 'A first edition in the original French. My father left it to me. Many consider de Sade's work to be the real precursor to Freud's. Surrealists hail him as enlightened and the embodiment of true freedom, and some prominent women writers can see a feminist approach in his work.'

'Is that so? Thought he was just a dirty old Frenchman, myself. Napoleon had him banged up, if memory serves right. On the reading list, is he?'

'This is my private study, Mr Frost,' Mrs Sidley answered sharply. 'I may keep in here what I wish.'

Clarke had mixed feelings. On the face of it she was bemused by the headmistress's taste in literature, but there was something surprisingly attractive about Mrs Sidley's erudition and confidence. The woman had class. And Frost, she felt, knew it too.

'Mrs Sidley, was Vanessa Litchfield close to anyone in particular here?' Clarke asked.

'Mrs Sally Cooper. That's Julie Hudson's form teacher, whom you met here the other day.'

Clarke remembered the short, plump blonde in her ridiculously tight, purple-corduroy trouser suit.

'I believe Mrs Cooper and Vanessa were good friends,' added Mrs Sidley.

'This Mrs Cooper, does she have pampas grass on her front lawn, too?' Frost asked, having replaced the book, and pulling out a Rothmans.

Clarke turned to him in surprise and then to Mrs Sidley, who was sitting very still. Eventually the headmistress helped herself to a cigarette from the silver box on her desk, lighting it from a small gold lighter.

The silence was becoming more awkward by the second.

'Well, if you think of anything that might help, give us a tinkle,' said Frost at last. 'Come on, DC Clarke, no point sticking round here. Before you know it we'll be trussed up and whipped.'

That's really helpful, thought Clarke. He didn't seem to have any control over what came out of his mouth, or didn't care, at any rate.

'Wait a minute, Mr Frost, please,' Mrs Sidley stood up as they were nearing the door, her aquiline nose catching the daylight from the windows.

Clarke was taken aback. Had Frost cracked this woman's painfully tough exterior?

'May I ask whether you think there's a connection between Mrs Litchfield's death and such ... practices?' Mrs Sidley said quietly.

'No, we have no evidence to suggest that. But what might start out as a bit of basic fun can often result in confused emotions, jealousy, et cetera, and who knows where that might lead,' said Frost.

Clarke realized that perhaps there was method to Frost's heavy-handed approach. She had misjudged him, again.

'Quite,' Mrs Sidley said, head now bowed.

'What exactly can you tell me?' Frost prompted.

'I'm afraid not much. Only an admission that I know it goes on among a few members of staff, out of hours of course, and most definitely not on school property.' She fixed Frost with a very stern look.

What an old vamp, Clarke thought. Mind you, Frost appeared to be visibly softening.

'Understood. But I may well want to have a word with Mrs Cooper,' he said, 'to get a handle on the local scene and practices. In the meantime, if you think of anything, please do get in touch.' He smiled sweetly.

'Goodbye,' Mrs Sidley said, with definite finality.

'What the hell was all that about?' Clarke said. They stood at the foot of the steps outside the main entrance, which was flanked on either side by a pair of badly weathered large stone lions.

Frost, despairing of his lighter, emptied the contents of his mac pockets on to the back of the nearest lion, found a Swan Vesta and struck it on the animal's flank.

'What do you mean?' he asked innocently.

'You mentioned pampas grass and she completely changed her tune!'

'And I thought I was the unworldly one,' he said as they walked across the gravel forecourt. 'Pampas grass might just be an ornamental shrub to you or me, something fluffy to decorate the front lawn . . . but to others, to those in the know' – he winked – 'it's a sign, an indication of intent.'

She looked at him, still not quite understanding.

'Swingers,' he clarified. 'You know, couples who are up for it with anyone. Group sex, orgies, all that. You're advertising it and you're not, if you see what I mean.

So either Mrs Sidley would get the reference or she wouldn't. And clearly she did.'

'Sidley, at her age?'

'Didn't think there was an upper age limit on that sort of thing,' said Frost.

'No,' said Clarke awkwardly, 'but it's not the sort of thing you want to dwell on.'

'No,' coughed Frost. 'Unless you're an old codger, I suppose.'

'Anyway, I'm impressed with the knowledge – if a little wary. How the hell did you know?'

'Scenes of Crime called while we were waiting for our audience with the headmistress; they'd found the archetypal little black book in the Litchfields' bedroom. Sally Cooper was listed under contacts headed *Pamper us*. They then asked if I'd noticed the pampas grass out on the lawn. I had, actually, on Sunday night. A woman had been creeping around it at the time. Which reminds me—'

'Hang on,' said Clarke, struggling to keep up. 'I still don't get where that leaves us with Vanessa Litchfield. How exactly she died, and just who was responsible.'

'No, but at least we know old Mrs Sidley is not as innocent and stuck-up as she looks.'

'Takes all sorts, I suppose,' said Clarke. 'Didn't know French history was your thing, though. You even knew all about Napoleon and de Sade.'

'I told you' – he smiled as she opened the car door – 'you'd be surprised what I read in my spare time.

Really we should have a word with Mrs Cooper, but that'll have to wait.'

'Oh, are those your gloves on that stone lion?' Sue Clarke said, stifling a yawn.

'Gloves?'

'Black-leather pair, by the looks of it.'

Frost turned to face the forbidding building. 'Shit, wouldn't want to leave those there – could get me expelled,' he said and hurried back. 'Right, now back to the nick for us – Johnny Johnson told me first thing this morning we have Lee Wright waiting for us in the cells.'

'You were in early,' Clarke said, surprised.

'Very.' Frost opened the Escort door for her. 'Just didn't have the energy to give him a grilling.'

Thursday (3)

'Jesus!' PC Simms exclaimed, as he felt the heavy glass door crack him in the back. He and PC Baker had been standing on the street, in Market Square, just outside Woolworths.

Simms spun round to see a skinny youth, with spiky yellow hair, trying to make a very quick exit. 'Steady on, son.' He grabbed the boy by his tracksuit top. 'What's the rush?'

'Late for school, aren't I,' the youth sneered.

'By about six months,' Simms said. It was that little tyke Kevin Jones, from the Southern Housing Estate, who, Simms was certain, had stopped attending Denton Comprehensive months ago, despite being only thirteen.

Gloria Jones, the boy's mother, was a serial shoplifter. His father, Mike, was a bouncer who took too much pleasure in his work. DI Allen had helped put Jones, Senior, away for ABH last year, after a brawl outside the Coconut Grove – not that he got long.

'What have you got there?' Simms asked, pointing to the pockets of the kid's tracksuit top, a Denton FC scarf doing little to disguise the bulges.

PC Baker had closed in for a better look as well.

'Keen to make amends, are we?' said Simms. 'Catching up on all the schoolwork you've missed over the years? Don't tell me. Pens, rubbers, pencil cases, perhaps a few sweeties to aid the concentration?'

The boy said nothing and stared down at his scuffed trainers, as if expecting the answer to leap out from under one of the grubby soles.

'Your own special night school, is it? Or perhaps – more likely – stuff to flog on the cheap outside the school gate,' Simms snapped. 'Hasn't your mum got enough to worry about without you nicking stuff from Woolies? Or did she show you the ropes, the mum's guide to shoplifting?'

'Right, you're coming with us,' PC Baker said, grabbing Jones's left arm.

The boy suddenly lost his swagger, clutching his right hand to his chest.

'What's the matter with your hand?' Simms said.

Jones looked sheepish, now trying to hide his clearly swollen and badly grazed right hand underneath his scarf. Simms noticed the scarf was in the team's away colours, though it didn't look as new as the PC knew it to be. It had a chunk missing too. 'Nothing,' Jones mumbled.

'Doesn't look like nothing to me. Here.' Simms grabbed the boy's right arm, before hastily dropping it. The wound stank. 'That's nasty, son. Badly infected, too.'

'What? Infected?' Kevin Jones said, alarmed. 'It's nothing, honest. Ferret took a nip at me.' The boy finally lifted his gaze.

'Ferret? Sure it wasn't a dog?' prodded Simms.

The boy was trembling slightly. 'Well, suppose it could have been a fox, but I—'

'Fox, ferret? Quite the little animal-lover, aren't you?' said Simms. 'You do know there's a full-on rabies scare in the county, don't you? Rabid foxes, ferrets, dogs, you name it, crawling all over the place.' Simms thought Baker was about to interrupt him, but then his colleague seemed to have second thoughts.

The boy was going very pale. Perhaps he'd missed the news announcing that the rabies scare was over.

Just then Simms was tapped on the arm. He turned to see an agitated man in a grey suit. 'What do you want?' Simms said to him.

'Andrew Morton, store manager,' the man replied, proffering a limp hand, which PC Simms ignored. 'Anything I can help with?'

'Ah, yes. Do you want to show the man your horde, son?' Simms nudged Jones.

Jones reluctantly dug around in the pockets of his tracksuit top. Rulers, pens, rubbers cascaded on to the wet pavement.

'Right,' Baker interjected, pulling Jones away, much to Simms's sudden irritation. It was Simms's nab. And he was already thinking excitedly that it might possibly smooth the way back into Sue Clarke's affections. Solving the blind man's death – she'd owe him, big time.

'We always press charges,' Morton was saying.

'Just what we wanted to hear,' said Simms, removing his handcuffs from his belt. The boy was beginning to struggle.

'I'd watch yourself,' Simms added for the store manager's benefit, while attempting to attach the cuffs, with Baker's help, 'he might bite.'

'Could be infectious, too,' said Baker.

Superintendent Mullett had come all the way down to the lobby to see DCI Patterson off the premises. He'd heard quite enough. Though, sadly, the shabby Anti-Terrorist Branch detective was due to return at noon, and with his local informer.

Mullett checked his watch – just gone eleven. His temples throbbed lightly. A fiasco, all right. Total and utter. Why the hell someone couldn't have told him they had an informer here, working as a second-hand-car salesman, Mullett had no idea.

Spinning round on his heels he glared at the front desk and the doleful Bill Wells. 'Get rid of these flowers, Sergeant, pronto.'

Wells glanced up suddenly, as if woken from a deep slumber.

'You heard me. This is a police station not a . . . What the hell?' The superintendent was distracted by a man in white overalls noisily positioning a ladder just down the corridor. The interior security door had been propped open, contrary to the most precise instructions.

Satisfied that the ladder was in the right place, the decorator walked back into the lobby, straight past the divisional commander, heading, Mullett could now see, for the stack of paint tins that had worryingly re-materialized underneath the notice board. He grabbed two tins and began to make his way back.

'Excuse me?' Mullett barked at the man. 'Aside from the fact that that door is never ever to be left open, not for one second, not unmanned, you're meant to be doing the corridors after six in the evening and before nine in the morning – not at eleven. That's why we're paying you lot such a ludicrous rate. Now drop what you're doing and get out of my sight.'

The man shrugged, left the paint and the ladder just where they were and made straight for the exit. 'Fair enough,' he muttered over his shoulder.

Outraged, and particularly so because he should also

have told the fellow to clear his stuff away, Mullett had no alternative but to shout at Wells again. But the station sergeant appeared to be trying to say something to him. 'What is it?' Mullett asked irritably.

'The garage, sir, phoned, about your car.'

'Yes, yes,' Mullett sighed. He didn't want to be reminded. 'Ah, Hanlon.' The great oaf was fighting his way into the lobby heavily laden with paper bags from the bakery. 'Any news?'

'Grace has run low, so I just nipped out . . .'

'Lord, man, you've enough to feed an army there.'

Hanlon frowned and continued across the lobby. 'We've got to feed the scum in the cells, as well,' he said, making for the corridor. 'Or else we'll be had up for . . . buggered if I know . . . something, anyway. And there's plenty of 'em.' With that he disappeared down the corridor.

Mullett shook his head despondently and moved back towards Wells. 'What does he mean, there's plenty of them?' He found his fingers drumming nervously on the counter.

'We're almost at capacity,' Wells said, opening the log. 'Four in last night. And one more this morning.'

Mullett's brow creased. 'Why am I never kept up to date? You had better elaborate, Sergeant.' He scratched the back of his neck nervously.

'Aside from Liz Fraser and Simon Trench, a drunk was picked up from outside the Coconut Grove; he'd taken a pasting, all right. There's a note here – having trouble with Johnny's handwriting . . .' Wells squinted at the log. 'And then Desmond Thorley popped back yet again at some godforsaken hour – I guess Johnny wasn't sure what to do with him.'

'Don't tell me, Thorley got scared all on his own out in the woods? This is most irregular.'

'The problem was, according to the log, he thought he *wasn't* alone.'

'He should be so lucky,' said Mullett. 'The child-killers can stay, but the drunk and the tramp! What the hell is this, some sort of charity? Get Thorley out of here, at the very least.'

'Yes, sir. Would have already,' Wells mused, 'but I haven't been in long myself. I had to go to the dentist.' He clutched his jaw. 'An abscess.'

'And what about the one that came in this morning?' Mullett snapped.

'Could be trouble with him.'

'What do you mean? We've got enough trouble as it is.'

'Kevin Jones – he's a minor. Mouthy little sod. PCs Simms and Baker have just brought him in.'

'A minor? Surely not! What possible charge?' Mullett could feel his blood pressure rising so fast he felt he might explode. While the cells were stuffed with drunks, time-wasters, and now schoolboys, in the real world an armed gang, possibly with IRA connections, was still at large, with £1 million of the Fortress's money. Not to mention the money they'd nicked from the Rimmington and Wallop heists.

'Shoplifting,' said Wells, peering at the log. 'Oh, and murder.'

'Murder?' scoffed Mullett, incredulous.

'That's what PC Simms wanted me to write down.'

Thursday (4)

DC Arthur Hanlon slid a pastry across the table in Interview Room One. The boy, with his spiky yellow hair, simply sneered at him, ignored the food, lit a cigarette, leant back and brazenly released a reel of perfect smoke rings. Hanlon gagged – his hangover was at its peak. Thank Christ he wasn't stuck in a car with Jack Frost this morning.

'How old are you, Kevin Jones?' Hanlon asked. Frost had detailed Hanlon to make a quick assessment of all those in custody. This was Hanlon's first call.

'Thirteen, aren't I.'

'Too young to smoke, then.' Hanlon swiped the fag from the boy's mouth. Ground it out under his foot. 'So what happened to your hand? Looks a mess.'

'There ain't no rabies,' Kevin Jones snapped.

'No, but that doesn't mean you weren't bitten by a dog. A guide dog at that.'

'Don't know what you mean. So I nicked a couple of rulers?' Jones said. 'You going to send me to borstal for that?' The boy leant forwards, glaring at Hanlon, his pitch-black pupils an uneasy contrast with his shock of peroxided hair. 'My mum'll be on the blower to Social Services by now—'

The interview was interrupted by a tap on the door and Hanlon turned to see DC Sue Clarke beckoning to him. 'Come in,' Hanlon mouthed.

'Mr Mullett wants everybody in the canteen for an emergency briefing,' Clarke said from the doorway.

'Emergency briefing?' Hanlon said, exasperated but already getting up.

Clarke looked momentarily vexed, before saying, 'Something like that.'

'Why the canteen? Actually, don't answer,' Hanlon said. 'Jones, you'll have to wait in the cells.'

The look on the boy's face went from utter contempt to vehement disgust. 'Oi, fatty! You can't do that, I'm a minor! I know my rights!' he yelled.

Hanlon leant across and pulled the scarf from the boy's neck. 'You won't be needing this.'

Out in the corridor, Clarke said, 'I just heard he's here – he's mine.' She rubbed her hands together.

'Don't worry, Sue, you're more than welcome to

him. Thought you might need this.' Hanlon handed Clarke the torn scarf.

Her face lit up. 'Thank you, Arthur, I'll just pop that along to Forensics.'

'I thought there was an emergency briefing?' said Hanlon, supporting himself against the wall to tie his shoe.

'Did I say "emergency"?' She smiled sweetly. 'Oh look, you've got something on your jacket. Paint, is it?'

Hanlon saw that the arm of his jacket, where he'd just leant on the wall, now bore a wide smear of magnolia emulsion. 'Shit!' he said. 'Mullett's bloody renovations.'

'Right. Everybody here?' said Mullett.

Mullett was standing in front of what Hanlon presumed to be the new serving hatch. Beside the superintendent was some form of easel, precariously supporting the incident board, which was covered with photographs, maps, artist's impressions, names, arrows and markers.

Hanlon found it difficult to make much out at this distance. He, Frost and a pale PC Pooley happened to be standing at the very back. Though Hanlon was being careful not to lean on the walls.

The canteen was barely recognizable. Gone were the wooden tables and benches of old, and in their place were new Formica-topped lozenges and stacks of orange chairs, their legs still encased in thick brown wrapping paper. The walls were pristine magnolia. It had certainly been swift work, Hanlon thought. If only Mullett had seen fit to direct that much effort to upping the division's manpower.

Standing a little way over to Mullett's left were two men Hanlon couldn't immediately place. One well built, with shoulder-length dark hair, a scruffy leather jacket and a good two days of stubble; the other – who did appear vaguely familiar – a gangly youth in a cheap grey suit. Next to them was assistant chief constable Winslow, looking particularly bald, shiny and self-important today.

'The assistant chief constable is very kindly going to give us an overview of where we're currently at with the Fortress investigation,' Mullett said.

Winslow stepped across to the incident board, and addressed the audience. 'In Wallop, Rimmington and now Denton, there were three gunmen in, as you all know, various disguises. There was also probably a getaway driver. Detectives in Wallop and Rimmington believe that only one vehicle was used – to pick up the cash. It seems they made their way separately to the building societies, and pulled on their masks just before they entered the premises—'

'But,' interrupted Mullett, stepping forwards and nodding at Winslow.

'Go ahead, Superintendent,' said Winslow.

'A different tactic was used here in Denton,' said Mullett. 'We believe the gang arrived in the centre of town all together in the white van, which was then used, highly effectively, for the decoy bomb hoax. The registration was false. The mannequin parts, found by DS Frost in the box inside the van, appear to have been lifted from a skip at the back of Aster's department store.'

Hanlon looked at Frost, who shrugged, as if to say, first he knew of it.

Winslow moved back to take position by the incident board, forcing Mullett to step aside. 'So here in Denton,' Winslow reiterated, 'the gang arrive in the white Transit van, park it up in Market Square, and make their way on foot to the Fortress. Someone rings the police station on the way, saying there's a bomb.'

Not to be outdone, Mullett shuffled a little closer, and said, 'The gang, once masked, brazenly threaten the Fortress staff at gunpoint, smacking a couple of people in the face with their pistols to show they mean business, before helping themselves to the contents of the tills and then moving on to the safes. They then leave from the back of the building, where we believe the waiting getaway vehicle was. All three branches had customer parking at the rear, though not a rear public entrance or exit. They appear to have barged through well-secured and alarmed fire exits, knowing exactly who'd be waiting for them.'

Winslow, pushing his spectacles up his nose, added, 'Interestingly, whoever was waiting for them in Denton, Rimmington and Wallop aroused no suspicion at all. There've been no outside-witness reports of anything untoward.' He paused. 'In each raid, the gang clearly knew their way around the buildings, inside and out, and were well aware what security measures were in place. None of the raids took more than six minutes. It seems more than likely that some inside knowledge had first been obtained.'

'Do we know for sure they all jumped in the same car for the getaway?' Frost piped up from the back, giving Hanlon a start. 'You see, two or so individuals could have slipped away on foot down side streets, while the masks and the loot were bundled up in the car, the gang then regrouping sometime later. Spreads the risk. We're asking for witnesses to four blokes in a car, but for all we know it might have just been the driver, or the driver and one passenger.'

Nods and grunts of approval filled the room.

'That's possible, of course,' conceded Winslow.

'But in the Fortress raid,' interjected Mullett, 'much of the centre of Denton was roped off. A couple of blokes wandering around inside a security cordon would probably have been spotted. A quick getaway, certainly in Denton, seems the most likely scenario.'

'But DS Frost managed to evade the security cordon,' pointed out PS Webster, from the far side of the canteen, where the hot-food counter had once stood.

'Not without drawing attention to himself,' said Mullett.

A titter swept around the room.

'Have any prints been found in the white van?' asked DC Sue Clarke, over by the door.

'Only yours, DC Clarke, and Frost's,' said Mullett, to a much louder chorus of laughter.

'Regarding the use of the van as a decoy,' said Webster, 'is this simply a change of tactics, or are other people now also involved with this gang?'

'Too early to say for sure,' said Mullett. 'But what is clear is that the raid on the Fortress was more sophisticated and audacious than the Rimmington and Wallop raids – besides the fact, of course, that they got a much larger haul.'

'What about security cameras?' Frost asked. 'What's been captured?'

'The Fortress has a new closed-circuit camera system,' answered Winslow this time, 'though the rear camera overlooking the car park appeared not to have been working.' He moved back up to the incident board. 'While at Rimmington and Wallop we have some pictures from inside the buildings, but there were no exterior cameras. As I've said, this gang knew exactly what they were doing.'

'And some,' said the man in the leather jacket standing next to Mullett. He had a faint, but definite Irish accent. 'The code word they gave with the bomb warning had been active up until July of this year.'

'Everybody, if you don't already know,' said the superintendent, 'this is DCI Patterson, from the

Anti-Terrorist Branch. He's exploring any potential links this gang might have, with' – Mullett cleared his throat – 'the IRA.' He coughed again, then continued, 'What most of you don't know is that the ATB have been keeping a close eye on Denton for some time. It's possible, apparently, that an IRA sleeper cell is holed up here.'

'Despite being a quiet little backwater,' said Patterson, 'Denton is well positioned for both the Midlands and London, and not a million miles from the Irish Sea. Brendan Murphy here' – Patterson pointed to the gangly young man standing next to him – 'has been here on the ground since the summer, helping to keep us informed.'

Hanlon caught Frost shaking his head resignedly. Frost whispered, 'I knew there was something fishy about that lad.'

'You sell fancy motors for Steve Hudson, is that right?' Hanlon asked, the face now having clicked into place.

The gangly lad nodded, a sly smile spreading across his sunken cheeks. 'That's right,' he said.

'But what about this code word,' DC Sue Clarke now asked, 'how are these things decided upon?'

'I can't go into too much detail, for security reasons,' said Patterson, straining to see exactly who'd asked the question. 'Though these code words do occasionally get out over time, and certain opportunities arise. With the help of Mr Murphy here, I'll be looking at all links, active and inactive.'

'Could a former Provisional be at work?' Clarke persisted. 'Someone who was a terrorist but who's since swapped bombing people for robbing them?'

'We'll be looking at that possibility,' Patterson replied. 'But that's not to say former Provos are any less dangerous, or don't still have a vested interest in the cause. With these people there are a lot of grey areas.'

Trying to take it all in, Hanlon was being badly hampered by his hangover, and the uncomfortable sensation of whisky repeating on him. He turned to see how Frost was faring, but he had disappeared.

PC Simms marched up from the cells feeling more than pleased with himself. He'd all but nailed a case for Sue, and now he'd just thumped the jerk – the child killer who'd upset her so much yesterday evening – bang on the nose.

Passing Bill Wells on his way out, Simms shook his sore right hand in triumph. 'Mr Trench down there seems to have had an accident.'

Wells looked up from a black bin bag, a limp bunch of gladioli in his fist, like a casualty from a wedding. 'You'll get yourself into trouble one day, son,' said Wells. 'Stupid young hot-head.'

'Someone seems to have kicked over a pot of paint, as well,' Simms said, before exiting the building.

Frost could hear one hell of a racket coming from the cells below. Trying to ignore it he nodded brightly at the uniform guarding the door, and slipped into Interview Room Two where Lee Wright had been waiting for some time. Wright was younger than Frost expected, short, thin, with receding hair a touch too long. Even clearly having been in something of a scrap – there were grazes and bruises on his face and tears to his clothing – he didn't look like he'd done a ten-year stretch for armed robbery. After all the fuss, Frost expected someone more substantial.

'Morning,' Frost smiled. 'I'm DS Frost.'

'Afternoon, more like,' said Lee Wright.

'Been in the wars?' said Frost, searching his pockets for his cigarettes, eventually flinging the packet on to the desk.

'Wars?' Wright shrugged. 'Seems like war's breaking out all over round here.'

'How do you mean?' Frost asked.

'Bank robberies, bomb scares – in a quiet little town like Denton. What's happened to the place?'

'Let's not forget the kidnapping of a minor, too,' said Frost, pressing the Record button on the cassette player. 'Right, Lee Wright, let's work backwards, shall we? Why were you turfed out of the Coconut Grove late last night? Couldn't hold your booze after all that time inside? Got too friendly with the entertainment? History with the owner, Harry Baskin?'

'I should press charges against that bastard Harry Baskin,' Wright mumbled. 'Him and his heavies. Baskin's got way too big for his boots.'

'What do you mean, exactly?' Frost leant forwards, and stabbed the Off switch on the tape recorder. 'Come on, Lee, you're in one hell of a lot of trouble. You help me, and I'll see what I can do for you.'

'Tell me where Julie is first. I want to see my daughter.'

'Of course you do,' said Frost, gently. 'She's being well looked after.'

'By her mum? Has Wendy got her?'

'You haven't heard?' said Frost.

'Heard what?'

'Wendy's in Denton General. Fractured jaw, among other injuries.'

Wright slumped in his chair, the colour draining from his battered face. 'I didn't do it. I didn't harm her. I wouldn't. Would never. She's the mother of my child.'

'It's all right, Lee, I don't think you did do it.'

'That wanker of a husband of hers,' Wright said, 'it was him, wasn't it?'

'Yeah.' Frost offered Wright a Rothmans. 'It was him.'

Wright took the cigarette. 'I'll have him.'

'You're in enough trouble. Don't push it.'

'So where's Julie? With my mum?'

'I believe Social Services are in charge of her for

now,' said Frost, 'until Wendy's better. Your mum's still got a few questions to answer.'

'They better bloody well be looking after her,' Wright fumed.

'Like you did? Whipping her away from her mum at Aster's? Down a fire escape?'

Wright looked at Frost quizzically with his one good eye. 'She came quite willingly,' he said, 'once she knew who I was.'

'Must have been quite a shock for her, all the same.'

'She's a big girl. Put up with all sorts at home by the sound of it. Her mum was never happy. Her stepdad was always knocking someone off – a tart bang across the road most recently. Can you believe that?'

'Julie tell you this? Or Wendy herself when you popped round there last week?'

'How do you know I was there?'

'Fingerprints.'

'Right. Yeah, well, so I did go to see Wendy, to see whether we could come to some arrangement. But she was terrified of what her bloke would do if he found out Julie wasn't his kid.'

'For good reason, it turns out,' said Frost. 'So you decided to steal your daughter, then?'

'I wouldn't put it like that. Look, I'd been away a long time. Things go round and round in your head. I couldn't wait. I didn't mean for her mum, for Wendy, to get bashed up. Look, I'm sorry.'

'Half the division was out looking for Julie, too,' said

Frost. 'One way or another, you've taken up a lot of our time.'

'Look, I said I'm sorry. I just wanted to see my daughter.'

'So what were you doing at the Coconut Grove last night?'

'Drowning my sorrows, I suppose. When I knew you lot had been to my mum's and taken Julie – I saw you – I didn't know what to do.'

'And Harry Baskin didn't like the look of you? Come on, Lee, you've got to help me now. Missing your appointment with your probation officer in Bristol is one thing, kidnapping a minor another altogether. As I see it right now, bit of spin here and there from us, and we can play it either way.'

'I was drunk. I don't know, Baskin obviously didn't want me around.'

'Why would that be?'

'I don't know, I really don't.' Wright reached for another of Frost's cigarettes. 'Can I?'

'Sure,' said Frost. 'The thing is, you and I both know there are some new faces – or even old, should I add – in town. And Harry Baskin will no doubt be doing his best to provide some scantily clad entertainment. Now he's not going to want an old lag stumbling around, mouthing off.'

'Not my style anyway,' said Wright.

'Isn't it? That's how you got caught the first time, wasn't it?'

'I've changed, Mr Frost. I don't want any trouble.'

'Really? So you kidnapped a twelve-year-old girl?'

'You know what I mean. I've given up all that big stuff – I only ever got involved in one serious job anyway.'

'And screwed that up too.'

'I don't want to go back inside.'

'From where I'm sitting, that looks exactly where you're headed,' said Frost. 'It's just a quick call to your probation officer.'

'Please,' pleaded Wright, 'give me a chance.'

'All right, *one* chance,' warned Frost. His conversation with Lee Wright's mother, Joan Dixon, had been on his mind the whole time. 'Who's the Irish fellow you saw in town the other day . . . when you shat your trousers?'

'Don't know what you're talking about.'

'OK,' said Frost, grabbing his cigarettes and standing, 'have a good trip back to Bristol.' He stepped over to the door, turned the handle.

'Wait,' Wright called out.

Frost swung back round, faced the room and the sad, pathetic figure of Lee Wright.

'This could get me killed.'

'It's your choice,' said Frost, pulling the door open.

'Joe Kelly,' Wright said. 'I was banged up with him for a short while in Dartmoor. Him and George Foster.'

'I'll see what I can do for you,' said Frost, walking out of the room.

What had Derek Simms done now?

Sue Clarke, in the general CID office, stood up and walked over to the window. Jack Frost was getting into his car in the station yard.

Apparently Simon Trench was screaming blue murder down in the cells, claiming that PC Simms had broken his nose. Clarke was hardly going to feel sorry for the child-killer, but she didn't trust Simms's motives one little bit.

She supposed she should have thanked Simms for nabbing Kevin Jones, and putting two and two together over the little tyke's ripped Denton FC scarf, in the new away colours, and Graham Ransome's death.

But she was still livid with herself for getting involved with Simms – talk about possessive. And now, with his assault on Trench, was Simms trying to ingratiate himself further, knowing how upset she'd been yesterday?

Frost's car pulled out of the yard and disappeared up Eagle Lane. Clarke returned to her desk despondently. Despite the sudden progress with the Graham Ransome case – she was just waiting for Forensics' opinion on the scarf before she formally interviewed Kevin Jones – she couldn't help feeling marginalized.

Frost was preoccupied – with Williams's death, she presumed – while everyone else was tied up with the

Fortress investigation. It was reaching fever-pitch, with the top brass down from London and County, and all this talk of undercover operations, inside knowledge and the IRA.

Even though she'd tried to make herself heard at the briefing, she felt she was being kept out of the loop. Also, it had just been confirmed that Simon Trench and Liz Fraser were to be dealt with by officers from National with psychiatric training.

While the Prime Minister might be a woman, Clarke decided policing was still far too much a blokes' world.

She'd have to toughen up.

Thursday (5)

It was approaching mid afternoon, the light already fading. Frost sat on a cold, damp swing in the kiddies' play area of the all but deserted Denton Rec.

Mike Ferris, Frost's contact at the British Telecom exchange, had come up trumps. Though now Frost needed to think, somewhere quiet and on his own.

Frost stared at the names and addresses Ferris had provided, along with a series of logs detailing the dates and times of the calls between those numbers and the phone box on Bert Williams's road.

The information would probably have taken weeks to get had Frost had to apply for individual warrants. And while not all of it made sense, a couple of key things stood out.

Saturday last, there'd been two calls between Aster's department store and the phone box. There'd also been a number of calls between Aster's and an address on Carson Road, registered to the one and only George Foster. Frost had a suspicion that this was the house opposite Steve Hudson's, with the gleaming Jag outside and the underdressed floozy inside.

Over a period of several weeks, there'd also been numerous calls between this Carson Road address, number thirty-seven, and Hudson's Classic Cars.

Frost knew he couldn't go arresting people for making phone calls, particularly when he wasn't legally in possession of that information. Yet a clear picture was emerging: Blake Richards, Aster's new security guard with, of course, the very chequered career as a Met detective, had to have been in contact with Bert Williams on the day that Bert disappeared. It looked likely that Richards was also in contact with someone at 37 Carson Road – probably former Denton hardman and one-time Coconut Grove bouncer George Foster.

The number of a Bath Hill telephone box also kept cropping up. Frost's money was on it being where Joe Kelly, the ex-IRA gunslinger, ex-Dartmoor inmate and now full-time bank robber, kept in touch.

Bert's death and the masked gang were linked, of that Frost was increasingly sure, though he still didn't know why Bert had kept so quiet about it all. What was also rankling was the fact that Frost had had no idea that George Foster still owned a property in Denton; for such a big-time name, who'd been in and out of the nick, it should have been common knowledge at the station. Such people needed to be kept an eye on.

Frost lifted his head to see a couple of mothers pushing babies in prams in the freezing late-October gloom. Bert had children, Frost found himself thinking; he'd been a grandparent. Everybody had somebody, until they were dead.

A woman in a headscarf approached the play area with two small children, tutting at the sight of Frost taking up one of the swings. He took a final drag on his cigarette, flicked it wearily to the ground and got up, smiling at a small boy who giggled nervously back at him. The mother tugged the child towards the slide. Frost sidestepped an old, white dog turd and walked slowly away.

He was arching his back, feebly attempting to stretch some life into his knackered body, when a couple of people a short distance away caught his eye. They were walking slowly down the central path that crossed the recreation area.

A woman, in her thirties, blondish, short, plump, was with a man, much taller, thinner, of a similar age but already balding.

Frost hurried towards them, nearly tripping over a Golden Retriever as he crossed the wet grass. The dog bounced off happily enough.

'Mind if I join you?' Frost asked, catching up with them.

The pair recoiled. 'Mr Frost?' the man said nervously.

'Mr Litchfield. Coping all right?' Frost looked into the lean man's cold, pinched face, his eyes red-rimmed. 'And Mrs Cooper, isn't it, from St Mary's? Out for a stroll?'

Mrs Cooper nodded at Frost, but said nothing.

'It's not what you think,' Maurice Litchfield said defensively, his voice strained and shaky.

'You know what I think?' Frost said. 'Please do tell me. Because I don't, half the time.'

Litchfield stopped and turned to face Frost. The woman wandered to the side of the path.

'Shouldn't you be out catching whoever murdered my wife?' Litchfield said firmly, collecting himself.

'Haven't quite worked out who that is yet, I'm afraid,' Frost said, sniffing. 'So far, it seems it could be any number of people. I'm guessing your friend over there might have some idea, the circles you two swing in.'

Frost could see Litchfield getting agitated again.

Frost fished in his pockets for his cigarettes. 'If we don't get a break soon we'll have to go public on this. Amazing what crops up when we put something juicy on the telly.'

'What do you mean, "go public"?' Litchfield asked anxiously.

'Do I really need to spell it out?'

'Yes, I think you do, Detective,' Litchfield said, his bravado surprising Frost.

'Your wife had a very active sex life, to put it mildly. You too, I'd bet, and your friend over there. A TV appeal for information would certainly attract the public's attention.' Frost paused, focusing on Mrs Cooper, who was well within earshot. He caught her glancing at Maurice Litchfield, a look of resignation across her face. 'Do you want me to carry on?' Frost asked, exhaling. 'In fact, perhaps you can help me out with some of the more extreme practices and equipment. It's a whole new world to me. A real eye-opener.'

'How dare you!' Maurice Litchfield spat. 'My wife was raped and then murdered. My poor darling wife, my Vanessa . . .' Tears of rage formed in his raw, swollen eyes.

'How dare I?' Frost snapped. 'How dare you waste police time. Your wife wasn't raped and murdered, and you know it. Your wife was asphyxiated while monkeying around in the sack.' Drysdale's quiet words came back to him. 'Plastic bag over her head, maybe? Except this time someone left the thing on for too bloody long and she sodding well died.'

Frost stopped, suddenly feeling very wretched. He looked up at the heavy sky, and said, 'I don't know how many of you were present, I'm not sure I really care. But stop wasting my time.'

Litchfield looked ruined, his bottom lip quivering,

his shoulders beginning to shake uncontrollably.

Frost had to step aside to let a gang of boys hurtle past pushing a pathetic Guy Fawkes in a shopping trolley.

'Oi, you lot! Watch where you're going!' Frost yelled.

'Up yours!' was the collective retort.

'Tell me, Mr Frost,' Mrs Cooper said, stepping forwards, as the noise of the boys died down, 'is it usual police procedure to interrogate the recently bereaved so brutally in a public park? You should be ashamed of yourself. Look at him' – she gestured to Maurice Litchfield – 'he's in a state of collapse.'

'He's only got himself to blame,' Frost said, turning to leave. He wanted to get to Aster's before it shut.

Hanlon walked into the CID office, saw DC Sue Clarke sitting at the main desk, her head hanging low over a Forensics report. She hadn't heard him come in.

'Good read?' he asked cheerily.

'Just what I wanted,' she said, looking up. 'Kevin Jones's scarf matches the piece of fabric I picked up down by the canal. Plus they found a couple of short, peroxide-blond hairs on that scrap, too. What's more, they found teeth marks on it and the rest of the scarf, consistent with a large animal – a Labrador or Alsatian.'

'Can't believe the lout was stupid enough to hang on to the scarf,' said Hanlon. 'Do we need to get the doc to have a look at Jones's hand, see whether they're definitely bite marks from a dog?'

Clarke took a sip of lukewarm coffee, threw the near-empty polystyrene cup into the bin. 'Not sure we'll need to. I've just been on to Harbinger's, the sports shop on Gentlemen's Walk. They recalled selling football scarves to a bunch of young yobs – in Denton's new away colours – only a week ago. There hasn't been much call for the new strip.'

'There's a surprise.'

'Be easy enough to organize a line-up starring young Jones. He looks distinctive enough.'

'We'll still need to get him to confess.'

'To what, exactly?' said Clarke. 'Affray? Actually attacking the man and pushing him into the canal?' She suddenly looked more resigned. 'I suppose I thought we had enough evidence to pin him to the location and to the fact that he was set upon by a guide dog protecting its master.'

'Hardly enough for a murder charge, is it?' said Hanlon. 'Let alone one involving a minor.'

'I suppose, then, I just need an admission that he was there, with some others, and that they got into a scuffle with Graham Ransome, who ended up in the canal, dead. And hope the jury does the rest. I want a result.'

'From what I gleaned of Kevin Jones earlier,' said Hanlon, 'it's not going to be easy. You'll need to scare the little shit. That way he might at least point the finger at whoever else was there with him. That lot have got no scruples, and if we round up the others, interview them separately, the true picture might emerge.'

'I'll try my best.' Clarke rose from her chair, and gathered her papers. 'But it doesn't seem like a priority right now, with all this Fortress stuff. It's going to be an uphill struggle.'

'It always is,' said Hanlon. 'Guess what Liz Fraser's up to now? She wants to retract everything she said yesterday, while Simon Trench says he's going to sue us for brutality.'

'Shit,' said Clarke.

'Fortunately,' continued Hanlon, 'Drysdale's toxicology report came in this afternoon. Becky Fraser's blood contained a huge amount of Temazepam. Seems she drank it with her milk. The little girl was as good as dead before she was suffocated. I already know Liz Fraser was prescribed the drug.'

'How? I thought medical records were out of bounds.'

Hanlon retrieved the empty brown plastic bottle from his jacket pocket and held it up. 'Just found this in the bin in her bathroom. She was only prescribed these last week.' He pointed to the label. 'Should have lasted her a month.'

'So that's where you've been this last hour. But where's Frost gone?'

Hanlon shrugged his shoulders. Buggered if he knew.

Frost carefully scanned the ground floor of Aster's. It was near to closing time on a dismal Thursday afternoon, and there were no crowds around the bargain bins at the front. No crowds around any counter or display stand, in fact.

What staff were there looked bored, desperate to get home.

There was no trace of Blake Richards, or the other security guard, whose name Frost had forgotten, either. Frost headed for the manager's office.

The access to the admin floor, five flights up, was unmanned, all doors open. Frost walked straight to Ken Butcher's office, remembering the layout from his visit with Hanlon last Sunday. The door was ajar and Frost strolled straight in, saying, 'Busy time of the day?'

The smartly dressed and bearded manager of Aster's had his feet on the desk and was reading the *Racing Post*. Startled, he quickly removed his feet, flung the paper to one side, sat up and straightened his tie.

'Do you usually just barge into people's offices?' Ken Butcher said. 'DS Frost, isn't it?'

'There was no one to stop me. What's happened to the security around here? Didn't see either of your esteemed store detectives on patrol, either.'

'Ah,' Butcher said. 'We're slightly understaffed today.'

'I bet you were understaffed yesterday, too,' said Frost.

'I'm not sure I get your drift, Detective.' Butcher shifted uneasily in his chair.

'Blake Richards, not in today?'

'No,' said Butcher.

'Or yesterday?'

'I do believe he didn't report for work either yesterday or today. Most unlike him. He's been completely dependable up to now.'

'And your other chap?' asked Frost, searching his mac pockets for his cigarettes. 'You have two security guards, don't you?'

'Keith Nelson's been ill,' said Butcher. 'Flu.'

'So what is it, a free-for-all downstairs?'

'All my staff are trained to be vigilant,' said Butcher. 'We all do our best to keep an eye out for any untoward behaviour.'

'No one spotted twelve-year-old Julie Hudson being dragged out of here,' said Frost, lighting his cigarette. 'And that's not to mention fire exits being left unalarmed, and bits of your mannequins turning up at major crime scenes.'

Butcher was looking more and more uncomfortable. He was now loosening his tie. 'Yes, I heard about the mannequin parts being found in that van. Someone from your station rang me this morning. But for the life of me, I have no idea how they got there.'

'Easily enough, I imagine,' said Frost. 'You've got a

skip full of them out the back, haven't you? Someone just helped themselves.'

'But why?' asked the store manager. 'Why would they do that?'

Frost wasn't going to admit he had no idea. Though it seemed like someone was trying to make a point by it. 'That's what I was hoping you'd tell me.' Unless it really was coincidence – that the mannequin parts were already in the van when the armed gang stole the vehicle. The van having previously been owned by a low-rent, opportunistic thief. Frost disconsolately exhaled a large plume of smoke.

'I just can't help you, Detective,' said Butcher. 'Sorry.'

Frost wasn't getting anywhere here. 'Don't suppose you've tried to contact your missing security guard?'

Butcher stood up. 'Of course we have. When there was no answer on his phone, I even sent a lad round to his home. The curtains were shut, no one in.'

Frost wasn't surprised. Blake Richards had probably well and truly scarpered by now. 'Did he ever mention any friends, acquaintances he had round here?'

'Not to me,' said Butcher. 'I barely knew him. Just seemed to be a rather solitary figure.'

Butcher walked with Frost to the door. 'Why are you so interested in him, anyway?'

Frost laughed, walked down the corridor, and threw over his shoulder, 'Armed robbery, murdering a police officer . . . and that's just for starters.'

* * *

'I want my mum,' said Kevin Jones. 'I want to go home.'

Were those really tears welling in his eyes? 'You should have thought about that before pushing a blind man into the canal,' said Clarke.

They were in Interview Room One, just her and him, in clear contravention of the procedure governing the formal questioning of a minor. But Clarke didn't care. She was going to break him down.

'I didn't,' Jones said. 'Want me to say it again? I didn't, I didn't, I didn't.'

'Who did, then?'

'That would be telling, wouldn't it.'

Though it wasn't strictly a formal interview, Clarke had made sure it was being recorded. She knew she could always dispose of the tape if things didn't go according to plan – that's what everyone else did.

'At last, you admit you were there,' said Clarke. 'Don't bother denying it. We've got all the evidence we need.'

'Me and my mates always go down to the canal. What of it?'

'Kevin, things aren't looking very sunny for you, are they? You've admitted you were down by the canal, you've admitted you know who pushed a poor, defenceless blind man into the drink. At the very least you're looking at accessory to murder – that's still a life sentence. You won't be going home for a very long time indeed.'

'He attacked us,' Jones suddenly said, brightening up.

'With what?' said Clarke. 'His white stick?'

'Yeah, yeah, that's it.'

'How would he see to do that?' protested Clarke. 'He was just waving it randomly about, was he? You stupid little shit.'

'And then he fell in,' Jones added, with a smirk.

She slammed her hand on the table top and stood up, kicking her chair back. 'If you don't start co-operating . . .' She calmly walked round the table, leant in close to him, seeing something resembling panic cross his face, and shouted in his ear, 'I'm going to make sure you never see daylight again.'

As she slowly backed away, towards the door, Kevin Jones looked up and straight into her eyes, and said, 'It's not my fault he died. We were just messing about with his dog and stuff. Having a laugh. We didn't kill him. Not our fault he couldn't swim. You can ask my mates, they'll tell you the same.'

'And who are they?' said Clarke, returning to her seat. 'I want all their names, addresses. Miss anyone out and you, me and a few of my friends from the station – and they're all bigger than me – will be going back down to the canal. See if that jogs your memory.'

Thursday (6)

Feeling an increasing sense of urgency to confirm his suspicions about the gang – and to start making some arrests – Jack Frost pulled into the Coconut Grove's weed-strewn and pot-holed, dimly lit car park. He knew he was clutching at straws. But Blake Richards wasn't the only collar he wanted. There were at least three other members of the gang.

It was just after five, and Frost realized he was starving, realized also that there was unfinished business with Maurice Litchfield.

Turning the engine off, he lifted the handset and called the station, leaving a message with Control for DC Clarke: she was to meet him at Maurice Litchfield's place in Denton Close in twenty minutes.

He didn't expect to enjoy the Coconut's exotic hospitality for very long.

He climbed out of the Cortina and stepped straight into a massive puddle. He swore, and lit a cigarette. He started to walk round to the entrance of the sleazy strip joint, but was overwhelmed by an acute stab of pain in his lower abdomen. 'Christ,' he uttered, bending double. As the pain eased a little he shuffled on until he was thumping at the heavy, fortified door, bearing a brass plaque with the words *Gentlemen's Club*.

Eventually a mountain of a man opened up, eyeing Frost suspiciously. 'Yeah?' he barked. His head was round and bald and shiny, like a huge billiard ball.

'Harry Baskin in?' Frost wheezed.

'Depends. Who wants him?'

'An old friend,' Frost said, the pain now rapidly easing – yet he found it had brought him out in a sweat. He wiped his forehead on the sleeve of his mac.

'He's got plenty of those,' the man said. 'Doesn't need any more.'

'Really? You can never have enough friends in this business.' Craning round the man Frost saw some punters in the bar; looked like a performance was going on. 'Wasn't aware you had an all-day licence for this joint.'

The bouncer stepped forwards, blocking Frost's view. 'Auditions, isn't it. What's it to you, anyway?'

Frost produced his warrant card and waved it at the

bouncer. 'Tell Mr Baskin that Jack Frost's here to see him.'

Two minutes later Frost was in Harry Baskin's office. The black gloss walls were studded with chrome-framed photographs of Harry with an array of long-forgotten VIPs and strippers. Baskin's desk was also black, glinting under the soft spotlights. Baskin was smiling away, his dyed-black hair slicked back and glinting too, along with his gold front tooth.

'Snifter?' Baskin said, picking up a smouldering cigar from a huge chrome ashtray.

'Don't mind if I do, Harry,' Frost said. 'Thought I'd stop by and thank you personally for giving us the nod with Lee Wright.'

Baskin laughed deeply. 'Think nothing of it – well, not for now, at least.' He retrieved a bottle of Scotch and two tumblers from a desk drawer.

'But I'm not sure Wright's who we really want, Harry,' Frost said, before taking a long sip of neat whisky. He felt it working its way straight to his empty stomach, and feared another stab of pain.

'Is that so?'

'Seen any other blasts from the past?' prompted Frost. Thankfully, the whisky seemed to be going down well. He scrabbled for a light and Baskin leant over with a hefty, gold-plated Ronson.

'To be honest, I try not to look too closely at my punters. Ugly lot.'

'Come on, Harry, you always know who's who,' said Frost. 'George Foster been in recently?'

'Georgie Boy? Haven't seen him for years. I'll tell you who was in here yesterday, though. Sir Peter Farnsworth, chairman of the Fortress. Nursing his wounds, I guess.' Baskin stubbed out his cigar. 'Big raid, wasn't it?'

'Know anything I don't?'

'I just keep an eye out for my birds, you know that, Jack. I leave the big-game hunting to the big boys.'

'Why did you chuck us Lee Wright?' Frost winced as a wave of pain shot through him. He knocked back the rest of his whisky, took a last drag of his cigarette.

'He was making a fool of himself. I don't like gropers and I don't like big-mouths. He might have seen a few things inside but he needs to learn to keep his gob shut. Or one day I fear someone will shut it for him, for good. Not a nice lot, those ex-cons.'

'Who duffed him up – Baldie on the door?'

Baskin slicked back his Brylcreemed hair with a meaty palm. 'Don't think he was working yesterday.'

'How convenient,' said Frost, rising from the chair. 'Well, thanks for the drink, anyway.'

'A pleasure,' said Baskin uncertainly. He remained behind his desk. 'Look, Jack, for what it's worth George Foster's niece is in town – Louise Daley. She did the odd performance for us too, when she first arrived. Saucy little brunette. Seems to have recently found other employment.'

As Frost reached the door he turned back to Baskin, and the wall of tacky photographs behind him, tits looming everywhere. He could still picture clearly the slim, foxy Louise Daley, tousled dark-brown hair, hazel eyes, in that skimpy, maroon dressing-gown, trying to shut her front door on him. Bright and early, Sunday morning, Carson Road – a different world. 'I'm surprised her knockers were big enough.'

Baskin laughed. 'She had other assets. Quick off the mark, if you know what I'm saying.'

Frost stared at Baskin, took a deep breath as he waited for another stab of pain to subside, then asked, 'Bloke by the name of Blake Richards mean anything to you?'

'Never heard of him,' Baskin said, too quickly.

'Joe Kelly?'

'Look, Jack – go easy. Evil breeds evil.'

'As if I don't know that,' said Frost.

Thursday (7)

Superintendent Mullett was standing in front of the new canteen serving hatch, tapping the makeshift incident board with a ruler and addressing a sparse crowd, uniform and plainclothes. Hanlon, Frost could see, was among them. As was DCI Patterson.

Frost marched straight up. 'What exactly do we know about Blake Richards and his life in Denton?'

Mullett looked bemused. 'Ah, Frost, good of you to join us at last.'

'He works for Aster's,' Hanlon said hopefully, 'though as a temp from a company called Security Guard. They provide both manpower and security installations.'

'Who else uses this company?' Frost asked, lighting

a cigarette to ease the ache in his stomach – the waves of pain were coming faster now.

'Everyone from banks and building societies to department stores and clubs, from what I've managed to find out so far. However, they're a cagey lot – perhaps not surprisingly. If you ask me, the company must possess some interesting security information,' Hanlon replied.

'More than useful, if you're planning to rob a bank,' said Frost.

'I imagine they are very particular about who they employ,' offered Mullett, stroking his moustache.

'Like the Met,' said Frost.

Mullett looked away. Patterson looked more interested.

Mullett turned back to the group. 'I'm not sure where this is all leading. Perhaps you'd like to explain, Frost.'

'We need to haul Blake Richards in,' said Frost, torn between revealing everything he knew and suspected, and trying to keep some information to himself. He still didn't know what Bert's rationale had been for keeping so quiet, and why Bert had even been in contact with Blake Richards. 'Urgently,' Frost added, knowing he'd have to give his superior something more. 'I've got a pretty strong idea that Blake Richards was involved in the raid on the Fortress, and probably the raids in Rimmington and Wallop.'

'Am I right in thinking this is Blake Richards,

formerly of the *Met*?' Mullett's brow furrowed.

Just then there was a loud clatter behind them, though no sign of who or what was causing it.

'Who'd have thought a bit of painting and decorating would create such mayhem.' Mullett glanced over his shoulder and shook his head in dismay. 'Where was I?'

'Richards, sir,' Frost replied. 'He's been providing the intelligence, at the very least.'

'Richards? But the man's been put out to grass,' countered Mullett.

'His past connections and his present job mean he's ideally placed,' persisted Frost. 'And he's a violent sod.'

'Ideally placed for what again, Frost?'

'For providing the information a gang would need to pull off a series of raids,' said Frost. 'What the hell do you think I'm talking about?'

'Is this another one of your hazy hunches, Frost?'

'For God's sake, Super.' Frost was suddenly aware of Patterson, standing just to the side of the group, staring at him. 'It looks more than likely that George Foster is involved too, and this ex-IRA man Joe Kelly. Foster and Kelly met in Dartmoor nick, and Blake Richards knew Foster in London. That's been clearly recorded.'

'Just because someone might once have met someone doesn't mean they're involved in a criminal gang together,' said Mullett loftily. 'Precisely what evidence have you got?'

'Phone records,' Frost said, exasperated.

'Phone records?' huffed Mullett. 'I don't remember sanctioning a warrant on anyone's phone recently.'

'Neither do I, which was why I had to resort to other means, given the urgency of the situation.'

'For God's sake, Frost,' said Mullett. 'How many times have I told you that if evidence is not legally obtained, so that it won't stand up in a court of law, then I simply don't want to know about it. Bring me something solid, and we'll have another chat.'

'It'll be too late by then,' pleaded Frost. 'Believe me. You think they play by the rules?'

'Have you even spoken to this chap Richards?' said Mullett. 'What does he have to say for himself?'

'He's gone missing,' said Frost. 'We'll need to search his house.'

'And how do you propose I'm going to justify a warrant for that? Get me something more substantial to go on, Frost, and I'll get that warrant. We do things properly here, by the book, or not at all.'

Mullett looked about the room, as if he were dismissing Frost. Though, appearing to have second thoughts, he quickly added, 'By the way, I hear the forensic report regarding the late DI Williams's car is in and has been delivered to your desk. What's it say?'

'It says, sir' – Frost looked away himself for a moment, gathering his strength and his thoughts – 'that the damage done to the car, most noticeably to the near-side wing, was consistent with an impact of no more than twenty miles per hour. The car went down the ditch at an angle, rising up and hitting the steep bank the other side.' He coughed, suddenly thinking he was going to be sick – he shouldn't have had that whisky with Harry Baskin. He should have had a sandwich instead.

'Did they manage to lift any prints?' asked Hanlon keenly. He and Mullett were now the only people left by the incident board, Patterson having walked away.

'No,' answered Frost, 'not on the car. Inside or out. Let's hope they've done their job properly.'

'As I suspected,' said Mullett, tutting. 'A tragic accident. Narrow lane like that. Bert no doubt taking the back route home from that fancy country pub out on the Rimmington Road. Not realizing how much he's had to drink – and the next thing he knows he's in the ditch, mortally injured. We must make sure we go to town this Christmas on our drink-driving campaign. Too many lives are needlessly wasted.'

'The thing is,' said Frost quietly, clutching his side, 'while that's what Forensics say, the pathologist, Dr Drysdale, is certain that Bert's injuries are consistent with an impact of much greater force. A crash at forty or fifty miles an hour at least, with the victim slamming into the steering wheel. Bert's chest was all but caved in, his ribs crushed. Yet, as Forensics noted, there's no real damage to the steering wheel – it's not even buckled.'

Frost felt he was breaking out in a sweat again. He

really wasn't well. But it was no time to be ill. Wiping his brow, he continued, 'He was smashed up first, outside the car, probably by one or two severe blows to his chest with a cricket bat.' He felt in his pockets for his cigarettes, before resuming, 'They've found traces of linseed oil on his clothes.'

Mullett was speechless, whilst Hanlon became more animated. 'I think I know what's coming next,' Hanlon said, nodding at Frost. 'He was put back in his car and the car was either pushed or shunted into the ditch, the door flying open.'

'Looks like it – from the blood found in the car and on the inside of the door. Forensics also found some unexplained pressure marks both on the rear bumper and the boot.' It was dawning on Frost that perhaps he hadn't been as appreciative of Hanlon as he should have been over these last few days. He'd make amends.

'I see,' Mullett finally said sternly. 'But the area was roped off. Scenes of Crime must have found corresponding tyre marks and footprints nearby.'

'They weren't so lucky there,' said Frost, his queasiness now passing. 'Some berk parked his Rover in the wrong place.'

Clarke was waiting for Frost in his filthy office, standing in the corner of the cramped room in the only free space. She was livid.

Frost eventually ambled in, making straight for his

desk. He slumped down in his chair, not bothering to remove his mac. 'Ah, Sue,' he said brightly, acknowledging her at last, 'popped by for a cup of tea and a Penguin?'

'Where the hell were you?' she said.

'What do you mean, where the hell was I? Trying to knock some sense into the super. There are three or four people out there we urgently need to talk to, regarding this Fortress raid, not to mention the death of a police officer, and bloody Mullett is fussing about dotting the "i"s.' Frost paused. 'Still, I do believe I'm getting somewhere, Sue.' He smiled up at her. 'I feel it here.' He patted his heart.

Disarmed – his eyes did have a twinkle when he was cheerful – Clarke calmed down a little. 'Well, I've been hanging around Denton Close for the last half an hour, when I could have been rounding up some little hooligans on the Southern Housing Estate.'

'And you're complaining?' Frost searched in his pocket for his cigarettes, and offered Clarke one.

She took a cigarette, then leant over his lighter. 'Maurice Litchfield, remember him?' she said, standing up.

'I'd stay clear of him – the dirty sod.'

'For God's sake, Jack. I was waiting for you, outside his home. You left a message for me to meet you there and I got the impression it was urgent.'

'To be honest, Sue, I suddenly didn't feel up to joining in. Bit of a pain in my stomach.'

'Pain in my arse, more like,' sulked Clarke.

'You sure you didn't pop in to see Maurice?'

Just then Hanlon entered the room, out of breath. 'So what are we looking for, Jack? A man who carries a cricket bat around in the boot of his car? Can't be too common this time of year. Still, it's a tall order – even if we had a stop-and-search in place.'

'Maybe we could speak to our friend Patterson,' said Frost. 'Perhaps he can set up an armed roadblock, single-handed. Doesn't look like the type to put up with any nonsense.'

'Something I'm missing?' said Clarke eagerly.

'Anything else to go on, Jack?' asked Hanlon, ignoring Clarke.

'Let me see,' said Frost. 'Where's that report?' Cigarette between his lips, he rummaged around on his desk. 'Ah, here we are.' He unsealed the large manila envelope. 'Let's see what it says.'

There was silence in the room for a couple of minutes. Clarke looked at Hanlon for an explanation. Hanlon just shrugged.

'Got the speed wrong,' Frost finally said. 'The damage to the car – it couldn't have been going more than ten or fifteen miles per hour. I tell you, they don't make chassis like they used to.'

'The cricket bat?' Hanlon prompted.

'Might have been a snooker cue,' said Frost. 'Same thing.'

'But you said Forensics had found linseed oil on Bert's clothes,' said Hanlon seriously.

'Did I? Look, Arthur, you couldn't fetch me something from the food trolley, I haven't eaten all day and my stomach's playing up.'

'Meals on wheels ran out of food ages ago and the bakery will be shut by now,' said Hanlon.

Clarke looked at her watch. It was gone six and she suddenly felt very tired. 'We could nip over to the pub. And you could both fill me in. I've spent most of the afternoon feeling out of the loop.'

'Tell you what,' said Frost, staring at Clarke, with his mischievous dark eyes, 'I'll fill you in, and Arthur can do his best to get a warrant to search 37 Carson Road. Owned by one George Foster and most recently occupied by his niece, an ex-stripper turned getaway driver, Louise Daley.'

'You've got to be kidding,' said Hanlon.

'I don't think so,' said Frost. 'Come on, Sue.'

Dragging Clarke out of the room and into the corridor, Frost shouted over his shoulder, 'Arthur, if you have any luck twisting Mullett's arm, you might want to get the artillery lined up ready, too. Could get heavy. Failing that we'll have to pop round ourselves.'

'Jack,' said Clarke as they hurried towards the exit, 'I hate to remind you again, but Maurice Litchfield's place?'

'You *are* desperate, Sue. We'll get there eventually.'

Thursday (8) ⎯⎯⎯⎯⎯⎯⎯⎯⎯⎯⎯⎯⎯⎯

Mullett rang down to the cells. He'd got wind that nothing short of a riot was about to erupt, though he wasn't going anywhere near the cells himself, knowing he'd never get out of the place tonight if he did so. He and Mrs M had a Rotary Club dinner.

'Simon Trench is banging his head against the wall,' said Duty Constable Jordan, on the other end of the line.

'At least no one's doing it for him,' said Mullett.

'Says his human rights have been contravened, that he's going to sue, et cetera. He has got a bit of a swollen nose and a black eye.'

'He should have thought about that before he removed his little girl's human rights, for good,' said

Mullett, searching his desk for the latest arrest-and-charge sheet. It wasn't to hand, and Miss Smith, as usual, was long gone.

'Tell him he can see a lawyer in the morning. With any luck, the National shrinks will have taken him off to Broadmoor by then.'

'The lad, Kevin Jones, is none too happy either,' Jordan continued. 'Making a hell of a lot of noise for a thirteen-year-old. His mum and someone from Social Services are still hanging about in an interview room, not being much quieter by all accounts, saying they won't go home without him, and if we don't watch it they'll come down on us like a ton of bricks. They're muttering about child abuse, you name it.'

'Blast,' sighed Mullett. 'I meant to talk to DC Clarke about him, find out the latest. Well, we can't put him up for the night without everyone and his nanny having a say. He'll have to go home, but on the understanding that he needs to be back here at nine in the morning, or we'll have him picked up and slapped with yet another charge.'

'Steve Hudson spat at me through the food hole,' said Jordan.

'Spit at him back,' said Mullett. He really didn't have time for this. He paused. 'Steve Hudson, you say? Wait a minute.' Mullett looked across his desk at the photograph of his beloved wife, standing outside their fine, new Denton home, part financed, as it happened, by a large mortgage from Bennington's.

'By God, I thought he'd been released.' Mullett tried hard to think back to his last conversation with Frost about Steve Hudson. All he could remember was Frost storming into his office and being unspeakably rude to Steve Hudson's uncle Michael, who was only there to discuss bank security and the Fortress raid. 'Is there a charge?' Mullett demanded.

'Yes. Says on my sheet that he's being charged with attempted murder.'

'Who the hell signed that?' Mullett retrieved a handkerchief from his top pocket and quickly blew his nose with one hand. He felt like he had hayfever, wondered whether all the decorating was beginning to trouble his sinuses. 'Don't tell me—'

'DS Frost,' said Jordan.

Mullett could hear shouting and clanging on the other end of the line. 'What's going on now?' The super wasn't sure what staff were left in the building, how many troops he could rally in an emergency. Briefly his mind alighted on the unnerving image of DCI Patterson: SAS-trained, he'd probably be able to quell a riot by himself. But Mullett had little idea what Patterson had really been up to since he'd arrived. He'd been assigned a room down near Records, and hadn't been seen much since.

'It's the lad Kevin Jones and the child-killer Simon Trench,' said Jordan. 'They seem to be acting up in unison. They're across the corridor from each other.'

'Maybe you should put them in together,' said

Mullett wearily. 'That could solve a few problems.'

'And create quite a few more,' said Jordan drily. 'The only prisoner who's not saying a word is Lee Wright. In fact, time I checked on him. He was rather upset earlier. Almost remorseful, I'd say.'

'I should hope so!' yelled Mullett. 'Abducting a child is no laughing matter, whether it's his own daughter or not. The sooner he's sent back to a proper slammer, rather than taking up our valuable space, the better. Why haven't the prison service picked him up yet? Make some calls, Jordan. I want him removed.'

Thursday (9) _____

'Had you heard of erotic asphyxiation before today?' Frost said loudly, pushing into the bustling, smoky pub. What a relief to be out of the station.

'What do you think?' Sue Clarke said, shaking her wet head and shoulders and looking around for somewhere to put her coat and umbrella.

'Young thing like you, thought you'd . . . well, finger on the pulse, or what have you.' Frost felt for his cigarettes.

'Even I have limits – you should know that by now.'

Clarke found a small table, and Frost shuffled over to the bar, returning with their drinks and two packets of crisps. 'Dinner,' he said, chucking Clarke a packet of salt and vinegar. He was having smoky bacon.

'What I don't quite understand,' said Clarke, shrugging, 'is why there weren't more marks on Vanessa Litchfield's neck, even if she'd agreed to be near-asphyxiated.'

'They're very careful, apparently,' explained Frost, eyeing Clarke keenly, 'about what techniques they use. Otherwise, as far as I can work out, half of Denton would be wandering around looking like they'd been half choked to death.'

'Jesus! It's that popular? Where have I been?'

'You tell me.' Frost couldn't help smiling. A Space Invaders machine was beeping away nearby.

'So has Maurice Litchfield come clean?' Clarke said. 'Why did you want me there this afternoon?'

'He hasn't quite admitted to it yet – but he will. I thought your calm, soothing presence would seal the deal.' Frost took a drink of his beer, the warm liquid settling nicely in his stomach.

'You should have heard me interviewing Kevin Jones. I was anything but calm. I could have murdered the little sod. At least I got all the names of his cohorts.' She sipped at her rum and coke. 'Frankly, I'm getting a bit sick of being pigeonholed as a soft, easy touch, just because I'm a woman. Heard of women's lib?'

'All for it,' said Frost enthusiastically. 'What do you want to wear a bra for, anyway, when you've got such lovely—'

'I could strangle you sometimes, Jack Frost.'

'We could give it a go.'

'Just get back to Maurice Litchfield, will you.'

'I bumped into him in Denton Rec earlier this afternoon,' said Frost, wheezing slightly. 'He was with Sally Cooper. While Maurice and I got into something of a heated discussion, I think it dawned on Mrs Cooper what he could be facing if he doesn't come clean. We'll get round there first thing tomorrow morning, give him another night to sweat over it. Don't think I've got the energy right now, anyway.'

'So what's he looking at – manslaughter?'

'At the most, if he gets the right judge. It's the public humiliation that I think will sink him though. He works in the City, for God's sake, one of those posh commuters. What are they going to say on the train in the morning? Strangely sensitive chap as well, even with his hobby.'

Clarke got up to go to the Ladies, and Frost watched her turning heads as she weaved through the crowded bar, remembering how Mary used to have that effect. Mary had been a cracker, no two ways about it, and she'd known it, too.

Shit, he said to himself. He'd blind forgotten their wedding anniversary tomorrow. No box of Black Magic, no flowers, no table booked. It wasn't much of a marriage any more, but that wouldn't stop the little firebrand from going ballistic. He'd have to think of something.

The moment he saw Sue Clarke returning his mood lifted.

'That bloke from the ATB is over there,' she said, sitting down. 'Patterson.'

'Oh, him. Don't know what he does all day, except earwigging other people's conversations.'

'I suppose that's what they're meant to do, isn't it? All that covert stuff?' Clarke gave him a big smile. 'So what's all this about snooker cues, George Foster and strippers driving getaway cars? You can't be serious.'

'I thought you were all for equal rights and women's lib,' said Frost. 'Why can't women drive getaway cars? Christ, you drive quick enough.' Frost suddenly felt nauseous. When he went for a piss earlier it hurt like hell all down his right side. Something was up and he knew it.

'Jack, you still with us?' said Clarke.

'Yeah, sorry. Stomach-ache, that's all. Where was I?'

'Getaway drivers – of the female variety. You look pale, you need to look after yourself.'

'I'll be OK.' He lit another cigarette. 'If I'm right, the getaway car used in the raid on the Fortress, and the other recent building society jobs, was driven by a woman: Louise Daley. A right little mouthy handful who happens to be the niece of George Foster. He no doubt roped her in – sort of thing he'd do.'

'I know who he is,' said Clarke. 'We studied him as part of our training: a hardcore criminal who graduated from Denton's seedier side to the big smoke. In and out of prison.'

'I've got Lee Wright to thank for steering me in the right direction and confirming the worst. The thing is, Foster, it seems more than likely, has hooked up with a nasty little Irishman named Joe Kelly. Lee Wright was banged up with those two for a short while. Foster and Kelly then recruited this ex-cop turned security guard, Blake Richards. A right violent bastard. On paper, it's a gang made in heaven – or should that be hell?' Frost looked around the smoky pub. He couldn't see Patterson anywhere.

'Go on,' urged Clarke, staring at him, a worried look still on her face.

Frost suddenly knew he was going to tell her everything. Knew he had to get it off his chest. 'Bert Williams was on to them. He'd been looking at Blake Richards's old Met file, came across the connections to George Foster and Joe Kelly, too.'

Clarke looked at him, wide-eyed, fresh-faced, her whole career stretching ahead of her.

'Where he died,' Frost continued, 'the more I think about it, is exactly where you'd meet someone for a quiet chat.'

Clarke was leaning in closer.

'Bert met someone out there, on that remote lane. There's no other possible reason why anyone would go that way, even if you were taking the back route back from the Chequers. Even if you were blind drunk.'

'But why would he meet anyone there, anyway?' asked Clarke.

'Bert thought he was getting some information. About the imminent Fortress raid, is my guess.' Frost lowered his voice. 'Someone could have been paying Bert back – Bert let a few things go in his time, we all do – or maybe they had an axe to grind. Perhaps both. Except that whoever Bert met on Saturday afternoon had changed their mind. Or they'd always been stringing him along.'

'Or someone else got wind of the fact Bert was sniffing around,' said Sue Clarke excitedly, 'that the gang was about to be rumbled, and decided to intervene.'

At that Frost leant right across and kissed Sue Clarke, full on the lips. Pulling back, he said, 'I wonder if Lee Wright told me absolutely everything.'

Bill Wells couldn't reach anybody he needed. One minute the station was buzzing, everyone running around frantically, leave cancelled, blanket overtime. The next it was completely dead. Just the pong of new paint and a growing sense of frustration as the hours slipped away without any serious breakthroughs.

He stuffed a stale digestive into the right-hand side of his mouth and tried to chew, but his sore gums were still giving him grief.

It was nearly eight. Johnny Johnson wouldn't be here until ten. Now the flowers were gone, Bert's memorial dumped into a black bin bag as per Mullett's orders, Wells only had the Denton Round Table Poppy Appeal to look at.

When the phone went he was almost relieved. Yet another disturbance in Denton Close. But this one was more specific: a man was digging up his front lawn, in his dressing-gown. Wells knew Frost wasn't in the building, so he tried Hanlon's extension, to no avail. Control was undecided as to whether an area car should be dispatched – there was no law against gardening at night, or gardening in your dressing-gown, after all. However, the address was ringing alarm bells with Wells.

He needed Frost here to make a decision. Failing that, Hanlon. Failing Hanlon, Clarke. Failing Clarke, himself, Wells supposed. He was interrupted from frantically dialling their extensions by a thin lad, in an anorak a couple of sizes too big for him, pushing open the door and ambling up to the front desk. The station sergeant recognized him as the informer who had come in earlier with DCI Patterson. Being an informer seemed like a cushy number to Wells, though not without certain risks, he supposed.

'Got a light, mate?' Brendan Murphy said, resting an elbow on the counter.

'Just a sec. Sure there's one here somewhere.' Wells rifled through the drawers.

'I was hoping to catch DCI Patterson,' Murphy said.

'Saw him walk out of here a while ago.' Wells offered him some matches.

'Right. Well, that's a bummer,' Murphy said, lighting his cigarette and then putting the box in his pocket. 'Is a DS Frost here by any chance?'

'No luck there, either,' said Wells. 'Anything I can help with?'

'No – it's Patterson I really need. I'll see if I can find him elsewhere.'

'You could try the pub. The Coach and Horses, just up Eagle Lane. Lot of officers head there after work.'

'What's that stink?' Murphy said, sniffing, and helping himself to a poppy.

'That'll be the emulsion.'

'Doesn't smell like paint to me.'

'No, it's not, you're right,' said Wells, as Desmond Thorley appeared at the counter.

'Jesus,' said Murphy.

'Not you again,' said Wells dismissively. 'Sneaking up on us too. Scared we'd lock the door if we saw you coming? Well, I can tell you, Desmond Thorley, we're not putting you up for another night running.'

'Only trying to help,' grumbled Thorley.

'What is it this time, then?' said Wells.

'Found this in the woods.' From the folds of his stinking rags, Thorley pulled out a black leather mask, a zip for the mouth, a beak for the nose, two tiny round holes for the eyes, and flopped it on the desk.

'I've seen and smelt enough,' Murphy said, looking up from fixing the poppy in his lapel and pushing through the station doors back into the sodden night, leaving a curl of cigarette smoke.

'Where exactly did you find it?' Wells asked Thorley. He'd studied the Fortress raid incident board in the canteen, determined as ever to pull one over on his higher-ranking colleagues and escape the drudgery of the front desk. Scant praise he'd got for helping to organize the Market Square evacuation.

'Some fifty yards or so from my humble abode, near a big clump of rhododendron bushes,' explained Thorley. 'Where I saw those people the other night. There's been some strange goings-on, as I've been trying to tell you all. I reckon this was dropped.'

'Looks in pretty good nick to me. It certainly hasn't been out in this weather for long.'

'I know what it is,' volunteered Thorley eagerly, 'what it's for.'

'Number of uses,' muttered Wells.

'Evening all,' Arthur Hanlon announced gamely, as he emerged from the interior of the building, pulling on his coat. 'Looks filthy out. I've done all I can for today, so it's a nice hot bath and an early night for me,' he added smugly, now halfway across the lobby.

'I doubt it,' said Wells. 'I've been trying to reach you. Where've you been?'

'Oh, sorry, Bill. Down in Records with Webster. What's up?'

'What isn't? Another disturbance in Denton Close.'

'That's definitely Frost's patch,' said Hanlon quickly.

'And Desmond's turned up with this.' Wells pointed to the mask.

'That's interesting.' Hanlon moved closer. 'Very interesting. Where did you get it?' he said directly to the tramp.

'I'll show you, if you like,' said Thorley.

Hanlon huffed, looked at his watch, and shrugged. 'Come on, then.'

Thursday (10) _____

They barged out of the pub and straight into a full-blown storm. Frost pulled his mac over his head, while Clarke battled with an umbrella.

'Sue, come under here,' Frost offered, fearing they were both in danger of losing an eye or two.

Giving up with the umbrella, Clarke ducked her head and nestled in close under Frost's mac. 'Thanks. You all right, Jack?' she shouted, as they were striding towards the station, into the driving rain.

Frost realized he was clutching his stomach with his right hand. 'I'll be fine. Spot of indigestion – ate my supper too quick.'

'You didn't have any supper.'

'Two packets of crisps. What more do you need?'

Turning into the station yard, they were suddenly forced back against the opened gate as an ambulance sped out, closely followed by a panda car. The panda slowed as it passed them, then accelerated, blues and twos cranking up.

'Your friend Simms needs to watch his temper,' said Frost, who had clocked the driver of the panda. 'One of these days he's going to land himself in a lot of trouble.'

'If he hasn't already,' said Clarke. 'He's not my friend, either. Though to be fair, he helped nail Kevin Jones.'

They started running towards the entrance, as much to get out of the rain as through any sense of urgency.

Wells was behind the counter, sipping from a steaming mug. 'You've just missed all the fun,' he said.

'What's happened?' asked Clarke anxiously.

'A prisoner tried to take his life.'

'Don't blame him . . . the conditions down there,' said Frost.

'But the fool only managed to make himself pass out,' Wells continued.

'Who was it?' Clarke asked.

'One Lee Wright,' said Wells.

'I don't believe that little weasel would top himself for a minute,' Frost said. 'Cunning little bugger, from what I could make out. How?'

'Concealed razor blade. Slashed his wrist.'

'Jesus, and I bet I know where he stashed it. He'll

have learnt that inside. Who booked him in, then, that berk Jordan?' Frost said.

'Jordan, I presume,' Wells said. 'There was a lot of blood, Jack. Right mess.'

'I bet,' Frost replied. 'All for show – oldest trick in the book. Damn, I wanted a word with him.'

'We can ring ahead to the hospital,' Clarke offered.

'Let's hope he hasn't already leapt out of the ambulance,' said Frost. 'Where's Hanlon? Has he copped off for the night already, having failed to get me that warrant?'

'Nope – he's gone off with Desmond Thorley,' said Wells. 'Denton Woods.'

'Thorley, really?' said Frost, searching his pockets for his cigarettes and retrieving a crumpled packet. 'What on earth for?'

'Desmond found a black leather mask, Jack,' revealed Wells. 'Yep, one of those, if you ask me. And for once I'm beginning to think it's more than the sherry doing the talking.'

'OK, Bill,' said Frost, his mind whirring over the number of black masks he'd come across recently. 'For the sake of my overloaded and underpowered brain, can you just run through all this again?'

Before Wells could open his mouth there was a blast of cold air. Frost and Clarke turned to see a drenched DCI Patterson hurry into the lobby.

'You following us?' asked Frost.

'Lucky I've caught you, Frost,' said Patterson. 'Just

heard from my informer that something's going down in Denton Woods tonight.'

'Don't tell me, an S&M orgy?' quipped Frost.

'The joke will be on you lot if you don't move it,' said Patterson. 'Joe Kelly and his gang have been stashing their cash there. According to my lad Murphy, they're going to divide up the lot and get the hell out of the country. They know we're on to them.'

Frost coughed, catching Clarke's eye; she was looking startled. 'You mean,' he said, 'they know the Denton Division is on to them. Thought the ATB was only interested in real terrorists.'

'Don't think it's time to squabble about who's doing what to catch this lot,' said Patterson calmly.

'What about Hanlon?' interrupted Wells loudly. 'He must be there by now, bang in the middle of it, unarmed and without back-up. Seems Thorley wasn't seeing things, after all.'

'Shit, of course!' exclaimed Frost, turning towards the station exit. 'Patterson, you better come with us. Sue can drive.' Over his shoulder he yelled, 'Bill, you alert Mullett, and see who you can rally and get on to Tactical. Direct them to Thorley's lair.'

A terrific downpour forced Hanlon and Thorley to hurry straight inside the rickety old carriage. As the rain drummed on the roof, leaks spurting here and there, and the wind rattled the windows, threatening to lift the roof off, Thorley searched everywhere for a drop of booze. On not discovering any, he stoked up the wood-burner and prepared his guest a cuppa from an old, used teabag.

'It's not every day I have the pleasure of company,' he said theatrically, making space on the bench he clearly slept on, for Hanlon to sit down.

Thorley then relayed once again the story of how he had found the mask, and what he was certain he'd seen the other night as well: a couple of men carrying something heavy over by the wall of rhododendron bushes. There'd been nights of odd noises and goings-on, which weren't just the badgers and the foxes, he was sure of that. People had been coming and going, hiding stuff here, he thought. He'd seen them, hadn't he?

Remaining on his feet, Hanlon gingerly sipped his insipid brew; there was no milk or sugar. He had no idea where Thorley got his drinking water from. At least the rusty old kettle had boiled.

When the wind and rain eased, Hanlon, desperate to get out of there, said eagerly, 'Right, Mr Thorley, time for us to have a quick look around.'

Thorley opened the carriage door and climbed down. Hanlon, holding a heavy torch, tentatively followed. Deep in the woods, the sudden calm was more unnerving than the earlier squall, and Hanlon began to question the wisdom of having driven out there at such an hour and in such sodden conditions. He should have waited until the morning. At the very least, he should have alerted Frost to this development and his immediate plans.

But it had been raining so hard, and once he was in the car with stinking Thorley, it had seemed churlish to stop first at the Coach and Horses and barge in on Frost and Clarke's love-in. Besides, Frost hadn't looked well, and knowing Thorley, it would all more than likely lead to nothing.

The pitch-black, creaking wood quickly seemed to close in around them. They hadn't gone more than twenty, thirty yards, edging past a huge shrub, and Hanlon was finding it hard to keep his beam focused on Thorley and the way ahead, plus what was underfoot. His feet were soaked and freezing already and he'd nearly tripped twice.

It was as he lifted the beam, somehow missing Thorley entirely, that Hanlon felt something hard rammed into his back.

'Don't turn round.'

Thursday (11)_____

'Come on, Sue, step on it!' Frost sat forwards in his seat as they skidded round the Wells Road roundabout and headed up New Lexington Road. 'I'm getting a bad feeling about this.'

'I'm going as fast as I can,' protested Clarke. 'The road's wet.'

'You should have let me drive,' said Patterson, in the back.

'You stick to loading your shooter,' said Frost dismissively. The ATB DCI had been fiddling with his Smith & Wesson Special since they'd left Eagle Lane.

Powering up Denton Road, the rain beginning to ease, Frost noticed the turning to Denton Close approaching. 'Ah, look. We really ought to check on Maurice and his nocturnal gardening.'

'Uphill struggle in this weather,' said Clarke, keeping her eyes firmly on the road for once.

'Uphill gardening's one of his specialities, I should think.' Frost coughed, as they sped past the turning and Clarke shot him a worried glance.

'Control should have sent an area car,' she said. 'Dread to think what Maurice Litchfield's going through.'

'We don't have time to worry about that now,' Frost said. 'Keep your eyes on the road, love.'

'I'm looking forward to seeing what the Denton Division can mobilize,' said Patterson. 'Once your boss has been located.'

'You'll be surprised,' said Frost.

'Of that I'm sure,' said Patterson.

Clarke gunned the Escort up Green Lane, the perimeter of Denton Woods on their right. 'Which entrance?' she asked.

'The north one. That's the nearest to Thorley's place,' replied Frost, as they roared past the turning to the south parking area, and continued round the woods. Trees were swaying in the headlights and huge puddles lay across the narrow road. 'What's this Joe Kelly look like?' Frost glanced back at Patterson. 'We don't want him getting away.'

'Small, wiry, dark-haired, mean little fucker,' said Patterson.

'Takes some balls to set up in competition with the IRA, I suppose.'

'How do you know he's definitely going to be there?' Clarke asked, as she slowed the car.

'As I said when I caught up with you at the station,' said Patterson, 'my boy Murphy heard through his sources that there's going to be a distribution of the spoils of war, so to speak. What's left of the cash, arms, you name it. They've obviously decided it's time to disband and get the hell out of here.'

'And all along the cache has been in Thorley's backyard,' said Frost. 'Bloody hell.'

Clarke swung on to a track, keeping up a swift pace. The car bounced wildly, spray and mud from the puddles flying up.

'This means, though,' said Frost to Patterson, 'that you ATB lot thought you were spying on the real IRA, when in fact you've been watching a has-been turned bank robber, who's hooked up with one of our home-grown talents and an ex-copper from the Met.'

'Don't forget the stripper,' added Clarke.

'You need to listen and watch a bit more carefully,' said Frost.

'Nothing's completely black and white with the likes of Joe Kelly,' said Patterson, ignoring Clarke. 'According to our intelligence, and I shouldn't really be telling you this, Kelly's still in contact with the IRA and we still think a cell might have gone to ground around here.'

'Couldn't you have intervened earlier?' asked Clarke. 'Would have saved an awful lot of trouble.'

'And a bloody life,' muttered Frost, thinking of Williams.

'We didn't have enough to go on,' said Patterson. 'Besides, it was more important to us that we tracked down this cell. We had to see if Kelly could lead us there.'

'And now, I guess, he's about to scarper.' Frost flicked a cigarette end out of the window. 'So you've suddenly decided you better nab him red-handed. So what, you can cut him a deal? Get some names and numbers off him?'

'We're doing what we can to help, aren't we?' sniffed Patterson, flashing his weapon. 'So what do the others look like? Who exactly are we after?'

'George Foster,' began Frost. 'Haven't seen him in years, but I shouldn't think he's got any smaller. Big meat-head, in his early fifties now, I'd say, always wore a lot of jewellery. Shaved head, et cetera. Blake Richards, he's a little younger, though every bit as solid. Neat beard. Tidy hair. Too concerned about his appearance, if you ask me. Never trust a bloke with a beard,' he added for his own benefit.

'And the girl?' said Clarke.

'Oh yeah – Louise Daley, the driver. Now you couldn't miss her, Patterson. Lovely bit of crumpet.'

'Shit,' said Clarke, bringing the car to a sudden stop

and looking over her shoulder at Patterson. 'Seems like your informer was right.'

The headlights revealed three other cars in the parking area: Hanlon's Escort, hemmed in by a Range Rover and a dark Jag.

'What do I do now?' Clarke asked, suddenly sounding nervous.

'Cut your lights and pull in over there, between those trees,' Patterson told her urgently.

Frost leapt out of the car, feeling the sickening pain in his stomach as he stood. Hanlon's safety was suddenly Frost's most pressing concern, and then nailing Kelly and the gang. Behind him the radio squawked into life as Control told them the Tactical unit was on its way, along with two area cars and Superintendent Mullett, who was rushing from a dinner.

'Somehow didn't think Hornrim Harry would miss out on the kill,' muttered Frost.

Clarke gave the station their exact location, and said it looked like company had already arrived.

'Remain where you are,' Control ordered. 'Back-up is on its way. Repeat, remain where you are.'

'Sod that, Hanlon's in there,' said Frost, limping towards the path, one hand pulling his mac together, the other clutching his gut and a torch awkwardly.

Patterson followed close behind, Clarke taking up the rear. Frost, holding the Maglite, pushed his way through the dripping foliage, stumbling over ruts and roots, through puddles the size of small lakes, his mac snagging on brambles, but going as fast as he could, as fast as the cramping pain in his stomach would allow him.

'Hold up,' Patterson whispered loudly. A sudden break in the clouds afforded them some moonlight as they approached a clearing, where the path diverged. 'Where are we, Frost?'

'It all looks different in the middle of the night, but from memory,' Frost said, 'the left fork leads straight to Thorley's carriage, the right continues through the woods.'

'If you go right, any way back round to the carriage?'

Frost could make out Patterson had drawn his gun and he could hear Clarke breathing hard behind him. 'Through a right load of crap, I'd imagine. It's like a jungle over there.'

'We'd make too much noise that way, anyway,' said Patterson. 'OK, here's what we do.'

'Since when have you been in charge?' objected Frost.

'We're not playing cowboys and Indians,' said Patterson.

'Shush. Someone's coming,' warned Clarke.

Hanlon was all too aware of Desmond Thorley fidgeting and grunting uneasily in what little space there was beside him on the filthy, damp carriage floor. The poor old tramp had taken a bit of a kicking.

Hanlon had fared better at the hands of the gang, complying with their demands to walk back to the carriage without turning round, and then to being trussed up, gagged and blindfolded. With what felt like a double-barrelled shotgun in his back he wasn't going to do anything else. Thorley, the fool, had expressed his outrage at the inconvenience.

There'd been at least four of them, an Irishman and a woman among them, so Hanlon had clearly heard. Though he hadn't managed to see any of them. They were pros, knew what they were doing.

Hanlon didn't know where the gang had gone now. He was badly shaken, but at least he was now thinking he might not actually die.

Then, instinctively, Hanlon ducked, or tried to, banging his head hard on the floor as the unmistakable crack of a pistol shot, then another, ripped through the woods, the carriage. It was met by two blasts from a shotgun. And one further, single crack.

Clarke, her ears ringing from the blasts, could just make out Patterson hunkering down behind a tree, both hands on his revolver. She and Frost were on the other side of the path, crouching half inside a rhododendron bush in the dark, a small branch jabbing her right in the ear. Shaking, she was clutching on to Frost for dear life, terrified of moving even an inch.

Some twenty yards further down the middle of the path lay a body. Just to the right another body was sprawled in the dirt, a shotgun on the ground a couple of feet away.

From the moving shapes and panicked voices and one high-pitched scream during the initial volley of shots, Clarke reckoned there were at least another two gang members in close proximity. She was relieved that Patterson was proving to be such a good shot, but knew he could easily be out-gunned. Clarke prayed that they didn't work out only one of them was armed. Though those still alive must have been sensing that if they didn't make a move soon they'd be facing a whole lot more.

Clouds were scudding overhead as near-pitch darkness fell on the woods, to be replaced, almost as quickly, by eerie moonlight.

Then suddenly a short, wiry man, clutching what looked like a holdall in one hand and a sawn-off shotgun in the other, appeared right in front of them. Clarke screamed – she couldn't help herself.

Frost immediately dived forwards, knocking the man to the ground.

There was the deafening crack of a pistol again, a groan of agonizing pain, swiftly followed by two more shots. Another figure was pelting away up the path, someone smaller, more nimble, with long hair. A woman.

Standing up, Clarke saw that both Frost and the man he'd tackled were lying twisted together and far too still on the wet ground. Patterson hurried towards her, breathing heavily, as she moved nearer the bodies.

'Frost, is he alive?' said Patterson, crouching. 'Not easy to tell in this light.'

Clarke, kneeling by Frost's body, and finding a wrist to feel for a pulse, could hear someone struggling to breathe. Leaning closer, she realized it was Frost.

Patterson quickly pulled the other man off, and returned to Frost.

'He's still alive,' said Clarke. 'Jack's still alive.'

'Of course I bloody well am,' croaked Frost, trying to sit up.

Clarke attempted to help him, but he was heavier than she expected, and he wouldn't stop clutching his stomach. 'Have you been shot?'

Patterson was running his hands over Frost, trying to move his arm away, looking intently. 'He hasn't been shot,' he said.

'It's my gut,' Frost groaned. 'Terrible pain.'

'He must have ruptured something,' said Patterson to Clarke, still checking him over.

Realizing how relieved she felt that Frost hadn't been shot, she said, almost joyfully, 'Or eaten something dodgy.' She stroked Frost's head and, wiping the mud from his face, said, 'You'll be all right, Jack.'

'Who's been shot?' whispered Frost.

'Joe Kelly, for sure,' said Patterson. 'That's him there, dead.' He pointed to the man Frost had tackled to the ground, dark blood visible in the moonlight pooling by his head and torso.

'Could have done with him alive, at least,' said Patterson. 'Oh, well, he didn't give me a lot of options. Thought he was going to put one in you, Frost.'

Patterson walked down the track, stooping over the other two bodies. 'One's still alive. Guy with a beard. But he's in a bad way.' Patterson kicked the nearby sawn-off shotgun further down the track.

In the distance Clarke could hear sirens and a helicopter. 'The woman got away,' she said.

'She's quick that one, all right,' said Frost, still half prone on the ground.

'If they set up some roadblocks fast enough, they should get her,' said Patterson.

'I somehow doubt it,' said Frost.

'What about Hanlon?' said Clarke, worry in her voice. 'Where could he be?'

'Try Thorley's carriage,' suggested Frost weakly, as torch beams and the sound of men running moved rapidly towards them.

'I'll check it,' said Patterson, drawing his gun. 'You wait with Frost.'

'You're quite handy with that thing, aren't you?' said Clarke.

'Needs must,' said Patterson. 'But it's never easy taking someone's life,' he added, walking off in the direction of the tramp's shelter.

Hanlon heard footsteps closing in, and the carriage door opening. Was this it?

'You two all right?' an Irish-accented voice asked.

It took Hanlon a moment to realize it was Patterson. But because of the gag, he couldn't answer, and only managed to nod his head weakly. Then he felt Patterson cutting the ties around his hands and feet. Once free, Hanlon struggled to sit up, pulling the gag off, as Patterson attended to Thorley.

'Who's been shot?' said Hanlon.

'Three of them,' replied Patterson.

'Any of us hit?'

'No. We're all OK. Except Frost.'

'What do you mean?' Hanlon stood up. 'What's happened to Jack?' He felt dizzy. Then he heard a helicopter hovering overhead.

'Got a problem with his stomach.'

'Is that all?' huffed Hanlon, stiffly making for the carriage door. Stepping through the opening he saw a blaze of torchlight, and the beam from the helicopter highlighting swarms of armed officers. Mullett, in a penguin suit, was striding into the clearing.

'Will I get a reward?' said Thorley behind him.

Friday (1)

In full ceremonial uniform Superintendent Mullett sat awkwardly at his vast desk. As much as he enjoyed being able to display the totality of his medals and ribbons it was impossible to get comfortable. The collar of his shirt had been starched stiff as cardboard, and the serge of his jacket and trousers was so thick and itchy he could barely bend his limbs, or scratch himself where he needed to. The only thing the fancy garb was good for was standing to attention on a freezing parade ground.

However, he'd thought that the seriousness of the situation and his impending national exposure warranted a certain gravitas. Elsewhere in the building the press were already assembling – local and national, print, TV and radio.

Mullett sighed, attempting to gather his thoughts. He was tired out. He'd managed no more than two hours' sleep last night. In fact, he'd been deprived of a proper night's rest the whole week, as Mrs M was only too keen to remind him over the breakfast table.

There was the briefest of taps at his office door before Assistant Chief Constable Nigel Winslow marched straight in, his right hand outstretched. 'My dear Stanley.'

Mullett struggled to his feet, struggled to reach across the desk to shake Winslow's hand, struggled to move his arm as he did so. 'Nigel.' He'd already had two telephone conversations with the assistant chief constable that morning.

'I think congratulations are in order,' said Winslow, helping himself to a seat. 'Bit bloody though. You'll need to think very carefully about what you say to the press.' Winslow grimaced. 'Patterson's role in particular. We still don't want the public alerted to the fact that an anti-IRA undercover operation was in place – and that comes from above.'

So Mullett was going to have to explain away the carnage, was he? And to think there'd be inquiries, inquests, endless probing questions from all and sundry about, among other things, why his own Tactical unit had not got there in time.

'I'm still livid that there's been some kind of undercover operation going on here for months, without my knowledge,' said the superintendent, his uniform

438

giving him courage. 'Why the hell was I not informed at the time?'

'As you know, the ATB moves in mysterious ways, in these troubled times,' said Winslow, looking flustered, and making Mullett wonder once more how much he really knew.

'And then there's the issue of you accusing the Denton Division of harbouring a mole . . .' persisted Mullett.

'Crossed wires, I believe,' Winslow said, wiping his brow. He changed the subject. 'I hear DCI Patterson did remarkably well under the most testing of circumstances last night. He'll be up for a commendation, I expect.'

Mullett walked over to the window. After the storm it was a beautifully crisp, autumn day. Though, there, lurking in a corner of the station yard like a black cloud, was a BBC van, a massive aerial extending up through its roof at that very moment. 'I have to say, my unarmed officers on the scene were every bit as brave, not to mention the fact that one of my men was bound and gagged at gunpoint.'

'Shame they couldn't stop the woman, though,' said Winslow, now frantically polishing his lenses. 'Not sure how she could have evaded the roadblocks, presuming they were put in place quickly enough.'

'We did everything we could,' countered Mullett, 'including calling up the helicopter.'

'At some expense.'

'Well, at least this Joe Kelly is out of the picture for good, and George Foster too – finally. While Blake Richards has a bullet lodged in his spine, and will probably never walk again.' Mullett rubbed his hands. 'The masked gang has been well and truly smashed, and we've recovered most of the money. All thanks to our solid detective work.'

'I thought it was the ATB's informer who gave the crucial lead on the night?' queried Winslow.

'Merely confirming what we already knew. DC Hanlon was on the scene first. I have to say, Denton CID is a credit to the force.'

'I take it, then, you'll have a good idea where to find Louise Daley.'

'Absolutely,' bluffed Mullett.

'Just make sure her picture is handed to the press in any case – they'll love this one,' said Winslow.

'I bet they will.' Mullett could just see the headline: STRIPPER FOXES DETECTIVES. 'Maybe we do need to parade Patterson in front of the press, after all. Have him explain himself. We don't want this … young woman in the limelight.'

'As I said, Stanley, we need to be very careful about exactly what we tell the press. I fear also it would be putting Patterson under too much pressure.'

Mullett coughed grumpily. As if *he* wasn't under enough pressure.

'You handled that rabies nonsense with some panache,' continued Winslow. 'I'm sure you won't let the force down with this one. Just keep any mention of the IRA well and truly out of it. It's possible this cell is still here in Denton.'

'And DI Bert Williams's death?' said Mullett, looking the assistant chief constable in the eye. 'What do you suggest I say publicly about that?' There was no scenario there which would provide Mullett with much comfort.

'Tell them that new lines of inquiry are being followed up. For God's sake, Stanley.' Winslow replaced his glasses, put away his lens cloth, stood, and smoothed his jacket. 'If stuck, that's *always* the answer.'

Friday (2)

'How you feeling, Jack?' said Hanlon, by Frost's hospital bed, having adjusted the curtain to afford them some privacy.

'Not so bad,' said Frost weakly. His stitches were beginning to irritate him as the anaesthetic wore off. 'Be better when I'm out of here, though.'

'I got these for you, Jack,' Clarke stuck her head through the curtains and smiled sweetly. 'For saving my life.' She made to hand Frost the flowers she had bought from the stall in the lobby, a bunch of white roses, then placed them gently on the bedside locker. 'They'll need a vase,' she said.

'No need for that. They look lovely just as they are. Thanks, Sue.'

Hanlon thought Frost looked terrible, his skin all waxy. 'Well, you've got Richards for company. And the super's coming down later.'

'Even more reason to get the hell out of here,' said Frost.

'You need to rest – when did they operate?' asked Clarke.

'Sometime last night,' said Frost.

'Appendicitis, eh? You need to stay put, Jack,' said Clarke, flicking her hair off her face. 'You could have died from a ruptured appendix.'

'We all could have died last night,' grumbled Hanlon, rubbing his wrists. They were badly chafed and bruised.

'Goes with the territory,' said Frost dismissively. 'Where is Blake Richards exactly?'

'He's under police guard on the second floor,' said Hanlon. 'Don't think he'll be walking again.'

'I messed up.' Frost struggled to sit up. Clarke rushed forward and helped position the pillows behind his back. 'You are making a fuss of me, Sue. I hope you'll be lending a hand when it's time for my enema.'

'You didn't mess up,' said Hanlon. 'Any more than any of us.'

'Should have been on to the girl sooner.'

'One-track mind,' said Clarke.

'And bloody Blake Richards,' added Frost. 'The signs were all there. Once a bent copper, always a bent copper. Shouldn't have let him out of my sight.'

'You think Bert was on to him?' asked Hanlon.

'It appears so. But something's still troubling me.'

'Jack,' soothed Hanlon, 'something's always troubling you.'

'I need to have a word with Richards. I still don't quite get why he was in contact with Bert. And then why he killed him – if it was him.' Frost shook his head wearily.

'There'll be plenty of time to grill him,' said Hanlon. 'Though Scenes of Crime have found a bloodied snooker cue in the back of Richards's Range Rover, the one parked up in Denton Woods. You reckon that could have been the weapon?'

'Quite possibly. We'll need to see whose prints are on it, anyway. And if the blood matches.' Frost coughed painfully.

'You really mustn't worry about that for now,' said Clarke. 'The gang's been smashed.'

'But the bird got away,' grumbled Frost, rubbing at his stubbly chin.

Clarke nudged his arm and said, 'You'll be able to go after her, when you're better.'

'She better bloody well have been caught before then. Come to think of it, I know just the person who might be able to help.'

'Oh?' said Hanlon.

'Steve Hudson.'

'Steve Hudson?' said Hanlon and Clarke in unison.

'He's been knocking off Louise Daley. Hadn't I told

you? Bet he might have some ideas about where she's gone.'

'Hudson's still banged up,' said Hanlon, 'on an attempted murder charge.' He looked enquiringly at Frost. 'Or was, earlier this morning. With all the fuss Mullett seems to have forgotten about him.'

'Attempted murder? You could probably get that changed, say, to common assault, if he leads us to Daley.' Frost sighed. 'I'm dying for a smoke. Can either of you two help me out?'

'It's not allowed on the ward,' said Clarke.

'You think that would stop me?' said Frost.

'What makes you think Steve Hudson wasn't part of this gang?' said Hanlon. He certainly wasn't going to fetch Frost a cigarette, and hoped Clarke wasn't, either.

'He's a lightweight,' explained Frost. 'Besides, if that was the case, that gang wouldn't have carried out the raid on the Fortress, knowing Steve Hudson was already helping us with our inquiries.'

'Good point,' said Hanlon.

'I shouldn't think he had a clue about Louise Daley's involvement,' added Frost. 'She was probably just using him to tune up her motor.'

'I wonder if that informer, Brendan Murphy, knew anything of Steve Hudson's entanglement with Louise Daley, given that he was working with him at Hudson's Classic Cars,' Hanlon speculated. 'And whether Murphy knew about her link to Joe Kelly?'

Frost shrugged, looking dejected.

'Well, Murphy found out about what was going to be happening in the woods. He must have tapped into Joe Kelly's network somehow. And you have to say Patterson came good,' said Clarke.

Frost coughed, then said, 'Where's Patterson now?'

'At home, I should think,' replied Hanlon. 'Suspended, pending the usual inquiries following a fatal shooting, or two.' He looked at his watch. 'Mullett's giving a press conference about it all right now, though apparently he's not allowed to mention the ATB's involvement. The IRA is off-limits, for operational reasons – they still think a sleeper cell might be in the vicinity.'

'Yeah, Patterson said as much. I'd love to hear Mullett explaining what went on last night.' Frost laughed weakly. 'Any water anywhere?'

Clarke moved to get the plastic jug, which had been perched on the windowsill, and poured him a glass of water.

'My throat's killing me,' complained Frost. 'No air in here. How's Lee Wright, by the way? What ward's he on?'

'He appears to have made a remarkable recovery,' said Clarke. 'With all the drama last night, he wasn't being properly guarded, and he's legged it.'

'I thought he'd do as much,' said Frost.

'Mullett doesn't know yet,' admitted Clarke. 'He'll hit the roof.'

'Still, Wright was very useful, coming up with those names. He'll turn up one day soon, I expect. In a load more trouble. Shame, I would have put a word in with his probation officer. The person who's really wasting our time is Maurice Litchfield.'

'Not any more,' Hanlon said.

'He's confessed?' asked Frost brightly.

'No,' said Clarke. 'He's killed himself, I'm afraid. Earlier this morning an area car found him hanging from a tree in his front garden. He was naked.'

'Used the belt from his dressing-gown, did he?' said Frost. 'Jesus wept. I suppose he wasn't going to make a mistake. Shit. Another tragic waste.'

'Quite a shock for the other residents of Denton Close, too, I should think, doing it like that,' said Clarke. 'Horrible.'

'I don't know,' said Frost, clearly trying to lighten the mood, 'they'd probably got used to some strange sights around there. Which reminds me, I never did get to the bottom of who it was I saw crawling around that garden on Sunday night.'

'A peeping Tom?' said Hanlon.

'It was a woman.'

'So?' said Clarke. 'There are women who get off on all sorts of strange things. You should know that by now.'

Just then the curtain was swept aside and a formidable-looking nurse, holding a clipboard, barged to the foot the bed. 'Time to take your temperature,

Mr Frost,' she said. 'Then time for a little nap!' She was holding a formidable-looking syringe.

'Time for us to leave,' said Hanlon, not sure which way to look as Clarke reached over and squeezed Frost's hand.

'Take it easy,' she said.

Walking down the long corridor towards the lifts, Clarke said, 'While I'm here I might as well drop by to see how Mrs Hudson's getting along.' She couldn't quite face going straight back to the station.

'I wonder what will happen to her marriage,' said Hanlon. 'Curtains, I should think.' He tapped the call button by the lifts.

'Some people hang on for very odd reasons,' Clarke said, as the lift arrived and the doors opened to reveal a petite, red-haired woman wearing a fitted, knee-length, red leather coat, with a matching handbag and black leather boots. Clarke was immediately struck by her presence. Her shoulder-length hair had been tightly permed and she had a freckled face and green eyes and was, Clarke guessed, in her mid thirties. She was smiling brightly – too brightly.

'Hello, Mrs Frost,' said Hanlon.

'Hello, Arthur,' she said, stepping out of the lift and warily eyeing Clarke from head to toe. 'Where's William?'

'Ward at the end of the corridor,' said Hanlon.

'*William*?' said Clarke, as the redhead walked away.

'Jack's real name,' said Hanlon. 'William Edward Frost.'

Detective Inspector Jim Allen had to park on Eagle Lane, back by the Territorial Army headquarters, as the station yard was filled with cars and vans he didn't recognize. He presumed the press conference, which he'd been watching at home on television, would have ended by now.

Then it occurred to him that the cars could well belong to officers from other divisions, and lawyers, independent advisers, people from the Police Complaints Board and government officials, you name it. A shoot-out in the woods. A notorious gang smashed. Everybody and his dog would want to be involved, himself included.

He hurried up the steps, feeling surprisingly fit and refreshed, despite the fact that his wife had just left him, and pushed open the doors to the lobby.

Coming the other way was *Denton Echo* reporter Sandy Lane, a fag in his mouth, a pork-pie hat askew on his mop of hair. 'Ah, Mr Allen,' he said. 'Where have you been all week? Tucked up in bed? On your own too, nowadays, if a little bird told me right. Marital difficulties? You wouldn't be the first.'

'Piss off,' said Allen, barging the sleazy hack out of the way and striding straight up to Bill Wells at the counter. 'Hello, Sergeant.'

Wells raised an eyebrow. 'Bit late, aren't you, Inspector?'

'Still some clearing up to do, isn't there? At least that's what Superintendent Mullett implied on the TV – what with this stripper on the loose. Got here as soon as I could.'

'You and everyone else,' said Wells.

'Been a hell of a journey trying to get back,' said Allen, 'train strikes, roadworks, demonstrations, riots, you name it. The country's in a right mess.'

'Where were you? The Peak District, wasn't it?' said Wells dismissively.

'Somewhere like that. Any idea where Mr Mullett is?'

'About to hold a briefing, so I understand, in the canteen.'

'In the canteen?'

'Renovations,' said Wells, wearily. 'Final phase.'

'Right,' said Allen, confused. Just what the hell had been going on? It was like he'd landed on Mars.

The moment he caught a flash of red coming down the corridor, Frost shut his eyes, feigning sleep. There was the unmistakable clip-clop of her heels, like a Welsh pony he'd often thought, and she could certainly kick like one.

Presently he heard the curtain being pulled shut around them and his wife sitting down in the chair beside his bed, and the creak of that bloody expensive coat. He could smell her, her perfume, the faint whiff of her make-up and of new leather.

'Haven't seen you in bed for a while, William,' she said.

Frost opened his eyes slowly, but made little effort to sit up. 'Oh, hello, love,' he said, yawning. 'What are you doing here?'

'The station were good enough to let me know that following an armed exchange in Denton Woods my husband had been hospitalized. It wasn't until I got here that I was informed that you hadn't actually been shot but were suffering from appendicitis.'

'They've whipped it out already,' Frost said gamely.

'Is that all they've whipped out? Must be plenty of other rotten stuff inside you they could have cut out while they were at it.'

'You're in a good mood, Mary. Makes a change.'

'William' – she leant closer, put her hand on the edge of his bed – 'I've been sick with worry – all week for that matter. Which has not been so different from the week before and the week before that. You have no idea what it's like being married to you.'

'I've only been doing my job,' he replied.

'You only ever do your job. That's the problem.'

'Please keep you voice down, Mary, people are trying to die in here.'

'Why can't you get a normal job? It's not as if they even appreciate what you do. You've been there for years, slaving away, and you're still only a sergeant.'

'Detective sergeant,' Frost said with a sigh.

'When are you going to be made an inspector? A superintendent? Someone with a bit of status, like your boss – what's his name? The one who is always on the telly.'

'It's not all about a few gold stripes and fancy medals. You'd be surprised – not all superintendents are quite what they're cracked up to be.'

'That's as maybe, we're all human.'

'Mullett's not,' insisted Frost.

'He did a good impersonation of being one – one who cared. He made it sound like the police smashed this gang with real guts. No mention of you, mind.'

'If I'd wanted my name in lights, on telly, I'd have joined *The Sweeney*, not Denton Police Station.'

'You're impossible,' Mary sniffed. 'Why can't you go into business then, the private sector? You could get a job as one of those security guards, couldn't you? Earn some proper money, too.'

'Nick it more like. Which reminds me, love,' Frost said, making more of an effort to sit up, 'there's someone I need to see.'

He pulled back the sheet and tried to get out of the bed, remembering he was wearing not pyjamas but a hospital-issue nightshirt. The injection had made him feel so much better, but there was still a terrible pain in his stomach. 'Be a love and pass me my mac, will you,' he wheezed. 'I think you're sitting on it.'

His raincoat, he could just see, had been draped

over the back of the visitor's chair. 'I need a smoke,' he added.

'Get back into bed. You're in no fit state to go anywhere.' Mary looked over her shoulder and, realizing she'd been sitting on his mac, quickly stood up. She lifted the garment up at arm's length, as if it were infected with something fatal. 'William, what the hell has happened to your mac? Dirt, rips . . . are those bloodstains? I only bought this for you the other week. Your birthday present, ruined already.'

'Nonsense, now give it here.'

'You just don't care, do you? Not about me. Everything I ever do for you gets thrown back in my face.' She brushed at the mac with a neatly manicured hand. 'I suppose you've forgotten what day it is today, as well.' There was a quiver in her voice. Tears were imminent.

Frost sat on the edge of the bed, thinking hard, frantically looking about him. 'Friday?'

She threw the mac at him, stamped a foot, and turned to go. 'Only our bloody wedding anniversary.'

His eyes settled on the flowers on top of the locker. 'I know that, love.' He reached over, managed to grab them by the stems. 'Here,' he said, holding them up, 'these are for you.'

Mary turned back. 'Oh, William.' She was surprised, all right. 'Didn't think you'd remember.' There really were tears in her eyes now.

Friday (3)

With the briefing over, officers were starting to come through the lobby, while others could be heard milling about the newly painted corridors, laughing and joking, an air of jollity sweeping through the station. Webster and Pooley were already standing just outside the entrance doors, chatting on the steps in the late-autumn sun. Mullett was no doubt back in his gleaming office, contemplating the successes of the past twenty-four hours.

And DI Allen, who'd now be in his cramped inspector's office, beating himself about the head for not having been around when it really mattered. Wells had an idea what that felt like.

The phone rang, disturbing Wells from his reverie.

Similar accent, but different code word. Bill Wells looked at his watch, then at the clock behind him. They had been given twenty minutes, and something told him that this time it wasn't a hoax. He readied himself to make the Tannoy announcement, but before he could speak into the contraption, Sergeant Webster was at the front desk. 'What now?' he said.

'Bomb alert: TA headquarters,' said Wells.

'Shit!' exclaimed Webster. 'That's just across the road.'

Frost swore under his breath when he saw it was Simms outside the door to Blake Richards's private room. Just his luck. He shuffled up, clasping his mac about him, his head clearing by the minute. 'This what you have to do to get top-class treatment round here – rob a bank?'

Simms gave Frost a disdainful look. 'Forget to put your trousers on this morning?'

Frost peered down at his bare legs – he was still wobbly on his feet. He'd be for it if the sister caught him out and about. 'A young nurse helped me out of them last night. Don't know what she's done with them.' He edged up to the door, peered through the small porthole. 'Conscious, is he?'

'Yeah,' said Simms. 'Can't move an inch, but he can talk, all right.'

Frost turned the handle, pushed open the door.

'You can't go in there. That's the super's direct orders.'

'Look, Simms,' said Frost, turning back and squaring up to the PC, 'why don't you shove off. You've been getting on my nerves all week.' Frost walked into the room, shutting the door in Simms's face. He knew the constable wouldn't rush in after him. The boy had no real bottle when it came to it, making do with easy targets. Frost knew his type, all right.

The private room was awash with wires and drips, cylinders and canisters of this and that, an array of monitors flashing and quietly beeping away, all centred around the bed where Blake Richards lay, one tube stuck up his nose.

Frost paused as he noticed the second-floor room had a spectacular view of Denton: there was the clock tower of the town hall, the spire of St Margaret's, the copper cupola on the roof of Aster's, the rows and rows of quiet semis, the tall Victorian warehouses lining the canal, the floodlights of Denton FC, the grim sprawl of the Southern Housing Estate and, on the horizon, the brown, autumnal belt of Denton Woods.

He turned back to the bed and leant over Blake Richards. Seeing Frost, his eyes widened, his brow furrowed. Panic slowly crept across his bearded face.

'Remember me?' threatened Frost, anger welling up. He was on the verge of pulling out every tube he could find, and then burying Richards under all the equipment he could dump on top of him.

'I didn't do it,' Richards whispered, frightened and hoarse.

'Didn't do *what*?'

'I didn't kill Bert Williams.'

'What was that snooker cue doing in the back of your car, then? Covered in Bert's blood.' Frost found he was pinching one of the tubes, the tube that ran into Richards's nose, knowing he was gambling with the facts, but knowing too that Betty Williams needed the truth.

'Someone borrowed my car that day. It's my cue, sure, it's always in the boot – I play snooker. But I don't know anything about any blood on it. Haven't used it all week.'

'What day are you talking about? What day did they borrow your car?'

'The Saturday, wasn't it.'

Frost felt a wave of dizziness – perhaps he should have waited until tomorrow before making bedside visits. He let go of the pipe and clutched the railings at the side of the bed, sweating and breathless. With relief he found a half-crushed packet of cigarettes in the pocket of his mac.

'I was at work all day, Frost. Easy enough to check,' Richards added, his voice bone-dry and growing fainter.

'Who are you trying to pin it on now, Richards? I need to know what happened to Bert. I hardly need to remind you that convicts don't like bent coppers any more than coppers do.'

'You think I care about that? Look at me! I can't

bleeding move. Paralysed from the waist down.'

'But you arranged to meet Bert on Saturday, right? Why?'

'Look, he'd had a tip-off about the Wallop job and he was on to me. Truth be known, we'd met a few times. We had this procedure, knowing we had to be careful. He didn't trust me much – don't blame him, I suppose. But he really wanted this one, I could tell. Wanted to hand it all wrapped up straight on to his new super's desk. Made out that no one at the station took him seriously any more.'

I did, Frost wanted to say. 'If I've understood this right, why were you snitching on this gang anyway? You were right in there, part of it.'

'I was stupid. Thought it wasn't too late. Thought I could get out. Look, George Foster had been black-mailing me one way or another for years, whether he happened to be inside or not. OK, I made a few mistakes when I was in London, but that was ages ago.' Richards struggled for air, to clear his throat. 'But when Foster hooked up with Kelly, after they'd both been released from Dartmoor, he got a whole lot nastier, a lot more ambitious. Started leaning on me because I was working for Security Guard.'

'Likely story. You just wanted the money, like the rest of them.'

'I couldn't have refused to help them. They'd have killed me. I suddenly knew too much and that's how they worked. But I wanted to come clean, honest. I wanted a clean break. That's why I came to Denton. That's why I started spilling the beans to your colleague. I did used to be a copper.'

Frost exhaled heavily, not thinking as he tapped the ash straight on to the floor. 'What happened to Bert, then? Who killed him?'

'OK, I set up the final meeting, down that lane – that was where we always met. I had no option, you see. They were suddenly on to me, Foster and Kelly. Nothing escaped Kelly – I should have realized that from the beginning. You see, they'd found out I'd been meeting Williams. Thought I could bluff my way out of it, told them, yeah, that was where I was getting a lot of my information from, about the police response procedures, that sort of thing. I said Bert was as bent as me. A washed-up drunk, too.'

Frost glanced towards the door. It was still firmly shut, no sign of Simms peering in.

'So come last Saturday they decide they want to check him out for themselves, see if he was as bent as I was making out. They took my Range Rover – knowing Bert would have been expecting me. The thing is,' Richards continued, 'Bert knew those roads, he'd picked that spot. If he'd thought anything unusual was happening, he would have known how to get away. I thought he'd be all right.'

'You could have warned him.'

'I tried, I promise. I rang, two, three times.'

Frost dropped the cigarette end on the floor and

stood on it, before realizing he wasn't wearing shoes. 'Arseholes!' he yelled, hopping on one foot. He quickly caught his breath. 'There's still a number of things I don't get. If they were so suspicious, why didn't they snuff you out too? Why take a risk?'

'I don't know. Maybe Bert convinced them he was bent but they decided to get him out of the way anyway. He was tough, wasn't he. Maybe they had plans for me later, after the Fortress job. Who knows. They left that snooker cue in my car, didn't they – could have been trying to frame me. Kelly was smart, well trained.'

'He wasn't that smart. He's flaming dead.' Looking up, Frost glanced once again at the Denton skyline. 'Who did he take with him when he went for Bert? Just Foster?'

'What's it matter?' said Richards.

'Heard of closure?' snarled Frost. 'Think of Bert's widow. You can't have been a tosser all your life.'

'Yeah, it was Foster, Kelly and Foster, and the tart. She would have driven them.'

'Louise Daley's the only one we don't have,' said Frost. 'Are you going to help us find her?'

'What's it worth?'

'Your life.' Frost was running his hand through a mass of tubes, deciding which one to yank out first.

'I'm not going to have much of a life, whatever happens.'

'My heart bleeds,' said Frost. 'Well, why not do

something good for once? Can't believe you ever signed up to be a copper. What a fucking disgrace.'

Richards took a breath. 'You could try the Hope and Anchor, a strip pub in Bermondsey, south-east London. That's where she came from.'

'I thought she was George Foster's niece,' said Frost.

'Don't think they were related by blood, if you know what I mean.'

Frost had heard enough – enough depravity for one morning.

He had a sudden urge to ring Betty Williams. He wanted her to know that her husband hadn't died in vain, that he had stuck his neck out, had shown the temerity to go after someone like Blake Richards, and the others, single-handed. That he was courageous. A hero. The best bloody copper Denton had ever seen.

Bert would never be forgotten, Frost would make sure of that – he would carry on where Bert left off.

Making for the door, Frost was stopped in his tracks by a massive boom, and then felt a shockwave wallop him in the back.

He immediately spun round, saw the window flexing and, beyond, a dark cloud of smoke mushroom into the sky.

If his geography was right, it was rising over Eagle Lane, home to the Territorial Army HQ and Superintendent Mullett's spruced-up Denton Division.

Acknowledgements

Thanks to Bill Scott-Kerr, Doug Young, Katie Gurbutt, Nick Reeves, Nicholas Shakespeare, Peter Straus, David Miller, Philip Patterson, Rob Nichols, Sam Evans, Sarah Neal, Sarah Adams, Selina Walker, Rachel Potter, Tony Stewart, Phil Wingfield.

Don't miss the next novel
by James Henry . . .

fatal
FROST

OUT IN 2012!